SWEET AS SIN

Also by J.T. Geissinger

The Night Prowler Series

Shadow's Edge
Edge of Oblivion
Rapture's Edge
Edge of Darkness
Darkness Bound
Into Darkness

Novella

The Last Vampire

SWEET AS SIN

A BAD HABIT NOVEL

J. T. GEISSINGER

Montlake
Romance

This is a work of fiction. Names, characters, organizations, places, events, and incidents are either products of the author's imagination or are used fictitiously.

Text copyright © 2015 J.T. Geissinger, Inc.
All rights reserved.

No part of this book may be reproduced, or stored in a retrieval system, or transmitted in any form or by any means, electronic, mechanical, photocopying, recording, or otherwise, without express written permission of the publisher.

Published by Montlake Romance, Seattle

www.apub.com

Amazon, the Amazon logo, and Montlake Romance are trademarks of Amazon.com, Inc., or its affiliates.

ISBN-13: 9781477830864
ISBN-10: 1477830863

Cover design by Eileen Carey

Printed in the United States of America

For my father, in loving memory.
You are missed.

Whatever our souls are made of,
his and mine are the same.

– Emily Brontë, *Wuthering Heights*

Chapter 1

Had I known my horoscope would be an accurate indicator of just how bizarre and life altering my day would turn out to be, I might never have gotten out of bed in the first place.

After a lengthy absence, Saturn returns to your sign today, bringing strange luck, creating problems, changing your plans, and exposing your faults. There's no avoiding it: today is a major turning point in your life.

Sprawled in bed with my iPad and my second cup of coffee, I made what my best friend Grace calls my "period cramps" face, and snorted. The only turning point I was looking forward to at that moment was the on-ramp to the 405 South at the end of the day, followed by two—okay three—margaritas when I returned home.

I had at least ten grueling hours ahead of me on a job I'd been dreading for weeks: the over-hyped, over-budget, and completely over-the-top shoot for the video for the infamous rock band Bad Habit's latest chart-topping release—the shoot that had already been rescheduled three times due to one band member being briefly jailed on a weapons charge, another flying on a whim to a beach party in Thailand without bothering to notify anyone, and another deciding to give an impromptu concert at a local bar and ending up mobbed, mauled, and hospitalized overnight for the many minor injuries one suffers when a room full of drunk, horny females makes a collective attempt to rip off your clothing and jump your bones.

Don't get me started.

I hate celebrities. I hate rock music. I hate celebrity rock musicians. None of which matters, because no one gives a rat's ass about my opinion about any of the foregoing. I'd been hired to do the hair and makeup for the video, not spout my personal feelings about entitled, pampered, immature adults with too much money and too little common sense. However, I'd met too many of them over the past six years working as a makeup artist in "the industry" not to have some pretty strong feelings on the subject. Models, actors, musicians, producers, newscasters, athletes . . . the list goes on, but one thing they all seem to have in common is a big overestimation of their own worth in relation to that of the common people.

Meaning me.

I tossed the iPad aside, gulped down the dregs of my coffee, threw on some clothes, and suffered a minor heart attack when I realized I was running fifteen minutes late. It probably wouldn't matter because undoubtedly the band would be way later than that—if they showed at all—but I'm one of those people who has to get everywhere ten minutes early, just in case. In case of LA traffic, for instance, which, being that today was Friday, was sure to be a nightmare.

I was right. What should've been an easy twenty-minute trip from my place in Venice to Greystone Mansion in Beverly Hills turned into a forty-five minute, curse-filled, heart-hammering drive straight out of the movie *Death Race*. By the time I arrived at

Greystone, I was sweating like a farm animal. I cleared security at the massive iron gates to the estate, parked my Fiat at the far side of a parking lot the size of a football field, and hustled inside with my makeup kit in tow.

And immediately heard, "Kat! You made it!"

I turned toward the familiar voice. The girl bounding toward me with the enthusiasm of a puppy and the blond, sporty good looks of a cheerleader was my other best friend, Chloe. She's always sunny, always smiling, always dispensing these chest-crushing hugs that might be weird coming from anyone else, but from her are adorable.

In fact, that's the perfect word for her: adorable. She's like one of those insanely happy Labradors you can't help but love, even when it's clawing your legs and slobbering all over your new dress.

"Finally," I said into her shoulder as she threw her arms around me. When she pulled away I had to look up to meet her eyes; at five four, I'm a good six inches shorter than Chloe. With her waifish figure and perfect skin, she should really be a model, but she's a florist instead. And an extremely talented one. Looking around the vast entryway of the manor, there wasn't a flat surface without a spectacular flower display. Even the carved wood banisters that flanked the sweeping main staircase had garlands dripping with roses and lilies.

"Amazing job, Lo," I said, impressed.

She wrinkled her nose. "It looks like a funeral. Nothing classy about it, totally overdone and gaudy, Vegas meets Turkish bordello. But that's what the client wants, so that's what the client gets." Her blue eyes glinted with a mischievous twinkle. "And they've got deep pockets, so I can't complain."

"What time did you get here? Traffic was a freakin' nightmare this morning." Chloe was the one who'd recommended me to the production company for the job, so I felt doubly guilty for being late.

"My crew's been setting up since midnight, but I only got here at four."

I stared at her in disbelief. "As in, *a.m.*?"

In my opinion, there are only two acceptable reasons to be awake at four a.m.: earthquake or zombie apocalypse. If I don't get my eight hours of beauty sleep, it's as if the Kraken has been released. All over my face.

Chloe looked chagrined. "I know. I totally overslept. Miles came over last night with a bottle of wine, and, well . . ." She looked away.

"So you're back together?"

I couldn't keep the disapproval from my voice. Miles was a douche bag, no doubt about it. One of those Ivy League, trust-fund guys, he'd been an on-again, off-again presence in Chloe's life for the past two years. He was a jerk and didn't treat her very well, but she loved him. So for the most part, I kept my mouth shut. I didn't have a leg to stand on, anyway.

Bad taste in men and a history of disastrous relationships are two things Chloe and I have in common.

She ignored my question, pointing to a pair of French doors at the opposite end of the long marble entry hall. "They've got you set up in the front drawing room, through there. C'mon."

Gazelle-like, she darted away before I could ask any more Miles-related questions. I dutifully followed, dragging behind me the rolling luggage carry-on that contained all my supplies.

I'd worked once before at Greystone, and knew the general layout of the place. The Tudor-style former home of an oil tycoon had been turned into a public park owned by the city of Beverly Hills, and was now used for special events, film sets, and posh weddings. The main house had fifty-five rooms on over forty thousand square feet. The grounds sported formal gardens, terraces, reflection ponds, fountains galore, an Olympic-sized pool, and sixteen acres of some of the most expensive land in the northern hemisphere.

In comparison, it made my tiny bungalow in Venice look like a skid row cardboard shanty.

Not that I'm complaining. I love my shanty. Owning a house at the age of twenty-five in LA is about as miraculous as the second coming. A million bucks in LA gets you a house the size of a Cheez-It, built in the fifties. And forget about a yard.

But as a little girl I'd dreamed of owning my own house the way other girls dreamed of marrying Ryan Gosling, so I skipped college, went straight to work out of high school, saved every cent, and made a few lucky investments. And now I was the proud owner of a Cheez-It myself.

Between the mortgage, the property taxes, the upkeep, and my demanding margarita addiction, I was dead broke. Hence my acceptance of today's dreaded job. A girl's gotta eat.

Or, in my case, drink.

Chloe had stopped just inside the French doors of the drawing room, and was looking back at me with a look I interpreted as either a warning or the sudden onset of abdominal cramps.

I stopped beside her. "What?"

"You know who that is, right?" She jerked her chin, and I followed her gaze.

Of course I knew. The entire *world* knew. Across the room in front of a lighted vanity, dressed in a plain white robe that did nothing to hide her amazing figure, lounged Avery Kane. Supermodel. Darling of the fashion world. Sometimes girlfriend of Bad Habit's lead singer.

And, if the rumors were true, a world-class bitch.

"What's she doing here? She's supposed to be in Cannes for a Louis Vuitton shoot."

"Word is, she's playing Nico's bride in the video. Had a fit when she found out that leggy redhead from the last season of *So You Think You Can Dance* had been hired, threw her weight around, got herself hired instead."

"I thought Avery and Nico broke up?"

Chloe slid me a look. "For someone who says she hates celebrities, you sure know a lot about them."

"I was channel surfing the other night and caught a segment of TMZ. Apparently Avery caught Nico with some groupie in the ladies' room at The Ivy."

Chloe eyed the miles of gleaming bare leg Avery had propped up on the vanity. "Anyone who would cheat on *that* needs to get his head checked."

"Maybe she's dumb as a post," I suggested cheerfully. "And has BO."

"*Look* at her, Kat. That girl does not have BO. Her farts probably smell like rose petals."

I sighed. "If she even farts at all. Which she obviously doesn't."

The room bustled with cameramen, lighting crews, production assistants scurrying around with Starbucks cups in hand. Judging by the sheer amount of people and equipment, it looked like the shoot would be both indoors and out, but the band was nowhere in sight.

"All right. Can't keep the beautiful people waiting. Want to go to Lula's after?"

Lula's, my favorite Mexican restaurant, was the one place they made margaritas exactly how I liked them: salty, sour, and wicked strong.

"Sure! Text me when you're finished. I should be out of here soon. We're pretty much done with the setup."

"Figure on six or seven, I've gotta stay until the bitter end for retouching."

"Perfect. Gives me time for a nap. I'll tell Grace to meet us."

Just as Chloe was about to go, it happened.

At first it was like this weird current of electricity surged through the room. Voices hushed, people stood straighter, the clamor of activity quieted. There was a sudden energy, as if everything were charged, but also an expectant stillness, like a held breath. Then the stillness gave way as a restless murmur moved through the crowd. The sense of energy ratcheted higher. Chloe and I turned, following the direction everyone else was looking, and there he was.

Nico Nyx. Lead singer for Bad Habit. Adonis in the flesh.

Chloe breathed, "Dude."

In Chloe-speak this can mean anything from "wow" or "shut up" to any number of curse words. She never curses, being that she's too ladylike, but I myself am afflicted with no such modesty.

"Ho . . . ly *shit*."

Standing in the foyer I'd passed through only moments before, Nico filled the space not only with the significant bulk of his gym-hardened body, but also with the power of his presence. Even standing still his energy was larger than life, a raw magnetism that encompassed the room and the people, the air itself. I'd met a lot of actors, made up a thousand models, worked with a ton of people both famous and obscure, but I'd never known anyone who could electrify an entire room of people just by stepping inside it.

Chloe's eyes were wide. "Now *that* is a *man*. My ovaries just fainted."

"Mine are doing the Macarena."

My gaze traveled up and down Nico's body. He wore scuffed motorcycle boots, faded jeans, a black T-shirt so tight it looked painted on. His hair was black and his eyes were brilliant cobalt blue, the same blue I'd once seen in a picture of the Caribbean Sea.

He was the most beautiful thing I'd ever seen in my life.

It slowly dawned on me I knew the exact color of his eyes because I was staring into them. He stared right back at me with a look so charged I thought he might ignite me with it.

Happy to simply bask in the enormity of his atmosphere and focused attention, a nervous tingle coursed through my body as I experienced a moment of infinite delirium. Looking into his eyes, I felt a bone-deep, blood-rocking rightness flare through me. A *connection*, wild and melodramatic, sinful and impossibly sweet.

And stupid.

I knew better. Nico Nyx was a superstar, one of the most desirable men in the world. I was a broke, foulmouthed, possibly alcoholic makeup artist with an overactive imagination. He was only staring at me because I was blocking the view of his supermodel girlfriend behind me.

Face flaming, I turned away. "Please tell me I didn't just get nailed checking him out."

"*Everyone*'s checking him out, Kat. But, um, you're the only one *he* seems to be checking out in return." Chloe's gaze dropped to the cleavage displayed by the little black camisole I'd thrown on earlier. "Which may or may not have something to do with the way your girls are on display in that shirt. That's some serious boobage you're rocking, hon."

My pulse pounded so hard I felt it jumping in my fingertips. "Okay. Acting natural. Going about my business now. Not freaking out at all. See you later, Lo."

"Later, Dolly Parton."

"Shut up." I wished I'd worn a different shirt.

Chloe giggled. "Good luck with the Brazilian Bombshell."

I waved good-bye to Chloe. With all the grace of C-3PO, I walked to the dressing table on the other side of the room, pretending to ignore the feeling that I'd just been struck by lightning.

Which I so. Totally. Had.

The French have a word for it: *abasourdi*. The rough translation is "love at first sight." Until that very moment I'd thought it an idea so sappily romantic I would be sure to make the "gag me" motion by sticking my finger in my mouth if it was ever brought up in conversation. After the past few years of bad relationships, my opinion of men in general, and love in particular, was lower than low. It was subterranean. I wanted nothing to do with either one.

So I'd decided that what I felt was simply hormones. I just needed a little one-on-one with Maximus, my trusty vibrator. He was far and away the most reliable male in my life.

I referred to him as my soul mate only half jokingly.

"Hi!" I said to Avery with brittle brightness when I arrived at the vanity where she was lounging. "My name's Kat. I'll be doing your makeup today." I stuck out my hand, expecting any kind of reaction other than the one I received: a loud, sputtering snore.

Avery Kane was dead asleep.

Sitting upright in the chair, her head rolled to one side, her mouth open and her face shiny, she looked less like a supermodel, and more like a soccer mom who'd been hitting her kid's supply of Ritalin. In fact, the closer I looked, the worse the view became. She had purple-blue shadows beneath her eyes, unwashed hair . . . and *holy*, the girl stunk like a brewery. I'd met homeless people who smelled better. I recoiled with a hand over my mouth.

Well, shit. Sleeping Beauty wasn't asleep. She was passed the hell out.

I looked up, hoping to catch the eye of the chubby PA in the Metallica T-shirt who was barking into a cell phone nearby, but instead saw a sight that made my heart flutter.

There across the room stood Nico Nyx, looking around, his eyes hunting for something. He turned his head. Once again his eyes locked with mine, and I had to lean back against the edge of the vanity to steady myself.

Because he'd apparently found what he was looking for.

Breaking free from the adoring knot of people surrounding him, he stepped away from the French doors, and headed my way.

Chapter 2

In a freak of timing that was either an act of divine intervention, a cruel joke played by a spiteful universe, or a simple case of Karma, the unconscious Avery Kane chose that exact moment to wake from her stupor.

She stiffened abruptly. Her head snapped up. Her eyes, red rimmed and watery, blinked open. She closed one eye and squinted the other, then stared at me for a long, silent moment.

Finally, in a slurred voice sweetened by the lilting accent of Portuguese, she said, "You're sitting on my foot."

I leapt in horror from the vanity I'd rested my weight against and looked down.

Damn. She was right. I'd parked my ass on the foot of the most beautiful woman in the world. That was probably a stoning-level offense in some countries. Maybe even this one.

Mortified, I dropped my kit and held my hands in the air as if I were being robbed at gunpoint. "Fuck! Sorry! My bad!"

"Mah." Avery waved an unconcerned hand and shrugged her shoulders. She yawned, exhaling fumes, then absently scratched her head.

I took that to mean I wasn't in imminent danger of death by stoning. And, because the sexiest man alive was about to make an appearance and his girlfriend wasn't exactly looking her best, I took pity on her.

Under my breath I said, "You're about to get a visitor, Ms. Kane. Nico's less than twenty feet away. Should I . . . ?"

It wasn't my business. I should've simply made myself scarce for a few minutes and watched discreetly from the sidelines until it was safe to return and perform an Oscar-worthy makeup transformation on the derelict in that chair. But all I could think of at that moment was that if it were *me* sitting there, slurring, stinking, looking train wrecked, I would've really been grateful if someone had my back.

There were dozens of people in the room. Not a single one of them paid her any attention. How long had she been here like this? Where was her assistant? Her entourage? She was one of the stars of the show, but as far as the room was concerned, she was completely invisible.

Then it hit me: To everyone else here, Avery Kane wasn't a person. She was a *prop*.

That royally pissed me off.

So of course I went all feminazi on Nico when he stopped next to her chair, stared down at her with fury darkening his eyes as he assessed her condition, and growled, "Goddamn it, Av, not *again*!"

Bristling, hands on hips, I stepped between them.

I've never been known for good decision making under pressure.

"Excuse me! We're working here. You're welcome to come back when we're finished, but I'm going to have to ask you to leave. *Now*."

His gaze cut to mine, and there it was again: connection. Like a plug into a socket. Only this time it was heightened by the anger rolling off him, palpable as a punch in the stomach.

After a long moment, Nico's question came deadly soft. "What's your name?"

I swallowed. Clearly snapping at the pretty, pretty rock star hadn't been such a brilliant idea. He seemed about to explode. I wondered if he had a history of violence. If I survived the next few minutes, I'd Google him later to find out.

"Uh . . . Kat. Kat Reid."

"Lemme ask you a question, Kat Reid. You gettin' between me and my girl?"

His voice was rich and sexy, with more than a hint of Matthew McConaughey southern drawl. I didn't have time to really appreciate it, because the two of us were locked in a stare down, arguing over his inebriated girlfriend. The space between us sizzled. There were sparks coming off him. Or maybe they were coming off me.

From the corner of my eye, I saw people staring.

But I didn't care. Another thing I hate in addition to celebrities, rock music, and celebrity rock musicians: bullies. There was no way I was going to let this guy intimidate me, no matter how beautiful and famous he was.

No matter how much I wanted to find out if his full, sensual lips were as soft as they looked.

After a quick mental slap to redirect my wayward thoughts, I squared my shoulders. "My work space is a dick-free zone, so if you're going to be a dick to her, then *yeah*. I'm getting between you and your girl."

His gaze never left mine. We stood there silently for a few seconds that felt like a geological epoch. Then his eyes softened, and he said something that shocked me.

"Good for you."

His lips curved into a smile that left me stunned, both by the beauty of it and by my sheer surprise of its appearance. Then he pulled a cell phone from his back pocket, punched in a number, and waited for whomever he was calling to answer.

"Barney." He spoke into the phone, but his eyes were still honed on me, sharp as a wolf's. "Bring the car 'round back. Got a situation." He didn't wait for an answer before disconnecting.

Avery slurred, "*Mi amorrr.*"

Nico and I turned to her. Probably because the room was still spinning, she was still doing the one-eye-closed thing.

Sighing, Nico stroked his hand over her mess of long tawny hair. "I'm gonna take you home, baby."

His voice was so intimate it made me feel gross, like a Peeping Tom. I turned to the vanity and began unpacking my bag, mainly for something to do. I knew I'd be packing it up again in a few minutes anyway. The shoot would have to be rescheduled once again.

Avery started to plead with Nico. "No. I can work. I'm fine, I jus' need a few minutes. Jus' need to clean up . . . " She slid her long legs off the vanity, set her feet on the floor, and attempted to stand. I saw every move reflected in the vanity mirrors, so I was treated to a front-row view of her collapsing as she lost her footing.

Nico caught her before she hit the floor. He swept her up in his arms as if she weighed next to nothing, which she looked like she did. She buried her face in his neck.

Nico caught my eye in the mirror. "Kat," he said gruffly. "A little help." His gaze went to Avery's behind.

I saw with horror that her small white robe had ridden up, exposing her ass. She was naked under the robe! Nico stood in a position that hid that fact from the rest of the room, but he couldn't walk away without giving everyone an eyeful.

I looked frantically around for anything to cover her with, and saw the PA in the Metallica T-shirt who'd been shouting into his phone earlier. He was bent over a snarl of electrical wiring a few feet away.

I ran over to him. "I'll give you fifty bucks for that shirt." I pulled a wad of cash from my skirt pocket. I looked down at it. "Make that forty."

He stood, glancing without surprise at the cash I was holding out as if complete strangers had offered him money many times in the past for his ratty T-shirt. He eyed me, pursing his lips. "This is my favorite shirt. It has sentimental value."

Great. A negotiation. "Look, I've only got forty bucks on me, but if you give me your number I'll call you later and get your address and I'll send you . . . "

His brows lifted.

"A hundred?"

The pursed lips again. "A *lot* of sentimental value."

"Seriously?"

He shrugged, and began to turn away.

"Okay! God! *Two* hundred bucks!"

He turned back, grinning, then pulled the shirt over his head. Except for a smattering of freckles across his breastbone, his skin was as white as a pearl. "I'll take the forty, I just wanted to see what you'd do."

He held out the shirt, I tossed him the cash, then I stomped back over to where Nico waited, muttering to myself about idiotic men and their idiotic games.

Why did so many men act like screwing with a woman's mind was an Olympic sport they were in training for?

Without a word, I arranged the T-shirt in such a way that Avery's butt was incognito. I had to touch Nico to do it, slipping the fabric between his arms and her body, making a cradle of it under her behind. Every time I touched him it felt dangerous, like I was doing something wrong but utterly thrilling.

The way he kept looking at me didn't help.

When I was done, I stepped back to inspect my work. "Okay. She's all covered." I glanced up to find them *both* looking at me.

"Thanks." Avery spoke in a small little-girl's voice. She looked guilty, like a child who'd been caught doing something bad.

My heart went out to her. She wasn't at all what I'd been expecting, the diva everyone tried to make her out to be. The word that came to mind was broken.

Nico was silent. He gave me one last, inscrutable look, then turned and strode through the room, carrying Avery away, ignoring the whispers that rose in his wake. Confused by my interaction with Nico, conflicted by my response to him, wondering what would happen next, I watched until they vanished around the corner.

"No. Oh no no no *no*!"

Startled, I turned to see a young Asian guy standing a few feet away, staring after Avery and Nico in dismay. With his shaved head, smoky eye makeup, and long, leather trench coat, he looked like a Mini-Me of Morpheus from *The Matrix*. Beside him was a mobile garment rack bursting with white wedding gowns in various lengths and designs. His zebra-print platform boots added enough lift to his tiny frame that we stood about the same height.

"Don't tell me girlfriend fell off the wagon again."

I wasn't sure how much to divulge, especially since I'd already decided to take Avery's side. So I went with a nonchalant expression and purposeful vagueness. "Let's just say . . . I don't think girlfriend will be back anytime soon."

Asian Matrix Guy's sigh was weary. He closed his eyes and pinched the bridge of his nose. "Sweet baby Jesus, what did I do to deserve this shit?"

I stood there awkwardly. Clearly I was not sweet baby Jesus, so his question didn't require a response.

He sighed again, then lifted his gaze to the ceiling far above. He waved an imperious hand. "Fine, then, universe! Bring it! Kenji will *not* be defeated!" He turned to me with a dazzling smile, all anxiety forgotten. "Hello, lovey. I'm Kenji, stylist for the band. Who're you?"

"I'm Kat, the makeup artist," I said, charmed by this zany character.

We shook hands, then he squealed. "Cat! Of course—because of the eyes, right?"

That wasn't the first time I'd heard that. The shape and color of my eyes were distinctly feline. "Actually, no. It's Kat with a k. Short for Katherine."

Eyes narrowed, Kenji looked me up and down. "What are you, Japanese and Irish?"

My mouth must have fallen open, because Kenji grinned.

"You're the first person to ever guess that right! "

"Well, now that we've got the introductions out of the way, Kitty Kat, we're going to be best friends, yes?" Kenji batted his fake lashes at me.

"Yes," I replied firmly, "and you *have* to tell me where you got those lashes because they're *amazing*."

Kenji preened. "Right? They're my signature lashes. I never leave the house without them. These and my Laura Mercier lip plumper make me the goddess I am."

"Have you tried the Smashbox O-Plump? It's just as good as the Mercier, and cheaper."

I turned to dig in my kit, found the tube, and held it out to Kenji. The two of us started an impromptu discussion of the merits of different lip plumpers and fake lashes, which led to a discussion about the best foundation to conceal five o'clock shadow, which then led to a raunchy, in-depth debate about whether Spanx was meant to be worn with or without panties.

In the middle of what I considered a brilliant line of reasoning about how fabrics that don't breathe can cause yeast infections—or, in Kenji's case, an unsightly rash of the nether regions—Nico showed up.

"Moist environments? Sounds fascinatin'."

I spun around, saw him leaning with a smirk against the rack of wedding dresses, and wished the floor would open up and swallow me whole. My mouth closed with an audible snap.

"A subject close to your heart, no doubt, you *rogue*." Kenji eyed Nico with a combination of disapproval and affection that seemed almost maternal. "And get your dirty paws off that Donna Karan! It's on loan!"

"Only thing dirty about me is my mind."

Nico was talking to Kenji. But he was looking at me.

Now that is a world-class asshole. Avery wasn't even ten minutes gone, and already he was putting the moves on the makeup girl, who he probably assumed would wilt and swoon like every other female in his orbit.

Okay, *inside* I was wilting and swooning, but there was no way in hell I was letting Mr. Egomaniac Rock God Jerkoff know that.

I sniffed like I smelled something bad, turned to my makeup bag, and started shoving things in.

"Goin' somewhere, Kat?"

Nico's voice had changed from a playful drawl to something a little more tense. *Weird.*

"The production company knows how to get in touch with me, so when the shoot's rescheduled—"

"Rescheduled?" Nico's tone was sharp. "What makes you think it's gonna be rescheduled?"

I turned to look at him. He wasn't smirking anymore. In fact, he now looked downright scary: glowering, arms folded over his broad chest, cobalt eyes piercing me through. I glanced at Kenji. He was examining Nico with his head cocked, frowning.

"Um, yeah. You know, because Avery . . . oh—are you just going to shoot around her?"

Nico's gaze roved over my face, my chest, my bare legs beneath my denim mini. Under his intent inspection, heat spread across my cheeks, a combination of anger on Avery's behalf and undeniable attraction on my own. His eyes found mine again, and my heart skipped a few beats at what I saw there. He stepped toward me, stopping an arm's length away. It took every ounce of my willpower not to step back.

"No," he said with calm authority. "We're not shootin' around Avery. We're replacin' her."

I went hot, then cold, and began silently to pray. *Please don't say it. Please God do not let him say what I think he's about to—*

"With you."

Kenji's head snapped around. He sent me the same "what the fuck?" look I knew showed on my own face. I drew a breath, determined to stay in control though adrenaline was lashing through my veins. There seemed to be an invisible fist squeezing my windpipe.

"You're joking."

Nico shook his head.

"No," I said. "That's not an option."

He waited, silent, unblinking, while I flailed around for a rational explanation as to *why* it wasn't an option. Judging by his expression, that was required.

"I—I'm not a model. I'm not an actress. I have zero desire to be in front of the camera. Thank you, that's very flattering, but the answer is no. Absolutely, positively, *no*."

Nico smiled. It was devastating.

"Darlin', I wasn't askin'."

Chapter 3

Kenji leapt up and down, squealing and clapping.

Shocked out of my wits by the turn of events, and my new best friend's traitorous embracement of said events—and simultaneously horrified that the entire room had turned to stare at us—I made an unattractive noise, akin to a cat trying to cough up a stubborn hairball.

Kenji was beaming. "Fun! Kitty Kat, I get to dress you!"

Oh dear Lord. This wasn't happening.

Examining my face, Nico's expression went from a sexy glower to an even sexier smirk, this one ridiculously self-satisfied.

"I do not accept." I enunciated each word carefully, holding Nico's gaze. My heart pounded as if it were trying to break out of my chest. "As I said, I'm not interested. The answer is no."

Completely ignoring me, Kenji danced around the rack of wedding dresses and began rifling through them, first whistling in happiness, then muttering something to himself about sample sizes and girls who ate too many carbs.

I made a mental note to remind myself to stab him later. Ten times for ignoring every word I'd said as if only Nico's opinion mattered, and another twenty for that crack about the carbs.

I made another mental note to myself to lay off the chips and salsa.

Then Nico Nyx uttered a sentence that made me reconsider my position. "Avery's day rate is thirty thousand bucks; you'll get the same."

All the breath left my lungs as if I'd been punched in the solar plexus.

Thirty.

THOUSAND.

Dollars.

I can't speak for the rest of the world, but for me that was a fuckload of money. For basically doing . . . what? Prancing around in a wedding dress for an afternoon?

He's still a world-class asshole, chastised my feminist side. *His sweet, beautiful, helpless girlfriend shows up wasted on set, and he has his driver take her home? Epic boyfriend fail. Do NOT go into the light!*

Yes, he's an asshole, countered my pragmatic side. *A RICH asshole, who just offered you more money for a few hours' work than you make in half a year. Don't be stupid. You can put half of it toward the mortgage, and use the other half to pay down your credit cards, then never see him again. Go INTO the light!*

But what about Avery?

It's not your fault she can't stay sober!

What if seeing another woman in her man's video will push her over the edge?

Bitch, PLEASE!

The two sides of my conscience were screaming at each other, and I was beginning to feel like a candidate for a mental institution. I had to make a decision, quick.

I took a breath and made it. "No nudity."

Nico lifted one shoulder. I took it as an affirmative.

"And no other . . . funny business."

Nico chuckled. "It's a music video, babe, not a porno. You don't even have to talk. Just stand there and look sexy."

Just look sexy? Did I look like I knew how to "look sexy"?

Did *he* think I looked sexy?

Kenji chimed in. "Trust me, lovey, you'll do great. I've done a million of these things. They'll do a few takes of each scene, and make it look perfect in editing. No sweat." He turned away from the rack of dresses to look at me. "So, I'm thinking you're a size four?"

I hadn't been a size four since about the sixth grade. I figured he was trying not to embarrass me in front of Nico, so I merely nodded, trying to look cool.

Kenji winked, confirming my suspicions, and turned back to the dresses. "This," he enthused, pulling out a slinky, side-slit number, "is it!"

Nico grunted his approval. I stared in disbelief at the gown. The fabric was so thin, and there was so little of it, I could have folded it up like a handkerchief and stuck it in my back pocket.

"No way, Kenji! And Nico, isn't there some kind of paperwork I should sign? You know, like a contract?"

He tipped his head back and examined me from beneath his lashes. "Why, you think I'd stiff you for the cash?"

God, every word this man said sounded sexual to me. Hearing him say "stiff you" made my ears go hot. "I'm not about to find out, because that's what contracts are for."

I smiled sweetly at him. I was rewarded with his chuckle again, which I liked far too much for my own good. He pulled out his cell phone and dialed.

"Barney, bring me thirty Gs from the safe when you come back, man. Yeah. See you then." He disconnected and sent me a slow, knowing smile.

I was floored. "You're paying me in *cash*?"

"You'd prefer a payment plan?"

This whole situation was amusing to him, evidenced by the twinkle in his eyes and the way his lips pressed together, as if he was trying not to laugh. I, on the other hand, was so flustered I was finding it hard to focus.

"That's a little . . . unorthodox, don't you think?"

He grinned. "That's rock 'n' roll, baby. Just go with it."

I narrowed my eyes at him. I didn't like him calling me "baby." He'd called Avery "baby." He'd also, in the span of mere minutes, called me "darlin'" and "babe." I guessed he called every woman other than his mother one of those three. I decided then and there that this little flirtation had gone far enough.

"Okay," I said, all business. "I'll go with it. One day of filming, thirty thousand bucks. But let's get something straight. My name's Kat. If we're going to work together, you need to call me by my real name, because that's the only thing I'll answer to."

His grin vanished. A muscle flexed in his jaw. He nodded, then directed Kenji, "Twenty minutes, then bring her up to the master suite on the second floor." He looked back at me. "We're shooting the bedroom scene first. *Kat*." He turned and walked away without another word.

The bedroom scene? My pulse went arrhythmic. What the hell had I gotten myself into?

"Oh, no you *didn't*!" Kenji laughed under his breath as he watched Nico stalk away, shoulders stiff.

"Unfortunately, I think I just did."

I grew frantic. Twenty minutes wasn't nearly enough time to do my makeup and hair, and squeeze myself into a dress two sizes too small. This was a disaster!

"Don't panic, honey, it's bad for your skin. What about this one?" Kenji held up another dress, a froth of tulle and satin with a fat cluster of pink fabric flowers at the waist.

I snorted in contempt.

"You're right. Too Trailer Trash Barbie. You need something a little more . . . " He pursed his lips, surveying the remaining dresses, then his eyes lit up. "Ethereal!"

From the rack he pulled the most gorgeous gown I'd ever seen.

It was in two pieces. The underlay was a long, simple cream silk sheath with a plunging neckline and a scoop back that dipped below the waist. Atop the sheath floated a delicate, sheer lace overlay in palest blush, shimmering with seed pearls and tiny crystals. Together the two pieces had the look of extremely expensive lingerie.

Awed, I reached out and slid my fingers over the lace, gossamer fine. "It's amazing, Kenji. But my ass will look the size of Texas in this dress."

"Tch! What is it with you girls and the size of your asses? Your rear end is beautiful, Kat, and totally proportionate to your body. Don't you know men love a nice juicy booty on a woman?"

There was something vaguely unappetizing about the term "juicy booty," but I decided to be gracious and say thanks when he left me speechless.

"And judging by the way Nico went all jacked-up junkyard hound dog when he saw you, I'd say he's *definitely* one of those men.

Can't say you're his usual type, but I've never seen him so wound up." He whistled. "The man was *en fuego*!"

On fire? Wound up? I recovered after a moment only to launch into a stuttering denial, face flaming with heat. "I . . . he . . . that's silly . . . he didn't . . . he wouldn't—"

Kenji sighed extravagantly, rolling his eyes. "*Please* don't tell me you're one of those girls who eats self-loathing for every meal, and has so little confidence she can't even admit when a man finds her attractive." He waited, brows raised in disapproval.

I felt defensive because I probably was one of those girls. But there was no way I was going to admit it. I wasn't *that* lame. I went with humor instead. "I'll have you know I only eat self-loathing for breakfast! Lunch and dinner I usually have margaritas."

He giggled. "Oh, honey. Is it too soon in our relationship to tell you that I think I love you?"

I regarded him seriously. "You actually said aloud that you thought I was a size four, so it should be *me* saying I love *you*."

"Well, don't thank me yet, lovey. I've still got to get you into this thing, which is going to take a miracle. Even Avery would've had to suck it in, and she's a size zero long."

"*Zero long?*" I was astonished. "That's not a size, that's an oxymoron! Please tell me she has to puke three times a day to keep herself that thin."

With a *tsk*, Kenji sent me a pointed look. "Green isn't your color, honey. And you didn't hear it from me but . . . well, let's just say girlfriend has to do a *lot* of things to keep her figure."

I felt a twinge of regret at being petty. Avery obviously had a substance abuse problem. Who knew what other horrors of self-abuse she underwent to keep looking perfect. Today excepted, of course.

"Well, I wish I knew her trick for getting booze to dampen the appetite. After two margaritas, I eat everything in sight."

Kenji looked startled. "Booze? What makes you think she was drunk?"

It was my turn to be startled. I'd had enough hangovers in my life to know what a really bad one looked—and smelled—like. "It was kind of obvious, Kenji."

He shook his head sadly. "No, honey. What Avery's into isn't obvious." He turned away, muttering under his breath. "Unless you know where to look."

It wasn't my business. Only it sort of was, because I was going to stand in for her, possibly making a colossal ass of myself in public in the process. I just *had* to ask. "What do you mean?"

He turned back to me, reluctant to answer. After a moment of lip-chewing, he sighed. "She's a good girl, but she's fucked up, and she's got good reason to be. So I don't judge. I just keep my fingers crossed that Nico can figure out how to help her before it's too late. It's not for lack of trying, that's for sure. That man has put his heart and soul into . . . "

His expression clouded. He seemed lost in a memory. Then he shook his head and waved an imperious hand, a gesture I was beginning to recognize as his trademark. "Anyway! Loose lips sink ships, lovey, so please don't repeat a word I've said."

He hadn't said much of anything, not exactly. But one thing stood out in screaming neon like a Vegas marquee: "His heart and soul."

Avery was Nico's heart and soul.

If I was going to get through today, I'd better remember that.

Chapter 4

When I stepped into the chaos of the master bedroom exactly twenty minutes later, it took mere seconds for the hubbub of voices and activity to die down, and for everyone to turn and stare.

Standing inside the doorway with Kenji beside me, I fought the urge to turn and run.

The sense of critical inspection was suffocating. Dozens of pairs of judging eyes raked over me, no doubt finding me a pathetic substitute for the woman who was supposed to be standing in this spot. I'd done my best with my hair and makeup, curling my long dark hair so it hung around my shoulders in loose waves, and using a pale palette on my skin and lips, with a contrasting dramatic, smoky eye. A pair of cream Louboutins with Swarovski crystal appliqué on the heel completed the look, adding six inches to my height.

I thought I looked pretty good. For *me* anyway. But I was no supermodel. Or any kind of model.

Which, judging by the looks on their faces, everyone in the room knew.

I swallowed hard and took a step back. A firm hand settled on my shoulder.

"Chin up and smile, sister," murmured Kenji. "It'll be worse if they think you're afraid. Sharks can smell fear, you know."

Since fear was leaking through my pores like giant, sweaty gumdrops, I assumed I was about to become chum.

Kenji gently shoved me forward, and I took another step into the room. A mincing step, because the dress was so tight I couldn't walk normally. I squared my shoulders, careful not to breathe too deeply so I didn't split any seams. On my lips I plastered a big, fake, shit-eating grin.

But when I saw Nico, sans shirt and shoes, lying atop a huge four-poster bed across the room with his hands behind his head, the shit-eating grin died a quick death.

Tattoos.

Muscles.

Burning eyes.

Bronzed skin.

The impressions came quick and fast. Blinking, I had to look away so I didn't just stand there and gape like an idiot.

"I know. Sears the retinas, doesn't he?" Chuckling, Kenji linked his arm through mine.

The master bedroom was as cavernous as the rest of the mansion, elaborate with antiques and oil paintings. The cameras were set up opposite the bed. A field of white-hot halogens on telescoping stands lurked behind. Rock music blared through speakers wired to the walls, and the air reeked of stale coffee and sweat.

I was ninety percent sure I was going to faint.

"Replacement girl! Yo!"

A young man swaggered up. Pasty and skinny, tatted from wrists to shoulders on both arms, he wore a red baseball cap reversed on his head, a sleeveless T-shirt, cargo shorts that looked as if he'd slept in them, and an enormous gold cross on a chunky chain around his neck. He looked all of fifteen years old, like a white kid from the burbs playing dress up in a rapper's clothes.

In other words, he looked like Justin Bieber.

He jerked his chin at me. "'Sup?"

I took this as an inquiry into my general state of being. My response was to recall the shit-eating grin. He grinned back, revealing a gold front tooth.

"So here's what needs to happen, yo? We only got half an hour for this scene, so we gotta work quick. You and Nico are on the bed, and it's right before the part where you run out on the wedding—"

"Run out on the wedding?" What woman in her right mind would run away from Nico on her wedding day? This sounded like a stupid video already.

Kiddie rapper looked at me as if I were mentally challenged. "Yeah. You know. Like in the song."

"The song?"

This was the wrong thing to say. Kiddie gangsta's pale face turned an interesting shade of red. He looked at Kenji.

"Yo."

There was so much emotion packed into that one syllable. Disappointment, disbelief, anxiety, anger. It was as if he'd just given an entire speech about his artistic dreams being crushed and the impossibility of working with such an idiot, using only two letters.

Kenji dug his elbow into my side. "Of course she knows the song, Obi! *Everyone* knows the song! She's only playing." He turned to me with a brittle smile. "Right?"

I realized I'd made a gaffe of epic proportion and would have to quickly backtrack. Whoever kiddie rapper was, he was apparently important. "Of course," I lied smoothly. "Who doesn't know the song!" Then I laughed.

It sounded, even to me, more than a little insane. I was beginning to crack from nerves.

"Ha! You got me!" Obi grinned, easily appeased.

I wondered how much worse this day was going to get.

Obi rattled off a list of instructions about how I was to act, stand, and stare off pensively into the middle distance while Nico lip-synched the lyrics as the song played over the speakers. I was tempted to give Obi another heart attack by asking about my character's motivation, but decided in the end to keep my mouth shut. I didn't want anything coming between me and that thirty grand.

"We good? You got it?" Without waiting for an answer, Obi turned and swaggered back to the bank of cameras, and started barking orders.

"*He*'s the director?"

"Yes, honey, he's the director. He's *the* director in music video at the moment."

"He looks like a teenager!"

Kenji chortled. "Among other things. But he's the real deal, lovey."

"What's with his name?"

"Random, right? It's a thing now. All these young directors are giving themselves nicknames, think it makes them sound badass. Obi is short for Obi-Wan Kenobi, the Jedi Master." He snickered. "Because, you know, our boy over there is so in touch with the Force."

I rolled my eyes.

Kenji added, "And by the way, *please* don't make any more jokes about not knowing the song. It's probably one of the best rock ballads ever written. It's a shoo-in for the Grammy this year."

I was going to tell him it was no joke. Really, I was. But then my gaze found Nico once again, and my thoughts flew right out of my head.

Still reclining on the bed, a wicked little smile on his lips, he crooked his finger at me, then patted the mattress beside him.

I'm sure my gulp was audible.

"Showtime," Kenji murmured, watching this exchange. He sighed. "Lucky bitch."

"Lucky" wasn't the word I'd use. "Screwed" would be more fitting. Because if my shaking hands, pounding heart, and sweaty pits were any indication, I was going to have a hell of a time remembering even a single instruction Obi had given me.

I was about to go lie on a bed with the most beautiful man I'd ever seen . . . and pretend I was his bride-to-be. While three dozen people watched. And filmed it.

Thirty thousand. Thirty thousand. Thirty thousand.

That was my mantra as I walked slowly across the room toward Nico, my pulse like thunder in my ears.

Chapter 5

"You look incredible."

Nico's voice was low and gruff. His eyes were unblinking, the look in them intense. I glanced away, picking at the delicate lace on my sleeve.

"You need powder."

Dear God, please tell me I didn't just say that out loud.

"'Scuse me?" Nico sounded confused.

Yep. I did say it out loud. Now if only I accidentally farted, my humiliation would be complete. "You, um . . . your nose. The lights . . . you should have powder."

"You tellin' me I need makeup, Kat?" His tone was gently mocking.

Did he know how much he affected me? Yes, of course he did. He'd been turning females stupid for years. I blew out a hard breath, and cleared my throat. "Everyone needs makeup for the camera."

He studied me. "Not everyone." A furrow appeared between his brows. "You covered your freckles."

He sounded disappointed. For some bizarre reason, he didn't like that I'd covered my freckles under a heavy layer of foundation. The freckles I'd hated my entire life. The freckles I would've sold my soul to permanently remove.

Obi shouted, "Replacement girl, on the bed! Quiet on the set!"

With horror, I realized there was no way I could lower myself to the mattress. That would require bending, which would no doubt cause multiple seams to split. Kenji had stuffed me into the designer gown so well it was molded to my body like a sausage casing.

"Replacement girl! *Now!*"

"Her name's Kat, Obi." Nico watched me from hooded eyes as he said this, one corner of his mouth curved up. "Apparently she doesn't answer to anything else."

Obi released a pained sigh. "Kat! Please! On. The. Bed!"

Well, fuck it. If the entire room was about to watch me bust out of a ten-thousand-dollar dress, at least I'd be getting paid triple that to do it.

I took a breath, closed my eyes, and, without bending at the waist, pitched forward.

I landed right on top of Nico.

His surprised grunt was almost drowned out by the laughter of the crew. I wondered how much humiliation a person could suffer before dying of it.

A pair of strong arms encircled me. Nico whispered playfully in my ear, "I'm flattered, Kat. I've had women throw themselves at me before, but never quite so literally."

Mercifully covered by my hair, my face flamed red with shame. I was contemplating never opening my eyes again when Nico gently rolled us both over, and tucked me into his side. He brushed the hair from my face, but I hid in the crook of his arm, groaning.

The bed began to shake with Nico's stifled laughter.

"Quiet on the set!" Obi's shout was shrill. He was immediately obeyed. By everyone but Nico, that is, who chose that exact moment to declare into the silence, "Fuck, you're adorable."

Ground, please open up and swallow me. Please.

"We're rolling! Cue music!"

A song began to play over the speakers. A lone violin note in plaintive high C, accompanied by the bass treble of a cello, filled the room. Then, sweet and soulful, aching with longing, a voice sang out.

My heart black as midnight on hell's darkest shore
Yearning for something, or someone, before
It's too late and I'm damned to this place
Of silence, and madness, and endless deep space

It was beautiful, that voice. Nico's voice.

I opened my eyes to see him there above me, staring down, the smile fading from his eyes. He swept his thumb across my lower lip, and began to sing along with the lyrics.

His voice was soft, intimate, as if meant only for me.

I've wandered and hungered and waited for you
I've prayed on my knees to find something true
And now that you've found me and claimed me for yours
You're taking me deeper than I've ever been before
Soul deep.
Soul deep.
Deeper than I've ever been before.

I was breathless. Wordless. Every cell in my body was aware of him, of his heat and weight, the wind-clean scent of his skin, the glow of the lights on his hair. Mesmerized, I couldn't look away.

In that moment, no one else but the two of us existed.

"CUT!"

Startled by the shout, I dragged my gaze from Nico. Obi stood with hands on hips beside a video camera, looking all sorts of pissed.

"Replacement—Kat! You can't just stare at Nico with your mouth open! *You're* the one with the power in this song, right? *You're* the muse. The bride who's about to leave him at the altar. Look at the wall, look at the ceiling, pretend to be bored. Look at anything but him! Yo?"

"Um, yo."

Obi nodded. "Good. We'll go again."

Nico shifted his weight. His leg slid over mine. I chanced a glance at him, to find him smiling, his hair falling into his eyes. He whispered, "Your heart's poundin', Kat."

He was flirting with me. The man was shameless. Even if he didn't remember he had a girlfriend, I did.

"It does that when I'm bored."

He grinned, clearly not believing a word I'd said. I had to be more convincing.

"Actually I have this condition where my blood pressure spikes when I'm near an overbearing asshole."

Wow, that slipped out much too easily. And apparently with convincing venom, judging by the expression on Nico's face. His jaw gritted so hard I thought his teeth might shatter. His voice came out in a growl.

"Why are you tryin' so hard not to like me?"

Obi shouted, "Cue music! We're rolling!"

I kept my mouth shut, looked at the ceiling, and tried to look like I wished I was anywhere else. The music started. After a tense moment, Nico again began to sing.

I stared off into the middle distance like a cat ignoring its owner's calls.

This time there was no shout of "Cut!" The room was quiet. The only sound I heard was the music and Nico's voice, soft in my ear, singing about finding love and losing it. Singing about longing, and loneliness, and loss.

Things I knew all about.

My throat got tight. I closed my eyes for a second, trying to avoid Nico's piercing stare. As his nose was only inches from mine, this was difficult. Closing my eyes helped.

We made it through the rest of the song in one take. I had looked appropriately disinterested.

"That was awesome, Kat!" Obi fist-pumped the air. "You looked totally turned off!"

A low rumble went through Nico's chest. I ignored it. "Thanks."

"Okay, everyone. Ceremony's next, yo. Let's get to it!"

People began to hustle. Nico stayed put, his arms hard around me, legs tangled with mine.

I lifted my head, and tried to move. This was like trying to move from beneath a boulder that's flattened you. "Um. Shouldn't we . . . "

"Yes, we should." His grin was wicked.

We weren't talking about the same thing.

"I meant shouldn't we get up. We should get up."

Nico stared at me, grin fading. The intensity in his eyes was more than a little scary. I blundered ahead. "You might have to help me a bit, though. This dress is—"

"I'm gonna ask you a question, Kat. And you're gonna give me an honest answer."

This didn't sound good. My heartbeat kicked up a notch. I swallowed because my mouth had turned desert dry. "Which is?"

He gave me a long, searching look. Then he bent his head and whispered into my ear, "Are you wet for me?"

My heart decided now would be a good time to have an attack. I couldn't blame it.

"Don't be disgusting!"

Of course I wasn't disgusted. I was too busy having a heart attack. Nico wasn't buying it, either.

"You are. I know you are. Your face is flushed. You're breathin' hard. Your heart's poundin'. And beneath your panties, your pussy is soakin' wet."

If my face was flushed before, now it went molten. It didn't help matters that he was right. I tore my eyes away, escaping the intensity of his gaze.

"You're an arrogant *prick*, Nico Nyx."

He chuckled. "Doesn't mean I'm wrong."

I hated that he could read me so easily. I hated how effortlessly I was falling apart in his arms. I hated how self-confident he was, how sure of the effect he was having on me. I hated it all, but I loved it, too, which was far more dangerous.

"Actually it does. My face is flushed because these lights are hot, and my heart's pounding because I'm nervous as hell. I've never been on camera before. It has nothing to do with you."

There was a long pause as he studied my face. "You lie for shit, woman. It has everything to do with me. You know it. I know it." His voice dropped. "And my hard cock sure as fuck knows it, too."

I laughed to cover my shock. No one had ever spoken to me the way he did. I couldn't believe the nerve of this man.

I couldn't believe how much I liked it.

This was all incredibly flattering, but I had to put a stop to this before it went too far. I wasn't going to be another notch on this arrogant rock star's bedpost.

"Well that explains a lot." My tone was withering.

His eyes narrowed. "Meanin'?"

"Meaning I know which of your heads is making all the decisions. Because I'm sure your *brain* would be reminding you right about now that you have a *girlfriend*."

I looked directly into his eyes so he would see that I meant business. I wasn't just another groupie or roadie or whatever those girls who threw themselves at rock stars were called. I had self-respect.

Battered though it might be, I still had it.

But Nico surprised me. He didn't flinch at my words. He didn't look one bit ashamed, as I'd hoped he would. He just stared right back at me with that intensity. His eyes were shadowed now, their color shifting like quicksilver with the light.

"Avery isn't my girlfriend."

Unbelievable. He thought I was an idiot.

"Oh really? You might want to tell Avery that. I'm no language expert, but I'm pretty sure 'mi amor' doesn't mean 'good buddy.' Besides, you already told me she was your girlfriend!"

"Said she was my *girl*, not my girlfriend."

What a load of bullshit. I turned away. "That's a pretty fine point of distinction. I'm sure my ex used the exact same line on one of the many chicks he screwed behind my back."

Nico took my chin in his hand, and turned my face to his. His eyes were flinty, his fingers on my jaw were firm.

"One thing you should know about me, Kat. I'm no angel. I've been runnin' wild since I was seventeen. But I'm not a fuckin' liar. I don't tell a woman she's mine and then mess around behind her back. If Avery and I were together, I wouldn't lay a finger on you. I wouldn't even flirt with you, no matter how bad I wanted you." His gaze dropped to my lips. His voice grew husky. "No matter how much I want that beautiful mouth all over my body. Suckin' me off. Screamin' my name when I'm buried balls deep inside you."

I lay there gaping, my mind blank. A flush of heat pulsed between my legs. His gaze came back to mine and that pulse of heat expanded to encompass both of us. Scorching. Intoxicating.

Wrong.

Whatever this madness was, I had to put a stop to it.

I tried to pull away, but he pinned me to his side. "Nico," I protested.

He shook his head, all hard eyes and hard jaw and hotness. "Not lettin' you run away just 'cause you're scared, darlin'. Not how it works when you're with me."

"I'm not *with* you!" It came out as a hiss. If it wouldn't have ended up splashed across all the tabloids, I would have slapped him across the face, he was so infuriating.

"Not yet." His voice was dark with promise. He sounded utterly certain, like it was a foregone conclusion that I would be his.

I would *not* be a foregone conclusion.

"Please help me up."

My tone was cold. Judging by the look on his face, Nico didn't like it.

"Kat—"

"Nico, no. Just no. Please stop it. I'm not a toy. You need to respect what I'm telling you. I'm flattered, but I'm not interested in anything except getting through today, and getting back to real life. Okay?"

He paused, gauging my tone. "Okay."

Relief swept through me. Disappointment, too, but I ignored that. I shouldn't have been too relieved, however, because Nico wasn't done with me yet.

"I'll let you up on one condition: prove you're not attracted to me."

I glared at him. "Would you prefer me to stab you with one of my heels, or gouge your eyes out with my fingernails?"

"Nah. A kiss will do the job."

Was I on drugs? Had I even gotten out of bed this morning? Maybe this was all an elaborate dream, and right now I was snug in bed with the covers pulled over my head. I stared at Nico, at a loss for what to do.

My body had a few ideas, but my brain wasn't on board with any of them.

"I don't kiss strange men."

"I'm not a stranger. We've been introduced." His fingers curled over the curve of my hip. His head dipped toward mine.

Breathing was becoming difficult. My face felt so hot it burned. "I don't kiss men with girlfriends."

"We already covered that. She's not my girlfriend. Next excuse?"

My hands were flattened against his bare chest as I tried to push him away. My voice came out small. "I don't want to."

Nico shook his head, his eyes hot. "Such a fuckin' liar," he whispered.

Before I could react, he lowered his mouth to mine.

Chapter 6

"*Dude!*"

"What a jerk."

"An insanely hot jerk!"

"Yet a jerk, nonetheless."

Grace wasn't nearly as impressed by my scorching encounter with Nico as Chloe was. Older than Chloe and me by five years, Grace was a marriage and family therapist in Beverly Hills who had no time for players, bullshitters, or cheaters. She clearly had put Nico Nyx into all three categories.

Rightly so.

We were at Lula's. It was past eight o'clock. I was on my second margarita, halfway through telling the story of my incredible, insane, impossible day.

"Please tell me you slapped him. Or at least didn't kiss him back." Grace waited for my answer, a chip loaded with salsa poised in the air on the way to her mouth.

"Um."

Grace was scandalized. The chip fell to her plate. "Kat!"

"I couldn't help it!"

Chloe was practically swooning at the thought of me kissing Nico. "Oh, God, I bet he tastes like sunshine. Does he taste like sunshine?"

No, Chloe. He actually tastes like crack. Or what I assume crack must taste like: heaven.

I made a noncommittal noise instead of voicing my thoughts, and shoveled more chips into my mouth.

"Kat."

Oh, crap. I knew that tone. I gulped down the dregs of my margarita, motioning to the passing waiter to bring me another.

Grace folded her manicured hands over the tabletop and leaned forward, piercing me with a death glare. With her flaming red hair, steely gray eyes, and take-no-prisoners vibe, she always reminded me of an Amazon warrior. I could totally picture her in a Raquel Welch fur bikini and boots, sword fighting a saber-toothed tiger. I bet she scared the shit out of the husbands who came to see her, seeking help for failing marriages. Maybe that was the secret to her success.

That, or that she'd suffered a traumatic brain injury in the car accident that killed her parents when she was a teenager, and had no recollection of life before her senior year of high school. Tragedy has a way of toughening you up. If it doesn't kill you in the process.

Which was one of the reasons Chloe was so sweet and happy. Nothing bad had ever happened to her. Knock wood.

Grace continued, "I see this every day in my practice. You take a rich, handsome, charismatic man, who's used to getting whatever he wants whenever he wants it. His ego is galactic. He thinks he's invincible. Everything comes so easily, he's frankly a little bored. Then one day someone tells him 'no,' and he simply can't fathom it."

Grace talked like this all the time. She actually used words like "galactic" and "fathom" in regular conversation. She was the one in our little group who read those Pulitzer Prize–winning novels with all the incomprehensible words and big ideas.

I love books, too. The movie versions of them.

"So how does he react when he hears a 'no,' this man who's so assured of his power?"

Chloe made a few guesses. "He starts to drink heavily? He hits things? No? Um . . . he sinks into a deep depression?"

"He digs in his heels."

This sounded ominous. Chloe and I exchanged a worried glance.

"He's so used to a yes-filled life, a 'no' simply isn't acceptable. He does whatever it takes to turn that 'no' into a 'yes.' And, as soon as it is, he loses interest. End of story."

The horrible mariachi music playing in the background began to annoy me. I really needed that drink. "So, this is good! I kissed Nico back. He got what he wanted. Now he'll leave me alone."

"You think so?" Grace didn't sound like she thought so.

"But you just said—"

"Let's recap. So far in this story of meeting Mr. Wonderful, you've said it was *you* who walked away when you first saw each other. And the first words you spoke to him were to ask him to leave, followed by calling him a dick. With me so far? Then, when you informed him you were leaving the shoot because your services were obviously no longer needed, he offered you a job." She paused for dramatic effect. "And thirty thousand dollars."

"Like she's going to say no to that kind of money!"

Chloe always stuck up for me when Grace pointed out my lapses in judgment. She was a good friend.

"*Then*, you had to lie on a bed with him, and pretend you had absolutely no interest in his bare-chested, muscular, sexalicious body. And the director commends your performance, no less! At which point Nico breaks out the really big guns, so to speak, and starts talking like he's auditioning for the part of Christian in the film adaptation of *Fifty Shades of Grey*."

"They already made that," Chloe pointed out.

"My point is that he's digging in his heels! Every time Kat gave him a verbal or nonverbal 'no,' Nico upped the ante. And finally, when she flat-out said she didn't want to kiss him, he couldn't stand it anymore. He kissed her anyway."

Nico was beginning to sound like a rapist.

"So you're saying in order to get rid of him for good, I should sleep with him?" That was vaguely insulting.

"No. I'm saying you should stay the hell away from men who are used to always being told 'yes.' You don't have the necessary level of conniving bitch to manage them."

So it was unsuccessful, unattractive losers for me for the rest of my life. Great.

"I don't see how a little flirtation could hurt." Chloe sounded crestfallen by the turn in the conversation.

"She's right, Lo." I sighed. The waiter brought my fresh drink. I smiled at him as if he'd handed me a winning lottery ticket. He seemed disturbed by my enthusiasm, and skittered away. "Aside from the obvious mismatch of Adonis with a mere mortal, he has a girlfriend. And we all know I've had a bit too much experience being on the other side of that equation. Plus, you know. My dad."

I cleared my throat and studied the hideous velvet Elvis on the wall above Grace's head. "It was just a weird . . . fun . . . crazy day. And now I'm thirty grand richer. That's it."

Chloe hadn't heard enough of the story yet. "But you didn't even tell us what happened after the bedroom scene!"

"We'll talk about it later." I looked at Grace. "After Grandma goes back to the rest home."

Grace threw a chip at me. It landed in my cleavage. I picked it out and ate it.

"You'll thank me someday, Kat. These movie stars and rock stars and famous athletes, they're not real people. They don't function in the real world. They don't have rules like we do. It's just smarter to avoid them, that's all. And you're the one who said it: your dad. You know exactly what the story is with men like Nico. They can't be trusted."

To manage the uncomfortable silence, I took a swallow of my drink.

Chloe muttered, "Killjoy."

"All right, ladies, enough of my sad story. Grace, any news on the man front?"

Grace made a face like she'd just been served a steaming pile of shit. "After the story I heard today in session, I think I might swear off men forever. Honestly, it's like they're a different species entirely. A race of giant walking penises with peanut brains. Or small penises with giant peanut brains."

I snorted. "You're just *now* figuring that out?"

"What happened? Spill!" Chloe was excited. She loved to hear how depraved people were, even if Grace had to change the names and certain details to protect the innocent. She guarded her clients' privacy ferociously, even with us.

"Did you know that dressing up like animals is a thing?"

Chloe's eyes grew wide. "What, like a *sexual* thing?"

Grace nodded. "Role play. Costumes. Even a whole unique language. I had a client today who walked in on her husband having sex with his secretary at his office. They were both dressed like Bugs Bunny. The secretary was shouting, 'Yiff! Yiff!' Welcome to the world of furries, my friends."

"That must involve some strategically placed holes in the bunny outfits."

That was my contribution to the conversation. I had become distracted by my cell phone, buzzing in my purse. I dug into my handbag as Grace and Chloe continued to talk. It was a number I didn't recognize.

"Hello?" As Grace did an impression of Bugs Bunny achieving orgasm, I put my finger into my other ear to muffle the cackling.

"Kat."

One word, and the world fell out from under my feet.

"Are you there?"

Three more, and all the blood drained from my face. It was a moment before I composed myself enough to speak. "How did you get this number?"

Grace and Chloe stopped cackling to stare at me. Chloe mouthed, *Is that him*? Grace mouthed, *That better not be him!*

"Can you talk?"

Barely. But that wasn't what Nico meant.

"Hang on a sec." I put the phone to my chest and looked at the girls. "So. It's Mr. Galactic Ego. He wants to know if I can talk."

Simultaneously, Chloe said, "Of course!" and Grace said, "Absolutely not!"

I looked at them. "Guys. This isn't helping."

"Did you give him your number?" Grace demanded.

"No. He asked for it, though."

"You see? That's exactly what I'm talking about! The man can't take 'no' for an answer! Hang up! And change your number! And, by the way, *he has a girlfriend*!"

Grace had an excellent point.

"Give him a chance! What if he and Avery really did break up? He's obviously into you!"

Chloe's enthusiasm was met with another death glare from Grace. I sat for a moment, nursing a minor nervous breakdown, trying to decide.

"Okay. I'll be right back."

"Kat!"

I slid from the booth and walked quickly to the restroom before Grace could tackle me and wrestle the phone from my hand. Once inside, I hid in a stall and sat on the toilet. I put the phone against my ear, waiting.

"I can hear you breathin'."

"It's something people normally do."

"Yeah," said Nico, "except you seem to be doin' it pretty loud. Were you runnin'? Like you ran away from me earlier?"

"How did you get this number?"

The silence that followed was deafening. Then: "You're not happy I called."

"I had a stalker once. I didn't like it."

"Did you call the police?"

"I shot him."

There was a longer, even more deafening pause.

"I'm kidding. I just had to move, and change my phone number."

"Just? That's more than a just."

"Well, yeah. Which brings me back to my original question."

There was some rustling on the other end of the phone. It sounded like he was sitting up, or lying down. I pictured him reclining in bed, and resisted asking him what he was wearing.

"Hungry Man."

That was the production company that hired Chloe for the job, who in turn recommended me. This meant Nico had probably only had to make one or two calls to get my number. That wasn't very stalkerish.

Only it sort of was considering I'd told him I had a boyfriend when he asked for my number at the end of the shoot. Grace would have a field day with that little tidbit.

"You're not sayin' anything."

"I'm trying to decide if this relationship is going to end with me calling the police on you."

I felt his grin through the phone. "So we're in a relationship now."

Rubbing my forehead, I closed my eyes. "Remember earlier today, when I said I had a boyfriend?"

"Yeah, I do. And remember before that, when I said you were a liar?"

"Do you think you're being cute?"

"I'm a lot of things, Kat, but cute isn't one of 'em."

He said the word "cute" as if it tasted really bad coming out of his mouth. I had to smile at how much that irritated him.

"Well, my friend Grace would agree with you there. She thinks you have a huge ego, you never hear the word 'no,' and you're only interested in me because you hate not getting your way."

The pauses in this conversation were growing longer and longer.

"Hmm. Your friend already hates me, and we haven't even met yet? Bummer."

"Well, Chloe doesn't hate you. She thinks I should give you a chance."

"I like Chloe better than Grace," Nico said immediately.

I had to laugh. Talking with him felt good. Also incredibly strange, but mostly just good.

"Love that fuckin' laugh of yours, Kat Reid."

His voice had gone all low and rough. Which, in turn, made my face get hot. I didn't know what to say. I fiddled with the toilet paper dispenser.

"I wanna see you again."

I closed my eyes. "I'm not that girl, Nico," I said softly.

"We have chemistry that's off the fuckin' charts, Kat. You ever felt like that before, first time meetin' someone? Because I sure fuckin' haven't. There's somethin' between us. I wanna get to know you, find out what it is. Gimme a chance."

His words thrilled me. But then again I was a closet romantic with a long and glorious history of shitty choices in men. My judgment couldn't be trusted.

However, he cursed more than me, which was no small achievement. I liked it. And I liked hearing him talk. I liked the deep, lilting timbre of his voice. It did something to me.

All that was beside the point. The glaringly obvious point.

"Avery—"

"Is *not* my girlfriend." His voice was rough, but in a different way. He was frustrated. "I told you, I wouldn't ask you out if she was."

Did I believe him? Could I? I'd unrolled half the toilet paper onto the floor before I spoke again. "Is that what you're doing? Asking me out?"

"Just tryin' to get to know you. We can go out, we can stay in. We can just drive around in my car if you want. I do that sometimes, drive around, nowhere in mind. Just to clear my head."

"Me, too."

I was surprised we had that in common. Why would Nico Nyx need to drive around and clear his head? Too many choices about how to spend his money?

"Is that a yes?"

I heard the hope in his voice. My heart, which to this point had been doing a reasonable job of not bursting, threatened to do just that. Determination wavering, I bit my lip.

"My boyfriend wouldn't like it."

"Yeah, if he fuckin' existed, he probably wouldn't. Quit playin' games with me, Kat."

I faked offense. "How do you know I don't have a boyfriend? Do I look like I couldn't get a boyfriend or something?"

I might have been fishing for a compliment there.

Nico didn't take the bait. He made an aggravated sound, halfway between a sigh and a growl. "All right. Here's the deal. If you really don't want me to, I won't call again. I'm not a stalker. But I think you're bullshittin' me about havin' a boyfriend. At least be up front about it."

He was quiet for a moment, just breathing. "Well?"

Again, that hope in his voice. Who was this badass rocker/hopeful boy with the filthy mouth and that beautiful, sweet soulfulness? The combination made me crumble.

"I don't have a boyfriend."

His exhalation was relieved. Hearing it, my stupid, never-learning heart soared. "Do you have a girlfriend?" I asked.

"No." His response was immediate and unequivocal, as hard as two fingers snapping.

We were quiet. Something was happening here. I felt it, I *knew* it, but I couldn't trust it. Not yet.

But I could be real about how I felt. I could own my confusion. If nothing else, at least I could be honest. I took a breath, and leapt.

"I don't get it. The whole thing with Avery. I want to believe you, but it seems really weird. And honestly like *you* could just be bullshitting *me* to get me to sleep with you. I've been down a lot of crappy relationship roads, Nico. Yes, today was amazing. Yes, I loved meeting you. Yes . . . I'm attracted to you."

His intake of breath thrilled me. I imagined Grace wagging her finger in my face.

"But I'm not interested in being the on-the-side girl. The one-nighter girl. The meaningless-fuck girl. That's just not me."

There was silence. When he finally spoke again his voice was quiet. "You ever have somethin' in your life you can't talk about, not just because people wouldn't understand, but also because keepin' your mouth shut was the right thing to do? For someone else?"

That one was a no-brainer. A painful bitch of a no-brainer. "Yes."

"It's that. With me and Avery. And honestly? I've never had to explain this shit before, because the women I usually run into don't give a fuck about who else I'm with."

I formed a mental picture of Nico's dick "running into" several women, and grimaced.

"But you do. So I'm explainin' it. Because I want you to understand, and to believe me. Because, like I said, I wanna get to know you. Avery isn't my girlfriend. She's important to me, and I care about her, but not in that way."

I had finally managed to unroll all the toilet paper from the plastic dispenser on the stall wall. I stared down at the pile at my feet, debating with myself. Trying to convince myself I didn't really think he was telling the truth.

Only I did.

"Okay."

"Okay, what?"

"Okay, I believe you."

Silence. Then, softly, "Fuckin' A, Kat."

He was happy. More than happy, judging by his voice. Ridiculously, that made me happy, too.

But first, some rules.

"This doesn't mean I'm sleeping with you. Or that we're going to date, in any normal sense of the word. It only means that I get you need to protect whatever it is you have with Avery, and I believe you when you say she isn't your girlfriend. Everything else is still up for debate."

"Well, let's get to it, then."

I frowned. "Get to what?"

"Debatin'. I'm outside Lula's now. I'll be right in."

Nico disconnected the call.

Chapter 7

My stomach dropped to the general vicinity of my ankles. I shot off the toilet, slammed out of the stall, and ran back to the table.

Grace took one look at my face and knew. "Shit. He's coming here, isn't he?"

I sank into my chair, too freaked out to respond.

"What? Here? When?" Chloe jumped up, craning her neck, looking around the restaurant in terror as if it were a mafia hitman she was expecting.

And not just, you know, one of the most famous, handsome, sexy, *famous* men in the country.

I managed a rational question. "What do I do?"

"You ask him how the hell he knew you were going to be at this restaurant, is what you do! Did he *follow* you here?"

Grace was indignant. I could tell because she threw her napkin on the table, leaned back in her chair, and crossed her arms over her chest. Plus, her nostrils were flaring.

Chloe took her seat again, looking chagrined. "I . . . uh . . . I might have said something about it."

I was confused. "You talked to Nico?"

"Not exactly. I mean, when I was leaving Greystone, Jeff asked me what I was doing later, and I told him I was meeting you guys here for drinks around seven."

Jeff worked for Chloe. He was one of her event setup and strike guys. "I don't get it."

"Well, when I turned around to go, Nico was kind of right *there*. He overheard."

"Did he say anything to you?"

Chloe shook her head. "He just smiled at me. And then I forgot how to talk."

Yes, I was familiar with the effect.

"I mean at that point, I had no idea that you guys . . . that you and Nico . . . " Just then, Chloe's mouth fell open. Looking over my shoulder, she'd stopped paying attention to me.

"Kat, introduce me to your friends." Low and amused, the voice from behind me sent a shiver up my spine.

Chloe gulped. Her eyes were so wide they took up half her face.

Nico took the empty seat beside me. He turned to me, slung an arm over the back of my chair, stretched his long legs out beneath the table, and grinned.

Damn, he made a black leather jacket and a pair of jeans sexy. His dark hair was a little disheveled, as if he'd been running his hands through it. His jaw was shadowed with stubble. If possible, he was even more beautiful at night. Or maybe it was the candlelight. Either way, the man looked positively edible.

Ignoring the hubbub arising around us, the looks and whispers coming from every direction, I tried to act nonchalant, as if this kind of thing happened to me every day.

As if I wasn't about to pass out.

"Well. I'll start with the one least likely to cause you bodily harm."

"Nice to meet you, Chloe." Nico nodded at her. He hadn't even needed me to tell him which one Chloe was. He could tell by the "die, asshole, die" vibe coming off Grace that she wasn't his biggest fan.

"And you must be Grace. Kat tells me you don't approve."

Grace raised her brows at me. Apologetically, I lifted a shoulder.

Always direct, Grace turned her attention back to Nico, and went right for the jugular. "I've seen her through too much shit to sign on for what's sure to be a shit storm of epic proportion. So no, I don't approve."

If I had to decide on the top five most embarrassing moments of my life, today would account for at least four of them. I chugged the remains of my margarita, wishing for another.

Nico smiled at Grace. I wondered how she managed not to combust. "Good. I like it that Kat has protective friends. Pleasure to meet you."

He'd also liked it when I'd stuck up for Avery. Bossy women seemed to be his thing.

"But really it's me who needs protection from her. Did she tell you the story of how she threw herself at me today?" He glanced at me, gently teasing. "*Shameless.*"

That sexy drawl, paired with that sexy grin, warmed me from the inside out. Oh, I was in so much trouble with this man.

Heading off what was sure to be an arctic response from Grace, Chloe chimed in. Unfortunately it was to blurt a sentence that made me slouch lower in my chair in horror.

"She only told us up to the point where you kissed her on the bed and her panties melted."

Thank you, Chloe. Who needs enemies with friends like you?

Looking at me, Nico's grin faded. His expression became distinctly hungry. I looked away and cleared my throat, squirming.

With a loud, aggravated sigh, Grace reached for the chips and salsa. "I can hardly wait to hear the rest." She bit down on a chip, crunching violently.

I sent her a warning look. *Don't be so harsh, Grandma, he's trying to be nice!*

She narrowed her eyes. *We'll see.*

"Turns out our girl Kat can act."

Our girl?

I still didn't look at him. Not even when I felt his thumb brush my shoulder. He began to sweep it slowly back and forth across the space between my shoulder blades. As I was still wearing the little black camisole, this meant his fingers were on my bare skin.

I tried to pretend I felt nothing. Which was like trying to pretend I wasn't being electrocuted. I started to breathe shallowly. I could smell him, sitting so close. Leather and cigarettes and manly musk. Did he smoke? I didn't care. I wanted to kiss him again. And again.

And again.

"So she was good!"

Chloe sounded proud of me. Of course she would be. If I decided to be a serial killer and went on a murderous rampage with a kitchen knife, she'd find some way to be supportive. She'd probably buy me a set of monogrammed cleavers.

"She's very natural in front of a camera," said Nico. "Obi wants her to star in the next video, too."

"I think I'd rather have all my teeth pulled out with pliers. Without anesthesia."

Nico's gaze flashed to mine. "Thanks."

I admit I felt happy he seemed so taken aback by my comment. It felt like it put us on more of an equal footing. He was so self-confident, and I was so off-kilter. But I backtracked a little, anyway.

"It's just . . . all those people. Watching. Judging. It's weird. I couldn't deal with that on a regular basis. Once was more than enough for me."

Fleeting and dark, a look passed over Nico's face. "Yeah. Livin' in a fishbowl has its drawbacks."

There was so much behind that simple comment, it even made Grace pause. She cocked an ear in her "I'm a good listener" therapist way, looking at him a little closer.

As if on cue, the waiter arrived.

He was visibly shaken. He obviously knew what shining star had joined our table. I wondered if he might curtsy. Or vomit. Across the restaurant, peeking around the corner of the hallway to the kitchen, a group of workers had clustered together, staring.

And was that a crowd gathering on the sidewalk outside?

"Ladies, uh, *sir*, can I get you anything?"

Nico looked at me. "What're you drinkin'?"

"Margarita. Rocks."

"Patron Silver?"

Yes, it was now official. This was my dream man. I nodded.

Nico ordered another for me and asked the girls what they wanted.

"Nothing for us, thanks. We have to get going, anyway. You know, work in the morning. Regular people stuff."

Grace sent him a pointed look, but it wasn't as frosty as before. That fishbowl comment might have made her begin to thaw toward him. Grace was very sensitive about the burdens people carried. Probably because she carried so many herself.

Nico ordered a whiskey for himself and sent the waiter away, which was when I noticed the restaurant manager herding a cluster of squealing teenage girls away from the front door. I began to feel distinctly uncomfortable with all the attention we were getting.

He was getting.

Yet he sat there as if no one else existed but the four of us. It was like a super power, the way he could ignore how people stared at him. One busty blond waitress had made four salivating passes by our table already, and we weren't even in her section. But he never even glanced in her direction.

He was, however, regularly stealing glances at me. God, those eyes were blue.

"If you go now, you'll miss all the good stuff. Kat and I were just about to have an interestin' discussion. A debate, I think you called it?"

He slid me a heavy-lidded look. A smile quirked his lips.

"Oh? About what?" Grace perked up.

Damn those sharp ears of hers. She could tell he was up to something.

"Well, she's already said she's not gonna sleep with me."

Chloe's eyes looked as if they might pop out of her head. Grace merely pursed her lips, unimpressed. She was a much harder nut to crack.

"And she's also said she's not gonna date me. So that only leaves us at friends." His smile now gone, he looked back and forth between Grace and Chloe. "And I don't wanna be just friends."

Hands down, most bizarre moment of my life. As hiding seemed like a reasonable response to the situation, I dropped my face into my hands.

"There doesn't seem to be a need for a debate if she's already told you what she wants."

As always, Grace's logic was impeccable.

Bitch.

"That's just it. She hasn't told me what she wants, she's told me what she *doesn't* want. So I think since you're her two best friends . . ." When Nico paused, I peeked at him through my fingers. "They are your two best friends, right?"

I nodded. He turned back to them.

"So since you're her two best friends, and she's not tellin' me what she wants, I think we should all figure this out together." His voice lowered. "Because I wanna get to know her. Because I think she's beautiful, interestin', and sexy as fuck, and that laugh of hers knocks me on my ass. And I think she wants me, too, only she's afraid."

He paused to draw a breath. "So. Tell me what I need to do to make her mine."

Chloe's gasp was soft and thrilled. Grace actually looked like she was impressed by his honesty.

The man was an evil genius.

"Being single would help, for starters."

Though my ovaries had just exploded from hearing Nico Nyx say "make her mine," I had the presence of mind to stick up for him.

"He told me he is, Grace. And I believe him."

She didn't miss a beat. "That doesn't change the fact that he has a bad reputation. With women, I mean."

"Yep." Nico nodded at her. "And half the shit the press writes about me isn't true."

"Which means the other half is."

He nodded again. "Never been a choirboy, that's for sure."

I could tell Grace liked that he didn't try to make excuses.

"Frankly, that's the problem, Nico. It's not only the women. It's everything together. Your entire lifestyle. You have no credibility. The way to earn someone's trust is to be trustworthy. And that takes time. You can't expect Kat to believe you're not going to hurt her just because you told her so the first day you met. You have to prove it to her. And since we're being honest here, I don't think you can."

"I can't if she doesn't give me a chance. That's all I'm askin' for: a chance."

Chloe watched this back and forth in wordless fascination. My face was getting very hot. From the corner of my eye, I saw a camera flash though the front window, and my heart sank.

Paparazzi. They followed Nico like sharks.

"Why should she risk it? What's in it for her except public humiliation when she sees a picture of you with some other woman on the cover of a magazine? I mean, of course, it's a nice dream. The glamorous rock star boyfriend, what woman hasn't fantasized about that? But it's not reality. Not the reality Kat needs, anyway."

This conversation had spun off from the merely strange into the twilight zone. "You guys. You realize I'm sitting right here, right?"

Chloe shushed me.

Nico took his hand from the back of my chair and ran it through his hair. The loss of the warmth of his touch left me aching.

"Okay. I hear you. And I get where you're comin' from. But you should consider the possibility that what Kat needs might not be what you think she needs."

With a glance over his shoulder, he stood. He'd noticed the paparazzi, too. He'd probably developed a sixth sense for them by now.

"Ladies. Been a real pleasure. But it looks like the fishbowl just got a little smaller. Time for me to go."

He looked down at me. He bent and kissed me softly on the mouth. Somewhere outside, another flash went off. Then another. With his lips on mine, I was too far gone to care.

"Think about it," he said quietly, holding my gaze. Then he turned and strode away.

He'd never even gotten his drink.

Chapter 8

So I thought about it. For the next week straight, I thought about it. When I still hadn't come to a conclusion, I thought about it for another week after that.

I thought so much about it, I wore out the batteries in my vibrator.

I didn't contact him. Though I looked at his number in my cell about fifty times a day, I didn't call. Even Grace was impressed by my restraint.

"Though it's probably only making him want you more. A man like him can't be used to waiting. Or is that what you're counting on?"

We were talking on the phone as I pushed a Swiffer over the hardwood in my living room on a sunny Wednesday afternoon. Dust bunnies were multiplying in every corner with the speed of . . . well, bunnies.

"Give me a break, Grace. You know I have zero game. I just haven't called because I have no idea what I'm going to say."

"Well, you could always talk about that lovely picture of the four of us in *Star* magazine."

She was still pissed about the grainy, long-distance shot some paparazzo had snapped of Nico leaning down to kiss me in the restaurant while Chloe and Grace sat at the table, looking on. The headline had screamed, "Nico Nyx and His Harem!"

My face wasn't recognizable, but Chloe's and Grace's were. The article theorized Nico had such sexual stamina he had to have at least three women at a time to satisfy him. Grace had gotten a fair bit of grief from her clients over it.

And Chloe had spent days trying to convince her douche-nozzle boyfriend, Miles, that she wasn't part of Nico's harem. Miles had insisted they go on another "break" while he thought about it. Ass.

"Speaking of which, did you read the story about Avery going to rehab?"

For "exhaustion" the article said. Ha.

"Yes, I did. And ninety days seems like a pretty long time to catch up on your sleep."

My phone chirped, announcing the arrival of a new text. I decided I'd check after I hung up with Grace. "Are we still on for dinner Saturday?"

"It's your birthday, knucklehead, of course we're still on! You only turn twenty-six once!"

"Ugh. Don't remind me. I thought I'd be an actual adult by now."

"You're an adult." She paused. "Ish."

"Hey!" It was one thing if *I* said it. It was another thing if she agreed with me.

"Although you do have a mortgage, so, technically, you're an adult. What can I bring?"

We were going to do our annual pajama party at my house,

complete with feather boas, champagne, ice cream, and chick flicks. I'd already picked out the movie: *The Notebook*. Because nothing says "we're having a good time" like ugly crying with your single, drunken girlfriends on a Saturday night.

Plus, Ryan Gosling. *Hello!*

"That seven-layer dip thing you made last July fourth. I don't want any real food, just snacks, appetizers, and desserts."

"And alcohol."

"That goes without saying. Seven-ish?"

"Sounds good. See you then."

We hung up. I checked who my text was from. When I saw, I might have cursed a little. Or a lot. And started pacing.

Are you still thinking?

Boy, was I. But how to answer? I chewed my lip and continued pacing around the living room, the Swiffer abandoned in the middle of the floor. Another text came through.

Because I'm still thinking about you. I can't stop.

I flopped onto the couch.

Okay, it was time to shit or get off the pot. I blew out a hard breath, mentally went over my pro-and-con list one final time, and decided.

Ditto.

I admit: it was possibly cowardly. And definitely lame. And I swear I wasn't trying to be all cool and unaffected. I had the trembling hands and sweaty armpits to prove it.

My phone rang. I looked at the number and tried to maintain some level of sanity. I clicked Answer and held it to my ear.

"You're doin' that loud breathin' thing again, Kat. You tryin' to have phone sex with me?"

"You didn't give me a chance to say 'hello.'" My voice had gone strangely breathy, exactly like I *was* trying to have phone sex with him. I took a few deep breaths, holding the mouthpiece away from my nose.

"Oh. Sorry. Go ahead."

I heard the smirk in Nico's voice. He was enjoying my discomfort. Damn him.

"Um. Hello?"

"Hey, Kat. Guess who?"

I cleared my throat and pretended to think. "Let's see. Bob?"

"No." Pause. "Who's Bob?"

Was he jealous? He sounded a little jealous. Was that weird, or thrilling?

"Bob's the guy at the corner store who calls me when he gets in a new shipment of Patron."

"Is he hot?"

Yes, Nico was definitely jealous. I felt a bit smug. "*So* hot. If you're into eighty-year-old men with six teeth and questionable hygiene."

"Hmm. Well, you never know. A lot of women like older men. Especially older men who supply them with tequila."

"True. Although I do have my standards. I require my men to have at least eight teeth. Ten is preferable, but a girl can't be too picky."

He laughed. It was soft, intimate, and utterly pleased. I smiled, loving the sound of it.

"Lucky for me I've got all my teeth, then. I think that should score me some bonus points."

I pictured his mega-watt, ultra-white smile. Yes, it did score him a few bonus points. But I didn't want him getting too cocky.

"Eh, you're okay. I'm very loyal to Bob, though. He knows exactly what I need."

Nico's voice lost all its laughter and lightness. It turned dark, serious, toe-curlingly sexy. "I know what you need."

And there went my heartbeat, surging to breakneck speed. Since we were at a safe distance, I thought a little light flirtation couldn't get me into too much trouble. I pretended innocence, just to see what he'd say. "Oh? And what's that?"

"Gimme your address and I'll come over and show you."

That's not what I thought he would say.

"What—now?" Frantic, I looked around the living room. The place was a mess. I wasn't much of a housekeeper, cleaning only when the dust became choking. I couldn't have Nico come over!

"Yes. Now. Made me wait two fuckin' weeks, Kat. I wanna see you. Now."

"Um. Maybe we should meet somewhere a little more . . . public."

"You afraid to be alone with me?"

"Well . . . yes."

He made a low, masculine noise in his throat. "Good. You should be. 'Cause I've spent the last fourteen days with a dick so hard it hurts. Gimme your address, Kat."

Whoa. Okay, this was all happening a little too fast, two-week interval notwithstanding. I couldn't just invite the man over with the expectation that we were going to have sex the minute he walked in the door.

Right?

"Here's the thing, Nico—"

"Don't overthink it, Kat. You wanna see me or not?"

My pulse was all over the place. I sat up, then regretted that move as the room began to wobble. "I do."

"What's the address?"

"I wasn't done talking."

He cursed. I ignored it. "I do want to see you, but I just want to lay a few ground rules before we start this whole . . . whatever this whole thing is."

I waited for him to respond. He sounded like he was listening hard, and he didn't answer, so I plunged ahead. "I don't want to just . . . um . . . "

"You got a three-date rule, sweetheart?"

I was relieved that he sounded amused. Thank God he had a sense of humor.

"Because I can respect that. But you should realize that when you see me today, it'll be the third date. So the next time you see me, all bets are off." His voice dropped. "And I wanna see you again tomorrow."

"We haven't even had *one* date yet!"

"The shoot, then the restaurant. That's two."

His idea of what comprised a date was seriously impaired.

"Those don't count as dates! We were *working* on the shoot, and you were only at the restaurant for like five seconds. If I see you today, *that* will be our first date."

I didn't mention that he'd gotten the details of the three-date rule wrong. It was sex *on* the third date, not after. I was trying to buy myself as much time as possible, because he was moving at the speed of a rocket.

"Okay. I'll give you the shoot. But the restaurant should count. Being with someone at a restaurant is textbook definition of a date. No matter how long it lasted."

I could not believe we were actually having this conversation. I sighed.

"I'll take that as a 'yes.' Now give me the fuckin' address, Kat, before I wear a hole in the damn rug."

He was pacing?

"What part of town are you coming from? Because I need, like, a half hour to get cleaned up."

Nico's response was a growl. I gave him the address.

"You're in luck. I'm comin' from the Hollywood Hills. It'll take me at least forty-five minutes to get to Venice in traffic." He paused. "Or I could take the bike. That'll get me there in thirty."

Was he screwing with me right now?

"You still there, Kat?"

"I'm still here."

"I'm gonna be there in thirty minutes. You gonna be ready for me?"

Oh, the dark promise in that tone. I felt like I was standing at the edge of a cliff, looking down. I already knew I was going to fall. The only question now was, how far?

And how hard?

And would the fall break me?

"I'll be ready," I whispered.

Nico's voice was almost a purr. "Darlin', that's *exactly* what I've been waitin' to hear."

Before I could say another word, Nico hung up.

Chapter 9

Thirty minutes passed at the speed of light.

I did my best to straighten up. I threw the dirty dishes in the sink into the dishwasher. I threw the dirty clothes on my bedroom floor into the laundry basket in my closet. The vacuum cleaner made its first appearance in six months. The entire time, I was frantically checking the clock.

I needed to brush my teeth. I needed to change my clothes.

I needed to take a Xanax.

When I heard the knock at the door almost exactly half an hour later, I was ready. Though not composed. I had no illusions about being "cool" for this. I just hoped Nico didn't notice how badly my hands shook.

I opened the door. He stood there, brawny and unshaven, just as beautiful as I remembered him. From one hand dangled a motorcycle helmet. Parked behind him at the curb was a fat, shiny Harley, which fit. He didn't seem like a sport bike kind of guy.

"Hey."

"Hey."

"You gonna invite me in?"

Visions of that moment when the unsuspecting homeowner invites Dracula inside filled my head. I brushed them aside, trying to maintain some semblance that I was a normal human being, and not the quivering mass of Jell-O I felt like.

"Of course. Sorry. Come in."

I stood aside to let him pass. He set the helmet on the table by the door, turned back to me, and before I could even get the door shut, took me in his arms.

He kissed me. Hard.

It was a take-no-prisoners kind of kiss. Or maybe it was a staking-a-claim kind of kiss. Either way, it knocked me off my feet.

When it was over, I opened my eyes to find him staring intently down into my face. "That was the longest two weeks of my fuckin' life. Don't pull that shit on me again."

The man had no filter. I couldn't help it: I cracked a huge grin. "It's nice to see you, too, Nico."

"Yeah?" He grinned back at me, and suddenly all the butterflies that had been having seizures in my stomach settled. It *was* good to see him. I liked having him in my house. "I mean, you don't compare to Bob, but I suppose you'll do."

He kicked the door shut with his foot, not looking away from me. "Can't compete with a man who sells you tequila, but I did bring you something."

Surprised, I perked up. "You did? What?"

From the inside pocket of his leather jacket, he produced a little black box. I may have blanched, because Nico laughed.

"Don't get all deer-in-the-headlights on me, now, Kat. If there was a ring in this box, it'd be a hell of a lot bigger. And we haven't even been on that third date yet."

I blushed, feeling like a total idiot. Then I started thinking about ring sizes. Then I blushed harder, screaming at myself mentally to pull my shit together.

Nico put the box into my hands. I opened it, and gasped. It was a necklace, gold and delicate, with a pendant in the shape of a Japanese symbol.

The symbol for trust.

My throat got tight. I looked away, blinking.

Nico mistook my reaction for disappointment. "You don't like it?"

"No, I . . . it's beautiful, Nico. I love it."

He put his fingers on my chin and gently turned my head back, so I was forced to look into his eyes.

"Then why d'you look like you're gonna cry?"

The waterworks have been a lifelong problem for me. I get choked up over all sorts of random things, from hearing the national anthem to those cat videos on Facebook. The word "sentimental" was invented for saps like me.

One of the many reasons I have to try so hard to pretend I'm tough. I don't have a thick skin, like Grace. I get hurt easily.

"How did you . . . this symbol . . . you know what it means, right?"

Nodding, Nico swept his thumb over my cheek. "Kenji told me you're half Japanese, half Irish. It was either this or a Trinity knot, which I thought might be a little too much. For a second date, and all."

A Trinity knot was a Celtic love knot, symbolizing eternal love. He was blowing me away with all this. "Nico . . . I don't know what to say."

He leaned down and gently kissed me. "Say you'll wear it."

Of course I would wear it. I was never going to take it off. I'd be wearing it when they lowered my coffin into the ground. I'd never received a gift as thoughtful, beautiful, or outrageously romantic in my entire life.

"Can I ask you a serious question?"

He nodded.

I had to gather my courage for a second before I could ask him what was on my mind.

"Why me?"

I promise I wasn't fishing for a compliment this time. I was just confused. This man could have any woman he wanted. Literally—*any* one. I thought I was better than average looking, but I certainly wasn't a stunner. Especially in a town like LA where beautiful women practically grew on trees. I could be funny on occasion, and I'd been told by past boyfriends I had a quirky, adorable charm.

But I wasn't on Nico's level. I was boxing out of my class. If he was Mike Tyson, I was the guy who emptied the spit bucket. I just needed to understand.

"Could be those freckles. First girl I ever loved had freckles. I was six." Nico regarded me very seriously, but I sensed the humor behind his tone. "Or it could be those Cleopatra eyes. Or that killer body. You got a woman's body, classic hourglass curves made for a man's hands."

I blushed again, looking down.

Nico's voice grew quiet. "Or it could be that when you look at me, I feel like I could fuckin' fly."

I looked up at him. Now he was deadly serious, staring at me with something like wonder.

"I don't have a lot of real in my life, Kat. You're real. Knew it when you stood up to me when I got mad at Avery. Protectin' a girl you didn't even know, puttin' yourself out there for someone else. And not backin' down an inch. I liked that. Liked it too that you didn't let me push you around or intimidate you. You'd be surprised how old that shit gets, people bowin' and scrapin', thinkin' they're gonna get somethin' outta you if they kiss your ass just right. And then you demanded I explain what the deal was with me and Avery before you'd even consider talkin' to me about there bein' anything between us. Which I loved, by the way. Shows you got class. And self-respect. To top it all off, you got two girlfriends who obviously love you and have your back, which means you're a good friend. Which means you're trustworthy. Which means fuckin' everything to me."

I let it all sink in, just breathing. I wasn't sure if I trusted myself to speak.

"So that's why I got you the necklace. That's what we're gonna have: trust. It's important to me, and it's important to you. All this other stuff . . . " He squeezed me into a tight embrace, nuzzled his face into my neck, and inhaled deeply. "Is just a bonus."

"Other stuff?" I sounded like Minnie Mouse I was so breathless.

He chuckled. "The way my dick gets hard just lookin' at you. The way you get wet when I touch you."

Oh, God. We were back to the dirty talk. And we were in my house. *Alone.*

I tried not to hyperventilate.

"First date, remember? And we still haven't established anything about me getting . . . you know. I never admitted to that."

Nico had one hand on my ass, pulling me against him, and one hand fisted in my hair at the nape of my neck. My arms were wrapped around his shoulders, the necklace box in a death grip in one hand.

"So you're saying you're *not* wet right now?" He trailed soft kisses from my earlobe to my collarbone, lightly nipping me with his teeth, lapping his tongue against the pounding pulse in my throat.

"Uh . . . uh-uh."

"So if I did this, it wouldn't affect you at all?"

He slid his hand up from my ass, across my hip and up my rib-cage, to the underside of my breast. He cupped it in his hand, then swept his thumb over my nipple.

My hard-as-rock nipple.

"Um. Nope. Not feeling anything."

Had anyone, anywhere, *ever* told such a colossal lie?

His chuckle was dark. "Hmm. Funny how you're shiverin' then. Must be cold in here."

His thumb stroked back and forth over my aching nipple, while his mouth—soft and wet, Jesus so incredible—sucked on a sensitive spot on my neck.

I may or may not have moaned. I couldn't tell you with any sort of accuracy, because my mind was no longer running the show. I arched into him, utterly lost.

He pinched my nipple, and I jerked, gasping.

"Anything yet?"

Teasing bastard.

"I was just . . . thinking that I need to . . . put some laundry in the washing machine—"

He brought his lips to mine. The moment his tongue invaded my mouth, I knew I was toast. Damn, but the man could *kiss.*

He pulled back after a moment. "Tell me you're wet for me," he murmured, panting. "Admit it. I wanna hear you say it."

Fine, Nico, you win. You win the battle, but not the war.

"Drenched. Soaked. Yes, okay, *yes*!"

I pulled myself out of his arms, straightened my shirt, and ran a shaking hand over my hair. I looked at him. He was breathing hard, staring back at me with fire in his eyes. It gave me courage that he seemed just as affected by me as I was by him.

"But this is only date number one—"

"*Two.*"

Well, I could compromise. "One point five. So I'm going to have to ask that you keep your hands to yourself for the remainder of our time together today, Mr. Nyx. We have an agreement, remember?"

My smile was sweet. Or maybe it was the smile of a humongous bitch. Or a woman with no sense whatsoever. Who turned down the sexiest man alive?

Me, that's who. Like I said before, I've never been known for good decision making under pressure.

"Okay. Date number one point five." He repeated it as if it were a life sentence. Then he smiled a smile of such wicked sensuality I nearly melted into a pool at his feet. "But in another one and a half dates, you're mine, Kat. All mine. For good."

Gulp.

I shrugged as if this were something gorgeous men said to me on a regular basis.

"All right, then, Chastity, gimme a tour of your place. Start with the bedroom."

I quirked my brows. Did we not just establish the ground rules?

He saw my look. "Most personal space in a woman's home is her bedroom. I can learn more from one look in a woman's bedroom than from spendin' a week in the rest of the house. So that's what I wanna see first."

I quashed the ugly impulse to ask him just how many women's bedrooms he'd toured. Because a) I didn't want to know the answer, and b) I didn't want to know the answer.

What was that old cliché? Denial isn't just a river in Egypt?

"Okay. Follow me."

I led him through the house, acutely aware of every dust mote, streaked mirror, dirty patch of floor. I tried to calm myself with logic. Men didn't care as much as women about cleanliness. And rock stars probably didn't care at *all* about cleanliness. I forced myself to picture him living in a mess of a bachelor pad with dogs running in and out, empty frozen dinner boxes on the kitchen counter, crumpled beer cans behind the couch.

I failed to conjure it. Someone as beautiful as Nico most likely lived in a cloud palace.

My house is only fifteen hundred square feet, so we arrived at the bedroom in about four point two seconds. He did the Dracula thing at the threshold again, asking me to invite him in.

I suddenly felt shy. What would he think? "Um. Come on in."

And then he was in my bedroom.

Squee!

He roved around the room like a big cat, restless in a new cage, sniffing things out. I had to admit he was onto something about a woman's bedroom being her most personal space. I'd spent more money and time decorating this room than any other. The rest of the house had a casual California boho-beach vibe, with its distressed wood floors, ivory furniture, and gauzy curtains, but the bedroom was very Zen. Decorated in a cool palette of sage greens and charcoal grays, with a floor-to-ceiling window along one wall that looked over a tiny tranquility garden of stones and succulents, it was my little oasis.

Nico seemed to like it, too. "Nice. Restful."

He examined the four prints that hung on the wall opposite the window, featuring black bamboo leaves against a background of white. He saw the sliding screen that separated the sleeping area from the master bath, and went in for a look. I stood near the doorway, leaning against the dresser, waiting for him to be done.

"Your bathtub seems a little big for one person." He stuck his head around the edge of the screen. He smiled, eyes alight. "Did I mention how much I *love* baths?"

"Really?"

His smile grew wider. "Candles, too. I see you got a lot of candles in here." He winked.

What a flirt.

"I'm not sure the image of you soaking in a bubble bath surrounded by candles jives with the whole badass rocker thing you've got going on, but who am I to judge?"

He pretended outrage. "What, badass rockers don't need to get clean?"

I pursed my lips. "I suppose you're right. But please don't tell me you also get facials and pedicures or we're going to have to reevaluate the status of our relationship."

His grin returned. "There's that word again, Kat. 'Relationship.' You got it real bad for me, don't you?"

My face turned red. Because *of course* my face would turn red.

"Thought so." He disappeared behind the screen again, leaving me to fan myself.

After what seemed like an eon, Nico strolled out of the bathroom, holding something in his hand. He held it up, dangling from his fingers. It was a short, black, silk chemise with a slit from thigh to hip: my lingerie. The master closet was adjacent to the bathroom.

"This is interestin'," he drawled.

I covered my face and groaned.

"And there's an entire section of the closet with even more interestin' stuff than this. Care to explain yourself, Chastity?"

No, I didn't. The story involved an ex with a lingerie fetish. I never wore any of it anymore, but I'd spent so much on the stuff I couldn't bear to just throw it all out.

Nico chuckled. "You're takin' the Fifth, I see. All right, sweetheart, I see how it is. I've got your number now." He strolled across the room, twirling the chemise between his fingers. He stopped in front of me, set his hands on the dresser, one on either side of my hips, and leaned down to murmur into my ear. "Lady on the street, freak in the bedroom, hmm?"

God, I hoped he didn't look in the drawer next to my bed. Maximus the vibrator wasn't the only little toy in there. I'd been single for quite a while.

"I have no idea what you're talking about, officer. That's not mine. I've been set up."

"Hear that sad story all the time, ma'am. Sorry to say I'm gonna have to take you down to the station for questionin'." He took my wrists in his hands, put them behind my back, and tied my silk chemise in a knot around them.

I realized my playful little avoidance tactic had been misconstrued as an invitation to play. *Play* play.

"Um, Nico . . . "

"Shh." He set his finger against my lips. He looked into my eyes, all teasing gone. "Trust, remember?" He took the little black box I'd set on the dresser, opened it, removed the necklace. Brushing my hair aside, he clasped it around my neck, then set his hands on my shoulders. He looked into my eyes.

"You said another one and a half dates. I'm respectin' that. So what we're gonna do now is get to know one another better, so after that date and a half, you're gonna feel more comfortable with me, because you see I can keep my word. And the more I keep my word, the more comfortable you're gonna feel. Which is what I want. You feelin' comfortable. So that when I finally do have you, you're not gonna hold back, feelin' shy, or embarrassed, or unsure. I want you a hundred percent on board. Yeah?"

I swallowed. My voice came out soft. "Yeah."

He cupped my face in his hands, and kissed me.

I couldn't remember ever feeling so turned on. It was part fear, part thrill, all physical reaction to his amazing smell and taste, to that electricity crackling between us.

It was also that I knew, without a doubt, that this man could make me break any rule I might set to slow things down. If he'd really wanted to, he could make me beg him to fuck me, and I'd be helpless not to.

"Good," said Nico, and swept me up in his arms.

I yelped in surprise. He carried me into the living room, and sat down on the sofa with me in his arms. My hands were still tied behind my back. He settled me into a comfortable position on his lap, arranged one of the cushions behind me so I was propped up, and spread his big hand over my thigh.

"So. Let's talk. First item of discussion: where were you born?"

"You don't think you should untie me first?"

He sent me a smoldering look. I read it to mean he didn't think he should untie me first. I sighed. "Manhattan."

"You grew up in New York?"

"No. We moved to New Orleans when I was two."

"The Big Easy. Cool. Must've been fun to grow up there."

"I wouldn't know. We moved to Georgia when I was four. Then when I was six, we moved to Kentucky."

Nico cocked his head. "I'm sensin' a pattern here."

My father could never live in one place more than a few years. Said it stifled his creativity. It was only when I was grown that I realized he used "creativity" as an excuse for everything from avoiding conversations he didn't want to have to keeping up with the rent.

I avoided his eyes. "My childhood was a little . . . chaotic."

He squeezed my leg, making me look at him. "That why you don't have any family pictures anywhere, Kat?"

Talk about sharp eyes. I cleared my throat and sidestepped the question. "What about you? Were you born here?"

He studied me for a moment, his expression serious. He asked softly, "Family's a sore spot?"

Less a sore spot, and more a gaping, bloody wound.

I shifted my weight in his lap and focused on the coffee table. Seeing my discomfort at the topic, Nico reached around my back and untied my hands. Then he took my wrists and put my arms around his shoulders. He stroked his hand over my hair. I rested my head on his shoulder, and he began to talk.

"I grew up in Tennessee. Shitty little town, dirt poor. My dad was an asshole. Beat the shit outta me and my brother whenever he came home drunk, which was a lot. Mom left when I was ten. Never saw her again. Got into drugs pretty hard when I was young, got in trouble with the law, spent a while in juvie. Met a kid in there who played the guitar. We got to be friends. Hooked up after we both got out. He taught me how to play, too. Started writin' songs, playin' this piece of shit guitar I bought at a pawn shop. Didn't have much else to do."

He laughed, but it was hard. "When I hit seventeen, figured I was gonna die in that town if I didn't leave, quick. So I did. Moved to LA. Lied about my age, got a job at the Pig 'N Whistle."

He paused to run a hand through his hair, but I knew what came after Nico got the job.

The Pig 'N Whistle was a famous restaurant and bar on Hollywood Boulevard. They had open mike nights twice a week where aspiring musicians could take a chance onstage. Nico took his chances, and became a crowd favorite. He could play, he could sing, and he looked like a movie idol. He was spotted by an agent, and the rest, as they say, is history.

Not yet twenty years old, he became a star. That was over a decade ago.

"And now here you are."

He rested his chin on top of my head. "Yep. Here I am. With you."

I closed my eyes, inhaling his scent. Here we were.

"How old are you?"

He chuckled. "You didn't Google me? Not sure if I should be happy or hurt."

I *had* Googled him. I'd read two or three lines, then I saw a picture of him and Avery, arm in arm at a fashion event in Paris, smiling into each other's eyes. I clicked away from the page, and went and made myself a margarita. That had been my first and last attempt at finding out information about Nico Nyx.

Denial. De Nile.

"Thirty-one. You?"

"Twenty-five."

"Did you want to be a makeup artist since you were a little girl?"

It was an accident. I was so comfortable with him, it felt so right sitting in his arms, I just forgot to lie. "No, I wanted to be a doctor so I could help my mom."

The moment it was out of my mouth, I tensed. I didn't talk about her. I didn't talk about my past. What was I doing?

Nico kissed my forehead. His hand tightened on my leg. "Easy, darlin'. I won't go there if you don't want me to."

I was quiet a moment, gathering myself. Listening to the sound of Nico breathing.

I felt safe with him. Something I hadn't felt with a man in a very long time.

Maybe ever.

I said, "Sometimes, when things get really bad, I just remind myself that life is a boot camp. We all start out soft, weak. And then we're tested. Over and over. It's hard. It's painful. At the end of it—if you survive, if you don't give up—you're tough. You've earned your stripes. And you get to graduate to the next level."

That's what my mother had called dying: graduation. She'd believed death was just a change of worlds, but certain things—like suicide—could snare a spirit between worlds, where it would exist in a never-ending limbo. So no matter how bad things became, no matter how much pain she was in, she'd never consider ending her own life to escape.

Even when I'd offered to help.

You don't graduate if you give up! She'd been angry with me, her words a brittle rasp in the silence of the barren hospice room as she lay gray and wasted on the narrow bed, struggling for breath. *Never quit, Katherine, no matter how much you might want to. Never, ever give in.*

I took a breath, trying to control the waver in my voice. "So I just focus on not giving up. It's really the only thing I have control over."

And it was the only way I could honor the memory of my mother.

Nico put his hand on my face. I looked at him, biting my lip.

He whispered, "You have any idea how fuckin' beautiful you are, Kat Reid?"

Shit. I was going to cry.

He kissed me. A tear slid down my cheek, and he wiped it away with his thumb.

"Crème brûlée."

I frowned at him, confused. "What?"

"That's what you're like. Crème brûlée. Tough on the outside, layer of hard-ass sugar. But on the inside, you're all soft and creamy sweet."

His blue eyes. That's all I could see. Endless, fathomless blue.

"You know what makes me stop crying?" I sniffled.

His voice came very gentle. "What, darlin'?"

I tried to appear as pathetic as possible. I might have even batted my lashes. "Kisses. Lots and lots of kisses."

His look grew warm. His smile came on slow and wicked. "Careful what you wish for, beautiful."

Then he kissed me again, only this time it wasn't sweet. It was scorching. He laid me down on the couch and gave me the hottest, deepest, most soulful kiss of my life. I kissed him back, spinning into oblivion, not even remembering to worry about what happened next.

I had officially jumped off the cliff, and was falling.

Chapter 10

Nico and I spent the rest of the afternoon doing things I'd never imagined a rock star would do with a woman: Talking. Watching TV. Snuggling on the couch.

It was bliss. It was weird, but it was bliss.

He had to leave at six to go to a recording session. Apparently he'd been working on some new songs and was eager to lay down the tracks. I admit I felt a little relieved that he had somewhere else to be, because the more time I spent with him, the more flimsy my three-date resolve became.

When he kissed me good-bye at the door, it dissolved altogether. I had a sneaking suspicion he could tell, because he left with a chuckle and a gleam in his eyes.

The look of a man with a foregone conclusion.

I worked the next two days, so we didn't see each other, though we talked on the phone a few times every day. In between the phone calls, Nico would send random texts that said things like, "You know you're dying to see me right now," and "I'm in the mood for a mouthful of crème brûlée," and a simple, sexy, "Three, baby. Three."

He wasn't about to let me out of that one.

And then it was Saturday. My birthday.

Twenty-six years old. How the hell did that happen? Eighteen to twenty-five had gone by so fast, I felt like if I blinked, I'd wake up and be two hundred.

Every year, I'd dreaded my birthday as if it were an impending visit to the gynecologist to check on a suspicious-looking vaginal sore. So of course I didn't come right out and tell Nico it was my birthday. He'd had to drag it out of me.

"So. Tonight."

That was his way of asking me on another date. Or our first official date, or whatever. I wasn't sure exactly how I was going to count the next one point five dates, but I'd figure that out when I got there. He called me first thing Saturday morning, making me wake up with a smile.

I sat up in bed and rubbed my eyes, dying for coffee. "I can't tonight. I'm busy. I've got a . . . thing."

"A thing? I haven't seen you in two days, we got another one and a half dates to get down to, and now you have a *thing*?"

He didn't sound happy. The man hated not getting his way.

"It's . . . me and Chloe and Grace are doing a girls' night. That's all."

"Oh. Cool. Saturday is the girls' regular get-together night?"

"Um, no, you know, it's just whenever we can. Everyone's schedule is so tight, and Chloe works all these crazy hours because of the flower shop, so we . . . just try and make it a priority to see each other." I cleared my throat. "Whenever we can."

I heard a low, menacing grumble. "You already said that. You gonna tell me what the deal is, Kat, or am I gonna have to come over there and make you tell me?"

He'd emphasized the word "make." I wasn't sure if I should have been scared or turned on. Either way, a little thrill went through me.

"Okay. It's . . . kind of my birthday today. And the three of us spend it together every year. So. That's it."

I could have sworn a crackle of electricity burned through the phone. "Your *birthday*. And you were gonna tell me about this when?"

Bossy. I made a face at the phone, and tried to sound innocent. "I'm telling you about it now."

"Yeah, and I had to pull a few teeth to do it, too. What's that about?"

Why did he have to be so observant? I could never get away with the tiniest bit of avoidance with him. Most other men I'd known were too oblivious to the nuances of a woman's voice or expression to recognize trouble signs, but Nico was like a hunting dog with a champion nose. He didn't miss anything.

"I'm guessin' by you bein' quiet that means you don't wanna talk about it."

I almost sighed in relief. I should've known better.

"Which is exactly why we're gonna talk about it. Trust, Kat. Remember?"

Fuck. Fuckity-fuck-fuck!

After another moment of silence on my end, Nico said, "You still with me on that?"

Yes. I was. And holy hell was it hard.

"Okay. Here's the thing, Nico. I have a lot of sad stories. But I'm not the kind of person who thinks talking about them is a good idea. Dwelling doesn't help. Feeling sorry for yourself doesn't help. Brooding on all the bad shit that's happened only makes it worse. So, I don't dwell. I don't brood. I learn my lesson and move on."

Nico waited quietly for a moment before speaking. "Got it. You don't like to dwell, so we won't dwell. But you're still gonna tell me what happened on your birthday that makes you not like it."

I heard the determination in his voice. From prior experience, I knew this was only going to go one way: his. So as long as we weren't going to dwell, I might as well cough it up.

Trust. Right?

"My dad left us on my eighth birthday."

Silence. It made me nervous, so I kept talking.

"He actually didn't even remember it was my birthday. I had a little party with my friends at our house, ate some cake, opened some presents, but he never showed up. He finally came home late that night, and just started packing his bags. I was already asleep, but my mother said he didn't say much. He just told her to tell me he was sorry, then he left. I never spoke to him again. He lives in Ireland now."

My voice was steady. It didn't waver once. "With his other family. The one he left us for."

Nico's silence frightened me. I began to worry I sounded pathetic. Did he think I was trying to get his sympathy? Was I coming off like a whiner?

"Baby."

That's all he said, but I knew by his tender tone that he didn't think I was pathetic, or trying for his sympathy. Emotion swelled over me. I had to swallow a few times before I could talk again.

"Anyway, that's the deal with my birthday. So me and the girls will be sitting around the living room tonight stuffing our faces with ice cream and drinking too much, and watching Ryan Gosling be the most dreamy man in the world."

"Is that right? *The* most dreamy man?" Nico drawled. He was playing along, letting me off the hook, keeping his word that we wouldn't dwell.

For that, I fell a little harder for him.

"Yep. Definitely the most dreamy man in the world. Maybe in the entire universe. *No one* could compare to my Ry-Ry."

"So he's up there with Bob, the toothless wonder?"

"Whoa! Bob has *six* teeth, remember?"

"I stand corrected. So Ry-Ry is up there with Bob, the six-toothed wonder? Those are your two main men?"

I laughed. He was teasing, but I also heard the subtext loud and clear.

"Wellll . . . " I sighed, pretending to concede. "There may be a new contender for the title of *main* main man, but the jury's still out on that one. I have another one point five dates to get through before I could give you an accurate idea."

His low chuckle went all the way through me. "Keep me posted."

"I will. And . . . I'm free tomorrow night. I mean, if you are."

"For you, baby, I'm always free. It's a date." He paused. The playful tone he adopted made it obvious he was leading me, pretending to try to add. "Date number . . . "

"Two point five."

I must have said it a little too quickly, because the low chuckle came again.

"That's right. Two point five." His voice lowered. "After tomorrow, there's only half a date left between me and paradise."

And the girls around the world collectively swooned.

"And Kat?"

"Yeah?"

Nico's voice grew soft again. "Happy Birthday, sweetheart."

He hung up. I stared at the phone.

Maybe birthdays weren't so bad after all.

At exactly seven that night, Grace rang the doorbell. You could set the world clock to that woman's timing. I opened the door to find her dressed in a pair of black silk lounging pajamas, a red feather boa, and a pair of sky-high red heels. She held a shopping bag in her arms.

I took the shopping bag from her. She set her handbag on the console and shucked off her heels.

"Let's put this stuff in the kitchen." I winked at her. "Where the drinks are."

"Now you're talking!"

I'd made margaritas by the pitcherful, and had set out a smorgasbord of unhealthy, fattening snacks on the table. The ice cream was in the freezer. All six gallons of it.

I poured her a drink, we toasted to getting old, and I went to change into my PJs while Grace got to work on the nachos.

Forty-five minutes later, Chloe showed up, breathless.

"Sorry I'm late! Happy Birthday!" She crushed me into a hug, then sailed past me into the kitchen. She set a wrapped present on the counter, and immediately began stuffing her face with the seven-layer dip Grace had brought.

"Everything OK?"

She winced at me like a puppy that's about to get a spanking for peeing on the rug. Even her gulp looked guilty. "Uh. Yes?"

Grace and I shared a look. Chloe's lack of poker face was as legendary as Grace's anal need to be *exactly* on time. This could only mean one thing.

She was hiding something.

If that asshole Miles hurt her again, I was seriously going to take a bat to his skinny, Ivy League knees!

I crossed my arms over my chest. I'm sure I didn't look imposing in my pink cotton Hello Kitty pajamas and matching pink boa, but my voice was firm. "Chloe."

Usually that would be enough to get her to spill. But she shook her head and stuck her nose in the air. "Nope. You're not getting it out of me. It's a surprise."

Her face was getting red. Grace and I shared another look. "A surprise?"

Nodding, Chloe shoveled more dip into her mouth. She said something I interpreted as, "For your birthday," although it sounded closer to "Fuhr thurr burffy" because her mouth was full.

"Is Ryan Gosling coming to dinner?"

Grace asked it lightly, because *of course* Ryan Gosling wasn't coming to dinner, but Chloe looked as if she was about to choke. Seven-layer dip sprayed from her mouth like confetti.

Remembering a threat she'd made on my last birthday, I gasped. "Oh my God, Chloe, please tell me you didn't hire a male stripper!"

Grace clapped gleefully, bolting upright in her chair. "Please tell me you *did*!"

Chloe pressed her lips together, and shrugged. She started casually wiping dip from the tabletop.

"You've got to be kidding me." I couldn't believe this! A stripper? Was she crazy?

Judging by her braying donkey laugh, Grace thought the whole thing was the height of comedy. "We are *so* videoing this! What time is he coming? Or is there more than one?"

"More than one? *What?*" My voice kept getting higher and higher. More than one male stripper—oiled, sweaty, and probably married—grinding on me in my living room was my idea of hell.

"You're not getting any more out of me, girls, so just drink up and let the party happen." Chloe poured herself a margarita and drank it in one swallow.

Male strippers.

In the words of the famous Japanese philosopher, Kenji, "Sweet baby Jesus, what did I do to deserve this shit?"

So I resigned myself to the inevitable. We ate. We drank. We laughed. We put on *The Notebook,* and we drank some more, and all the while I was waiting for the doorbell to ring and deliver up a hot mess and a whole lot of humiliation for my birthday gift.

But when the doorbell finally rang, that wasn't what Fate had in store for me at all.

Chapter 11

"Oh, Kath-er-ine! Door for you!"

Grace, sitting cross-legged on the living room floor with her fourth margarita in hand and the red boa now tied around her waist because it kept shedding feathers into her drink, sang out the moment the doorbell chimed. When I groaned, she and Chloe fell into a fit of giggles.

"You are the *worst* best friends *ever*."

I was lying on the couch with my feet over the arm, gorging myself on rocky road. I dumped the near-empty ice cream container on the coffee table and stood. I adjusted my own boa, fluffed my hair, and took a few wobbly steps toward the door, girding my mental loins for what awaited me on the other side.

"Wait!"

Chloe climbed to her feet. Literally. She had to use the edge of the coffee table as a prop. It took several sloppy attempts before she finally made it upright, grinning like a loon, looking ready for Coachella in her cowgirl pajamas and rainbow boa.

We'd all had quite a few drinks. Margaritas, champagne, and possibly one or two shots of tequila at the end of *The Notebook*, when Allie and Noah die together in bed in the old folks' home, and I cried so hard snot ran down my face.

That goddamn movie gets me every time.

Chloe linked her arm through mine. "Grace, c'mere! Get her other arm."

Grace stood and did as she was told. I began to worry. "Support on both sides? Please tell me this isn't going to be so bad I'll faint."

In answer, Chloe hiccupped. She was still grinning madly, a wild glint in her eyes.

I looked at the closed front door. "Are there, like, a hundred strippers waiting on my front porch right now?"

Grace stared at me with a straight face. "Don't be ridiculous. I'm sure there's a hundred horny strippers. Who are into foot bondage. And what one of my clients refers to as 'wet work.'"

I stared at her. "Do I really need to ask?"

"Peeing on his partner."

I formed some very exotic mental images in the few moments it took the three of us to stagger from the living room to the front door.

With a grand flourish, Chloe swung wide the door. And there they were, standing proudly abreast in my front yard: an eleven-piece mariachi band, complete with giant hats, tight pants, pointy cowboy boots, and more machismo than a gang of Spanish bullfighters.

They were flanked by a pair of massive floral arrangements in urns. The grass they stood on—all the grass in the yard, as a matter of fact—was carpeted in lavender rose petals, inches thick. From the branches of the two gnarled willow trees near the sidewalk swayed hundreds of votive candles, casting flickering light over everything. Dozens of lavender hydrangea plants had been placed along the little white fence that ran the perimeter of the yard, lending to it a Martha Stewart garden party chic.

And the brick walk from the sidewalk to the front door was lined with glass bud vases. In each was a single, perfect lavender rose.

The mariachis launched into an enthusiastic rendition of "La Canción del Mariachi," a song I recognized as the one Antonio Banderas strummed on his guitar in the movie *Desperado.*

The movie Nico and I had watched the other day at my house.

The movie I had declared "totally romantic."

I turned to Chloe. She was beaming like she'd swallowed the sun. I tried to think clearly through the alcohol fog in my brain. "Chloe?"

She nodded enthusiastically.

"What is this?"

"It's your birthday present! From . . . " She gestured wildly to the sky, as if indicating God. "Guess *who*?"

I had a pretty good idea.

On my other side, Grace was confused. "Wait. So these are the strippers?"

"There are no strippers, dummy!" Chloe hopped from foot to foot as if she were fire walking. "That was just a decoy! For the *real* surprise, from Nico! Flowers! Music! *Love!*"

She was speaking a foreign language. She had to be. I did *not* just hear her say "love."

Grace squinted at the mariachi band. "So what you're saying is I'm *not* getting to look at all this hot Latin ass naked?" She let out a ladylike belch. "This party sucks."

I noticed old Mrs. Lewis from across the street peering out her front blinds. Then I noticed the man leaning against the Harley parked at the curb next door, watching me, and the next breath I took was sharp.

Our eyes locked. I stared at Nico. He stared at me. Before I even knew I'd made the decision, I was running down the brick path, through the line of mariachis and across the street, into his open arms.

In my enthusiasm, I might have knocked him back a step. I hugged him tightly, standing on my tippy toes, the asphalt rough and cool against my bare feet.

He laughed a low, pleased laugh, hugging me back, his lips on my hair. "She likes her birthday present?"

I spoke into his chest, avoiding his eyes. I didn't know if I could withstand those eyes. "She likes. She likes a lot. Everything is so beautiful, the flowers, everything. And the mariachis are like . . . wow."

"Couldn't forget mariachis. They were playing in the background on our first date."

I peeked up at him. He remembered what music was playing at Lula's?

"And on date one point five, in that movie you liked. So I guess this is our song."

Was this man for real?

Nico saw my look of disbelief. He swept his thumb over my cheek. His voice dropped, becoming almost inaudible. "Needed to make you some better birthday memories, sweetheart. Needed you to know I'm a man who's gonna take care of your heart."

Oh, oh, and *oh*. I squeezed shut my eyes, determined not to cry. I made a joke instead. "If this is a ploy to get out of my three-date rule, it's totally working."

He was silent for a minute, while the band played on, serenading the neighborhood. "Know you got your girls over, or I'd take you up on that, darlin'. You can take another half date off our total, though. Seein' as how there's flowers and music and all."

I laughed softly. "You drive a hard bargain, Mr. Nyx. But I think we can make an exception, considering the flowers and music. You have a deal. We've now officially been on *two* dates."

He took my face in his hands. My own hands were occupied with exploring beneath the hem of his untucked T-shirt. Against my fingertips, his abdomen was warm, muscled, and hard. His abs contracted as I brushed over them, giving me an odd and wonderful feeling of power.

Maybe it was the music. Maybe it was the balmy evening air. Or maybe it was all I'd had to drink. But suddenly I was struck with the fiercest need to get closer to him. *Physically* closer. I wanted to taste him. I wanted to trace every plane and angle of his body with my tongue. I wanted to gobble him up. I'd never felt so ravenous.

I'd never wanted a man as much as this one, right here, right now.

"But, you know, no date's complete without a kiss, Nico."

My quiet words sent a rumble through his chest. He looked straight at me, his gaze intense. "Not really askin' for a kiss, are you, sweetheart."

It wasn't a question. He knew. My answer came on the faintest breath. "No."

He bent his head, bringing his face to mine. With wonderful, slow strokes that made me shiver with desire, he brushed his mouth against mine, teasing my lips softly with his tongue. "What is it you're askin' for then, Kat? What is it you want, baby? Tell me."

He fisted a hand into my hair. He wound his other arm around my back. He held me in place against him, my head tilted up, my eyes staring into his.

I should have been scared, but I wasn't. I should have held back, or played it smart. I probably should have done something else—anything else—but tell the truth.

But deep down, I knew what I wanted, no matter how stupid it might be. And I'd always sucked at playing games. "You, Nico. I want you. *All of you.*"

His eyes went hot and dark. Silent, he held me there against him for a moment, just looking at me. Then, chuckling, he cracked a grin. "Hmm. She's had one too many, I see."

I was taken aback. That wasn't the reaction I'd hoped for. "That has nothing to do with anything! Didn't you hear what I said? I want you! You should be kissing me right now!"

His grin grew wider. "Darlin', that's real sweet, but I don't take advantage of drunk women."

Because I tended toward dramatic after an evening of cocktails and tragic love movies, I gasped in mock outrage. "What kind of rock star *are* you? Isn't that in the job description? Rape, pillage, etcetera?"

His face did a funny thing then. It was part flinch, part disgust, a bit of something I would have sworn was pain. But he closed off his expression so quickly it was almost as if it hadn't happened.

But it had. And it scared me. And because my verbal filter had been disabled by alcohol, I blurted the first thing that came to mind. "Oh dear God please don't tell me there's an ugly story involving rape in your past."

Had it been physically possible, Nico's gaze would have incinerated me. But if his eyes were fiery, his voice was the opposite: ice, ice cold. "That's what you think? That I'm capable of that?"

Not only was his answer evasive, but also it was one of those turn-it-back-on-you questions I absolutely hated. One of my exes used to wield that weapon with particular effectiveness. I stared at him a moment, trying to rein in my temper. "No."

He looked relieved. I wasn't sure if that made me feel better or worse.

"But . . . "

His relieved look vanished, replaced with wariness, and he stiffened.

"There's a story there, right?"

After a silent moment spent combing his fingers pensively through my hair, he nodded. "It's not my story, though," he added when I began to pull away, alarmed. He gathered me back into his arms, and rested his temple against mine. He spoke softly, his warm breath caressing my cheek. "That's not me, Kat. I would never . . . I could never do anything like that."

He was sincere. Or at least he sounded sincere. Into my mind, Grace's voice made an unwelcome comment. *Pathological liars are really good at that kind of thing.*

I was bummed that my pleasant buzz and the earlier sweet, sexy mood had evaporated, but I wouldn't be deterred. "Okay . . . so are you going to tell me whose story it is?"

The tension returned to his body. That didn't make me happy. I withdrew again, crossing my arms over my chest.

"Look. This whole trust thing has to go both ways. I know you had a life before me, and I don't expect a laundry list of all the things that happened in it. Strike that—I don't *want* a laundry list. Your past is your own business. But you're asking a lot if you expect me to take every strange thing you say on faith. Mystery is great. Mystery I can take, because mysteries eventually get solved. But secrets?" I shook my head. "I'm not so good with those. If we're going to get closer, you're going to have to let me in. That's part of the deal."

Seeing his stricken expression, I softened a bit. "Amazingly romantic gestures like a yard full of flowers and mariachis notwithstanding."

He stood there breathing shallowly. I couldn't tell if he was angry or not, until he pulled me against his chest and gave me a hard kiss, edged with desperation. He broke away suddenly. "Fuck. I'm not good at this. Please don't be mad at me. I just don't know what the fuck I'm doin' here."

A pang of pain speared my chest. "Doing here? You mean, with me?"

"No! God, no, that wasn't what I meant! I mean this—" he squeezed me—"us! I'm not a relationship guy, Kat. I've never done this shit before."

Shit? Our relationship was shit?

He saw my expression, and groaned. "Christ. She's thinkin' too much again."

"Stop referring to me in the third person!" I was so mad, I could have stomped my foot. I wanted to stomp *his* foot.

Suddenly he loomed over me. Large and intimidating, he grasped my face and held me inches from his own. "Listen to me!"

That got my attention. He began speaking in a rapid-fire, urgent voice.

"I'm gonna say a lot of shit that doesn't come out right and I'm probably gonna do a lot of shit that pisses you off because I'm a stubborn motherfucker who's used to answerin' to no one and doin' whatever the fuck he wants, *whenever* the fuck he wants! But I'm into you, and you're into me, and we're gonna give each other the benefit of the doubt until one of us fucks up, and then we're gonna talk about the fuckup and move past it! Because I'm not gonna let the girl of my dreams walk away over some stupid shit like my dumbass ways or her need to overanalyze every little thing!"

Ouch. That stung. Mostly because it was true: I *did* overanalyze. I could spend half an hour in the shampoo aisle at the store trying to decide which I needed more, moisture or shine. But then I forgot about that part and rewound, disbelieving what I'd heard.

I whispered, "Girl of your dreams?"

He shook his head, amazed by my ignorance. "You think I fly in the best mariachi band from Mexico for every crazy broad I know? You think I regularly buy jewelry for women I haven't even fucked? You think I'd stand here in the street with that old lady glarin' daggers at my back—" he jerked his head. Through her living room window, old Mrs. Lewis was indeed glaring daggers at his back—"lettin' you cross-examine me, if I didn't think you were the girl of my dreams?"

The sweet, sexy feeling was making a reappearance. I decided the cross-examination could wait until tomorrow, after all the alcohol had worn off. "I'm guessing . . . no?"

He said gruffly, "You're fuckin' right, *no*!"

Behind us, the mariachi band ended the song with a flourish. Grace and Chloe clapped enthusiastically, and Chloe squealed something that included the word "love."

Of course that was the only thing I heard.

Nico said, "Now gimme a kiss before I send you back to your girls and your main man Ryan fuckin' Gosling."

He didn't wait for me to say anything, he just kissed me again. When I was sure I'd pass out from want, he pulled away and stared into my eyes. "Tomorrow."

It was a promise and a threat, rolled into one. Tomorrow, if I saw him, would make date number three. I had the sneaking suspicion he knew all along exactly how the three-date rule worked, and whatever dance we'd been doing up to now would turn into something else entirely.

Something I was equally desperate for and terrified of.

I nodded. "Tomorrow." More softly, I added, "And thank you, Nico, for all of this. It's amazing. This is the best birthday I've had in a really long time. As long as I can remember."

Nico's smile was dazzling. His eyes glinted devilish blue. Without another word, he climbed on his bike, revved it up, and roared off down the dark street.

I watched him go. He hadn't worn a helmet.

When he was out of sight around the corner, I made my way back to Chloe and Grace, and stood arm in arm with them as the mariachi band launched into another song. Some of the neighbors strolled over to enjoy the music, and even old Mrs. Lewis seemed content, watching from her window, nodding her head.

I was happy. It was my birthday, and things were good.

But in one small, quiet corner of my heart, a voice had begun to repeat itself. It was a voice I was intimately familiar with. One I knew from past experience I should heed.

Watch out. Too good to be true always is.

I had no idea, then, just how devastatingly right that voice would turn out to be.

Chapter 12

Sunday morning arrived with all the pleasantness of a sledgehammer bashing my skull.

When I sat up in bed, I immediately wished I hadn't. Rooms weren't supposed to spin and tilt in that awful way. Groaning, I flopped back against the pillow. From beside me came an answering groan.

Apparently, Chloe had slept over.

We were sprawled on my bed, still in PJs and boas, the bedcovers a tangled mess beneath us. Obviously we hadn't had the presence of mind to get beneath them when we passed out.

Through the cotton in my mouth, I said, "I feel like I've been beaten with a bat."

Chloe's blond hair looked as if some angry nocturnal animal had made a nest in it. She winced, laying a hand over her eyes. "The infamous margarita bat strikes again. And why are you yelling?"

Her voice sounded like thunder to my sensitive ears. "Look who's talking, Miss Shouty Shouterton. They can probably hear you on Muscle Beach."

From the kitchen drifted the delicious scents of freshly brewed coffee and frying bacon. I assumed that it was Grace's doing, or I'd been burgled by a short-order cook. I waited a moment, breathing deeply, letting my stomach decide if it was going with violent barfing or if it could tolerate the grease and caffeine cure. After a moment in which my stomach stayed mute on the matter, I decided to try getting up again, this time with better results.

Once standing, I looked at Chloe. "You know what we need?"

She peered at me through her fingers.

"Hair of the dog."

"There's only one problem with that idea."

"Which is?"

"I'd have to stand."

I walked to her side of the bed. "Walked" is actually a generous description of the herky-jerky movements of my body, but nonetheless I made it in one piece. I held out a hand to Chloe. She took it and sat up, swinging her long legs over the side of the bed. In her wake she left a drift of rainbow feathers on the sheets.

She looked down at the boa lying listlessly on her chest. "This thing has definitely seen better days."

"So have we. Now get your ass out of bed. I need a transfusion of coffee and a Bloody Mary."

Chloe sent me a lopsided smile. Mascara was smeared beneath her lower lids, her eyes were bloodshot and puffy, and that *hair*, but she still managed to look pretty. I, on the other hand, would be avoiding any mirrors like the plague.

With the speed of ninety-year-olds, we made our way to the kitchen. Grace was reading a newspaper at the table, coffee cup in hand. She looked up at us, and snorted.

"Well, well, look what the cat dragged in!"

Chloe and I eased ourselves into chairs beside her. "How are you looking so bright eyed and bushy tailed this morning?" I distinctly remembered her keeping up with us drink for drink. At least until after the front yard mariachi serenade. After that, things were fuzzy.

Grace raised her chin in the air, arch as the Queen of England. "Because I'm not an amateur, clearly."

It was my turn to snort. "If *experience* counts, we're all professionals."

"Olympians," Chloe agreed. Sighing, she folded her arms and rested her head on them on the table. While I contemplated that Olympians were the exact *opposite* of professionals, Chloe appeared to be about to drift off back to sleep.

"Children," said Grace, rising to pour Chloe and me coffee, "there are three things one must do in order to prevent a hangover." She set the mugs in front of us, turned to the stove and began piling bacon and scrambled eggs onto plates. "First, never drink on an empty stomach."

"We ate!" This from Chloe, speaking to the tabletop.

"Not nearly enough, and not before you started drinking."

I thought about it. She was right.

"Second, you should drink a glass of water for every glass of alcohol you have. Two glasses of water is even better."

"I hate water," said Chloe. "It's so boring. And it takes up so much room in your stomach."

I agreed via grunt.

Grace ignored our input, setting the breakfast plates on the table. She took her seat. "Third, you should take an Alka-Seltzer before bed, along with a B-complex vitamin, and another of both in the morning."

"You could have told us all this last night." I crunched into a piece of crispy bacon. *Delicious.*

"Like you would've listened to me. Besides, this is so much more fun."

"For *you*!" Chloe warily eyed the plate in front of her. Her face turned faintly green.

"Yes, for me," Grace agreed. "What, you think I keep you two around for intellectual stimulation?"

I kicked Chloe under the table. "Grandma's grouchy this morning."

Chloe pushed her plate away, picking up her coffee cup instead. "Well, you know that old joke about women and menopause."

"There's at least twenty years between me and menopause, Einstein."

Chloe acted as if Grace hadn't spoken. "What's the difference between a pit bull and a woman in menopause?" She paused, smiling sweetly at Grace. "Lipstick."

Grace pressed her lips together in an effort not to smile, though I could tell she wanted to.

"You're not going to be twenty-five forever, princess. I'm going to remember that joke and trot it out at a very deleterious moment."

"If I knew what that word meant, I might be worried. By the way, how was it when they first discovered fire? Those must've been exciting times for you and the other Neanderthals."

Grace raised her mug to her mouth and sipped her coffee to hide her smile. "Homo erectus had fire way before the Neanderthals, sweetie."

This exchange was making me testy. "Someone please tell me we're not actually sitting here discussing cavemen, when we could be discussing something *so* much more interesting."

Grace and Chloe turned their attention to me.

"Like . . . my birthday present?"

Grace pretended ignorance. "I'm so glad you liked that Coach bag I bought you. That color will really go great with your—"

"Oh, shut up! Tell me what you thought! Was it too much? Was it weird? Was it sweet?"

They knew exactly who and what I meant, of course. I knew Chloe was on board with the whole Nico thing, but it was Grace's input I really wanted. Of our little group, she was the one with the most sense. Not that I regularly paid attention to it, but still.

"It was . . . " Grace pursed her lips in thought. "All of those. I'm leaning mainly toward weird, though."

"It was romantic, not weird!" Chloe protested. "You're just mad about not getting strippers."

"He *flew* the mariachis *in*, Chloe. Do you have any idea what a logistical nightmare that must've been, putting that together in one day? And the cost? All for a woman Nico's known for two weeks? To me that leads right back to our conversation in Lula's about men who aren't used to hearing 'no,' and what happens once they finally get a 'yes.' "

Grace's words chilled me. Was that all Nico's present was? Another attempt at getting to a "yes"?

If it was, it was definitely working. I'd admitted as much to him last night.

"I suppose I shouldn't tell you the other part, then." Chloe waited for Grace and me to take the bait. We did, leaning forward to talk over each other.

"What other part?"

"Did it ever occur to you, Kat, to wonder why Nico chose lavender roses instead of red?"

I blinked. "No. Why?"

"Because of what it means."

Grace and I shared the same expression of confusion. "Because of what *what* means?"

Chloe looked at the two of us as if we were speaking in tongues. "The color of the rose!"

"Red means love and passion," said Grace with authority.

Chloe nodded. "Exactly!"

That was a little disheartening. Nico had chosen a rose that *wasn't* about love and passion? "And lavender means, what? Like, friendship? Respect? Oh—trust!"

Chloe looked as if she had a piece of delicious cake in her mouth that she had to talk around. "No. Lavender means *love at first sight*."

It sat there between us all for a moment, heavy and huge, until Grace rolled her eyes. "Oh, for God's sake."

Remembering how Nico had looked at me the day we met, how I'd felt when I'd looked at him, I was at a loss for words. "Wow. That's . . . "

"Ridiculous. Seriously, love at first sight? What is he, twelve?" Grace obviously wasn't suffering from a loss of words at all. She didn't let Chloe's sour look deter her. "Chloe, even you have to admit that's just silly for a grown man."

"It's not about what I think. It's not about what you think, either, Grace. It's about what Kat thinks."

They looked at me expectantly. The words "hot seat" came to mind.

"Two weeks ago, I'd have agreed with you a hundred percent, Grace. And part of me still does. A big part. But I'm doing the best I can, trying to take it slow and see where it leads." When Grace sighed, I added, "Which might be nowhere, you're right. He might get bored as soon as he has me. I mean, I'm just . . . me. Not too many bells and whistles."

Grace scowled. "That's not what I meant, and you know it! Any man would be lucky to have you—"

"I know you're only trying to protect me. And believe me, I'm trying to protect myself, too. My eyes are open. But—and please don't kill me for saying this—it just feels different. It feels right. *He* feels right."

I left out the part about the little, worried voice telling me to watch out. *Ladies and Gentlemen, please welcome to the stage the Queen of Denial!*

"He said almost the exact same thing about you." Chloe's voice was quiet. "When he came into the shop to set this all up yesterday. It's why I was late getting here; I had to make sure things were all set before I left."

"Nothing like waiting until the last minute," Grace muttered.

"Actually, he didn't *know* until the last minute," Chloe corrected, looking at me pointedly. "Because someone didn't *tell* him until the last minute. *Anyway*, he wanted to know if you had any favorite flowers, and what all the colors of the roses meant, and how much he needed to spend to make it amazing. And when his buddies made fun of him, he just said you felt right. And that they could go fuck themselves."

"Nico brought his friends with him to go flower shopping for a woman?" Judging by Grace's startled expression that seemed to carry some deep meaning.

"Two of the guys from the band. Brody, the lead guitarist I think, and A.J., the drummer." Chloe made a face. "And that A.J. was a total jerk! Do you know he actually had the nerve to *growl* at me when I got too close to where he was standing on my way into the cooler? Like what—he's so important I can't even walk around my own shop?"

She huffed, which was the extent of her temper. I'd once seen her snap at a waitress who'd accidentally dumped a plate of spaghetti in her lap. Chloe felt so bad about snapping, she left a tip even bigger than the bill and wrote a five-page apology letter to the restaurant, even though the silk dress she'd been wearing was ruined. She was a marshmallow.

"Wait, back up. You're telling me Nico brought his *bandmates* to go flower shopping? From the *band*?"

Chloe frowned at Grace. "Yes, his bandmates from the band. As opposed to his bandmates from the IRS?"

I was worried now. "Why? Is that bad?"

"Well . . . no. It's just not what I would've thought a man like Nico would do. Showing his tender underbelly in front of the other predators, and all."

"Grace, has it ever occurred to you that not *every* man is a predator?"

Grace scoffed. "Show me a man who isn't a predator and I'll show you a woman."

"That's a terrible attitude for a marriage counselor!" Chloe had gone into prim schoolmarm mode, pinching her mouth and looking disapprovingly down her nose at Grace. Which of course made Grace laugh.

"You're right, Chloe. I'll try to remember your wise words during my next session."

"With Mr. Wet Work? Are you seeing him this week?" Chloe had already forgotten her disapproval. She wanted details. I thought that was a terrible idea, considering we were both nursing ugly hangovers. With a pounding head and a queasy stomach, there's only so much talk about urine you can take.

The doorbell rang.

"Who's ringing my bell at the crack of dawn?" I grumbled, making no move to get up.

"Eleven o'clock is hardly the crack of dawn, Sleeping Beauty." Grace rose from her chair and swept off to get the door. Since she was the only one of us who currently looked like a human being, I thought that was a good idea.

Boy, was I wrong.

Grace's shocked cry jerked me out of my seat. I looked over just in time to see her slam the front door in the faces of what appeared to be a small mob with cameras gathered on my doorstep, jostling and shoving one another in their eagerness to get a look inside.

Paparazzi.

From behind the closed door—which Grace had flung herself against—they began shouting questions.

"Miss Reid, what's your relationship with Nico Nyx? Is it true you're pregnant? Have you secretly married?"

Chloe's mouth hung so far open her jaw looked unhinged. Grace looked wildly around my living room, as if for a weapon. As for me, I was glued in terror to my seat, having absolutely no idea what to do.

From the corner of my eye, I saw movement in the yard outside the kitchen window. Standing there with a video camera on his shoulder was a guy in a TMZ T-shirt. He was grinning. He pointed to the lens and mouthed, "Smile!"

That did it.

I launched myself from the chair, stormed to the window, and, after giving him the finger, yanked the shades down. I then strode through the living room, cursing, pulling all the drapes closed, trying to keep the bacon I'd just eaten from making a reappearance.

"Chloe, call the police!" Grace made sure the front door was locked, then ran to the back door and did the same while I tried not to panic, or puke. Chloe dialed 911 and reported to the operator that we were under attack. The operator seemed to be having trouble understanding her story, because a near-speechless Chloe was uttering such enlightening gems as, "People! Cameras! Swarming! Help!"

I took the phone, identified myself, and gave my address. "Please, send officers right away, there's a group of paparazzi in my front yard trying to take my picture!"

There was a pause. "Ma'am, are you in physical danger?"

"What? Yes! I mean, no, they don't have guns or anything, but they're all over my yard! They're asking questions, and shooting video!" The operator was quiet. I tried to make myself sound reasonable. "They're trespassing, right? This is private property!"

"Do you live in a gated community, ma'am?"

"No." Did that matter?

"Is your home accessible from a public street, or behind gates or a private driveway?"

I could already tell this wasn't going well. I grudgingly admitted my house was indeed on a public street.

"Is anyone attempting to enter the residence? Have you been verbally or physically threatened with harm? Are there any minor children at the residence?"

"No to all three. But they can't just walk all over my property, can they? They're probably thrashing my lawn!"

I was dismayed to hear the operator's voice grow bored. "I'll send a unit to check on you, ma'am. Please stay indoors, and don't engage with anyone until an officer arrives. If you feel in imminent physical danger or there is any other emergency, please call us back—"

"Wait—you're not seriously telling me this is OK? They can't stalk me like this, right? This is my home!"

"I understand you're upset, ma'am. We'll send an officer as soon as we can."

She didn't sound as if she understood. She sounded as if she thought I was overreacting, and wasting her time, and taxpayer resources. Fury exploded inside me like a bomb.

"You know what? I know these calls are recorded. So if I get killed by one of those psychos outside my front door, I want the whole world to know it was because you couldn't be bothered to do your job! How are you going to feel when they play this back on the news after I'm dead? I bet if I was Angelina Jolie you wouldn't take such reckless chances with my life!"

Through the receiver came the faintest, weary sigh. "Ma'am, please calm down. If you like, I can stay on the phone with you until the officer arrives."

Through the closed kitchen curtains I saw shadowy figures moving around the side of the house. Dear God, were they looking for some way in?

"No, I do *not* like! I need help! Now!"

Beside me, Chloe looked worried that I was shouting at the police, the people who were supposed to come and help us. Only I had no idea if and when they actually would.

"Give me that!"

Grace snatched the phone from my hand. She launched a scathing verbal smackdown on the 911 operator. Her rant included some excellent points about common decency, constitutional rights to privacy, and the sanctity of a person's home. At the end of it, the operator was still unmoved. Finally Grace threatened to write a strongly worded letter to the mayor of LA—a client of hers—and hung up.

Almost immediately, my phone rang again. Without looking at the number, hoping against hope the police were calling to say a squadron was on its way, I answered.

"What's wrong?" Nico's voice was instantly tense. I supposed he could tell by the frantic way I'd answered the phone that all was not well in the land of Kat.

"Oh, thank God, Nico, it's you!" I was ridiculously relieved to hear his voice. Not only because it was him, but also because it had just occurred to me that if the paparazzi had my address, they also might have my phone number. Was I going to have to stop answering my phone?

"Kat! What is it?"

"The fucking paparazzi are camped on my doorstep! And tromping around my backyard! And asking questions about me and you—"

"Give me thirty. Don't answer the door, don't talk to them, don't go near the windows. Just hang tight. I'll be there in half an hour, and I'll take care of it. You hear me?"

He rattled off these instructions with the bluntness of a drill sergeant, fully expecting to be obeyed. I was even more relieved; he seemed to have some idea of how to handle this. Naturally he would, having probably handled this exact scenario many times before. He was much more reliable than that awful 911 operator who didn't care if I lived or died. I should have told her the house was on fire.

"Yes."

"Good. And pack a bag, enough stuff for at least two days."

He hung up. I stared at the phone, my head pounding, wondering if we'd yet had a conversation where I'd been the one to end the call. And pack a bag? WTF?

"What did he say?" Grace stood with her arms crossed over her chest, her face red with anger.

"He said he'll be here in thirty minutes."

"What then? Is he bringing a machine gun?" She looked as if she hoped this was a possibility.

Chloe said, "You have some strangely violent tendencies for a therapist, Grace."

"Trust me, if murder was legal, I'd have killed dozens of people by now."

In light of the situation, I let that disturbing statement go unchallenged. "I'm sure Nico's dealt with this a million times before. He'll know better how to handle it than we do."

"So, in the meantime, we just hang out?" Chloe glanced nervously around.

I understood her anxiety perfectly. Thirty minutes seemed an awfully long time to wait. Unless the cops got here first, which seemed unlikely.

"Well, if we're relegated to standing around like a bunch of cows awaiting the slaughter, we might as well make good use of our time." With that unattractive visual, Grace went to the fridge, and began rummaging through it.

"You're not seriously thinking of food right now." My stomach turned at the thought. The bacon I'd eaten was starting to put up a fight.

"Don't be silly. We need stronger fortification than that." She emerged from the fridge with tomato juice and Tabasco. She grabbed a bottle of vodka from the freezer, retrieved three glasses and the pepper shaker from the cupboard, and began to prepare a trio of Bloody Marys.

My legs no longer willing to support my weight, I sank gratefully into the chair at the kitchen table. I wasn't entirely sure if my shaking hands were the result of the hangover or current events.

"Grace, you're a genius."

She glanced at the front door, the kitchen windows, the drapes obscuring the patio doors. Then she looked back at me.

"Well, sweetie, *one* of us has to be."

Chapter 13

In less than fifteen minutes, I heard the distinct, high-pitched cry of sirens.

Peering out a crack in the drapes, my fortifying Bloody Mary clutched in hand, I spied three black-and-white LAPD cars roll to a stop in the middle of the street outside.

The red and blue lights were flashing, but the sirens only occasionally barked. It seemed more a crowd-clearing technique than the typical full-bore emergency wail. And it was working; the paparazzi began to dutifully traipse off my lawn to stand on the sidewalk across the street.

From their bored expressions and snail's pace, it seemed like getting rousted from private property by the cops was just another day at the office.

"That was fast." Over my head, Grace was looking out, too.

"Your threat about the mayor must've worked." Chloe had already guzzled her Bloody Mary. Grace had made her drink two glasses of water afterward and take vitamins and an Alka-Seltzer. She already seemed better. I, on the other hand, was too freaked out to have more than a sip of my own drink, an occurrence that had Grace wondering aloud if that might be a sign of the apocalypse.

"Maybe the 911 operator felt guilty about my imminent death." I watched six burly officers emerge from the parked police cars. Four of them started talking to the group on the sidewalk while the other two made their way up the brick path toward my front door.

I was right: the lawn had been trashed. Also, many of the bud vases lining the walk had been toppled, and one of the large floral displays in urns lay in ruins on its side. *Bastards!* At least the hydrangeas lining the fence still looked intact. Maybe I could plant them.

If I didn't have to move to Iceland in order to escape the paparazzi plague.

"I'm sure paparazzi don't actually kill people." Chloe sounded more hopeful than certain.

Grace said, "I have two words for you. Princess Di."

With that chilling pronouncement, the doorbell rang. I ran to answer it, Grace and Chloe at my heels.

"Miss Reid?" One of the officers—blond, dimpled, square-jawed—looked hopefully at Chloe. She looked back at him as if he were Prince Charming, just arrived on his trusty steed.

"That's me," I said, interrupting the mutual admiration society.

Blond Cop tore his gaze from Chloe to regard me with less enthusiasm. He inclined his head. "Ma'am."

Why wasn't I "Miss"? Christ, did I look that haggard?

"Thanks for coming so quickly."

"No problem," said the other officer. He was shorter, but no less broad in the chest, or intimidating, than his associate. "First time dealing with the paps can be scary, we know."

Grace pounced on that like a cat on a mouse. "How do you know it's the first time?"

Blond Cop provided the answer, smiling knowingly. "Your friend gave us a call."

Nico had the cops on speed dial? In my mind, he was beginning to take on the stature of Superman. Chloe, Grace, and I shared a dazed look.

"If you don't do anything interesting, they'll leave on their own after a while. In the meantime, we'll make sure they stay off the lawn and on the other side of the street. We know most of these guys. The TMZ crew is pretty harmless; it's the independents you have to watch out for. They can get a little aggressive."

I knew they were aggressive, but hearing a policeman describe them that way was on a different level, considering cops dealt with the worst of the worst of humanity in their jobs. I felt more and more sick. "They can just stand across the street, watching me? For how long?"

The officer didn't answer directly. Most likely he could sense my pending mental breakdown.

"There are loitering laws, but honestly it's best just to ignore them. Like I said, unless you do something interesting, they'll be on to the next thing pretty quick." He handed me a business card. "If you feel threatened, this is the number to the station. Officer Cox and I," he nodded at Blond Cop, "patrol this area and can usually be here within fifteen minutes."

"What if you're not on duty?" Chloe was wringing her hands in worry. Officer Cox looked at her as if he'd like to give her a hug. Or something stronger.

"Don't worry. We've got you covered."

I felt a little better. Then I wondered if I needed to have Chloe move in with me so Officer Cox would respond just as quickly to my next distress call. Because I assumed there would be a next distress call; it wasn't as if I was going to stop seeing Nico because of those paparazzi fuckers.

I realized he'd be arriving soon . . . and I probably looked like something the cat had coughed up.

"Thank you, guys. So much. Just having you here makes me feel better." *Now please leave so I can take a shower and scrape the moss off my teeth before Superman flies in and mistakes me for a cave troll.*

Officer Cox and his friend nodded at me and turned to go. After a few steps, Officer Cox turned back. He held out his own card to Chloe. "Just in case."

Biting her lip, she took the card. They stared at one another a beat. "Right. You never know. Emergencies and all."

He nodded. So did Chloe. It seemed as if something had been decided. He walked away, black baton swinging phallically at his hip, his swagger that of a man who'd just bagged an elephant.

Chloe couldn't take her eyes from him.

Well, I thought cheerfully, *so long, Miles*! Silver linings, etcetera. The three of us retreated inside, and I closed the door. Now seemed a good time to finish my drink.

"Did that just happen?" Chloe seemed a bit stunned.

"What? Your love connection with the LAPD?" Grace chuckled. "Yes, sweetie, I think it did."

"He was *hot*, right? And did you see the size of his *gun*?"

I wasn't going to touch that one.

Grace said, "I'm sure you two will make beautiful blond babies and live happily ever after as Mr. and Mrs. *Cox*, a name designed solely to amuse people like me. Now can we please discuss how we're going to get out of here without those vultures outside following us home?"

Oh. I hadn't considered that. At some point, Grace and Chloe had to leave.

"I need a shower in order to think. Just give me—"

From outside came the unmistakable screech of a vehicle braking hard. When we looked out the window, I corrected myself: *two* vehicles. With no regard for the fact that it was a two-way street, a pair of black Escalades with limo tint had parked opposite the police cars, blocking traffic. Their driver doors flew open. Out popped Barney and Nico, both of them looking like they were about to commit murder.

At the sight of Nico, the paparazzi went into a feeding frenzy that would have made a school of piranha proud.

"Uh-oh."

"Bit of an understatement, Chloe, but accurate, nonetheless." Grace sent me a sympathetic look. "This should be fun."

"Oh, God. What's he doing?" Turning away to pace in the living room because I couldn't bear to watch, I began to chew my thumbnail.

"Well . . . it looks like he's about to get into a fight with . . . " Grace began counting. "Eight guys. The rest are taking pictures. Who's the thug with him in the black Armani?"

Only Grace could spot a designer suit at three hundred paces.

"Barney. He's Nico's . . . " I thought of him driving Avery home, and returning to me with a briefcase of cash the day of the shoot. "Assistant, I guess? He's not a thug. He's really sweet."

Was I hyperventilating? I couldn't look out the window. I had no experience with fights, and didn't trust myself not to scream. I felt as if I might be having an out-of-body experience.

Grace winced, watching the action outside. "I think Barney just tasered someone."

I was horrified. "What? With a taser?"

She answered drily, "No, with his cell phone. It's a new Android app."

"*Dude!* I thought people only twitched like that for effect in the movies!"

"Chloe!"

Unimpressed with my outburst, Chloe drew in a low, thrilled breath. "Oh! Look at Officer Cox!" A moment later, louder, "*DUDE!*"

OK, now I *had* to look. I crossed to the window just in time to see Officer Nordic God Cox shove a man to the ground, toss him on his stomach, and wrap a pair of handcuffs around his wrists, faster than I could blink. Not that I was blinking, because my central nervous system was suffering from sudden-onset paralysis.

The scene outside had quickly devolved into chaos.

I spotted Nico again. Time seemed to slow to a crawl. He was shouting at a man with a video camera while the police officer who had come to the door with Officer Cox pushed him back, one hand flattened on Nico's chest, the other wrapped around the weapon at his waist. His face contorted in anger, Nico looked completely unhinged, like he might at any moment tear off the policeman's arm and beat the other man to death with it.

Nico broke away from the officer and headed toward my door. I had it open before he was halfway up the path. He brushed past me into the house, slammed shut the door, locked it, and turned to grip my upper arms. He pulled me against his chest.

"Are you all right?"

Though his voice was controlled, his expression, energy, and posture were thermonuclear with rage. His nostrils were flared, his breathing was ragged, every muscle in his body was clenched.

I'd never stood this close to someone so furious. I could almost *smell* the violence in him. It frightened me so much I stuttered when I answered.

"W—we're okay. Th—they didn't do anything."

Nico stared at me in silence, examining my face. I don't think he believed me.

"Grace."

She stood near the front windows, watching us. "Yes?"

Not releasing me, Nico cut his gaze to her. He jerked his chin. My guess was correct: he was looking to Grace for confirmation.

She answered in a quiet monotone. It was her professional lion-tamer voice, designed to soothe and support, yet without any shred of emotion.

"She's fine, Nico. We all are. We had a scare, but no damage has been done. The police arrived very quickly. Thank you for calling them. And thank you for coming so quickly as well. I know Kat feels much better now that you're here."

Her tone revealed nothing. Her expression revealed nothing. Her unflinching gray eyes revealed nothing. But I'd known Grace Stanton a long time. The moments she revealed nothing were the most revealing moments of all.

If she'd been withholding final judgment on Nico before, if she'd been inclined to dislike him for his womanizing and his life-style and his past, but was giving him the slightest benefit of the doubt for my sake, this situation had brought her to her ultimate, irrevocable conclusion.

I had zero hope it was positive.

Not privy to this information, Nico nodded, seeming grateful for her words. Seeming, if not *calmed*, at least slightly less explosive from hearing them. He looked back at me.

"Okay. We're outta here. You pack your bag?"

I was almost afraid to say "no." "Um . . . "

He didn't wait for more. "Do it. We leave in five." He looked at Grace, then at Chloe. "You girls get ready, too. Barney will drive you home."

"But my car—"

Nico cut Chloe off. "We'll get it to you later today. Just give Barney your keys, and he'll handle it. You don't want those guys outside following you home, trust me. Once they know where you live, you'll never get rid of them."

Never? Appropriately, Chloe paled. As did I.

"Why do I need a bag? Where are we going?" I asked Nico.

"My place."

He correctly interpreted my stunned look, but wasn't taking "no" for an answer.

"You're staying with me until this dies down." He jerked his head toward the closed door. "And we'll figure out what we're gonna do to get this place more secure. I know a guy who does great security systems. Gates, surveillance, the whole—"

"I'm not installing *gates* around my house, Nico. I don't want to live like a prisoner!"

And why had he just assumed I'd stay with him? He hadn't even asked! I'd stay at a hotel. This was too weird to be believed.

"Kat," said Grace, still with that quiet, unnerving voice, "he's right."

That was the last thing I expected to hear her say. I turned to stare at her.

"If you and Nico are going to be together, you need to be realistic about what that entails. What's happening outside today is the tip of the iceberg in terms of what you're up against. You have to start thinking about protecting your privacy, and your safety. Now that they know who you are, you'll be hunted."

Hunted? Chills coursed down my spine.

"They'll start going through your trash. They'll follow you to your car, the grocery store, the movies, the doctor's office. They'll climb the trees to get a better view into your yard, to see if they can get private pictures of you and Nico . . . " her face slightly reddened, "together. And if they do, they won't hesitate to publish those pictures. Or, God forbid, *video*."

Lurid and horrible, snippets of celebrity sex tape scandals flashed through my mind's eye. Was I about to join the ranks of such women as Pamela Anderson, Paris Hilton, and Kim Kardashian?

"This isn't making me feel better, Grace."

"Sorry, sweetie. But you've been through worse. I'm sure you can handle this. It's not the end of the world, it's just . . . a major adjustment."

Nico's fingers tightened around my arms. He was looking back and forth between me and Grace. I knew he was wondering what she'd meant by "been through worse."

The story I'd told him about why I hated my birthday wasn't the worst of my little Pandora's box of sordid stories. Not by a long shot.

"All right. I'll get my stuff." I didn't add that I'd be staying at a hotel. I didn't want to have that particular discussion with Nico in front of the girls. I knew how he was about getting his way.

"C'mon." Grace moved toward the bedroom. "I'll help you pack. Chloe?"

Still looking dazed, Chloe nodded, following Grace into the bedroom. Nico and I were left alone.

The first thing he did was pull me into a hard hug. He smelled like cigarettes again, and leather, and some kind of spicy cologne. He put his mouth to my ear, his unshaven cheek scratching my skin. "I'm sorry."

"It's not your fault."

"Yeah. Thanks for that, but it is."

My head tucked against his chest, I sighed. Then, realizing I hadn't yet brushed my teeth, I mashed my lips together in horror. And my hair. And my face!

I gently pulled myself from Nico's arms, noting as I did that he was still wound tight as a bowstring.

"Okay. Five minutes. Be right back."

Before he could answer, I dashed after Chloe and Grace, closing the bedroom door behind me.

I found Chloe sitting on the edge of my bed, looking lost. Grace had pulled my oversized duffel bag out from the closet, and was calmly putting a pair of folded jeans into it. I watched her cross to my dresser, pull out several pairs of panties, socks, and T-shirts, and add them to the duffel.

"Grace."

She didn't stop packing. "I already know what you're going to say, Kat. But you're wrong. I don't hate him."

"You don't?" I couldn't keep the surprise from my voice.

"No."

"Even after what just happened? What you just warned me that's going to keep happening if I keep seeing him?"

She glanced at me. Her hands fell still. I waited impatiently for her to speak. Even Chloe sat a little straighter.

"He's not what I would've wanted for you. It's too complicated, too risky, too . . . *much.* I still don't trust him. And I still think it's going to end in disaster, I've made that pretty clear. But—and this is a big, extenuating but—when a man acts as protective as Nico just did, it means he cares. A lot. He wasn't at all concerned about how he was going to look to the press, or with how the police might react to his crazy chest-thumping Tarzan routine; he was only concerned with you. So, if nothing else, I'm convinced at least that he doesn't see you as just another notch in his bedpost." She resumed packing the duffel. "Obviously I still think this relationship will be about as stable as the Titanic, but after watching him go ballistic because you were upset, I'm keeping my mouth shut from here on out. Well, except for this small public service announcement: no glove, no love."

I was touched. It wasn't like Grace to cut men slack. Especially men of the galactic-ego variety. "Gee, Grandma, I think you're getting soft in your old age."

"Shut up," she said mildly, "and go brush your teeth. That breath of yours is about to ignite something."

So, after giving Grace a hug, I followed her advice. I hurriedly washed my face, brushed my teeth, stuck my hair in a ponytail, and changed my clothes. Then Grace and Chloe helped me put together the rest of what I'd need for a few days away.

A few days away . . . with Nico.

Titanic, here I come. Hope there's room in the lifeboats.

Chapter 14

Getting from my front door to the Escalades waiting on the street was like something out of a Schwarzenegger movie.

In the few minutes that had elapsed since Nico had shown up, more police vehicles had arrived, two news vans with satellite dishes had set up shop across the street, and what seemed like every neighbor within a fifty-mile radius had gathered, sensing blood. The scene was so bizarre, I wouldn't have been surprised if psychotic assassin robots from the future leapt from the crowd, laser guns pointed at my head.

Not that I would have been able to see them. Grace, Chloe, and I all had jackets draped over our heads like burkas.

Or shrouds.

The jackets were Nico's idea, one with which Grace wholeheartedly agreed. Talk about doing a one-eighty.

"I won't be able to see where I'm going!"

My protest had been trounced by Grace's logic, which, in typical fashion, trounced everything. "We'll hold hands. Nico can lead.

But the paparazzi won't be able to see our faces, which is what they want. So, we win."

Chloe said mournfully, "I see the headlines already. 'Nico Nyx leads hidden harem from love den to limousines.' I can only imagine what Miles will have to say about this."

"I thought you and Officer Cox were going to be making beautiful blond babies," I reminded her.

She'd visibly brightened at the mention of his name. But it was short-lived. As soon as Nico opened the front door, all hell broke loose.

Then we ran the gauntlet.

Nico's grip on my hand was so tight it hurt. I could only see my feet, his feet, and the pavement. Oh—and a lot of other feet all around, from everyone crowding in so close.

Apparently the police had failed miserably at keeping the paparazzi contained across the street.

Worse than the feet was the shouting, which rose to a roar as we progressed from the yard to the Escalades. I couldn't believe this was happening.

"Why are there so many of them?" Chloe screamed.

Good question. She was behind me, gripping my right hand as tightly as Nico held my left. Grace, ever stalwart, brought up the rear. The four of us stumbled through the crowd to the cars, getting bumped, shouted at, harassed. Camera shutters sounded like gunfire. I held my breath, heart pounding wildly, adrenaline pumping through my veins, until finally we made it to the car.

Barney had apparently had enough of tasering people, because he helped Chloe and Grace into one Escalade, and me into the other. The minute he slammed the door shut, I sank low into the seat and clicked the Lock button. Then I tried to remember how to breathe.

A moment later—it could have been seconds or minutes, I was so terrified I couldn't tell—the driver door opened with a chirp of a remote, and Nico got in.

"Seat belt."

His voice was so rough he might have been swallowing rocks. He shut the door and revved the engine. A siren barked three times, and we began to move. We crept along for a while, until the sound of the crowd faded and we picked up speed. We *kept* picking up speed, until we were moving so fast I got even more scared than I was before. I stayed quiet as long as I could, until I couldn't stand it anymore.

"Are we being chased?"

Silence. The sound of Nico's ragged breathing. Then, curtly, "No. Had an escort from the cops, but they dropped off a few blocks back."

"So can I take this jacket off my head now?"

Nico exhaled hard. I peeked out from under the jacket. He had a death grip on the steering wheel. His hands were curled so tightly around it his knuckles showed white.

I took his nonanswer as a "yes." I pulled the jacket off, but kept it on my lap just in case. My heartbeat was beginning to slow to pre-freakout levels, but I was still hungover, and not operating on all cylinders. I needed a shower, and about ten more hours of sleep.

"You got to my house really fast."

Nico didn't take his eyes off the road. "Not fast enough. You sure you're okay?"

The mirrored aviators he wore reflected back harsh glints of sunlight over the dashboard and windshield. I closed my eyes, and rested a shaking hand on my forehead. "Other than feeling like death, I'm fine."

I felt his sharp gaze examining me. "Birthday party hangover?"

I nodded. He reached out and took my hand, rubbing his thumb against mine. I heard his hard exhalation again, followed by a muttered curse.

I glanced at him. A muscle in his jaw flexed, over and over. He stomped on the gas, and we barreled through a yellow light, narrowly missing a Prius trying to make a left turn.

"I'm okay, Nico," I reassured him softly, squeezing his hand. "Really. Just a little weirded out." *Hello, understatement of the year.*

"Those fuckin' jackals!" The words were snarled from between his clenched teeth. His pulse was pounding wildly in a vein in his neck. On impulse, I reached out and stroked it. He looked over at me, his jaw tight.

"Thank you for rescuing me."

He cut his gaze back to the road. "Yeah, I'm a real knight in shinin' armor."

I realized he was as mad at *himself* as he was at the paparazzi. He really did think this whole thing was his fault. I suddenly felt very protective of him, and angry at them. But considering his mood, I didn't want to say anything that could be misinterpreted as blame. So I just kept my tone soft and sweet.

"Okay, maybe not armor." I glanced at his jean-clad thighs. "You're my knight in shining denim."

This earned me a small, wry smile. It looked more like a grimace, but I'd take it. Leaning over the console between our seats, I pressed my lips to that angry pulse in his neck. He wound an arm tightly around my shoulders, kissing my temple. I tucked my face in between his neck and shoulder, breathing him in. I loved the way he smelled: purely masculine.

"Do you smoke?"

It took a while before he answered. "Only when I'm really stressed out. It's bad for my voice."

I'd only smelled smoke on him twice. Now, and that first night at Lula's, when he'd been waiting outside as he called. It gave me a little thrill to think he might have been worried about calling me. Maybe I hadn't been such a foregone conclusion after all.

We drove a while in silence, until we hit Sunset Boulevard and started into the hills.

"So. Your house." I sat back in my seat, but Nico kept his hand on the nape of my neck, gently squeezing. It was big and warm, and made me feel better.

"Yep. My house."

"Where your *bedroom* is."

Now his smile was genuine. I even got a flash of teeth. "Easy, Tiger. I'm not that kind of guy. You want me, you gotta work for it."

Playing along, happy that his thunderstorm mood might be lifting, I pretended outrage. "But it's our third date! You're supposed to put out on the third date!"

His head snapped around. Above the aviators, his brows shot up. His smile couldn't have been more brilliant. "Yeah? That how it works?"

Oh, shit. Foot, meet mouth. I mentally flailed around, grasping at straws. "Uh . . . unless you follow Steve Harvey's advice, which is that you shouldn't give up the cookie for, like, ninety days."

To his credit, he didn't crash the car. He merely stared at me, those blue eyes burning me straight through his sunglasses.

I looked out the window, pretending to examine the view. When I heard Nico's low chuckle, I knew I was in for it.

"Okay, darlin'. Game on. Consider your cookie safe for ninety days."

My mouth fell open. Ninety days! He had to be joking! Only I had the terrible suspicion he wasn't.

Commence Operation Backpedal.

"I mean, I'm not saying that *I* necessarily follow Steve Harvey's advice. I'm just saying there are a few different schools of thought on the subject."

"Hmm." He slid his fingers down my arm, picking up my hand in his own. Then he looked at me over the rim of his sunglasses, and sucked my thumb into his mouth. He bit it, lightly, eyes twinkling with mischief.

Son of a bitch.

He must've read my dismayed expression, because he looked mighty pleased with himself. "No, I think Steve Harvey has it exactly right, Kat. Man knows what he's talkin' about. A girl can't just be givin' away her golden cookie to every dog that comes sniffin' around. Gotta keep that cookie in the cookie jar. Keep it *fresh*, right?"

I retrieved my hand with as much dignity as I could muster. It was my turn to utter a noncommittal, "Hmm."

Okay. If the game was on, I wasn't about to lose. I was going for the gold. Even if it killed me.

I decided to change the subject by texting Chloe to make sure she and Grace were all right. She answered back that they were almost at her house, and Barney had promised to show her how to use his taser. I hoped Grace hadn't been volunteered as the subject.

"Will Barney get in trouble for using a stun gun on that guy?"

Nico shook his head. "Barney's ex–special ops. He knows the law inside and out, knows when he can reasonably plead self-defense and when he can't. The guy he tasered took a few swings at him, which equals the former. Plus he's in tight with the LAPD; he was a cop for a few years before he went into private security."

"Oh. So he's your bodyguard?"

Nico said quietly, "He's my friend. He's someone I trust implicitly."

His tone hinted at mysteries, at tangled history and buried bodies and closets full of skeletons. More secrets. Worried again, I fingered the charm on the necklace he'd given me, wondering exactly what having Nico's trust entailed.

I was lost in thought for the remainder of the drive. When we pulled up to a stainless steel gate at the end of a long cul-de-sac, the gate swung open on silent hinges, and we began to climb a steep gravel road lined with huge Italian cypresses. It went on for what seemed like forever, until finally we crested the top of a hill.

There sat Nico's house, a sprawling compound of glass and stone, perched right on the steep hillside so it seemed suspended in air.

I was flabbergasted. He actually *did* live in a cloud castle.

The views stretched all the way from Malibu to downtown LA. The city was laid out beneath us, vast and shimmering in the morning light. Far off in the distance on the winking blue Pacific, I caught a glimpse of the Channel Islands. I'd never seen anything quite as spectacular.

"Welcome to the Shack."

Awed, I laughed in disbelief. "Yeah, it's very shack-like. So small, and ugly. You poor thing."

Nico's voice grew dark. "It's a lot different from the trailer I grew up in, that's for sure." His face clouded with memory. After a moment, he shook it off. "So. I expect you'll wanna see my bedroom first. Get that outta the way, since you won't be spendin' any time in there for the next three months."

I stuck out my tongue. He laughed. He got out of the car, retrieved my bag from the backseat, then strolled around to my side and opened my door, grinning and so cocksure I had to roll my eyes.

"Outta my way, Romeo." Brushing past him, I lifted my chin and sniffed like a duchess dismissing the stable boy. He grasped my arm, spun me around, dropped the duffel on the paved driveway, and took my face in his hands.

"Get it right, baby. My name isn't Romeo." His voice was husky. His nose was touching mine, his body was pressed against mine, those blue eyes searing straight down to the bottom of my soul.

"No?"

Slowly, Nico shook his head. He brushed his lips against mine, gently sucked my lower lip into his mouth, and pressed his teeth against it just hard enough to sting. He released it and whispered, "I'm the Cookie Monster."

God, that voice. Those eyes. That wicked grin. The man was sex incarnate. Forget ninety days. Alone with him in the house, I'd be lucky to last ninety minutes.

My widened eyes made his grin grow wider. Without further ado, he grabbed the duffel, grabbed my hand, and led me into his house.

Chapter 15

Here's the thing: I'm no hick. And I don't say that in a mean way. My point is simply that I'm not an innocent country girl who's never been away from her little hometown to see the world. I'd moved all over the States as a kid, I'd met all kinds of different people, I'd lived in LA for years, and I'd worked in the industry, which meant even if I didn't personally have wealth, I was exposed constantly to people who did.

But not like this.

The art collection. The car collection. The guitar collection, which covered the walls of a room larger than my entire house. Larger even than the plot my house was *built* on.

Then there was the custom recording studio, the fifty-seat home theater, the elevators, the infinity pools (one on the roof), the terraced gardens, the tennis court, the gourmet kitchen with not one, not two, but *three* enormous double refrigerators, along with a formal dining room that could easily seat everyone I knew. And then some.

The décor was what I'd call *Architectural Digest* Macho Minimalist. All the furniture, wall coverings, and art was either gray, black, or white. Soaring ceilings, recessed lighting, fifteen-foot-tall glass walls that slid back so that inside was out, and vice versa, completed the look. No rugs or draperies softened the angles and starkness. No color brightened the rooms.

And not a shred of anything personal, anywhere. Other than the room of guitars and the music studio that hinted at the occupant, Nico's home was as antiseptic as a hospital, as impersonal as a hotel room. The sheer amount of space made it feel worse somehow, like he was living in a rented movie set.

Enormous and echoingly empty, the house made me feel strangely sad.

"What do you think?"

We stood in the living room together, beside a black leather sofa that appeared to have been designed to repel all but the most fearless of guests. The edges were so sharp, the cushions so unyielding, sitting on it might cause substantial bruising. Nico had given me the tour of everywhere but his bedroom. I assumed, contrary to what he'd said, he was saving the best for last.

I was hesitant to be honest, because I didn't want to hurt his feelings. "It's . . . incredible. I mean, really . . . there aren't words."

There. That should do it. Right?

He looked at me askance. "Pick a few."

Oy. "Well, it's just . . . um . . . very . . . "

I glanced away, focusing on the view stretching for endless miles in the distance. A weird thought struck me: was this how God felt, looking down on His creation, watching everyone busily living their lives from far above, alone?

I said quietly, "Lonely."

Silence followed, long and cavernous. Then, to my surprise, Nico pulled me into a hug. He wrapped his arms around me, dropped his face to my shoulder and sighed as if a weight had just been lifted from his own. I held him, enjoying the feel of his body, twining my fingers into his hair. He inhaled deeply against my neck, rubbing his cheek there as if he wanted to mark me with his scent.

"I knew you'd get it."

His words were muffled against my skin. I pulled back to look up into his eyes. He stared down at me, his expression serious in spite of the wry upward curl of one side of his mouth.

"You knew I'd get what?"

"Every single person I've ever brought here goes apeshit over this place, but I fuckin' hate it."

It took a lot of willpower on my part not to let random images of the "persons" Nico had brought here bother me. "Why do you live here, then?"

One broad shoulder lifted and fell. "Gotta live somewhere. High-end real estate's a good investment. And it's secure."

It certainly was. You'd need a helicopter to see into the living room, mountain-climbing gear to gain access from below, or some dynamite to blast through the high, thick stone wall that surrounded the property on the front and sides. For all intents and purposes, he lived in a beautiful, luxurious maximum-security prison.

"Have you ever thought about moving out of LA?"

Into his beautiful blue eyes came a look that was almost haunted. "And go where? And do what? Run away? Hide?" Nico shook his head. His eyes grew hard. "No. I don't hide. My life's not perfect, but it is what it is. I accepted it a long time ago, that everything good comes with a price. Happiness. Freedom. Success. Nothin's for free."

Oh, there was so much more beneath those words. So much *pathos*, as Grace would have termed it. Unutterable, unbearable suffering. It brought out my maternal instincts.

"Some good things are free," I whispered, staring into his eyes.

"Yeah? Name one."

I bit my lip. Heat rose in my cheeks. Nico didn't miss it, but he didn't comment on it, instead stroking a thumb over the flame on my skin, waiting.

I swallowed, deciding to be brave. "Love."

His eyes flashed. The muscle in his jaw flexed. He was quiet long enough for me to want to slink away into a corner and curl into a tiny little ball. But then he closed his eyes just longer than a blink, shaking his head.

"Baby, that's the costliest thing of all."

After an awkward moment, I said, "Excuse me, Debbie Downer, I was wondering if you could find Nico for me?" When he just looked at me, silent and smoldering, I prompted, "You know, the grand romantic gestures guy? The gold jewelry guy? The lavender roses guy? The unremorseful stalker? Any of this ringing a bell?"

He stared deep into my eyes. The depth of emotion I saw there took my breath away. "What's more romantic, Kat? Fallin' in love because you don't know any better . . . or fallin' in love, *knowin'* it's gonna ruin you, *knowin'* it's gonna rip out your fuckin' heart and smash you into a million little pieces, but doin' it anyway, because you'd rather pay the price and be ripped and smashed forever than never get a taste of it at all?"

My lips parted. A funny little noise escaped my mouth. The edges of everything grew fuzzy, because of the water welling in my eyes. "I'm not going to ruin you," I promised in a vehement whisper.

His lips curved to a sad smile. "Yeah, you are. You already have. Just the way you're lookin' at me right now has ruined me for any other woman." His quicksilver eyes grew intense. "And I'm gonna make damn sure I ruin you for any other man."

I felt the kiss he gave me all the way to my toes. It was hungry—no, it was *devouring*. I clung to him, feeling what little reason I had left regarding this relationship slipping away.

Because even if he was right, even if we were destined to ruin one another, I didn't want to stop. In my heart of hearts, I didn't care what happened in all my tomorrows, as long as I could have *this*, right now. His kiss and his smile and the fever that burned so brightly between us.

The fever that might just leave a smoking path of destruction in its wake.

He broke away first, breathing hard. His erection pressed against my lower belly. Even through our clothing I felt it twitch.

I cleared my throat. Trying for a light tone, I said, "I think you should probably show me your bedroom now."

His brows slowly raised. "You propositionin' me?"

"You complaining?"

He grinned. "Who, me? The Cookie Monster? No, ma'am, I am most certainly not." Leaning over to pick up my bag, he asked casually, "By the way . . . you pack any of that nice lingerie of yours, Chastity?" He took me by the hand and led me toward the curved staircase that rose to the second floor.

"Um, no."

He looked over his shoulder, and winked. "Good. 'Cause you're not gonna need it."

Yes, I was in trouble. Deep, deep trouble.

And I was loving every minute of it.

My euphoric mood lasted exactly three minutes, until Nico led me into his bedroom.

It wasn't the unmade bed; we already know what a slob *I* am. And it wasn't that I was envious of the view, or the size of his closet, or that he had an entire home gym in an adjacent, glass-walled room.

It was the fucking picture of Avery *on the nightstand beside his bed.*

There wasn't a single photo or personal memento in the entire house, yet he slept with a silver-framed picture of his ex-whatever two feet from his head. The shit-eating grin Avery sported in the photo seemed aimed directly at me.

Murderous jealousy reared up inside me, spitting fire. I had to look away for a moment and stare out the windows to stop myself from saying something really bitchy about how the Cookie Monster was about to die of starvation.

Nico set my duffel on the glossy black dresser across from the bed, then turned to me. His smile faded. "You okay?"

"Yep."

I wasn't looking at him, but I was pretty sure his eyes narrowed. I swallowed the bile in my throat and tried to maintain my dignity instead of exploding into the fit of screaming shrew threatening to come on.

Silent as a panther, he stalked toward me. "What's up, Kat?"

Damn Eagle Eyes! Can't you see I'm trying not to have a meltdown here?

I decided to lie rather than admit how angry I was at him, and how angry I was at *myself* for letting that picture get to me. He'd already explained she was important to him. He'd already asked for my trust. And I had—allegedly—given it. I knew Avery was a big part of his life, or at least she used to be, and I wanted, *so badly,* to be mature enough, secure enough, to be the kind of woman who would smile and say, "Oh, isn't that sweet," and actually mean it.

Clearly, I was not that woman.

But *screw that* if I was going to admit it to him.

"I'm feeling a little sick from last night, and all the excitement this morning. I think I might need to lie down. Or maybe take a shower and then lie down. Would that be okay?"

"Of course." He was concerned. "Do you need anything?"

A hammer. A flamethrower. A gun. I really wanted to destroy that stupid picture. Maybe even taser the fucking thing, and then destroy it.

"No. Just a couple hours' rest. I'm sure I'll feel better later. I'm sorry."

"Don't be silly," he said softly, taking my hand. He pressed a kiss to my forehead, then led me into the gleaming marble bathroom and showed me how to work the shower, and where the fresh towels were. Then he kissed me again, on the lips this time, gently and so sweetly it shaved an edge off my anger.

"Need someone to help you wash your hair?" he murmured, nudging his nose against mine.

In return, I could only offer a weak smile. "I'm good. Rain check?"

The pause before he spoke was longer than I was comfortable with. I glanced at his eyes, regretting it instantly when I did. The darkness from downstairs had crept back into them, shadowing the normally crystalline blue with a deep, ominous ultramarine, the color of the sea before a storm.

"Okay, baby. Whatever you say."

His voice was shadowed, too, but with what emotion, I couldn't tell. His gaze drifted to the necklace around my throat. He picked up the trust charm between his thumb and forefinger, and stroked it contemplatively. Then his lashes lifted, and he pierced me with his stare.

Without another word, without a smile, Nico turned and walked slowly from the room.

I sank to the edge of the enormous Jacuzzi tub, dropped my throbbing head into my hands, and sighed. I hated jealousy. It was such a petty, spiteful, insecure emotion. Unfortunately, being with a man like Nico—a man who women *literally* threw their panties at—practically guaranteed the green-eyed monster would become a permanent resident in my brain. If I wanted to explore this thing between us, if I didn't want to ruin it before it had even really begun, I'd have to find a way to manage it.

But how?

That question bothered me the entire time I was in the shower. I soaped my body, shampooed my hair, shaved everything that needed shaving, letting the hot water coax the tension from my muscles, half expecting Nico to walk in any minute and join me. Half hoping he would, and also half dreading it.

He never did.

When I finally finished showering, dried off, and padded barefoot into his bedroom to get the clothes from my duffel, the picture of Avery was gone.

Chapter 16

When I awoke, the sun had shifted low on the horizon, bathing the room in a soft golden glow.

It was late afternoon, or early evening. I blinked, squinting against the light. I remembered sitting on the edge of the bed, worrying about the picture of Avery, and then . . .

Oh. Right. I'd lain down, thinking it would be only for a moment and then I'd get up and change. Apparently the moment had turned into hours. For the second time today, I was waking up on top of the covers on a bed.

Also for the second time today, someone was beside me.

I turned my head to find Nico staring up at the ceiling, hands behind his head. He'd changed into a pair of loose black sweatpants, slung low on his hips. He was barefoot, and bare chested. When he turned his head and looked at me, he was so breathtaking I longed for a camera. That jaw of his could cut glass.

"Hey."

"Hey." He rolled to his side, lifted to his elbow, propped his head on his hand. He stared down at me with hooded eyes, his expression unreadable. Our bodies were mere inches apart, so close I felt the heat radiating from him.

I became acutely aware that the two of us were half naked. Beneath the thick white towel wrapped around me, I wore nothing at all.

I swallowed around the lump in my throat. "How long have you been there?"

"A while." He reached up and brushed a strand of damp hair from my forehead. "Feelin' any better?"

I inhaled and stretched my legs, assessing, then nodded. "Yeah. Headache's gone."

"Good." He trailed his fingers over my brow, across my cheek, down my neck. His hand lingered over my collarbone. He began to toy with the chain around my neck. Watching it instead of me, he asked, "And how 'bout that nasty urge to bury a knife in my chest? That gone, too?"

Busted. I sighed, embarrassed and annoyed all over again. "Was I that obvious?"

Nico traced his fingers over my chest, moving from my neck to my shoulders, along the top of my cleavage where the towel was cinched, up the line of my throat. Everywhere he touched, it felt like he left a trail of sparks. My breath hitched at the sensation.

"Told you the first day I met you, baby: you lie for shit."

He began to work the seam of the towel open where it was folded over on my chest. His fingers deftly pulled the two ends apart until the space between my breasts was exposed. He left it like that, open but not revealing more than a narrow strip of skin, and trailed his fingers lower. I was sure he'd be able to feel the jackhammer wreaking havoc inside my chest.

When I spoke, my voice was shaky. "I'm sorry for getting mad—"

"Don't be."

Nico's hand moved lower, then lower still, pushing the opposite sides of the towel aside to gain access to my bare stomach. My breasts were still mostly covered, as were my girly bits down below, but the rest of my skin was now exposed from my neck to beneath my belly button.

Several parts of my body began to tingle in the most fantastic way. When Nico swirled his fingertip around and around my belly button, then dipped it gently in, I had to bite my lip to stop from moaning.

"Don't be sorry for gettin' mad, Kat." His gaze flashed to mine. "Be sorry for lyin' to me. And don't ever do it again." He leaned in and rubbed his cheek against mine, nosing aside my hair to breathe into my ear. "You hear me?"

My unsteady exhalation would have to serve as an affirmative, because I found myself not fully in command of my ability to speak.

Warm and wet and wonderful, his tongue skimmed the rim of my ear. His teeth lightly pressed down on my earlobe, and he sucked it into his mouth. On my stomach, his big hand spread open. More tingling and sparks spread in its wake.

Lost in sensation, I closed my eyes.

Nico pushed the towel over the slope of my hips. Cool air brushed over my breasts and thighs, and I knew I was fully exposed to him. Curiously, I didn't feel shy. In fact, I was strongly fighting the urge to wantonly spread my legs and point to my crotch, shouting, "Eat that goddamn cookie!"

What a slut.

And—far worse—what a pushover. You'd think I'd been living in a convent for the last ten years, I was so horny. What the hell had he done with my resolve?

"Say it, baby," he whispered in my ear. His hand drifted south over my belly. "Tell me you won't ever lie to your man again."

Was it ridiculous, the sheer thrill I felt at Nico calling himself my man? I didn't know. I didn't care. All I knew was where I wanted his clever fingers to go. And that I'd do pretty much anything to get them there.

"Yes. Yes. I mean, no. Both. Whichever. I won't."

God, I was pathetic.

He pinched the flesh of my upper thigh, then stroked the sting away. His fingers drifted dangerously close to home base. "You won't *what*?"

His voice had grown hard. He leaned into me and sucked one of my nipples into his mouth. I gasped, arching against him. His tongue swirled around and around my nipple as his finger had around my belly button. Feeling as liquid as a tub of butter left out under the summer sun, I shuddered. "Ah . . . I sort of . . . forgot the question."

"C'mon, now, baby, you can do better than that," he chided, chuckling. He moved to my other nipple, lavished it with the same attention the first had received, laughing softly again when I squirmed, no longer able to hold back my groan of pleasure.

"I won't lie to you. I won't. I won't . . . oh, God. Please don't stop doing that!"

His teeth skimmed my nipple. He bit down, harder than before. I jerked, my hands clenched in the sheets. Feather light, his fingers brushed over my sex, and I whimpered his name.

Of their own will, my hips flexed up into his hand. I knew I was wet. I knew he felt it, as soon as I heard the low grumble of desire go through his chest. His thumb drew the softest of circles over my clit, and I sucked in a breath, my legs parting.

"Beautiful," he murmured against my breast. "Fuck. Kat. You're so beautiful."

The arm he was leaning on slipped beneath my back, dragging me closer to him, pinning me against his hard body. I sank my fingers into the thick softness of his hair, and pulled his head down, desperate to get as close as I could. His chest felt burning hot. His lips on my skin were even hotter.

"You make me feel beautiful, Nico," I whispered, my eyes shut, my body singing from his touch. "You make me feel like the most beautiful woman in the world."

He said, "That's because you are," and slid his fingers deep inside me.

I moaned. My head tipped back into the pillow. My knees drew up. My pelvis rocked against his hand.

What a way to wake up.

Nico's voice was a low rasp in my ear. "You're gonna come for me. And when you do, you're gonna be mine, baby. No other man can touch you. No other man gets that smile, those eyes, that laugh. You're gonna give it all to me, and me alone."

Oh, his fingers. And his words. Magic. I turned my face to his neck and sucked on his throat, desperate to taste him, desperate to get as close as I could. My body was arching in time to the slow, deliberate thrusts of his fingers inside me. I was shivering. I was flying. I was losing myself in him, and damn if I didn't want to get lost.

Naturally, Fate thought it would be funny to interrupt this beautiful interlude with a noise I was quickly starting to hate: the doorbell.

It rang with a chime that seemed to echo through the house like gunfire. My eyes flew open. Nico and I both froze. The doorbell chimed mockingly on and on, as if stuck on repeat.

Without removing his hand from its possessive, intimate position, Nico looked over his shoulder, to the clock on the opposite wall. He growled, and I don't think I'd ever heard a sound so frustrated. Not that I was thinking, really. I was *teetering*, caught on the razor's edge of release.

My voice was a croak. "What's happening?"

He turned to me. Those dark sea-storm eyes were back, along with a scowl. "Band's here. Forgot they were comin'."

Oh. Great. The band was here. What a wonderful end to a perfectly wonderful day.

I wanted to scream in disappointment. Or maybe pull the covers over my head and hide until the morning came and I could put today behind me, like a bad dream. Hungover, mobbed, jealous, jealousy exposed, and now sexually frustrated.

The last thing I expected to hear at that moment was a soft, satisfied laugh.

Damn. The man could read me like an open book. "Do *not* laugh at me."

Nico's scowl had faded, replaced with a look of amusement. The twinkle in his eyes was even more satisfied than his laugh. He slowly withdrew his fingers, making me shudder, then stroked them up and down my sex, focusing on the aching nub on top. He pinched it between his fingers and tugged. I gasped, stiffening, my eyes wide, staring up into his.

The doorbell rang on and on.

Nico ignored it. "You gonna hide your feelings from me again, Kat?"

Stroke. Tug. Stroke.

"I—I can't . . . okay yes probably." The last part came out in a breathless rush as the coil of pleasure deep in my belly wound tight.

Nico kissed me softly on the lips. "The correct response to that question is 'no,' baby."

Stroke. Pinch. Stroke. I couldn't help the soft, pleading whine I made. More stroking, firmer, quicker, as Nico intently watched my face. His own was hard with desire. My lips parted wordlessly when I felt a tiny contraction.

And then, bastard that he was, Nico stopped.

"No! Nico!"

Without breaking eye contact, he lifted his hand to his mouth and sucked on the two fingers that had just been inside me. He really made a meal of it, too, running his tongue all the way down to the base of his fingers, sucking all the way back to the tips. It was sexy as hell. Then he crushed his lips against mine and fucked my mouth with his tongue.

He wrapped an arm around my back, hard as an iron bar, and held me against him, kissing me with so much passion and possessiveness it took my breath away. He rolled on top of me, gripped both my wrists in his hands, and pinned them to the pillow above my head.

The doorbell fell silent. With all my heart, I hoped the band had decided to take a hike down the canyon and would never be seen again.

Panting, Nico pulled away and stared down at me. His eyes were wild. He looked even more undone than I was. He looked about to explode.

So, brat that I am, I laughed.

I flexed my pelvis against his, feeling the hard length of his erection through his sweats. "Aw, what's the matter big boy? Feeling a little frustrated?"

Fast as lightning, he sat up, pulled me along with him, flipped me over, and had me across his knees. Then he leaned down and sank his teeth into my bare ass.

I cried out, mostly from surprise. It stung, but didn't really hurt. I think my ego was more hurt that he could flip me around like a pancake and I could do nothing to stop it.

Or could I?

I looked at him over my shoulder. When he glanced at me, kissing the flesh he'd just nipped, I lifted my butt so there was a pretty arch in my lower back. In my best phone-sex-operator voice, I breathed, "So you're an ass man, then, Nico? Or . . . " Slowly, I rolled over, watching as his eyes devoured the sight of my naked body. I cupped my breasts in my hands. "Are you more of a breast man?"

When he remained silent, staring down at me in molten stillness, I smiled even wider. "No? Must be a leg man, then." I slid my hands down my ribcage, over my belly, and across my hips, then, catlike, stretched out to my full length, pointing my toes and lifting my hands over my head.

I was totally naked. Totally exposed to him. And, due to his expression of extreme desire, feeling totally fantastic.

Until he grabbed me by the ankles and dragged me across the bed, and on top of him. I wound up on his lap, legs around his hips, face in his hands, stunned by how easily he could manage my weight and get me exactly where he wanted me with minimal effort on his part.

Nico answered me in a gruff whisper. "When it comes to you, Kat, I'm all three. But make no mistake: I play to win. So if you wanna start this little teasin' game, I'm not gonna stop until you *beg* me to." He ran his tongue along my lower lip, and rocked his pelvis into mine, putting pressure in the exact right spot to make me softly gasp.

"*You* started it!" I might have already been begging a little. The band was a distant memory by now.

"Did I? Hmm." Nico cupped my ass and ground me against him. My nipples skimmed his chest, sending jolts of pleasure through me, jolts that grew hotter and stronger when he moved his hands to my breasts and gently squeezed. He stroked his thumbs back and forth over my aching nipples, watching my face all the while. Watching as my lids grew heavy, my breath grew short, my pulse went haywire.

Oh God. Could he make me come . . . just like this?

I whispered his name. A small smile played over his lips.

"Yeah, baby? What is it? You got somethin' to say?"

It was already on the tip of my tongue. Just one little word and I could fall apart in his hands. *Please.*

But that would be too damn easy. And if there was one thing I was determined not to be with Nico, it was easy.

Well, easi*er.*

I smiled a little smile of my own. "Yes. Actually I do." I reached between us, slipped my hand beneath the waistband of his sweats, and wrapped my fingers around his stiff, swollen cock. His eyes went wide. I was more than a little satisfied to hear his sharp intake of breath. Sweetly, I said, "*I* play to win, too, handsome. You're on."

I kissed him. I stroked him as we kissed, loving the low, masculine sound he made deep in his throat, loving how hard I made him, loving how his breath was just as ragged as my own. My thumb swept over the velvet crown, and he groaned my name, fisting my hair in his hands.

At precisely that moment, the band walked in.

Chapter 17

The first thing I did was scream. Then I dove off the bed and landed with a thud on the floor opposite the door, and hid.

Nico, on the other hand, decided that exploding in thermonuclear anger was the right way to deal with the situation.

"What the FUCK, assholes? Get the FUCK outta my bedroom!"

Amused chuckling followed his outburst. Then one of the assholes said, "Wouldn't have had to come up here to find you in the first place if you would've just answered the door, bro. But I can see now you were . . . occupied. Must've been why you forgot to lock the door in the first place." The voice rose, calling out to me. "Hi there, sweetheart! Kat, is it? Heard a lot about you. Don't worry, we didn't see much!"

I heard more amused chuckling, with a few snickers thrown in for good measure.

This day just kept getting better and better.

Suddenly the laughter was cut off cold by the sounds of surprised grunts, curses, and the unmistakable hollow thud and window rattling that occurs when a body is thrown against a wall.

"I said, GET THE FUCK *OUT*!"

Nico had descended once again into the unhinged zone. I peeked over the edge of the bed just in time to see him physically throw a big, muscular man with dark blond hair through the doorway, then turn and grab another man—brown haired, with a boyishly handsome face that stood in stark contrast to all the black leather he was wearing—and slam him against the wall, his forearm against the man's throat.

"Take it easy, bro!"

I recognized this one from the video shoot. He was Brody Scott, Bad Habit's lead guitarist, aka "Scotty."

Nico roared, "*You* take it easy, Brody! Do what I fuckin' said and get your ass outta here, or I'm gonna rain down so much nasty shit on your head it'll make the apocalypse look like a picnic! You feel me?"

After a moment, Brody said, "Yeah, bro. I feel you."

A tense silence followed as the two men glared at each other. Brody didn't look too happy about having Nico's arm against his throat, but his hands were held up in a gesture of surrender. Finally Nico let him go. He pulled away to stand with his hands curled to fists at his sides, his legs spread wide in a fighting stance. I couldn't see his face, but if the bunched muscles in his shoulders and back were any indication, Nico was ready to throw down in a major way.

And so was the woman inked on his skin.

Across the majority of his back was tattooed the figure of a woman floating in air. She was wrapped in a black gauzy sheet that barely covered her voluptuous naked figure, and had long black hair that waved in an invisible wind. There was something ominous about her, about her beautiful, unsmiling face, her piercing dark eyes. Something forbidding, and vaguely familiar. I felt as if she were staring right at me. Right *through* me.

Then Brody turned and stalked out the door. Nico slammed it behind him.

I exhaled a long, shuddering breath.

Nico stood staring at the door for several seconds. His hands flexed open and closed. He bowed his head, exhaled hard, then came to me. He pulled me up from the floor and hugged me, burying his face in my neck. I was surprised to find he was shaking.

"Well. That was fun." I was joking, because obviously that was *not* fun, but I didn't want to add any fuel to Nico's fire.

"They're lucky I wasn't inside you or I would've killed them both."

His tone was so murderous, his body so rigid and wracked with tremors, I didn't doubt he was telling the truth. His temper truly scared me. I wondered if it had ever gotten beyond his control. I squeezed him tighter, my arms around his shoulders, my bare chest pressed to his. Even though I was totally humiliated, horrified, and pretty sure I wasn't going to leave the room until the band was long gone, I felt it was necessary to try to defuse the ticking bomb in my arms.

"They didn't mean to make you mad. They didn't know I was here. It was just a mistake, Nico."

He lifted his head, slanting me a dangerous, cutting stare. "They saw you naked."

I laughed nervously, afraid of what I saw in his eyes. "Well, my gynecologist has seen worse. And, you know, I may have had one or two boyfriends before you. There are men out there in the world who've seen me naked."

Humor was definitely the wrong way to go. As was that last tidbit about other men. Nico's eyes bored into mine with a blazing fury that made me even more frightened. His brows pulled down low. A flush of color stained his cheeks. He settled a firm hand around my jaw and tilted my head up so our noses were almost touching.

"I wasn't kidding before, Kat, when I said no other man got to have you. That *especially* includes seeing you naked." He paused, his voice dropping. "And get a fuckin' female gynecologist. Any man that has that job is nothin' but a perv."

A strange sensation settled in the pit of my stomach. I recognized it, having experienced it many times before: dread.

I'd had two controlling boyfriends in my past. One of them, a narcissist named Ryan, had attempted to dictate every facet of my life, including my wardrobe, my work schedule, who I hung out with, what I ate, and how much sleep and exercise I got. I ditched him pretty quickly.

The other bad seed was an extremely intelligent and sophisticated Frenchman named Phillip. He was far more dangerous than Ryan, because his genius was in getting me to question myself. He never came right out and demanded I do anything. His style wasn't a kamikaze approach, as Ryan's was.

It was guerilla warfare.

Subtly, over the course of a year, I began to distrust my instincts. Had I really been flirting with that friendly bartender? Was my dress as revealing as his disapproving glances said? Phillip's influence was so roundabout, his technique so refined, my self-confidence eroded to the point I began to rely on him for the most mundane decisions. And, mission accomplished, he happily complied.

It took Grace giving me a walloping slap upside the head to set me straight.

So now, with those shitty experiences under my belt, I couldn't ignore the neon red sign flashing in front of my eyes, screaming, "Control Freak Alert!"

No man was going to tell me which gynecologist to see. That was just crossing the fucking line.

"Number one," I began, staring him dead in the eye, "you said after you'd made me come, I'd belong to you. I didn't come. You can work out for yourself where I'm going with that."

His nostrils flared. He leaned in closer to me, and now our noses were touching.

That only pissed me off more. My next words were biting.

"Number *two.* Until you have a freezing cold speculum shoved up inside you and winched open by ten different doctors before you find one that's actually nice and makes you feel comfortable and knows what the hell he's doing, you *do not* get to weigh in on my choice of a gynecologist. And, finally, the very important number three, stop being such an asshole!"

I spun out of his arms, retrieved the towel from the bed, rewrapped it around my body, and stood glaring at him from a few feet away.

Only after I'd done all that did it occur to me that poking an angry bear usually isn't the best tactic.

Nico's voice came deadly soft. "Don't yell at me."

I answered in the same tone. "Refer to point number three."

He stepped closer, eyes fierce. I refused to step back. "Nico, don't. I'm not letting you intimidate me. If you want this to go any further than today, than right this second, just *don't.*"

That stopped him dead in his tracks. Looking as if I'd just slapped him, he whispered, "You're not goin' anywhere, Kat."

I got so mad it was all I could do to answer him civilly. "Just to be perfectly clear: you don't get to make that decision. I'm not your toy."

He licked his lips. It reminded me of a nature show I'd once seen of an alpha wolf on the hunt for a caribou in the Alaskan wilderness. It didn't end well for the caribou.

He took a measured step closer, then another, until we were a foot apart. His eyes drilled into mine. I still refused to budge. "You're my *favorite* toy, baby. And I'm yours. So that makes us even."

I opened my mouth to protest, but he interrupted me.

"That also means I'm not gonna let you walk away 'cause you got your panties in a wad about me actin' like a man. Told you this yesterday and I'm sayin' it again: we're gonna give each other the benefit of the doubt. You're pissed at me, you tell me. I think you're bein' a drama queen, I'm gonna tell you."

What? Me? A drama queen?

"I can tell by that angry little noise you just made that you think I'm an even bigger asshole now that I said that, but just like you shouldn't be afraid to speak your mind to me, I'm not gonna be afraid to speak my mind to you." He glanced at my necklace, then back up into my eyes. "I wasn't playin' when I said we're gonna have trust, Kat. It might not always be pretty." He reached out and softly stroked my cheek. "But it is always gonna be real."

I considered all that, then decided to go for broke. "Okay. You want real? Here it is. And if you don't like it, you've only got yourself to blame."

He waited, still tenderly stroking my cheek. I wished he wasn't doing that, because it was messing with my righteous anger.

"I've had twelve lovers in my life." His hand on my face froze. "That's right, I said it. Twelve. Two of them were complete psychos, three of them had mommy issues, four of them were just fucking immature. The other three either cheated on me or roughed me up. One of them did both, and loved every minute of it. So that puts you at unlucky number thirteen. And if I were judging this relationship on my past experiences, I'd be out that door so fast right now your head would spin.

"I don't like aggression. I don't really like possessiveness, either, but at least that shows you care. But the anger? This stuff with you going ballistic on the press, and even getting physical with your friends? That worries me, Nico. All your secrets worry me, too. But I'm standing here, telling you this, because *I* care. I'm looking for reasons to stay. Don't give me any more to walk away."

Slowly, he withdrew his hand from my face. He stared at me a long, long time, silent, his expression a mix of frustration and conflict, and what might have even been fear. He whispered, "I only have two secrets, Kat. One that could ruin my life, and one that could ruin someone else's. If you want me to, I'll tell you both."

Oh. I hadn't been expecting that. But he wasn't finished yet.

"As for the anger, I don't have an excuse for that. Never felt possessive about a woman before. Or jealous, either."

Not even Avery? Not even that beautiful train wreck whose picture you keep beside your bed?

"Never," he insisted, reading the look in my eyes. "And I'm not gonna stand here and lie to you that it's not gonna happen again, 'cause it might. Hell, it probably will."

When I made a noise of frustration, he reached out and grasped my wrist, pulling me nearer. "But I get you don't like it. So I'll do my best to curb that shit. If . . . " he wrapped his arms around me and spoke into my ear, "you do your best not to compare me to every other fuckin' douche bag you've been with. I don't compare you to anyone else. At least give me that."

I settled my head on his chest, listening to the steady thumping of his heart. He brushed my hair off my neck and trailed his lips across my shoulder and up my throat, pressing soft kisses as he went. My arms, having a mind of their own, wound around his waist.

I didn't know what to think, or feel. Or *do*. What he'd said about his secrets unsettled me, and while I wanted to know what they were, at the same time I didn't. I decided that, for the moment, it was enough he'd offered to share. There was only so much my brain could deal with in one day.

I sighed, defeated. "Okay. Deal. No comparisons on my end, and you keep a leash on King Kong."

He cupped his hand around the back of my neck, nuzzling my throat. "Don't sound so put out, baby. This is a good thing."

I raised my head and gave him a disbelieving look. "Exactly how is what just happened a good thing?"

His blue eyes shone. "Got our first fight outta the way. Now we don't ever have to do it again."

I shook my head. His ability to transform from fire-breathing dragon to teddy bear was almost mutant. Time for a subject change before the dragon woke up again. I trailed my fingers over his skin. "What's this tattoo on your back?"

He bent his head to my neck again, breathing me in. "Nyx. Greek goddess of the night. According to their legends, she was so powerful she was feared even by Zeus himself. She was the mother of death."

My hands on his back faltered. *The mother of death? Seriously? That's what you have tattooed on your body?*

Secondarily, because I wasn't always the sharpest tool in the shed, came the realization that the man in my arms shared his last name with a mythical figure accredited with giving birth to death. Which made no sense at all, if you thought about it. But the point was: how could that be a coincidence?

Was Nico's last name not his real one?

I knew celebrities did that kind of thing all the time. Marilyn Monroe's real name was Norma Jean Baker. John Wayne's real name was Marion Morrison. But, and this was a big but, if Nico's last name wasn't his real one, why the hell would he choose Nyx, goddess of the night, mother of death? Creepy much?

Holy shit, I thought, suddenly breathless. *What if his first name isn't real, either? What if it's, like, Eugene?* I examined his gorgeous face in a whole new light.

"What?"

"I need to ask a question."

"Shoot."

"Is Nico your real name?"

He looked surprised. "Yeah. I'm Italian on my mother's side, Nico was my grandfather's name."

Not Eugene. Thank God.

Nico cupped my jaw, his eyes searching mine. "Why? Your real name isn't Kat?"

I burst out laughing. How could I not? "Yes, silly, Kat's my real name. And so is Reid," I added, subtle as a hammer.

But Nico was too busy being enamored to take the bait. His eyes went all hot and steamy, as did his voice. "Christ, Kat. That laugh. Gives me fuckin' goosebumps." He bent his head and took my mouth, sucking greedily on my lips like they were candy.

Would I ever tire of that amazing tingling his kisses sent winging throughout my body?

"Whoa, cowboy." I pulled away before my hormones could take over. "The band, remember?"

He closed his eyes. "Yeah. How could I forget." His tone was so sour I had to laugh again, which brought a smile to his face. He gazed down at me, smiling brilliantly, his dark hair falling into his eyes, golden light from the windows haloing his head. In that moment, something happened that I thought only happened in the movies.

My heart—literally—skipped a beat.

"There it is," he whispered, going from lighthearted to intense with whiplash speed. "There's that look I love so much."

The L word. He'd just said the L word! *Faint now, or wait until he leaves the room?*

Slowly, as if magnetized, our faces drew together. The kiss started out tender, but quickly turned greedy. His hands were greedy, too, shoving aside the towel to rove over my naked hips, bottom, waist. I rose up on my tiptoes. My arms tightened around his shoulders. When he began to walk me toward the bed, I had to intervene before I lost myself completely in him.

"The band, Nico."

We stood there breathing heavily, bodies fused. He pulled the towel away and discarded it so we could be skin to skin, then ran his hands up and down my sides, hips to armpits, lust and possession in every twitch of his fingers. I opened my eyes. His were still closed. He licked his lips again, as if needing to taste me.

I whispered, "Handsome."

His eyes drifted open.

"Go be with the boys. Go apologize for pulling a Rambo. Have a drink. Play some music. You'll feel better. Then, tomorrow, we'll forget about this shitty day and start fresh. Okay?"

He slowly shook his head. "Never gonna forget a single day, baby. Good and bad, they all add up to the story of us. I'm gonna take every one and cherish it, come what may."

Aw, shit. Here came the tears. "You're really good at the sweet talk," I said, my voice wavering.

He cracked a grin. "I'm a songwriter, darlin'. Kinda comes with the territory. Now get that beautiful ass in some clothes. I'm not goin' downstairs without you."

"You're not going to let me maintain my dignity and hide, you mean."

His thumb grazed my lower lip. "No hidin'. For either of us. Yeah? We're out in the open, with everything between us, and everything else. It's me and you against the world, baby. One day at a time."

Well, that did it. Water spilled over my lower lids and tracked down my cheeks. "Dammit. I'm supposed to still be mad at you."

But Nico only laughed and pulled me closer, cradling me against his chest. "I know. I'm an asshole. And you're my Drama Queen, who's gonna call me on my shit and keep me on my toes. And fuck if I would have it any other way."

So I went and got dressed. Then we went downstairs to meet the band.

And then all hell broke loose.

Chapter 18

It started out well enough.

Nico led me downstairs by the hand into a room adjacent to the music studio, where everyone had congregated. And by everyone, I mean Brody; the big blond guy Nico had thrown out of the bedroom; two heavily tattooed guys Nico introduced as Chris and Ethan, the bassist and keyboardist for Bad Habit; and six pretty girls in crotch-grazing minidresses and hair out to *there*.

Oh, fun! Groupies!

Not.

Two of the girls were hanging off the big blond guy like those leech-like fish who swim alongside a shark, cleaning its gills. The others were draped all over the rest of the men. The blond guy made an angry, bear-like noise deep in his throat.

Nico acknowledged him in a flat voice. "A.J."

So this was the infamous A.J., drummer for Bad Habit. I hadn't seen him at the video shoot because his scenes were filmed separately from mine and Nico's. Chloe had been right: the guy was a growler. I examined him with interest. He was hulking, roped with muscle, and taller than Nico by at least a few inches, maybe six foot six. I was a terrible judge of height, but I'd seen shorter NBA players. He reminded me of The Rock, if The Rock had shaggy blond hair and eyes the color of whiskey.

If he cut that hair and stopped channeling a grizzly interrupted during hibernation, he might have almost been cute.

Brody was lounging on one of the unwelcoming leather sofas, managing to make it look, if not comfortable, at least not quite the torture device the one upstairs appeared to be. His boyish face wore a wary expression as he looked back and forth between Nico and me. "And here's Mayweather now. We were just talking about you, bro."

The brunette who was plastered against Brody snickered. Nico's stony glare wiped the smile right off her face. She looked at the floor, mouth pinched. The other girls occupied themselves by examining me with narrowed, hostile eyes.

I'm sure my jeans, T-shirt, and air-dried hair failed to pass muster, but I did my best to try to look like I didn't give a shit what these girls thought about my outfit.

"My lady says I should apologize to you dumb assfuckers for goin' off on you upstairs."

Nico sounded as if he'd rather take a swan dive into a pool of cow manure. I squeezed his hand. He glanced sideways at me, and I nodded in encouragement. He exhaled, then turned his attention back to his band mates. They looked back and forth between Nico and me, wearing matching expressions of surprise.

I took it Nico didn't do much apologizing.

"So I am." He paused. "I'm also lettin' you know if you ever so much as *glance* in her direction again, naked or not, I'll rip off your fuckin' heads."

I sighed.

The woman on A.J.'s left side, a willowy blonde with remarkable cleavage in a BDSM-inspired black leather ensemble studded with silver grommets, pinned me with a stare so full of hatred I instinctively shrank closer to Nico.

"Your *lady*?" Her husky laugh was mocking. She slithered away from A.J. and came to stand in front of Nico with her hands on her hips, treating me as if I were invisible. Her perfume was gaggingly strong. "And here I thought *I* was your lady, loverboy."

All the breath left my body as if I'd been punched in the chest. Nico had slept with this . . . this . . . *maneater*! And holy . . . those legs! Those boobs!

Oh, God. How long had it been since he'd been with her? Two weeks? Two days? *Oh dear God I'm going to puke.*

But Nico, being Nico, made it all better with only a few well-chosen words.

With one side of his mouth quirked, in the most dismissive tone I'd ever heard, he said, "Nah, darlin', you were never my lady. Or probably anyone else's *lady*. More like the village bicycle. Haven't taken a ride on that rusty, second-hand bike in what, six months?"

The look on her face was so priceless, I wished I had a camera.

"You fucking *asshole*!" she shrieked, red in the face.

Nico shrugged, then winked at me. "Guilty as charged."

It all happened so fast. She took a snarling step forward, her right arm cocked back, her intent to slap Nico across the face as clear as daylight.

So, naturally, because I'm shit for making quick decisions, I slapped her first.

The *crack!* of my open palm hitting her cheek was immediately followed by her scream of disbelief. Her head rocked back.

Staggering sideways in her heels, she spun around and stared at me wide-eyed, cradling her jaw.

Holding her gaze, I quietly said, "Back off, bitch, unless you want another."

Across the room, the four other members of Bad Habit roared with laughter.

She lunged at me. Nico yanked me out of the way just in time, and she went flying by in a cloud of cheap perfume, screaming bloody murder. Her girlfriends were up on their stilettos before you could say "boo," lunging at me, too. It was six against one, and if the boys hadn't intervened, I would've been torn to shreds in a fury of red acrylic claws.

"Brody, get the girls outta here!" Nico shouted. He held me in a protective bear hug against his chest while the guys corralled the girls to the opposite side of the room.

"C'mon, hooker, you heard the man, party's over." Brody held the brunette firmly by the arm and began to pull her away.

"Don't call me a fucking *hooker*!" she hollered, struggling to get free.

Brody laughed. "You're right. That's an insult to hookers."

He ignored her squawk of anger and dragged her from the room, while A.J., Chris, and Ethan managed to get control of her friends. They were escorted out in a spewing hail of profanities, and promises to gut me like a fish the next time they saw me.

Dumbfounded, I stared after them. "Jesus Christ. Where do you find women like that? The ninety-nine-cent section of hell?"

Nico turned me around and held me against his chest. He looked as if he was holding back a smile. "Yeah, it didn't look like you got on too well with them, huh, baby? In fact, I think it's fair to say you even got . . . *aggressive*."

Shit. He had me. He so totally had me there.

"And I'm wonderin' why that might be? Feelin' a little . . . *possessive* maybe?"

"No!" *Hello, blatant lie, my new best friend.* "I slapped that cow in self-defense! She was about to hit you!"

"That's not *self*-defense, Kat. That's you protectin' *me.* Kinda like I was protectin' you against the paparazzi, and from my boys seein' you in all your bare-ass glory."

And there it was. The truth with a capital T. Which only meant one thing.

I was a complete hypocrite.

I rested my forehead against his chest, and sighed. "You know, if you're going to be right all the time, it's really going to get old."

He laughed. Really laughed, his chest shaking with it.

"And smug is really going to get old, too!"

"Yeah, but you bein' mad 'cause I called you out on some shit you were just pissed at me about is *never* gonna get old."

"Shut up." It was a halfhearted "shut up," because, once again, he was right. I would find the same thing extremely hilarious if the situation were reversed.

Nico tilted my face up with a knuckle beneath my chin. His eyes were warm and soft, his voice even softer. "Make me."

Still smarting from the encounter with Miss Thing, I reluctantly rose up on my toes and gave him a dry little peck on the lips.

"Yeah? That's all I get for bein' so right? A grandma kiss?" He clucked in disapproval.

"Try not to break your arm patting yourself on the back, there, *loverboy,*" I said tartly.

Nico gathered me in even closer. His chuckle was a deep rumble in his chest. "Love it that you're jealous over me, baby. But you don't have to be. I'm all yours now."

I might have harrumphed, but I loved hearing him say he was all mine.

Too bad it wasn't true.

"Nico."

We turned to find Brody, white faced and nervous, standing in the doorway.

"What's up?"

Brody cleared his throat. He glanced at me, and I knew. I just *knew* it was bad, before the words were even out of his mouth.

"Got a situation, bro."

Nico tensed. He stepped in front of me protectively. "Yeah? What?"

The sound of the air-conditioning kicking on seemed unnaturally loud in the brief silence that followed. "Think you should come see for yourself." Brody looked at me again. I went cold with fear.

"Stay here." Quiet and firm, this was directed at me. Nico should have known better.

"No."

"Baby—"

"No."

"Uh, Kat?" Brody chimed in. "I, uh, think that might be the best thing."

I glanced at him. "Well, then. *Definitely* no."

"What the fuck is up, Brody?" said Nico, bristling.

Brody cleared his throat again. "Got a visitor."

For a moment there was no reaction. Then, as if he suddenly understood, Nico muttered, "Fuck." He ran a hand through his hair. He turned to me, his eyes dark. "Need you to stay here, baby."

"Nico—"

"I'm askin' you to stay here. Please. Go up to the bedroom and wait for me there."

We stared at each other. In his eyes I saw the conflict, the anger and frustration. I wondered if he could see the disappointment in my own. Without thinking, my hand lifted to the charm resting at the hollow of my throat. Nico's eyes followed the motion, then flashed back up to mine.

To trust, or not to trust? That was the question.

Well, I'd come this far. If our relationship was the Titanic, I'd find out soon enough if we'd just hit the iceberg or were still sailing out on the open sea.

"Okay," I said softly. "I'll be upstairs."

I specifically didn't say I'd be going to the bedroom.

Without waiting for an answer, I brushed past him and left the room. It might have been my imagination, but I could have sworn I heard two relieved exhalations as I went.

Outside it was growing dark. The sun had dipped below the mountains, and the house was filled with shadows, stretching along the floors, crawling up the walls. I hurried up the grand staircase, hugging my arms around my body, desperate for answers.

I didn't know if I could count on them from Nico. I'd have to get them on my own.

Nico's bedroom was on the back side of the house, overlooking the city and ocean beyond. Which meant that there was a room on the opposite side that overlooked the driveway and courtyard where we'd parked. That's where I was headed.

It didn't take me long to find what I was looking for. My heart pounding, I crept into one of the many sterile, silent rooms on the second floor, drawn to the soaring windows. The long driveway came into view as I moved slowly forward through the room. I saw the large roundabout with the fountain at its center, Nico's Escalade, and a trio of other expensive sports cars parked haphazardly around that I assumed belonged to the other members of the band.

I crept closer. Was that shouting I heard?

Trying to stay out of sight from anyone who might glance up from below, I moved even closer to the windows, drawn by what I now realized was, in fact, shouting. Furious shouting. A woman was screaming at the top of her lungs. I couldn't make out her exact words, but every so often she said a word I recognized.

Nico.

The hair on the back of my neck stood on end.

I leaned in the final few inches and saw the tableau below. The six hoochie mamas who had arrived with the band were clustered together in a knot, all of them standing stock still. Brody, Chris, Ethan, and A.J. stood off to the right side of the driveway, surveying the scene with an air of solemn discomfort, but no great surprise.

In the center of the driveway stood Nico. His back was to me, but I could tell just by his posture that he was once again thermonuclear with rage.

A few feet opposite him, screaming like a banshee, stood Avery Kane.

I gasped. My hand flew to cover my mouth.

She was in rehab. She was *supposed* to be in rehab! Or . . . was that just a story that had been concocted for the press?

Was that just a story *Nico* had concocted for the press? Or *they* had, together?

My mind whirled furiously with speculation. I tried desperately to remember what I'd read about Avery checking in to rehab, or what Nico had told me about it, but couldn't focus on anything because I was drowning in quicksand.

Suddenly Avery threw herself at Nico, pounding his chest with her fists. He quickly subdued her, wrapping his arms around her to say something into her ear. She collapsed against him, sobbing. They stood there like that for a moment, Nico obviously trying to comfort her, before he led her over to his Escalade, put her inside, started the engine, and sped away, tires spitting gravel.

Shaking, I stepped back from the windows into the deeper shadows of the room. I felt as if someone had just driven a stake through my heart.

What the fuck? What am I supposed to do? Sit here and wait for him to come back . . . from where? Where is he going with her?

"He doesn't know you saw her," I said aloud. My words echoed eerily in the stillness of the room.

Nico had his back to the house. He couldn't have seen me. I was pretty sure no one else had seen me either, given they were too preoccupied with the drama playing out in front of them. And there were no lights on in the room . . .

So as far as Nico knew, I'd gone to his bedroom and didn't know squat about what had just happened.

I stood there in the gathering darkness for a few minutes, trying to calm myself. Then to the empty room I said softly, "Okay, Nico. I'm done playing. I call. Show me all your cards."

I turned and went to his bedroom, to wait.

Chapter 19

Night fell. Hours passed. He didn't call. He didn't return. I lay on my side on his bed, fully dressed, with my legs drawn up and a pillow under my head, watching the city lights shimmer far below, waiting.

And waiting.

And waiting.

Never in my life had I passed a night so long. It felt eternal. I couldn't sleep from all the buzzing in my head, all the clamor in my heart. Each minute that ticked by aged me incrementally, so that when the first, faint rays of dawn began to spread pink across the sky and I heard the front door open and close, I wasn't sure my ancient head would have the strength to lift from the pillow.

Footsteps on the stairs. My heart began a thundering gallop inside my chest. I closed my eyes, lay still, and let him come to me.

He paused in the doorway to the bedroom. I felt him looking me over, felt the weight of his gaze, felt the air grow thick with tension. Still I refused to turn. He moved slowly toward me. The mattress dipped with his weight. I heard a deep, quiet sigh, then the sound of rustling fabric. I wasn't sure if he was undressing, but I damn well *was* sure I wasn't going to turn around and look.

Then he was beside me, pressing the warm length of his body against mine.

His knees drew up. A heavy arm settled across me and squeezed. I felt his nose in my hair, his lips brush the nape of my neck. When I realized he was spooning me after being out all night with *her*, I almost grabbed the clock off the nightstand and beat him to death with it.

The fucking. *Nerve.*

He whispered, "Talk to me, baby."

He smelled like cigarettes.

"Those groupies of yours threatened to gut me, but it looks like you've got them beat."

His voice dropped even lower. "Don't say that. Please."

"Which part? About your groupies?" I knew I was being a bitch. I also knew no woman in her right mind would blame me.

A desperate edge came into his voice. "They're not mine. They just hang out with the band sometimes. A.J. likes to keep them around, but they're just . . . window dressing. They don't mean anything."

Words. Semantics. The man was a grand master at saying pretty things in order to dodge all the ugly underneath. He hadn't even bothered to address the important part of what I'd said to him.

"Kat—"

"Where did you go, Nico? Where have you been all night?"

A beat of silence. *C'mon, superstar,* I thought bitterly. *You've had plenty of time to concoct a really fantastic cover story. Let's hear what you came up with.*

His quiet exhalation stirred the hair on my neck. "Avery was the situation that Brody was talkin' about. She showed up here, high as shit, screamin'."

A shade of hostility faded from me. He was telling the truth, so far, at least.

"Then what?"

"Then I took her back to rehab."

That's all he said. I started silently screaming. *And? For the other ten hours?* But I didn't break. I just waited, breathing shallowly, rigid as a plank.

He rose up on an elbow and looked down at me. I stared at the ceiling, refusing to get sucked into his penetrating gaze.

"Do you believe me?"

"Do I have a choice?"

"You always have a choice, Kat."

"You're giving me nothing to go on."

"Nothin' except trust, you mean."

God, that made me furious, throwing that in my face. Had this whole insistence on having trust been a setup for situations just like this? So I was supposed to, what, feel bad for asking questions? For wanting to know what was going on?

Screw that. Screw that to the one millionth power.

"Let me ask you a question, Nico. I'd like to find out if you have a good answer for me, because I can't figure it out. What's the difference between trust . . . and blind, stupid faith?"

It was a while before he answered. Finally, in a voice whiskey rough and breaking, he said, "Love."

I gasped. Tears pricked my eyes. "That is so unfair!"

I made a move to leave, but Nico prevented that by rolling me flat on my back and straddling me. His big thighs pinned me to the bed. I'd been right in my earlier assumption; he'd removed his shirt, and his shoes, and was wearing only jeans.

His naked chest mocked me. His golden skin mocked me. Every tattoo and rippling muscle and stupid chiseled feature mocked me, as did his hair, his eyes . . .

Oh, fuck this. I hated him. That was it. I hated him, and I was *done.*

"Get off me!" Shoving had exactly zero effect. Nico didn't budge, but he did grasp my wrists and hold them against his stomach so I couldn't scratch his eyes out, as was my plan.

"Settle down!"

"Or what, you'll walk out for the entire night, give me no real explanations when you get back, and expect me to lap up all your bullshit like it's goddamn gelato? Been there, done that, OVER IT!"

His lips parted. Into his eyes came a look of fury so acute I quaked inside. There was a split second of stillness—*rabbit, meet the wolf that's going to snap your neck!*—then Nico bent down and crushed his mouth against mine.

His tongue was hot and invading, his hands around my wrists were hard. I jerked my head to the side to break the kiss, but Nico let go of my wrists and pinned my head in place with both big hands around my jaw. Pushing against his chest got me nowhere. Trying to shove him off got me nowhere. I was so frustrated I wanted to scream.

But then his kiss began to take effect.

Even through my anger and hurt, the taste of him, the sweetness of his mouth, thrilled me. Thrilled me and drugged my senses, making the world narrow to our lips and tongues and panting breaths, the unforgiving pressure of his hands against my head.

My traitorous body arched into him, wanting more.

He made a sound deep in his throat. Without breaking the kiss, he adjusted himself so he was lying flat on top of me. He was already hard; I felt it as soon as he pressed his pelvis against mine. One of his hands left my face to rove roughly over my body. He cupped my breast, pinched my nipple through the thin fabric of my T-shirt and bra, slid his hand down my thigh, and pulled my leg up to his waist. All the while his mouth was on mine, demanding, angry, and hot.

I pulled my other leg up to his waist so he was settled between my thighs and wound my arms around his back.

He finally broke the kiss to rear up. With one hard tug, he yanked my shirt off over my head. My bra followed, torn apart and tossed aside, then his mouth was on my breasts, greedily, brutally sucking.

I moaned. This was wrong. He'd been out all night with another woman. I couldn't let myself do this. He was using me, playing me, he didn't respect me at all—

Nico unzipped my jeans and yanked them down over my hips, tearing them off. He tore off my panties next. With one hand on my shoulder, holding me down, he unzipped his own jeans and freed his erection. Hesitating, he glanced up at my face, his eyes dark.

The question was there in his gaze.

Once, I thought, delirious. *One time and then it's over.* "Condom," I rasped, barely able to breathe.

He gave me his weight, leaned across to the nightstand, retrieved a condom from the drawer, tore it open, rolled it down the length of his cock, then shoved himself inside me with no preliminaries, without even so much as a word.

I cried out in shock. My nails bit into his back so hard I was sure I'd broken the skin.

He turned his face to my ear. "You wanna make me bleed, baby?" he said, his voice rough. "Go ahead. Won't be nothin' new. You been doin' it every single fuckin' minute since we first met."

He thrust even deeper into me. I groaned, wanting more, hating him, hating myself.

His teeth grazed my shoulder. His fingers dug into the tender flesh of my hips. He thrust again, and again, each time harder and more mercilessly.

This wasn't making love. This was fucking. It was raw and angry and hopeless and devouring . . .

And it was exactly what I needed.

I said his name on an exhalation, dragging my nails down his back, my hips moving in time with his. I slid my fingers beneath the waistband of his jeans and cupped his hard ass, pulling him deeper into me. He started a new rhythm, one thrust alternating with an amazing, fluid swirl of his hips that dragged his pelvis across my clit and around an incredibly sensitive spot inside me.

This time when I said his name, it was more of a helpless moan.

His hand gripped my throat with just enough pressure to alarm me. My eyes flew open. A flicker of panic winged through my chest.

"Come and you're mine," he panted, his face hard. "That's the deal, remember?"

"Fuck your deal! No deal!"

"Fine, then. Don't come." His smile was evil. His hips continued their torture. He bent his head and sucked my nipple into his mouth, and I couldn't stop the gasp of pleasure that escaped my lips, not for all the money in the world.

Against my breast, he chuckled.

"I hate you."

It was a whisper, nothing more, but Nico reacted as if I'd shouted it to the hills. He reared up on his elbows, sank his fingers into my hair, and said, "You're a fuckin' *liar*! Tell me the truth, Kat!"

Something inside me broke then. I felt it, like someone had taken my heart and just snapped it in two, as if it had no more strength or substance than a toothpick. I began to cry.

"*You're* the liar! And I do hate you! I do!"

Nico pressed his cheek to mine. His heart pounded frantically in his chest. "If you wanna call what you feel for me 'hate,' then I hate you, too, baby. I hate you with my whole heart."

I shuddered. Tears streamed from beneath my closed lids. There were no words to describe what I felt. I had never been more confused, more angry, more hollowed out. It was as if every emotion I'd ever felt had decided to run rampant at full throttle through my body.

Humiliation was near the top of the list.

Because even though he'd left me alone all night, even though I still had no idea if what he'd told me was the truth or not, even though I'd just told myself it was over, I still wanted him. I wanted more than one night.

I wanted *all* the nights, and all the days, too. All the highs and lows, all the wreckage. No matter how stupid or self-destructive it was, I wanted everything he made me feel, because, more than anything, he made me feel *alive*. I sobbed, clinging to him.

Nico whispered, "That's right, sweetheart. Give it to me. Don't hide from me. Give your man everything you've got."

He cradled my face, wiping away my tears with his thumbs. When he flexed his hips, driving himself deeper into me, my moan was broken. He cut it off with a kiss.

Then it was nothing but a frenzy.

There was so much urgency in our kisses, in the way our hands explored and our bodies crashed together, it might as well have been our last few minutes on earth. When finally I cried out, the first waves of orgasm gripping me, Nico's whole body shuddered, shaking mine. He slid a hand under my bottom and squeezed.

"Fuck, baby. I can feel that beautiful pussy milkin' my cock." He groaned as I continued to come, harder than I ever had, every nerve ending in my body honed to an exclamation point, my heart cracked wide open.

"Look at me!"

Though my mind had spun far away, my eyes obeyed his husky command. He hovered there above me, face strained, looking exactly as ruined as I felt. I took his face between my hands. He said my name, his eyes locked to mine. Then he fell apart in my arms.

He throbbed and twitched, deep inside me. His breathing stalled. All his muscles clenched. With an animal sound, he came, his fingers digging so hard into my hips I felt the bruises forming. Then he collapsed on top of me, panting.

I don't know how long we stayed like that. Long enough for our breathing to slow, for our hearts to resume a more normal beat. He pressed kisses along my jaw, to the corner of my mouth. He slid his arms beneath me, then rolled me over so he was on his back and I was on his chest, my head resting on his shoulder. He cradled me like that, stroking my hair, caressing my back, calming me.

Outside, the sky was lifting to a clear, blinding blue. Another perfect day in LA.

Watching that beautiful sky, I knew, to the marrow of my bones, I'd just signed my own death warrant. I'd just handed over the keys to my happiness to a man I knew almost nothing about. Except that he was volatile and came with more baggage than even the Titanic held.

And, if our ship was destined to sink, I was too smart to be so stupid. I had to buy myself a life preserver.

"Promise me something," I whispered.

Nico answered without hesitation. "Anything."

I swallowed, watching a lone seagull sail across the sky. "If I ever need to walk away . . . if I ever tell you it's over, let me go. Don't try to convince me to stay. Don't follow me. Just let me go."

He was silent so long I glanced up at his face. I'd wounded him.

I saw it in his eyes as he studied me. "If I say 'yes,' are you gonna tell me you're walkin' away right now?"

Sniffling, I shook my head.

He brushed the hair off my forehead. "You need that so we can move forward? Me givin' you my word that I'll let you walk away if you want to?"

I nodded.

"All right. I promise."

I felt relief tinged with sadness, mixed up with elation and fear. Until Nico spoke again, and then I just felt frozen.

"If you admit you don't hate me and tell me the truth about how you really feel."

My lips parted, but nothing came out. I looked away, but he held my chin in his hand and forced me to look at him. "Tell me, baby," he whispered.

I moistened my lips, closed my eyes, and told him the truth.

"I'm scared. I'm scared as shit. I've never felt anything like this before, and I'm pretty sure you could break me. And . . . and . . . " I faltered, my voice shaking. "I'm falling in love with you. And it's way too soon. Way too *much.* All I know is that you make me crazy and happy and miserable and insecure, and . . . fuck." My chest got tight. "I need a few days to figure this out."

He froze. His voice dropped to a dangerous level. "You did *not* just come all over my cock, give me everything I been wantin' you to give, tell me you're fallin' in love with me, and then say you need space. Tell me I didn't just hear that."

I opened my eyes, only to be pinned by Nico's burning stare. It was hard to swallow around the rock in my throat. "Can't you understand how hard this is for me? You, those girls, Avery . . . everything? If the shoe was on the other foot, how would you feel?"

He didn't answer. But his nostrils flared and his lips thinned, and I knew he knew he wouldn't like it one little bit.

Time to go for broke.

"Why did she come here?"

He knew who I meant, of course. A muscle worked in his jaw. "She's got nowhere else to go."

"And the next time? And the time after that? Are you always going to have to rescue her? Are you always going to drop whatever's going on in your life to take care of Avery?"

Into his eyes came a look of pure torture. He inhaled deeply before he spoke, as if he knew the effect his words would have on me beforehand, and was steeling himself for the blowback.

Nico whispered, "Yes."

That was it. There it was, in black and white. Funny, I never knew a heart could break more than once in the span of a single hour.

Then, with horror, I realized the man I'd just laid myself bare to, body and soul, had reciprocated by telling me that another woman would always be his first priority *while he was still inside me.*

Ice formed in crackling long fingers along the length of my spine. It became almost impossible to breathe. "You . . . you . . . "

I couldn't find the word. "Bastard" was too nice. "Son of a bitch" didn't cover it. "No good, lying, untrustworthy, piece of philandering shit" didn't even begin to make a dent.

I flew off of him before he could stop me and staggered to my feet, desperate to get the hell out of that room, out of that house. I found my discarded clothes on the floor, dressed in record-making time, went to my duffel on the dresser, and shrugged on my jacket. The entire time Nico watched me silently from the bed.

At least he had the decency to zip up his fucking jeans.

On my way through the door, Nico said, "You're not even gonna ask me why?"

He sounded bitterly disappointed in me, which pushed me past the breaking point. I spun around and shouted, "Why doesn't matter, Nico! It doesn't change anything! It doesn't change how you feel!" I put a hand to my head, almost dizzy with another sickening realization. "God," I whispered. "I should have known. I *did* know. What an idiot."

Nico sat up. He swung his legs off the mattress and sat staring at me with the light streaming in behind him. His face was in shadow, but I didn't need his expression to identify the anger in his voice. "Should've known *what*?"

I turned away. I walked out the door. It didn't matter. In the grand scheme of things, it really didn't. But I'd only gone a few feet past the threshold when I turned back to look at Nico one final time.

"You remember that story I told you about the reason I hate my birthdays?" I was surprised my voice was so steady when everything inside me was dissolving into dust.

Needed you to know I'm a man who's gonna take care of your heart.

Beautiful lies from a beautiful liar. I angrily wiped the moisture from my eyes.

"I left out one little detail. When I said "I should have known," I meant I should have known better than to get involved with a musician. Musicians are unreliable. There's always something more important to them than you."

He watched me, waiting, his shoulders rising and falling with his uneven breath.

"I know because my father was a musician, too."

Nico stood from the bed, moving toward me, but I was already gone.

Chapter 20

I went to Grace's.

I walked down the long hill, tears streaming down my face. At the end of the hill I called a cab and waited under the shade of a flowering jacaranda. It was only once I was seated in the back of the cab and had given the driver Grace's address that I realized I wasn't wearing shoes.

The soles of my feet were raw, blistered, and bleeding. The irony wasn't lost on me.

Grace lived in a high-rise condominium building in Century City that catered to wealthy older people, celebrities, and women recuperating from plastic surgery. The security was top-notch. There would be no paparazzi, and no uninvited visitors.

She opened the door, took one look at me, and said, "Oh, honey."

I fell into her arms.

Without another word, she led me to the guest bedroom, where she used an antiseptic wash on my soles and applied bandages, then covered my feet in a pair of ankle socks. She made me a cup of chamomile tea, and made me drink it, along with a Valium. Then she put me under the fluffy duvet on the queen bed and rubbed my back until I fell asleep.

Girlfriends are sometimes the only thing that make life bearable.

I slept deeply, without dreams. When I opened my eyes in the muted twilight of early evening, it might have been the same day, or a thousand years later. I used the toilet, avoided my reflection in the mirror, then shuffled into the living room to find Grace working on her laptop at the dining table.

"*Rocky Horror Picture Show* is on at the ArcLight," she said, not looking away from the screen. "You up for it?"

It's an incredible blessing, when someone who knows you well understands you're in pain, yet allows you to take a breath before expecting you to talk about it. Grace had long ago mastered the art of the gentle handling of wounded souls. It was comforting to know that if I didn't want to, I'd never have to talk about what had happened between me and Nico at all.

Even more of a blessing: there would never be an "I told you so." From Grace, anyway. My own conscience was already kicking and screaming about it.

"Sounds good." I went directly to the kitchen, opened the fridge, and poured myself a glass of wine from the corked bottle in the door. I sat across from her again. Grace didn't bat an eyelash at the size of the highball glass I'd poured the wine into.

"It goes on at nine. I was going to order from Electric Karma first." Her level gray eyes met mine above the lid of the computer. "Can your stomach handle it?"

Indian food might not have been the best idea under the circumstances, but, surprisingly, I was hungry. "Only one way to find out."

A smile lifted her lips. "Atta girl."

She phoned the order in. The food arrived thirty minutes later. In the meantime, I drank another highball of wine. I did a serviceable job with the naan bread and tandoori chicken, but the smell of the curry from the lamb tikka turned my stomach sour before I even had a bite.

Throughout dinner, I struggled to fight back tears. When they spilled over, Grace would just hand me a napkin and continue munching on her kebab.

"Don't you have that work thing in Santa Barbara this week?" she asked around a mouthful of marinated beef.

I'd been booked for a fashion shoot at the uber-swanky Bacara Resort, for the fall collection of the couture wedding dress designer Reem Acra. It was scheduled to be shot over the course of four days. I, along with a small army of models and support staff, were scheduled to arrive midweek and stay through the weekend. I'd been so excited about it—the trip was all expenses paid—but now I was grateful merely for the fact that I could escape LA for a few days.

I nodded, pushing my plate away. "Perfect timing."

Grace didn't have to ask to know what I meant. Better than anyone, she knew that burying yourself in work is one of the best ways to avoid real life.

Real, shitty, painful life.

"You can stay here as long as you want, kiddo. You know that, right?"

The tears began to spill over my lower lids again. I stared at my plate, watching the remains of my meal swim. "I hate men," I whispered.

Grace reached over, took my hand, and squeezed it. "Hey."

I looked at her.

"If you ever want to go lezbo, I'm totally on board. I've been a certified man-hater for years. The only thing they're good for is their cocks. And half the time they're not even good for that."

She grinned, and I had to laugh through my tears. "You like cock too much to give it up."

"That's unfortunately true. Maybe I could just be a part-time lesbian."

"I'm pretty sure that's not how it works."

Her grin grew wider. "Honey, you'd be surprised."

I groaned. "God, that just sounds like *twice* the heartache."

She squeezed my hand again, then rose from the table to clear our plates. "The trick, my love, is to not let your heart get involved in the first place."

I watched her scrape food into the trash, load the dishwasher, and tidy up, all the while contemplating what she'd said. I didn't think it would have been possible to not let my heart get involved where Nico was concerned, even from that first day we'd met. But Grace was a serial, short-term dater, never getting serious with anyone, never settling down. I knew her lack of memory about her past made her distrustful of the future, so she didn't count on anything but the here and now.

Most of the time that made me feel sad for her. Right now it made me think she was a genius.

"I'm going to change before we head out." I rose from my chair, rounded the table, and was about to give Grace a hug when something on her computer screen caught my eye. I stopped dead in my tracks.

She'd been checking her email. On the right side of the screen there was a bar of rotating ads, and the one currently appearing at the top was for TMZ. Its headline read, "Supermodel Goes Supernova."

The picture beneath showed a wild-eyed Avery Kane screaming at the photographer.

I couldn't help myself. I leapt on that computer and clicked on that teaser before you could say "glutton for punishment."

The article was short and full of speculation. Avery had disappeared from rehab the day prior without notifying staff, only to surface hours later at a prominent producer's house party in Malibu, where she was photographed pacing around a pool, shouting into a cell phone. She was next photographed on Rodeo Drive in Beverly Hills, emerging from the Hermès store wearing enormous sunglasses that did nothing to hide her sunken, sallow cheeks. A store employee, carrying an armload of boxes, accompanied her to the Rolls at the curb, where she got into a scuffle with a Japanese tourist who was trying to take her picture with his cell phone. The article quoted the tourist as saying Avery was "crazy" and "high."

Except for a few additional pictures of Avery earlier in her modeling career, there was nothing more. No mention of her returning to rehab. No sightings of her with Nico.

I collapsed against the back of the chair, stunned and sickened.

Where had Nico gone with Avery after they left his house?

It doesn't matter. It doesn't matter. I told myself that over and over. Except, of course, it really did.

I was about to rise from the chair when something in one of the pictures made me gasp.

It was a shot of Avery on a catwalk in Milan. Sleek and stunning, she was striding away from the camera wearing an evening gown that featured a back that plunged all the way to the dimples at the base of her spine. Her tawny hair was upswept in an elegant chignon so her entire back was exposed.

And there, in all her creepy glory, was the mother of death, Nyx.

Avery and Nico had matching tattoos.

At least I made it to the kitchen sink before my dinner made its way back up.

I stayed with Grace for the next two nights. We never did go see the *Rocky Horror Picture Show*. I went straight to bed and stayed there, rising only to eat and use the toilet. I was ill in every way a person could be: soul sick, heartsick, physically sick. None of the food I ate stayed down, but Grace kept forcing soup and crackers on me, keeping me hydrated with Pedialyte. On Tuesday morning, Grace went to my house and retrieved my kit and a few other things I'd need for the trip to Santa Barbara because I just couldn't face the possibility that there might be paparazzi still camped outside my door.

But Officer Cox had been right. The paparazzi had moved on to more interesting stories. Grace relayed that there wasn't a single cameraman in sight.

Nico and I were already yesterday's news.

I drove to Santa Barbara in Grace's Lexus because my Fiat was still parked in my garage, and she insisted she'd use a car service to get back and forth to her office. "I can write it off as a business expense," she said airily, waving my protests away. "Besides, I've always wanted to know what it feels like to have a chauffeur." And that was that.

And now I was in an ocean-view hotel room in Santa Barbara, sitting on the edge of the bed, staring at the cell phone in my hand. I'd turned it off on the cab ride home from Nico's, not wanting to hear any more excuses. Not wanting to know if he'd try another tack. Now I felt sufficiently far enough away to deal with it. With shaking hands, I hit the button to turn it on.

There were five voicemails.

The first was from Chloe from three days prior. "Just wanted to let you know I got home in one piece. Hope you're okay, too. Dude, that was *intense*." She paused, and I could picture her chewing her lip. "Um . . . so . . . how long do you think I should wait before calling Officer Cox?" She giggled. "I think I need to report a woman dying of being sex starved." She hung up after promising to send her crew over to clean up what remained of the trampled flowers in my yard.

Three days ago felt like another lifetime.

The next call was from the coordinator for the Reem Acra shoot, saying she'd emailed me the final itinerary and inviting me to a cocktail reception, which happened to be in just a few hours' time. I quickly texted her to confirm, then went back to voicemail.

The third call came in at two thirty in the morning. At first, no one said anything. Rock music pounded in the background, blaringly loud. Then, in a thick voice, Nico spoke.

"Gave you eighteen hours. Now ask me why."

My heart jumped into my throat. The music played a moment longer, then the call cut off. Another call came in the next day at almost 4:00 a.m. More loud music. Another pause. Then Nico's voice again, even rougher this time.

"Goddamn it, Kat." He hung up.

On his final call, Nico didn't say anything. It sounded as if a party had been raging wherever he was for days. All I heard was music, the sound of his ragged breathing, and, making my heart clench, a woman's faint laughter in the background, before the call dropped and I was left clutching the phone to my ear, shaking.

Maybe Nico was taking a ride on the Village Bicycle after all.

The phone in my hand rang. I jerked so sharply I dropped it. I put my hand over my thundering heart, took a few breaths, and leaned down to pick it up. Seeing the number on the readout, I made the decision to press Send before I was even conscious of it.

"Nico."

"Fuck," he breathed, "you picked up."

He sounded terrible. Actually, he sounded incredibly relieved, but also pissed off, strung out, and a little drunk.

"I had my phone turned off." Why was I explaining that to him? What was I hoping for here, something that would make sense? Something that wouldn't make me want to jump off my hotel room balcony? I should have learned my lesson by now.

"Runnin' away again. Always fuckin' runnin' away from me, Kat. And always comparin' me to some other dickhead that broke your heart. Even your dad."

Blood rushed to my face. My ears were scalding. "I'm going to hang up now."

"Yeah? Well before you do, ask me why."

I was shaking in anger, in hurt, in confusion. "I already told you, why doesn't matter. You made your choice perfectly clear. It is what it is."

His laugh was disturbing on many levels. "Don't kid yourself, baby. Why's the *only* thing that *ever* matters. Now ask me."

I stood and began to pace. "How long have you been up?"

"A while. Where are you?"

I didn't answer.

"'Cause I know you're not at home. Know you haven't been there in days. So where are you, Kat?"

He'd been by my house, more than once, looking for me. Why? He wanted to have his cake and eat it, too? "I'm working."

"Where?" His question was clipped and demanding.

"What difference does it make? You already told me everything I needed to know—"

"Not everything," he interrupted, his voice turning hard. "You left before you heard it all. Because you didn't *want* to hear it all."

My anger was growing, along with my impatience. Now this was *my* fault? "Okay, Nico. You win. I'll play your little game: Why?"

There was a long, deafening silence, then a ragged sigh. "I can't talk about this over the phone."

Fighting back tears, I looked out at the ocean. "You know what?" I whispered, shaking my head. "I think I'm all checkmated out."

"Don't fuckin' hang up!"

I'd never heard him so angry. Even when he was screaming at the paparazzi, even when Brody and A.J. had walked in on us in bed. His fury crawled right through the line and grabbed me around the neck, squeezing. I couldn't answer. But I didn't hang up.

"Tell me where you are! I'm comin' to get you!"

A lone tear tracked its way down my cheek. "No, you're not. You pursued me and convinced me she wasn't your girlfriend. Then you fucked me and told me you'd always take care of her. You love her, Nico. You have history. You have her picture next to your bed! You even have the same tattoo!" My voice was getting shrill. "How am I supposed to compete with that? How can you expect me to *want* to?"

The sound he made was part hiss, part growl. There was a loud bang, then he let out a string of curses. "Tell me where you are!"

Alarmed, I sat up straight. "What did you just do? What was that sound?"

"Probably broke my fuckin' hand punchin' this wall, is what I just did! Tell me where you are so I don't break the other one!"

"I'm not taking the blame for you acting crazy, Nico! If you want to be stupid enough to ruin your hands so you'll never be able to play the guitar again, that's totally on you!"

There was another loud bang, and another. He made a sound like he was gritting his teeth against pain.

"Nico! Stop it!" What was the matter with him?

"Tell me where you are!"

Another loud bang, and suddenly I just couldn't do it anymore. I couldn't take this kind of drama.

"Stop hitting things first!" I waited a moment. He seemed to be listening to me, because there were no more loud bangs. "Okay. You want to know where I am? Here's where: out of your life."

For the first time since we'd met, I hung up on Nico Nyx.

It felt like I'd just cut off my own arm.

Chapter 21

I worked. I ate. I slept. I made it through the next three days without checking my phone again, or dying, though it really felt like I would.

Then on the final day of the shoot, life decided it would be super fun to drop a nuclear bomb on my head.

I was applying contouring powder to the knife-edged angle of a model's cheekbone in one of the hotel suites that had been set up for makeup and wardrobe. She couldn't have been more than seventeen, snapping gum and fiddling constantly with the pink bedazzled phone in her lap, tweeting and Facebooking and all the rest. She clicked a link on the screen, and a song began to play. Her nose wrinkled in distaste. I tapped it with the handle of my brush.

"Don't scrunch your nose. You'll get bunny lines and will have to get Botox when you're twenty."

Obviously, I was feeling a little stabby.

"I can't believe anybody likes One Direction, they're such a bunch of little boys?"

The model, a wafer-thin El Salvadorian girl ironically nicknamed Gordita—Spanish for "chubby"—had the habit of ending sentences at a higher pitch than the beginning, so it always sounded like she was asking a question. I made a noncommittal noise and started working on her other cheekbone. They were so sharp they could draw blood if I accidentally touched them with my finger. I wondered what the last meal she'd had was. Probably water and an olive, followed by a piece of sugarless gum for dessert.

When I turned to get the eyelash glue from the vanity beside us, she squealed.

I whirled around, expecting to see a spider on her arm, or at the very least a cheeseburger that had made a sudden appearance on one of the trays of Evian an assistant was circulating through the room, but she was staring at her phone, enraptured by whatever was on the screen.

"Omigod! It's Bad Habit's new video! It was just released!"

My stomach did this funny thing where it tried to crawl up my esophagus and escape. Forgetting the lash glue, I plastered myself to Gordita's side, watching over her shoulder.

And there they were, in all their rock 'n' roll glory. Bad Habit.

It struck me for the first time how apropos that name really was. Greedy and unable to resist temptation exactly as if I were an addict, I stared with my mouth open as the video I'd made with Nico came to life.

Watching it was so surreal. Even on a four-inch screen, I could see the combustible attraction between us. The tension in our bodies, the way we looked at one another, even the way we *didn't* look at each other all screamed "want."

I was proud about how I looked. Like a vampy, old-fashioned pinup girl back in the days when having a good figure meant having tits and ass, not the body of a twelve-year-old boy like my friend Gordita beside me.

But if the camera had been kind to me, it absolutely worshipped Nico. He was undeniably gorgeous and charismatic in real life, and sexy as sin, but the camera brought out another facet of his beauty. He was a man of flesh and bone and blood, but onscreen there was this quality of otherworldliness about him, a glow, as if he'd stepped straight off a cloud from Mount Olympus.

He was a star, he was beautiful, and, for one infinitesimal moment in time, he'd been mine.

I bit the inside of my cheek so hard I tasted blood.

"*God*, he's so *hot*!" Gordita was practically drooling. I couldn't argue with her, but that didn't mean I didn't want to pinch the nonexistent fat on her upper arm and ask, "Have you stopped working out lately, dear?"

She puffed out her lower lip and blew out a breath, fluttering her bangs. "Too bad about what happened to him, though."

Dread descended on me as if a wet blanket had been dropped on my head. A surge of adrenaline flooded me, and my hands began to shake. "What do you mean? What happened?"

"That thing with his girlfriend?"

"G-girlfriend?" I nearly choked on my own tongue getting the word out. Gordita looked at me strangely.

"Yeah, Avery Kane? You must've heard of her, she's super famous? Anyway, they found her dead in rehab last night. Apparently she was getting drugs in the other rehab she was in, and was, like, a danger to herself? She went on some rampage or something. So Nico got some kind of court order and put her into this, like, mega-secret rehab for rich junkies where she couldn't, like, leave, even if she wanted to?"

She began inspecting her manicure, not realizing that my entire world had begun to spin out of control. The room was slipping sideways. "But I guess there's always ways to get drugs, even in rehab. She OD'd. Heroin, the news said? She'd shoot up between her toes so there wouldn't be any track marks on her arms." Gordita laughed a girlish, envious laugh that was like fingers down a chalkboard to my ears. "Smart girl."

I couldn't catch my breath. It felt like the walls were closing in around me. Everything in the room was too bright, too loud, too *close.*

"Hey. You don't look so good. Are you okay?"

Gordita reached for me, but I turned and ran from the room, already sure where I was headed.

The street outside the long driveway to Nico's house was mobbed. It was well past sunset, but it seemed closer to noon from the illumination of so many news vans, video cameras, and lights on portable stands. Overhead, a helicopter whirred. Its searchlight danced jaggedly around the neighborhood, but I didn't care if it caught me in its blinding beam.

All I could think about was getting to Nico.

It had taken me less than two hours to make the trip from Santa Barbara to Hollywood, my foot crammed against the gas pedal, my heart flying as fast as the car. I went through hell by the time I reached him, a hell of whys and what-ifs, blame and self-recrimination.

He hadn't lied to me about at least one thing. He'd taken Avery back to rehab, just a different, more exclusive one than the one she'd been in. He'd basically had her committed. But what about all the rest? The lost hours, the tattoos, what he'd said to me in bed about how he'd always take care of her?

The worst part was knowing that he would have told me before I'd left his bedroom that day when he came back after the long night away. He would have told me everything, if I'd just done like he'd wanted, and asked him "why."

Now I couldn't wait to know. I *had* to know, and I was going to try to get him to tell me. If—and this was a giant if—he'd even see me at all.

Because he wasn't answering my calls. His cell rang and rang, then an automated message came on saying the voicemail was full and to try again later.

Two police cars were parked in front of the gate to Nico's house, keeping the press and paparazzi at bay. I pulled up and rolled down the window, listening to the sound of a thousand shutters clicking as an officer approached my car.

"You're going to have to turn the car around, ma'am—"

"Please, no, you have to let me in. He's . . . " I swallowed. "Mr. Nyx is expecting me."

The officer paused, assessing me. I knew I most likely looked like shit, but wasn't going to break eye contact like I had something to hide. His gaze darted around the interior of the car. He was probably looking for weapons. "Who are you?"

"Friend of the family. Close friend. He'll be upset if he finds out I was here and got turned away." My heart pounded. Lying had never been my forte.

The officer's eyes were keen and penetrating. "Lady, if you're such a close friend, why don't you have the gate code?"

Shit. The damn gate code! I looked at the tall iron gate in desperation, willing it to open. It didn't oblige.

"Please," I begged. "He knows me. I've been trying his cell but . . . it's turned off. Look, his number is right here, I have it in my phone. I just . . . I don't have the house number."

The officer's look soured. I forged ahead, getting desperate. "My name is Katherine Reid. Nico and I did a video together, the one that was just released. Have you seen it?"

No answer. He didn't look impressed. Maybe he wasn't a fan of rock music.

"Please just call. Tell him Kat is here. He'll let me in."

I must have sounded more sure than I felt, because after another moment of silent inspection, the officer straightened and returned to his squad car. He conferred briefly with the officer from the other car, then retrieved a phone from his dashboard. He dialed, watching me.

The conversation was short. When I saw the officer's expression, my heart sank. He walked leisurely back to my car, his hand resting lightly on the butt of the gun strapped to the belt around his waist. He leaned into the window. I closed my eyes, defeated.

Nico didn't want to see me. He'd turned me away.

"All right, Kat. Up you go."

Luckily the officer straightened then, because all the blood drained from my face. God only knows what he would have thought of that.

The gate swung slowly open. I waited until there was just enough room, then revved the engine and blasted past it, roaring up the hill at top speed until I reached the circular gravel drive. I narrowly missed destroying the fountain at its center in my haste.

The house was dark. I slid to a stop, inches from the hedge that flanked the steps to the front door. I was out of the car, across the porch, and ringing the bell in seconds. Then I realized the door was already open. Literally open, cracked a few inches, not only unlocked.

Filled with trepidation, I pushed it open wider and stepped inside, into darkness.

"Nico?" My voice echoed off the walls. There was no response. I began to panic. "Nico, where are you?"

I crossed the empty living room. The dining room was empty as well, as was the kitchen, the theater, the recording studio. I took the stairs to the second floor two at a time, not bothering with the elevator. I couldn't be trapped inside an elevator at a time like this. As it was, I could hardly breathe.

Past the guest rooms, past the library, past the game room I hurried. When finally I stood outside Nico's closed bedroom door, I was trembling, freaked out, and not at all sure of what I'd find on the other side. A sliver of light spilled from beneath the door, beckoning me.

I turned the knob. The door swung open on silent hinges. There he was, seated on the edge of his bed, staring at the carpet, his hands clenched in his hair, elbows propped on his knees.

"Nico," I whispered.

Slowly, as if it pained him to move, he lifted his head and looked at me. His eyes were red. His cheeks were wet. If I'd thought I'd gone through hell on the way over, Nico's face proved he was still there.

"You're here." His voice was a lifeless, terrible thing. He sounded as if he were speaking from beyond the grave.

I went to him. He watched me, making no move to stand. When I was a foot away, he reached for me. His face crumpled. He slid from the bed to his knees, holding me around the waist, and buried his face between my thighs like a hiding child. He made a sound like he was choking. Feeling helpless, not knowing what else to do, I stroked his hair.

"I'm here. Nico, I'm here."

His shoulders shook. His fingers clenched into the fabric of my shirt. I heard him gasping. It seemed like he was trying desperately to hold himself together and failing in every possible way.

I knew this kind of grief. I recognized it like you recognize the face of an old friend you haven't seen in many years, but could never forget. I'd suffered through it before, and now Nico was suffering it over the death of Avery.

My God, how he must have loved her. I was ashamed at myself for wishing, however briefly, he might have loved me the same way.

I said his name again. Still kneeling, he looked up at me. In one long, shuddering breath, he said, "She was raped by her father almost every day from the time she was eight years old until she left home at fourteen. *Eight years old*, Kat. Can you blame her for gettin' into drugs? Can you blame her for bein' so fucked up?"

Goose bumps raised all the hairs on my arms. I stared down at the beautiful ruin at my feet, shocked into silence.

"She tried her whole life to get it behind her. But how can you escape somethin' like that? A betrayal like that? You can't." His voice broke. "Even when she was little I knew this day would come. Even after what I did to make it right." He swayed, clinging to me.

Beyond my confusion, I felt the first, cold pangs of fear arrow through my chest. "You knew her when she was little? What do you mean—make it right?"

Nico's eyes were glazed with fatigue, red with tears, filled with unbearable anguish. But oh, so blue. So sweetly, beautifully blue I almost didn't believe what next came out of his mouth.

"I killed him. I killed that son of a bitch and then we ran away and I never looked back, not once in all these years."

Frozen, I stared at Nico, my mouth open, my heart a stone inside my chest. A stone that shattered with his next whispered words:

"She was my sister."

Chapter 22

Only in a storybook does a tale like Nico and Avery's have a happy ending. He was right: some betrayals you can never escape. Some wounds are far too deep, and far too painful, to heal.

Avery's real name was Amy. She was beautiful from birth, one of those babies people are always saying should be in commercials, gurgling happy and picture perfect, a gem. By the time she was a toddler, men would stop their mother on the street to tell her how gorgeous her daughter was, and why didn't she move the family to Hollywood and put her in the movies?

Their father noticed little Amy's beauty, too. He noticed it all too well. When it finally came to light that he was molesting his own child, their mother—a former stripper, with no education beyond the ninth grade—blamed Amy. She walked out the door, never to be seen again.

Leaving her three children in the hands of a monster.

In comparison to what Amy suffered, the two boys fared fairly well. There were regular beatings, long, drunken rants where dishes would be thrown and broken, whole days when their father would be blacked out on the kitchen floor and they'd try to pretend everything was normal by going to school and pasting smiles on their frightened faces. That, at least, was bearable. Sometimes they'd get lucky. If you're quick enough, you can dodge a flying fist. You can learn to leap out of the way of that plate or vase or picture sailing toward your head.

But a little girl is helpless when she wakes in bed with a grown man on top of her. There's no dodging his groping hands, his brute strength, the horror of his body invading hers.

And if she loves her father, if, underneath all the terror and shame, she still *loves* him, she learns to deal with the reality of her life, and the unthinkable betrayal of the one man who's supposed to protect her, by learning to hate herself.

Amy's rage turned inward.

At eleven, she began cutting herself with a razor blade. At twelve, she began taking drugs. By thirteen she was sleeping around, the most promiscuous girl in school. When she had an abortion just shy of her fourteenth birthday—her father's baby? Some other, uncaring boy's?—Nico knew he had to get her out of that house and that destitute, godforsaken Tennessee town, or doom her to a life of misery, followed by an early death.

His father didn't think that such a good idea.

They tried to sneak out. Their father caught them. There was an ugly scene, a scuffle that turned into a brawl. A scared, seventeen-year-old Nico pushed his father down a flight of stairs in a fit of anger, and watched crying as the tyrant that had terrorized them for so many years lay broken at the bottom and didn't get up.

His brother and sister, holding hands behind him, were crying, too. They were still crying when the police came, still crying when their father's cooling body was taken away. There was an inquiry. Their father's death was ruled accidental; toxicology reports showed he'd been drunk at the time, of course.

They were scheduled to be put into foster homes, but when the social workers showed up, the kids were gone, riding a Greyhound out of town.

Their father only gave them a single thing of value in his life: the contents of his wallet. He'd had just enough to cover three student tickets to LA.

"We lived on the streets for a while, stealin' food, sleepin' in doorways, until Amy got caught tryin' to walk out a store with a loaf of bread. The owner woulda sent her ass to jail, but there was this woman in line who turned out to be some rinky-dink modeling agency owner. She paid for the bread and smoothed it out with the store owner, then bought Amy a meal. Told her she could be a star. Told her she'd give her a place to stay if she signed a contract with the agency. So she did. Amy started modelin' under some fake name, tellin' people she was eighteen. She could pass for it, too. All the shit she went through, she coulda passed for thirty."

We were lying together on the carpet at the foot of the bed. His head rested on my crossed legs. I stroked his hair and kissed him repeatedly as he talked, his voice hollow, his eyes closed, my heart breaking over and over and over.

"I lied about my age, too, got a job at the Pig 'N Whistle, bussin' tables, washin' dishes. My brother, Michael—he was the middle one, fifteen at the time—started runnin' drugs for some local dealer, sellin' to elementary school kids. I shoulda known, he was bringin' in so much cash, it shoulda been obvious what he was doin', but I was so fuckin' scared, always thinkin' the police would figure out what really happened and knock on the door and arrest me. I just shut my eyes to it.

"He used to bring this skinny Portuguese kid around the place we were stayin', the shitty apartment the modelin' agency rented for Amy. Name was Juan Carlos. Barely spoke English. Always gettin' the shit beat outta him 'cause he had a big mouth, but he had mad swagger, was a little fuckin' Napolean, and Amy fell for him hard. Wasn't long before he convinced her to go back to Brazil with him. He had family there. Said they'd get married, and she'd never have to worry about anything again."

For a long while, Nico was silent. His throat worked soundlessly, as if he was swallowing sobs. "So she went. Left me and Michael a note, took all our savings. Three years went by and not another word. Then one day I get a phone call, outta the blue. 'I'm coming back,' she said in this weird voice, all foreign soundin', no trace of Tennessee left. 'Just like that?' I said. 'What, your husband leave you?'

"There was this long pause, like she was thinkin' how to tell me somethin', lookin' up at the ceilin' like she used to do when she was gatherin' her thoughts. 'In a manner of speaking,' she answered, and the way she said it, all weird and quiet, I swear I got chills. I knew just by the tone of her voice that Juan Carlos was dead. And I knew she had somethin' to do with it."

Nico opened his eyes and stared up at me. "So she came back. I barely recognized her. Grew half a foot, bleached her hair, lost so much weight she looked anorexic. Had this crazy smile all the time, tryin' so hard to pretend she was someone else. This girl she made up named Avery Kane, an orphan from the slums of Sao Paolo who came to the US to make it big. She was such a good actress, spoke such perfect fuckin' Portuguese, had all the details down about her fake past, even I started to believe it. She was always smart, Amy. In another life, she coulda been a lawyer. A teacher."

He made an ugly sound, halfway between a choke and a laugh. "Instead she was Daddy's fuck toy, then Juan Carlos's. He had family all right. And the family business was brothels. He was a recruiter, came to the US a few times a year to find new talent. You can guess what happened once Amy got to Brazil."

I was horrified. "Oh, God."

"When she came back here, she had enough money to rent an apartment. Probably stole it, I didn't ask. So she starts modelin' again. Sellin' herself, one way or another, 'cause no one ever taught her she was worth anything except for the way she looked and what was between her legs. I tried to get her to stop, go back to school, find somethin' she really loved doin', but she was stubborn as fuck." He paused for a moment, breathing raggedly. "You remind me of her that way."

I thought I might remind him of her in other ways, too. Secrets. Lies. A dark, painful past. I wondered if that's what attracted him to me. I wondered if, deep down, he knew he couldn't save his sister and hoped to save me instead.

"She picked up the heroin habit in Brazil. The brothel boss made sure all the girls were high; made 'em easier to handle. Even when she came back to the States, Amy could never shake the habit. I put her in a dozen different rehabs over the years. She'd do fine for a while, then somethin' would set her off and she'd slide right back into it."

I smoothed my hand over his skin, down the muscles of his back. My fingers trailed over the shadowy figure of Nyx. She stared up at me, mysterious as the sphinx. Nico saw where I was looking and sighed.

"Amy always used to say she had nothin' but death and darkness at her back, so much sin it would devour her if she ever turned around. One day we were watchin' this show about Greek mythology—this was right after she got out of another rehab—and they showed this painting of Nyx. When they said she was born from Chaos, and was the mother of death, darkness, pain, and deceit, we just looked at each other. Guess we kinda felt like, she's our people, you know? She's *us*. Went right out and got inked. Michael, too. Made us all tighter, in a way. Had another little secret between us, but this one felt almost like . . . I don't know. Protection, maybe. Like a talisman that could keep us safe." Nico's voice broke. "So fuckin' stupid."

Gently, I smoothed the hair off his damp forehead. "It's not stupid, Nico," I whispered, desperate to offer him anything that would help soothe his pain. But he only shook his head, disagreeing.

"Changed my last name then, too. Real one's Jameson, by the way. So one lie became two, and two became ten, and suddenly the press thinks Amy is my girlfriend 'cause we're gettin' photographed together so much, even though we tried not to. And it was fuckin' weird at first but then I figured, why not? It made it safer for us, in a way. One more layer of make-believe to take us further and further from anyone who might suspect the truth. So we went with it. It got to be this big game to her, pretendin' to be jealous over some random chick, bein' all coy when some interviewer asked her if we were gonna get married."

The stories I'd heard, the photos I'd seen of them together . . . none of it was real.

What a terrible way to live.

"Who else knows?"

"Kenji knows a little. I doubt Avery told him anything, but he's sharp as a tack. I think he figured out a few things on his own. But only Barney knows the whole story. I know him from way back, when we all first came to LA. He was a bouncer then, workin' the door at the Pig 'N Whistle. Got jumped by three big guys one night. I saw it, stepped in to help, took a knife in the ribs before the fight was over. Spent almost a week in the hospital. When I got back to work, Barney said he owed me his life. I thought he was just bein' dramatic, but years later when he started workin' for the LAPD after he got out of the military, he called me up, said if I ever needed anything to let him know.

"Turns out I *did* need somethin'. 'Round that time, Amy landed a contract with Victoria's Secret to be one of them 'angels.' Some old, dirtbag photographer thought she looked a lot like this teenage model he'd worked with years before. That first modelin' agency Amy signed with closed its doors way back, but this asshole was still around. Knew there were probably pictures of her from that time still around, too. So I told Barney. He took care of it. Made everything disappear, every trace of evidence that Amy ever existed before she became Avery."

"And the photographer?"

Nico's hesitation was loaded. "Never heard from him again."

It hung there between us. Nico watched me with those beautiful eyes, waiting. Waiting for me to react, to decide if what he'd just told me about him getting Barney to make the photographer "disappear" would be the thing that would finally send me running.

That he was telling me all this, trusting me with such a huge thing, not only his fate, but Barney's as well, made my heart swell until it felt close to bursting. I loved him so much in that moment it physically *hurt*.

I took his face in my hands. He stared up at me, tense, his eyes still red and wet. In a trembling whisper, I said, "You know what I think?"

His jaw tightened. He shook his head.

"I think you did what you had to do to protect her. You protected Barney, too, when you didn't have to, and I've already seen how protective you are of me. And now you're laying it all out for me, telling me the truth, even though it's ugly and would get you in all kinds of trouble and fuck up your career if I told anyone else . . . and all that makes me think I can trust you with anything. Even my life."

His relief was enormous. I saw it in his eyes, felt it in his body. He sat up, pulled me into his arms and lifted me from the carpet. He carried me to the bed and lowered me to the mattress, then undressed me with quiet intensity as if I were a gift he was unwrapping. I knew from the desperate look in his eyes that he needed me, he needed to lose himself in me, and I was happy to let him get lost.

I needed to get lost in him, too. We needed to lose ourselves in each other.

This time it wasn't fucking. Nico made love to me with an almost desperate tenderness, his kisses gentle, his hands gentle, his eyes so soft and unguarded my heart felt squeezed by an invisible fist when I looked into them. And when it was over and we lay quietly panting in each other's arms, Nico hid his face in my neck, wrapped his arms around me, and cried.

Love washed over me, fierce and burning. Love and a feeling of protectiveness so strong I knew that I'd do anything in my power to keep him from feeling this kind of pain ever again. With every shake of his shoulders and softly choked sob, I vowed he'd never again have to suffer like he was now, not if there was anything I could do to prevent it.

After a while, he quieted. His body relaxed. Quickly afterward, he fell asleep, as if he'd been released.

I held him until the sun came up. Through the tall windows, I watched the sun rise over LA. I felt my center of gravity shifting to him, felt a clear and quiet recognition that the love between us was the only thing of true beauty I'd ever known in my life.

Nico and I had each other. We were safe now.

We were both finally home.

Chapter 23

When I awoke sometime later, Nico was still wrapped around me, snug as a python. Though his weight was substantial, and his body heat was making me sweat, I loved waking up entangled with him.

Unfortunately, I *really* had to pee.

"Sweetie," I whispered, trying to remove myself as gently as possible from his arms. His response was to drag my naked body closer to his and silently bury his face between my breasts.

I laughed softly. "No fair hiding in my cleavage."

His voice was muffled against my breasts and scratchy with sleep. "This is my favorite place in the world. Nothin' bad ever happens here."

Hearing that, my heart got squishy soft. Even the biggest, baddest alpha male is still a little boy inside. I stroked his silky dark hair, my smile growing larger as he made a sound like a purr.

"Something bad might happen if you don't let me up to go to the bathroom, superstar."

He lifted his head and blinked sleepily at me. "First I have to tell you something."

I cocked a brow.

Nico said, "I want kids."

Slam! went my heart against my breastbone. My mouth opened. Nothing came out.

"More than just a couple. Four, maybe."

My voice was a whisper. "You want four kids?"

He nodded.

"With . . . me?"

He looked around the room, then back at me. "You see anyone else here?"

The whites of his eyes were bloodshot, which made the blue of his irises all the more brilliant. He stared at me, waiting, utterly serious. I had a fleeting image of four beautiful dark-haired children running around a park, screaming in glee, as Nico and I watched on, holding hands and smiling.

My heart alternated between wild throbbing and stalling out altogether. I felt a little dizzy.

"I'm tellin' you this because I'm not gonna waste any more time on anything that isn't real. Always wanted a family. Not gettin' any younger. And now that I have you . . . " he pressed a soft kiss to my lips, "I can't see any reason to put it off."

There didn't seem to be enough air in the room. I was having trouble breathing. Memory was wreaking havoc with my emotions, and I was in danger of either breaking out in tears or throwing up.

"Um . . . can we wait to get started until after I pee?"

I should have learned by now that Nico would see past my attempt at lighthearted evasion. His sleepy gaze sharpened. He lifted to an elbow and hovered above me, searching my face. "What's wrong?"

I turned away, swallowing hard.

"Kat—"

"Just give me a second," I whispered, trying desperately to catch my breath. I pulled myself from his arms and sat up abruptly, covering my naked breasts with the sheet. Nico sat up beside me, tense and watchful, his gaze riveted to my face.

Gulping air as I stared out the windows to the city below, I flattened my hand over my heart. I knew I was going to ugly cry—my watering eyes, clamoring heartbeat, and shaking hands attested to that—but I hoped I'd be able to get through the next few minutes without breaking down completely.

I'd never spoken aloud what I was about to tell Nico. Not since it had happened, more than eight years ago. But he'd been so honest with me, risking everything, I had to be completely honest in return.

No matter how much it hurt.

"When I was seventeen, I got pregnant."

The first of the tears crested my lower lids and spilled down my cheeks. I didn't bother wiping them away. Beside me, Nico was silent.

"My mother was terminally ill with breast cancer at the time. She was sick a lot after my dad left, but this was different. Watching her die was the worst thing I've ever seen. It was brutal. Over the course of a year, she wasted away right in front of my eyes. I was just a kid, with no dad around, no siblings, facing the fact of being totally alone in the world, and I just . . . I just went crazy." I closed my eyes, the pain of remembering sharp as a blade scraped across every nerve ending. "I had an affair with the school counselor."

Nico slid his hand up my spine, beneath my hair. He cupped the back of my neck and squeezed. Somehow his support made me feel worse.

"Logically I can look back and understand I was just a scared teenager looking for a father figure, but at the time I thought it was love. Glenn wanted me to have an abortion. I can't really blame him. If anyone had found out about us, he'd have been fired, probably prosecuted. But I didn't tell anyone. And because I didn't want to have an abortion he cut off all contact with me. He quit his job right in the middle of the school year and moved away. I never saw him again."

Nico muttered, "Motherfucker."

My laugh was humorless. "Yeah. So there I was, a pregnant minor with a dying mother. I was friendly with the hospice nurse who was taking care of my mom, and confessed my condition to her. I couldn't tell my mother, of course. Obviously that wasn't a choice. But the hospice nurse referred me to an adoption agency, and I registered with them."

My voice kept breaking. Tears streamed down my cheeks, dripping onto my chest. Nico scooted closer to me, wrapping his legs around my hips. He pulled me back against his chest and I rested my head on his shoulder. I kept my eyes on the view, on the beautiful clear sky, focusing only on my next breath.

"I got to decide who the adoptive parents would be. There were a bunch of applicants; I had no idea so many people who wanted babies couldn't have one of their own. But there was this one couple, Brian and Diana. They were both from big families and always wanted kids, but she couldn't have any because she'd had cancer. The chemo had put her into early menopause. I decided on them. Because of my mom, and her cancer. I felt as if there was a connection. Like it was meant to be."

Nico hugged me hard. "That's beautiful, baby. You did the right thing."

My face screwed up. I couldn't see anything anymore because of all the water in my eyes, so I closed them tight, shaking violently in his arms. "I'm not done with the story yet."

It was several long moments before I composed myself enough

to continue. "By the time my mother died, I'd turned eighteen. The day they called me from the hospice to tell me she'd passed, I went into labor." From my mouth came a strangled sound. I gasped for air. "I wasn't due for almost another two months."

Nico fell completely still. His arms around me were crushing.

My final words were whispered. "It was a baby girl. She was so tiny. So frail. I couldn't believe she made it at all. For three days, Brian and Diana and I slept in the NICU at the hospital, watching her fight. And then on the third day, our little baby girl died."

Nico breathed in horror, "No."

"The doctors weren't clear if there was a genetic component, something wrong with the baby that would have made her premature anyway, or if the stress of my mother's death put me into labor, but I didn't have any money for testing, and what difference would it have made? My baby was gone. My mother was gone. And Brian and Diana suffered almost as much as I did. Maybe more, in a way. All their hopes and dreams, dead.

"And I felt responsible. Even though I hated myself for it, part of me wished I'd had the abortion like Glenn wanted me to. Part of me thought it was my own fault, all the suffering I'd caused this sweet couple. Part of me wanted to die, too."

Nico turned me to face him. He was shaking his head, tears welling in his own eyes.

I cut him off before he could speak. My own words were sobbed. "So I don't know—if there's something wrong with me—if maybe I can't have a healthy baby—"

"Angel." Nico crushed me against his chest, kissing my face, my neck. "Angel, stop! It doesn't matter! What matters is us—"

"But you want a family!" I wailed. "What if I'm broken? What if I can't give you what you want?"

Nico rolled onto his back, taking me with him. He hugged me

so tight I could barely breathe, but I didn't care. I clung to him, crying hard, my face in his neck.

His voice in my ear was gentle, but determined. "*You* are what I want. *You* are what I need. Anything else is a bonus."

"But—"

It was his turn to cut me off, his voice firmer. "No buts! There are doctors we can see if you're really worried about it. We can get answers from professionals before we make any decisions, okay? Jesus, I'm sorry. If I'd known anything about what you'd gone through, I'd have brought this up in a whole different way."

He kissed me again, stroking my hair away from my tear-streaked face. "How about this."

I blinked up at him through wet lashes.

"How about if we get married, and work out all the rest of this stuff later? Let's take care of the important thing first."

My tongue wouldn't work. In fact, none of my bodily functions seemed to be working. I felt like I was floating, weightless, in outer space.

Nico frowned. "I'm not likin' that look on your face, darlin'."

I managed, barely, to say his name. Whatever he saw in my face then made his own face crease into a smile.

"It's settled, then. We're gettin' hitched."

"Wait," I said, breathless, reeling. "Wait."

His frown returned. "What?"

"You can't propose without a ring."

His brows shot up. "No? 'Cause I just did."

"*Now?* But . . . yesterday. What happened with Avery." I hated to say it, but it had to be said. "And soon, the funeral."

Sorrow welled in his eyes. His voice was quiet. "Yeah. The funeral. Need to know I've got you there by my side. Need you standin' next to me. Gonna need you more than ever, that day. And every day after."

When I began to protest again, he shook his head. "No more secrets between us. And no more distance. It's you and me, a team. And I want to know you're legally obligated, baby, because you've got a bad tendency to bolt for the hills."

I studied his face, my heart racing. The future was rushing at me, enormous and beautiful. "Grace is going to have an absolute fit."

Into his eyes came a mischievous light, though his expression remained serious. "Almost worth it to say 'yes' just to see that, isn't it?"

"One more thing."

"What's that?"

I swallowed. "You haven't said you love me yet."

"Oh." He considered it. "That's true."

I waited. "So?"

Very seriously, he said, "You love me."

"Nico!"

He tried to look innocent, and failed miserably. "What? You said, 'You haven't said *you love me* yet.' So I did. Are you gonna be this difficult to please as my wife?"

Hearing him say "wife" recalled the tears to my eyes. "You're a jerk," I whispered, not meaning it.

All the teasing left Nico's eyes, his face, his voice. He gently cupped my face in his hands, staring up at me in a sort of wonder, as if the sun were shining right out of my head.

"What I am is yours. All yours, body and soul. And I can't live without you. I don't want to spend a single minute from this moment on without you. I sleep better with you. I feel better with you. Everything seems brighter when you're around. I can't imagine a future without you in it, and if that's not me tellin' you 'I love you,' I don't know what would be."

Overloaded with emotion, I burst into a fresh onslaught of tears.

Nico sighed. He lowered my head to his chest and let me sob against it, combing his fingers through my hair. "Woman, you're a damn handful."

I cried even harder, and let the man I loved hold me until I was all cried out.

Chapter 24

We agreed not to tell anyone about our engagement until an appropriate amount of time after Avery's funeral had passed. However, our opinions varied greatly about the correct definition of how long was appropriate. Nico thought a few days or weeks. I thought a few months, maybe even a year. For the time being, we agreed to disagree.

I was having a hard time processing everything. Part of me was convinced I was lying in a coma somewhere, dreaming up the whole thing. Another part of me was blissfully happy.

And another part, a darker part, was terrified. I kept waiting for the other shoe to drop.

I knew fairy tales were just that: tales. Made-up stories. How could I—Kat Reid, regular girl, sometime fuckup and full-time cynic—be in love with, and engaged to, the force of nature that was Nico Jameson Nyx?

An unanswerable question. The more pressing issue at hand was Avery's funeral.

Four days after her death, the memorial was held at Hollywood Forever, a sprawling cemetery adjacent to Paramount Studios, where some of the most famous legends in the entertainment industry were buried. When Nico and I pulled up in the Escalade driven by Barney, security was tighter than tight. Staff was denying to callers that there was a service for Avery Kane, even though it had been reported in all the papers. Police cars were parked in a line in front of the entrance, blocking the public from the grounds. Even the flower delivery vans were being searched. A large white tent had been erected over the burial site so the helicopters couldn't get photos of the grave, or of anyone who attended.

Goddamn helicopters. Just the sound of whirring could now make me jump a foot in the air.

Nico had insisted the funeral be family only. Which meant it was him, Barney, me, and Michael, Avery and Nico's brother, who'd flown in from San Francisco that morning.

The minute I laid eyes on him, I knew he was trouble.

The family resemblance was striking. He had Nico's height and coloring, the same square superhero's jaw. But where Nico had an indefinable glow about him, a compelling ease in his own skin, Michael was all hard angles and edges. Whippet thin and full of nervous energy, with sharp, darting eyes, he carried himself like someone who'd just robbed a bank.

I found him unnerving. He seemed to take an even stronger dislike to me. When Nico introduced us, Michael stared at me with such unconcealed hostility, my breath caught in my throat. But as soon as Nico turned to look at him, Michael's expression went blank.

"Nice to meet you, Kat. Nico's told me a lot about you. Sorry we had to meet under these circumstances."

When he turned and walked stiffly away, going to speak to the sad-eyed priest across the tent who would preside over the service, I squeezed Nico's hand.

"He doesn't like me."

"It's not about you."

"Why do you say that?"

Nico ran a hand through his hair and sighed. "He blames himself for introducin' Amy to Juan Carlos. He'd never admit it, but I know him. He's sufferin' as much as I am. You just met him at the worst possible time."

It sounded reasonable. But the little twinge in my gut had me thinking twice. I decided not to make a mountain out of this particular molehill. Not now.

"I'm sure you're right. Ignore me, I'm premenstrual."

Nico sent me a grateful smile. I knew I'd done the right thing by letting it go. But I decided to stay as far away from his brother as I could.

Unfortunately, Michael made that impossible. When the priest murmured that the service would begin, Michael came and stood right beside me, so close his shoulder touched mine. With Nico on my other side and Barney to Nico's left, we stood in a row beside Avery's dove-gray coffin, listening in silence as the priest began to speak. Nico held my hand so tightly my fingers went numb.

I noticed Michael's hands flex open and closed several times, as if he was itching for something to hit. I wondered if a tendency toward anger was another thing that ran in the family.

Then it was over, as abruptly as it had begun.

"May her soul and the souls of all the faithful departed through the mercy of God rest in peace." The priest sprinkled holy water over Avery's coffin. He made the sign of the cross in the air. All that was left to do was watch as the coffin was lowered into the ground.

Michael stepped away and crossed his arms over his chest, avoiding Nico's eyes. I thought it strange the two of them didn't embrace. "See you at the house later tonight?"

Nico frowned. "You're not comin' now?"

Michael shoved his hands into the pockets of his jeans and shook his head. "You know crowds make me twitchy. I'll be over after everyone leaves."

"It's just gonna be us, the band, and a few of her friends."

Nico hadn't wanted anyone but us at the funeral, but I'd convinced him to have a small wake afterward at his house for a few industry people, Avery's friends, her manager and agent, and the band, so they could pay their respects.

Michael's unfriendly gaze settled on me. "Like I said. Crowds."

It was official. Nico's brother hated me.

"Suit yourself." Nico pulled me close to his side and kissed my temple. Michael watched, his expression pained. He glanced away, but for a moment I could have sworn I saw pure rage cross his face, there, then instantly gone.

"Yep. Later." He turned on his heel and strode away, exiting the tent through a curtain. He shoved it aside with disdain, as if it had personally offended him.

I exhaled a breath I didn't know I'd been holding.

Nico's voice was as dark as his eyes as he stared at the curtain Michael had disappeared through. "We were never that close. Not like me and Avery. And if I'm bein' honest, which I always am, I probably blame him for Juan Carlos, too. Just as much as I blame myself for everything else."

I saw how much he was hurting. Though his logical brain realized he wasn't responsible for Avery's overdose, I knew he couldn't shake the guilt. I knew there was a voice whispering in his ear that he'd failed her.

I also knew—by the way he wouldn't let me out of his sight, the way he now had to know where I was and what I was doing every moment in the past few days—Nico had transformed his guilt into an iron-clad determination to ensure he'd never fail me.

The two of us were going to need a shitload of therapy.

Barney laid his big hand on Nico's shoulder. "You did everything you could, man. And then some. Not everything can be fixed. Not everyone can be saved."

Nico looked around the tent. He looked at the forest of flowers. He looked at the priest. He looked at the coffin. He said, "Let's get the fuck outta here." And so we did.

"Oh, Kitty Kat, it's good to see you again," said Kenji, embracing me tightly. "Wish to hell it wasn't because of this, though. Life's a real twat sometimes, right?"

He released me, shaking his head. We stood in a corner of Nico's living room, near the wall of windows where I'd stationed myself in an attempt to remain mostly invisible to the smallish crowd of Avery's friends as they milled around the tables of food set out by the caterer. I felt beyond awkward, and didn't want Nico holding my hand or showing other outward signs of affection, which, naturally, aggravated him. But I wasn't giving in. Fondling your new girlfriend at the wake of (who everyone assumed was) your late ex-girlfriend was in the worst possible taste.

It was beginning to hit me just how delicate the situation really was.

I didn't want to invite questions, or attention. I didn't even think I should be there. But Nico had refused to consider the possibility. "Wherever I go, you go," he'd said, all growly and Nico-ish, and that had been that.

My cover story, in case anyone asked, was that I'd done Avery's makeup on a photo shoot at some indefinite time in the past, and we'd hit it off and become quasi friends.

The only problem was Kenji.

Today he wore a shiny dark-purple suit, the color of an oiled eggplant. The coat, embellished with peacock feathers on the lapels, fell past his knees. His eye shadow matched his suit, and his platform boots matched his vest: searing vomit green. The overall effect was startling. He was only missing a top hat and cane to pass as a ringmaster in an acid-trip circus.

Judging by the sadness in his eyes, however, his mood was anything but circus-like. I wondered how close he and Avery had been.

"So are you and Nico a thing now?" He glanced across the room to where Nico stood staring at me over a bald guy's shoulder.

"Um."

Kenji waved his hand. "Oh, lovey, don't worry, I won't tell. It's none of my business. If he's happy, I'm happy. And I'm guessing by the way the man is ogling you, that he's plenty happy. I'll never forget the way he looked at you the day you met—"

"Kenji!" I hissed.

He blinked, surprised. "What?"

Three tall women with the walk and bearing of models approached, accompanied by a short, fat man sweating bullets in a black suit a size too small. The women stopped and looked me over in silence while the fat man stepped forward with his hand extended.

"Hi. Ethan Grossman, Avery's manager." His face reddened. "Former manager."

I shook his hand, smiling tightly. How unnecessary to add that caveat. I disliked him already, especially since he seemed to be looking at my chest with a little too much interest. I'd worn a very simple black sleeveless dress that showed no cleavage, but that certainly wasn't stopping Mr. Grossman from trying to find it.

"Kat Reid. Nice to meet you."

"I'm Kenji, stylist for the band." Kenji proffered his hand, which Ethan shook, then quickly dropped, turning his attention back to me.

"You a friend of Avery's?"

Oh shit. Here we go. My tight smile got tighter. I'm sure my mouth looked as puckered as an asshole. Without looking in Kenji's direction, I said, "We worked together."

Technically, that wasn't a lie. It was definitely stretching the truth, however. I hoped that's all I'd have to say on the subject, but one of the models perked up, recognizing me.

"You're the girl in the band's new video, right?"

The other two models murmured in agreement, assessing me with sharp, calculating eyes. Ethan's gaze turned wolfish.

"Oh? You're a model? Do you have representation?" He grinned. "I'm always on the lookout for fresh new faces. And this Christina Hendricks look—" he waved his hand, indicating my figure—"is definitely coming back in style."

Jesus H. Christ, these people were unbelievable. He was recruiting at a wake? I let my smile drop and just stared at him. He took my look for one of confusion.

"She's the curvaceous redhead in *Mad Men*."

"I know who she is. And I'm not looking for representation, thank you."

The three models seemed a little too satisfied to hear that. My guess was that they were clients of Ethan's. I'm sure they didn't like hearing that zero percent body fat might not be in vogue for much longer.

"Hey."

The gruff greeting from behind made me jump. I hadn't realized how tightly my nerves were strung until then. I turned to find A.J. standing there, staring down at me.

"Can I talk to you for a second?"

Relief swept over me. Saved in the nick of time. "Of course." I nodded to Ethan and the three models, who'd never even bothered to introduce themselves. "Excuse me." I squeezed Kenji's arm. "We'll talk later, okay?"

"Okay, lovey. Whatever you say."

He seemed distracted, not even offering a smile or meeting my eyes, and I sensed there was more to his mood than the solemnity of the occasion. He kept stealing glances at Nico across the room, then frowning and shaking his head, as if in answer to some silent question he'd asked himself.

Trying not to worry about what the problem might be, I shot a final glance at Ethan, said a silent prayer he wouldn't ask Kenji anything more about me, then turned to A.J. "Should we go over there?" I motioned to a nearby sofa. A.J. nodded, then walked away as abruptly as he'd walked over. I saw Nico watching us and sent him a one-shouldered shrug. His guess was as good as mine at this point.

When I got to the sofa, A.J. was pacing in front of it. With his shaggy blond hair, loping stride, and bulk, he reminded me of a lion. A jittery lion. His hands were on his hips, his gaze on the floor. He hadn't bothered with a suit for the occasion. Neither had Nico, for that matter. I supposed head to toe black counted as dressing up for a rock star, even if it was jeans and a leather jacket.

A.J. stopped pacing and lit a cigarette. He exhaled a cloud of smoke and fixed me with an intense stare. Even in heels, I had to crane my neck to look up at him: the man was a giant. On one side of his neck, a tattoo peeked above the collar of his black T-shirt. I couldn't make out what it was.

"Your girlfriend," he said gruffly. "The blonde."

I didn't know what I'd been expecting, but that definitely wasn't it. "Chloe?"

He nodded curtly, his eyes hard. Something in his demeanor put me on edge. I remembered how Chloe had said he'd been mean to her at the flower shop, and I prepared myself to hear something bad. Was he going to have the balls to talk shit about my friend? At Avery's *wake*?

"What about her?"

He licked his lips. In an accusing tone, he demanded, "What's her deal?"

Oh, no. Oh, no he didn't. I had to remind myself to maintain my shit, because this was not the time or place to get into an argument with the surly drummer from Bad Habit.

I spoke softly, holding his gaze. "Her *deal* is that she's the sweetest, kindest, most loyal person I've ever known in my life, and if you so much as speak a negative *word* against her, I'll . . . I'll . . . I don't know what I'll do but it won't be pleasant."

A.J.'s brows shot up. He sucked hard on his cigarette, blew smoke into my face, and folded his arms across his chest. He stared at me down his nose. "Did you just threaten me?"

I waved the cloud of smoke away. "You're damn straight I did. No one talks shit about my girls."

His eyes were a gorgeous golden amber, the color of aged whiskey.

Though his face was stone cold, there was a hint of warmth in those eyes. I suspected he was laughing at me.

"I can see that. Guess I'll have to be more careful in the future."

"You do that." I mimicked his posture, crossing my arms over my chest.

We stared at each other. He took another hit from his cigarette. I noticed his knuckles were scarred and abnormally large. The back of each finger was inked with a small tattoo. The only one I got a good look at was a flower with initials on each petal. A.J. saw me looking, transferred his cigarette to his other hand, and shoved the hand with the flower tattoo into his pocket. *Weird.*

"Are you always this feisty, or am I getting special treatment because you're still mad about me and Brody walking in on you and Nico in his bedroom?"

My face went molten. I'd been doing a relatively good job up until that moment ignoring the fact that he'd seen me naked. With my hand wrapped around his friend's dick.

Ugh.

"I wasn't really that mad about that. Totally embarrassed, but not mad. I know it was an accident."

Examining me, A.J. drew a thoughtful hit on the cigarette. Like a dragon, he exhaled the smoke through his nose in two long plumes. "It was. And thanks for calming Nico down. I think if you'd asked him to, he'd have ripped out both our throats on the spot. In case you couldn't tell, he's more than a little obsessed with you. Never seen him like this before."

It was then that I noticed it. A.J. had the faintest echo of a Slavic accent in his voice, a certain way of pronouncing his vowels that sounded vaguely communist bloc. How interesting. I thought a change in the course of conversation was in order.

"Just out of curiosity, where are you from?"

His reaction was so unexpected it took my breath away. He stiffened. The warmth in his eyes turned into an arctic chill. Bristling, he leaned toward me as if he were about to grab me around the neck. "Nevada. Why the fuck do you ask?"

I had the good sense to be terrified, at least. This was not a man to be trifled with. But I didn't step back, though I suddenly, desperately, wanted to. "Your accent."

A.J. leaned even closer to me. "I don't. Have. A fucking. Accent." He enunciated each word, each syllable, his gaze burning mine.

All the tiny hairs on my neck stood on end. An intuition that A.J. had his own set of dark, dangerous secrets blossomed in my stomach, setting my nerves alight. "Ookay," I said on a shaky exhalation. "But even if you did, I won't mention it to anyone else. Your past is your own business."

"We weren't talking about my past. We were talking about you hearing something that's not there."

We were almost nose to nose at this point. I thought people might be beginning to stare. My temper flared; what an asshole!

"Actually we were talking about Chloe. And she was right about you."

He blinked. Hostility drained away from him as fast as it had come. "She mentioned me? What did she say?"

I waited a fraction of a second, in order to give my words a little more punch. "She said you were a total jerk. Which I'm thinking is the understatement of the decade!"

Heart pounding, I spun on my heel and headed for the kitchen. I'd had enough socializing for one day. It was margarita time.

And lo and behold, who did I find sitting on the marble island in the middle of the cavernous kitchen but Michael, nursing a Scotch and staring glumly at the floor. When I came in, he looked up with a start.

"Oh. Sorry." I didn't know why I was apologizing, but I thought I'd probably be the last person on earth he wanted to see at that moment. Turns out I was wrong.

"Kat. I was just thinking about you. Come in." He set his Scotch on the countertop and slid off the island to stand facing me. He motioned to the army of alcohol bottles lined up on the kitchen counter near the sink, courtesy of the caterer. "Need a drink?"

"Yes, please." I was grateful. Maybe Michael wasn't as bad as I'd first thought. Anyone who offered me a drink couldn't be all bad. I walked closer, inspecting the bottles. "You think there's any Patrón in here?"

"I'd guess yes. Nico isn't a skimper when it comes to the good stuff." His gaze flickered over me. A ghost of a smile touched his lips. "Or anything else, for that matter."

I didn't know precisely what that meant, but it made me uncomfortable. Between Ethan Grossman, the cryptic exchange with A.J., and now this, I was getting a headache.

Michael fished a glass from one of the cupboards, and poured me a shot of Patrón, no mixer or ice. He handed it to me, and hoisted his glass of Scotch and somberly made a toast, all the while staring me in the eye as if down the sights of a gun. "Here's to new friends."

I raised my glass. "And new beginnings."

When I'd downed the shot, Michael was still looking at me with the same strange intensity. He hadn't taken a swig of his drink.

"Indeed. Nico tells me you're engaged. Congratulations."

Oh, Nico. Dammit! My face flushed with heat. "We weren't going to tell anyone. Under the circumstances, I thought it would be better to wait."

"You mean, seeing as how everyone thinks Amy—excuse me, *Avery*—was Nico's girlfriend."

My mouth went dry. Nico had told Michael I knew Avery was his sister. When? Why hadn't he told me? Was this bad, or good?

It felt bad.

"And since we're on the topic," Michael said, his voice getting rough, "has he told you what he was supposed to be doing that day she left rehab? Or why she came here, looking for him?"

Carefully, I set my empty glass on the counter. I stayed silent, bracing myself for what was sure to be something I didn't want to hear.

Michael said venomously, "Nico was supposed to have gone to visit Avery that day. It was her birthday, you see. But instead," his voice dropped an octave. "Instead he was with *you*."

I sensed the rage rising inside him. Heart pounding, I took a step back. "Michael."

"Rescuing you from the paparazzi, was it?" He sneered, shook his head, and produced a soft, ugly laugh. "Unbelievable. You do realize, Kat . . . "

He took a menacing step toward me. "That you *killed my fucking sister*."

Chapter 25

All the blood drained from my face. "That isn't fair, and you know it. I'm going to assume you're just upset—"

"You're goddamn right I'm upset." His voice was hoarse. His eyes were wild. "I'm beyond upset. I'm fucking *furious*."

He was, I could see that. I also saw how much pain he was in. The anguish in his eyes was unmistakable. It appeared he might at any second start to cry.

Remembering what Nico had said about Michael blaming himself for introducing Amy to Juan Carlos, I kept my voice gentle. Though I was angry at what he'd just accused me of, I also understood that he'd just lost his sister. He was hurting. He was lashing out, and I was a convenient target.

As gently as possible, I said, "I'm sorry, Michael. I'm so sorry she's gone. I'm sure she loved you very much."

His face turned ashen. "You don't know anything."

Taking a risk, I reached out and touched his arm. "I know you loved her. And that you and Nico did the best you could. I don't know if you blame yourself the way he does for not being able to save her, but I do know that it's not your fault. None of this is your fault."

I watched him crumble. His face was transfigured with misery. He put his hands over it to hide as he began to cry. "It *is* my fault," he whispered, his voice cracking. "She'd still be alive if only I'd never—"

"Shh. None of that, now. Stop."

He leaned toward me. I put my arms around him. He sagged gratefully against me, resting his chin on my head as he wrapped his arms around my shoulders. It was awkward and strange, but also sweet.

The men in this family weren't exactly what could be described as stable.

"I'm sorry I said that. I'm a fucking asshole." His voice was ragged against my ear. His body shook.

"Apology accepted. And you're not an asshole. Actually I don't know you well enough to make a determination, but I'll give you the benefit of the doubt under the circumstances. We'll start over from here and get to know one another, and then I'll let you know."

He laughed, or made a sound close to a laugh, and I was glad as that's what I'd been aiming for. After a moment, he pulled away and looked down at me. His cheeks shone with tears. I looked up at him, smiling.

"You're gonna be my sister-in-law. I've never had in-laws before." He sounded as if he was unsure if that was a good thing, or a bad thing, but had decided to go with it and find out.

That made me hopeful. My smile grew wider. "Well, that makes two of us."

He was still shaking a little. His eyes were still wet. His arms were on my shoulders, our faces were only inches apart. When his gaze dropped to my lips and he bent toward me, I experienced a moment of shock so profound I didn't react in time to pull away.

Michael kissed me.

Then I heard Nico's infuriated voice. "What the fuck is *this*?"

We broke apart. Michael spun around. There in the kitchen doorway stood Nico, his expression as black as his eyes.

"Nico, it's not what you think," I began, but he was already stalking toward us, his lips curled back over his teeth.

My heart leapt into my throat. I'd seen this look before. I knew what was coming.

"Brother." Michael held his hands up. Nico ignored the obvious surrender gesture, and launched himself at Michael.

Everything happened so fast.

Fists flying, snarling like a rabid dog, Nico collided with Michael. Instantly Michael began to defend himself and fight back. The two of them staggered around the kitchen, throwing punches, shouting, ramming into the cabinets with a sound like small detonations. They slammed into the rows of bottles on the counter, sending them tumbling to the floor where they shattered. Alcohol sprayed everywhere.

"Nico, stop! Michael! The two of you, cut it out!"

They ignored my shouts, not faltering for a moment as they continued to pummel one another. Michael's lip was split and bleeding, as was Nico's cheek. But Nico soon had the advantage, and dealt his brother a blow to the face so severe it knocked him off his feet and onto his ass on the kitchen floor.

"Touch her again and you're a corpse!" Nico shouted, standing over Michael with legs spread.

Nursing his jaw, Michael looked up at Nico. His laugh was low and sardonic. "Why, afraid she might like it too much?" He glanced at me. Nico's head turned sharply as he looked at me, too.

"Who kissed who?" he spat, breathing hard.

I gaped at him. Everything inside me went cold. "You've *got* to be kidding."

"Answer the fuckin' question!" Nico roared, stepping away from Michael.

Tears stung my eyes. "If you really think that I'd—"

He was on me before I could finish my sentence. He grabbed my arm and pulled me against his chest. "If you lie to me, I swear I'll—"

"What?" I cried, trying to pull away. "You'll punch me?"

Like an animal, he bared his teeth. "No. I'll *punish* you."

Dragging me away by my arm, he hauled me out of the kitchen, leaving Michael bleeding and chuckling darkly in a pool of alcohol and broken glass.

There was a door on the opposite side of the kitchen. Nico pulled me through it. It led to the empty dining room. Another door led to a corridor that led outside, to the backyard. Across the yard was a pool house, which was where Nico was headed.

"Let me explain—"

"Quiet!"

I huffed in outrage. He didn't notice, or didn't care, because he kept up his determined march to the pool house, dragging me along behind him like a piece of luggage. He stormed through the door, slammed it shut behind us, spun me around to face him, and kissed me. Hard.

I shoved at his chest. He didn't budge. His tongue invaded my mouth. I twisted my head but he held me in place with one arm banded like a vise around my back. His other hand locked around my jaw.

I bit him. He pulled away with a curse.

"Good, I hope that hurt! Try and kiss me again before apologizing and I'll bite your tongue off!" I was panting from our walk-run across the yard, from indignation, and from fury. I couldn't believe he'd actually had the nerve to ask if I'd been the one to instigate that kiss with his brother.

I had half a mind to rip the necklace he'd given me off my throat and choke him with it.

A low, dangerous noise rumbled through Nico's chest. His eyes flared animal bright. In one swift move, he bent, picked me up, and hoisted me over his shoulder. I found myself upside down, staring at a floor of polished terra-cotta pavers.

"Put me down!"

Instead, Nico slapped my ass with enough force to make me gasp.

"I said, *quiet*!"

He crossed the room in a few long strides. He flipped me upright, then pushed me down onto a sofa and stood standing over me, staring down in murderous rage, fists clenched, dark hair falling into his eyes.

My mouth went dry. He loved me. I knew he loved me. But at that moment, I would have sworn he was also perfectly capable of wringing my neck.

I kept my voice steady. "Before you do anything, you should know that if you lay a hand on me in anger, it will be the end of us."

Nico's lips thinned. Deadly soft, he said, "Katherine. So help me God. One. More. *Word*."

"Nico—"

He lunged at me. I squealed, sounding like a mouse when it spots the cat in midjump. But he caught me before I could bolt. His weight pinned me against the sofa cushions. His hands curled around my upper arms. He gave me a jolting shake, as you would give a naughty child, and started to yell.

"Every fuckin' time things go sideways, all you wanna do is run! You think this is a game, me and you? You think this is somethin' either of us could *ever* run from? It's not, Kat! You don't run away from what we have and keep on breathin'! This ends, it'll kill us both!"

With a strangled sound deep in his throat, he crushed his mouth to mine. I strained against him, wanting to bite him again, equally wanting to reassure him. How could he think I thought we were a game? Didn't he know how much I wanted him? Needed him? How every breath I took, every thought I had, was for him?

As he ripped at my clothing, shoving my dress over my hips, tearing at my panties, I realized there were no words that would reassure Nico of my love.

I had to show him. I had to show him in the only way he could accept, and understand.

I let him push me back against the sofa. I let him drag my panties down my legs. When he fell on me, ripping at his zipper, I wriggled from beneath him. With a murmur to shush his protests, I pushed him back to the cushion I'd just been lying against. Then I lifted my dress over my head, let it fall to the floor, unsnapped my bra and tossed it aside, unzipped his jeans, freed his erection, and took the entire long, hard length of it into my mouth.

Blowjobs aren't something I've ever had strong feelings about one way or another. I know men love them, the same way I've always loved it when a man with a skilled tongue goes down on me. These things were all a nice part of sex. But this felt like much more than a mere sex act. More than trying to give pleasure, far more than angling for control.

As I bathed Nico with my tongue, as he arched and brokenly moaned my name, his head tipped back into the cushions, his fingers clenched in my hair, every muscle in his body pulled taut with bliss, I felt as if this was a form of communion.

There was no him. There was no me. There was only *us*. Giving and receiving, trusting and sharing, divine and holy and raw and ugly and everything in between.

"Baby," he groaned, thrusting his hips helplessly, his fingers twitching against my head. "Please. Please."

He was begging me for mercy. He was begging me for release. I'd give him both, but not before making him pay for it.

I wrapped my fingers around the base of his cock and began to stroke him in time with the pull of my mouth. With my other hand I cupped his balls. He shuddered, widening his thighs. His taste, his smell, his sounds, his ragged breathing . . . with every audible tick of the clock on the wall, I surrendered myself to sensation.

I surrendered myself to him.

"Tell me what you want." I paused briefly to run my tongue around the velvet, throbbing crown of his erection. "Tell me what you need, Nico."

"You, you, angel, always you." His hips flexed into my hands. He opened his eyes and stared down at me, his face flushed with color, his hair stuck in damp strands to his forehead. His voice dropped to almost nothing. "For me it will always, only, be you."

I tortured him with my tongue. My lips. My hands. He made a pleading noise. His lids fell shut. When he groaned, long and low, his entire body stiffening, I knew he was close. I straddled him, guiding him to my entrance, and hovered there above him, waiting for him to open his eyes.

When he did, I said softly, "I love you, Nico. No matter what happens, I'll always love you. Do you believe that?"

His hands wrapped around my hips, pushing down, trying to enter me. I used my thighs to resist, stroking the head of his cock gently back and forth against my wetness. He groaned again, and I bent down to whisper into his ear.

"I *love* you. I will *always* love you. I belong to *you*, no matter what."

He kissed me, desperate for my mouth. His hips bucked. When I wouldn't let him slide into me, he grunted in frustration.

The next thing I knew I was on my back with his face between my legs.

I cried out as I felt the soft heat of his mouth on my aching center. He devoured me, roughly nursing my clit, sliding two fingers inside me, even sliding his tongue all the way inside me. I arched, gasping his name. His free hand caressed my breasts, pinching my hard nipples.

He lifted his head and turned it to my thigh. He bit me there, lightly, watching me with feral eyes. "Say it again."

I watched in fascination as his head slowly lowered. He stroked his tongue in a slow circle around my clit, still looking at me, ravenous as a wolf. Then he stopped, waiting for me to speak.

"I love you," I whispered.

He rewarded me with a dark smile, and his mouth. I moaned with the feel of him sucking hard on my swollen, sensitive nub. His teeth skimmed it, and my whole body jerked. He made a sound of male satisfaction, brought both hands up to squeeze my breasts, and did it again.

The sensation was so intense, I sucked in a breath. It felt like tiny explosions were going off in all parts of my body. Fireworks burst in blazing color beneath my skin.

I closed my eyes, and gave myself over to pleasure. My hips moved to their own rhythm, keeping time with Nico's tongue. Soft moans worked from my throat. Heat blossomed across my cheeks and chest. I began to spiral past rational thought, consumed by what he was doing to me.

"This is my pussy." His whisper was so soft he might have been speaking to himself.

"Yes, yes, yes," I chanted.

His hands tightened around my breasts. "These are mine, too, aren't they, baby?"

He swept his thumbs back and forth over my rigid nipples. My answer was a softly begging whine. He pulled himself up my body, positioned himself between my legs, and took my face in his hands. He kissed me. I tasted myself on him, salt and musk and wetness, and loved it.

"And this beautiful mouth is all mine, isn't it?"

His cock nudged my entrance. I arched my back, hungry for it, but Nico wasn't giving me an inch until I gave him what he wanted. His voice was no longer a whisper. It was demanding, and hard. "Answer me."

"Yes, Nico."

He flexed his hips, allowing only the head of his cock to sink inside me. I moaned, and he smiled, wicked as the devil.

"Those eyes are mine, too."

"Yes, God, yes."

He gave me another inch. "What else, baby?"

I clawed at his ass, desperate for more of him. "Everything, Nico! All of me! I'm all yours, I swear it—"

My babbling turned to gasps as he thrust inside me, burying himself to the hilt. He held my head, his fingers tangled in my hair, and began to fuck me, slow and deep. He dropped his forehead to mine. I felt his breath on my cheek, heard his rough whisper in my ear.

"For how long will you be mine, Kat? A day?" Thrust. "A week?" Thrust. "A year?"

Thrust.

Thrust.

Thrust.

As I stared into his eyes, lost, it occurred to me in a flash of comprehension that this is what real happiness felt like. Burning and flying and unexpected freedom, that last, breathless moment at the top of a roller coaster before you throw both your hands up in the air and let loose a thrilled scream as you begin the weightless drop.

Any final resistance inside me fell away. I belonged to this man, body, heart, and soul, and I grasped the full reality of it in the space of one heartbeat to the next.

On a trembling breath I said, "I'll be yours for as long as both our hearts are beating."

Nico stilled. His brow furrowed. His lips parted, as if he'd say something, but he made no sound. But his eyes spoke to me, and what they said was this:

Worship you, cherish you, love you more than anything on this earth.

Joy seared through me, brilliant as a sunbeam slicing through a thundercloud. I'd never felt anything so beautiful, or so powerful, or so perfectly pure.

I started to cry.

He pressed kisses all over my face, murmuring endearments. He started to move again, and I moved with him, and shortly thereafter the two of us made so much noise I was vaguely surprised someone didn't call the police to find out what all the screaming was about.

We tumbled off the couch in a mess of arms and legs. Sweating, panting, undone, we lay on the cool tile floor, staring up at the ceiling until finally Nico started to laugh.

"Something funny, superstar?"

He returned my sour look with a gentle smile. Swiping his thumb beneath my lower lids, he said, "Other than your raccoon eyes?"

I jabbed him with my elbow. He laughed louder, and pulled me against his chest. "Forgot she doesn't like to be teased about bein' such a softie."

"Right. You also forgot she doesn't like to be referred to in the third person." I jabbed him again.

He rolled over and nuzzled his face into my neck. I had no choice but to melt.

"Just fuckin' life," he murmured, sighing. His arms tightened around me. "One of the worst days can also somehow be one of the best days."

I knew why it was one of the worst. But . . . "How so?"

"Because, sweet girl, you finally gave up the cookie."

I frowned. "I hate to correct you on such a delicate subject, but I gave up the cookie a while ago."

"That wasn't the real cookie, baby."

I felt vaguely insulted. "Excuse me?"

Nico smiled at me. It was like being bathed in sunshine. "Don't get me wrong, now, that cookie between your legs is fine. More than fine," he amended with a chuckle when I glared at him. "But the *real* cookie's your heart, baby. That's the cookie I always wanted. You gave me little nibbles. You even gave me a couple of big bites. But you finally gave all of it to me today, right now." All traces of humor left his face. His voice dropped to a soft, wondering whisper. "And it's the sweetest thing I ever tasted in my life."

I let it sit there a moment, not daring to speak. Speaking might ruin it. And I wanted to remember this moment forever, remember exactly how he was looking at me, how it seemed as if we'd just discovered a new planet together. As if we'd just opened the door on an entirely different world.

"You know," I said, voice breaking, "if I didn't know better, I'd think you sat around making up this stuff in advance only to trot it out at the right moment, just to see if you can get me to cry."

He glanced at a square of black fabric bunched beneath my hip, a square of wrinkled fabric, sporting a suspiciously wet stain. "Well, if you weren't cryin' before, you might start now."

Nico hadn't worn a condom. At the last minute he'd pulled out. "Oh, shit. That's my dress, isn't it?"

"'Fraid so, baby."

Monica Lewinsky and I suddenly had something in common. "Tremendous. You think anyone will notice?"

"Nah." He paused, looking me over. "Might notice that big hickey on your neck, though. And that just-been-righteously-fucked hair. And I probably shouldn't mention what's happenin' with your makeup. Raccoon eyes are the least of your worries in that department."

I'd applied a deep berry-pink lipstick earlier today. I wondered how far away it had migrated from my mouth. I sighed, defeated. "Well, then. I'm hiding in the pool house until after everyone's gone."

Nico's eyes darkened. "Probably not a bad idea, considerin'."

Considering his brother, the new monkey wrench in the clockworks. As if we didn't already have our fill of those.

I stroked his cheek, wiping away a bead of blood on the small cut beneath his eye. The area was bruised and beginning to swell. Damn him and his hair-trigger temper. No man was perfect, but this particular character flaw of his had me seeing an alarming number of stupid fights in our future.

At least the make-up sex would be amazing. As would the make-up sweet talk.

Those alone were practically worth a fight.

"Tell me you know I didn't . . . Michael. I didn't start that. I would never do something like that to you."

He whispered, "I know, baby. And I'm sorry for bein' an idiot. But walkin' in, seein' that, *today* of all fuckin' days . . . I just lost my shit." He sighed deeply. "I shouldn't have taken it out on you. I should've known how it happened."

"I actually don't know exactly how it happened." As an afterthought, I added, "I'm not even sure he meant anything by it."

Nico gathered my hand in his and kissed my fingertips. The gesture was gentle, but his eyes were still dark, and his lips had thinned to a line. "You don't know Michael. He doesn't do anything without a reason. But it doesn't matter what he meant. He put his hands on you. He's lucky he's still breathin'. Does it again, he won't be."

I thought it smart to avoid further discussion in that area for the moment. We'd had enough death for one day. "Come and get me when it's over?"

Nico stood, lifted me to the sofa, draped a throw over me, and quickly dressed. Turning his gaze to the main house, visible through the windows, he muttered, "Yeah. When it's over."

He kissed me, then he was gone.

Chapter 26

I didn't see Michael again. When Nico came back to the pool house, and I asked what had happened, Nico only said that Michael wouldn't be a problem for us again. Judging by the look of cold resolution on his face, I believed him.

Then, as it does, life went on.

After a few weeks, Avery's death took a backseat to other stories in the news, and Nico and I settled into something resembling normalcy. I worked. He recorded songs for Bad Habit's upcoming album. I hung out with Chloe and Grace, he hung out with the band. I spent most nights at his house, he pestered me about when we could announce our engagement.

"It's still too soon," I'd always answer gently. "Really, there's no rush. Let's just enjoy this time together."

Every time I said that, his mouth thinned to a hard line.

But I knew as soon as we announced the engagement, life as I'd known it would be over. For now we existed in a private little bubble, under the media's radar, evading the paparazzi by laying low at the Shack. When I needed to leave the house, Barney drove me. Even with the blackout windows on the Escalade, and Barney's expert ability to lose a tail, I still felt exposed. I wanted to put off life in the fishbowl as long as possible.

On this particular day, Chloe and I were lying on chaise longues by the pool, enjoying the warm September sun. Nico and the band were in the recording studio downstairs, where they'd been for hours. I had a day off from work, and Chloe was playing hooky from the flower shop.

"So what's the 411 on you and Officer Cox? Is it loooove?" I asked, munching on a potato chip.

Chloe blushed at my teasing. She and the good officer had been on multiple dates over the past few weeks. It looked like her ex–douche bag, Miles, was finally out of the picture.

"Something like that," Chloe muttered, glancing away.

I sat up, shading my eyes from the glare of the sun. "What's wrong?"

"Nothing! Everything's great, silly!" She laughed, waving a hand, but I sensed something behind her dismissal. Like me, she'd always been a terrible liar.

"Really? Is that why you're not looking me in the eye when you say that?"

"It's just . . . " She sighed extravagantly and rolled her eyes. "God, I can't believe I'm going to tell you this."

Now she had my full attention. I swung my legs over the chaise, peering at her through my sunglasses. The deck was hot beneath my bare feet, the sun warm on my shoulders. "Don't tell me he's not nice to you."

"No, nothing like that! For someone who wears a gun to work, he's surprisingly sweet." She sipped from the glass of iced tea on the little table between us, then set it back down and began to apply more suntan lotion to her legs.

"So?" I prompted, impatient.

She paused, looking sheepish. "It's just that . . . " she cleared her throat. "Well, to be totally honest, he's not a very good kisser."

"Oh. Well, that's not fatal. You can teach a guy to be a better kisser."

Chloe just stared at me. She obviously had her doubts.

"Okay, like how bad? On a scale of one to ten, with one being the kiss in the rain between Allie and Noah in *The Notebook*, and ten being slobbered over by a Great Dane with a bad case of halitosis?"

She considered it a moment. "Forty-seven."

"Oh my God, seriously?"

"Seriously. I have to wipe my face with a towel afterward. And my tonsils are sore. He's an *aggressively* bad kisser. I just feel too bad for him to say anything. How could I even bring that up? 'Excuse me, dear, but you're tickling my lungs with your freakishly long Gene Simmons tongue. Mind dialing it back a notch?' Yeah, that's not a conversation I can see myself having with a man authorized to use deadly force."

Picturing a horrified Chloe being slimed by a smitten Officer Cox, and her being too nice to clue him in, I started to laugh. It was hilarious.

"Dude," said Chloe, unamused.

"I'm sorry," I replied, gasping with laughter, "it's just too funny!"

"Uh, *no*, actually it's not. The worst part is Eric is otherwise a really great guy. We have a lot in common, and we laugh the entire time we're together, but," here Chloe shuddered, "now every time he gets near my face, I have a panic attack." She sighed. "I think I'm going to stop seeing him. We haven't done the deed yet, but I can't imagine having sex with someone I'm afraid will drown me in a tsunami of spit."

I had to cover my face with my hands I was laughing so hard. Chloe fished an ice cube from her drink and threw it at me.

Finally I calmed myself enough to speak. "Okay, I have an idea."

"If you're going to tell me we should make an appointment with Grace, I will throw you in the pool."

"No, no, listen. What if *you* took charge of the situation?"

Chloe merely blinked at me.

"So, for instance, what if you told him you'd always wanted to play 'Interrogation,' and you handcuffed him to the kitchen chair?" As Chloe's brows rose, I started to really warm to the idea. "Maybe he's a spy, and you're an FBI agent, and he has top secret information you need. Maybe the only way you can get it out of him is to *tease* it out. Maybe he has to sit in the chair and let you do all the . . . um . . . stuff, so that you can be in control."

Chloe sucked thoughtfully on her straw. "So he couldn't even kiss me back, or I'd win, like that?"

I nodded. "That way the whole pace of it is in your hands. If he gets too, um, enthusiastic, you stop. If he controls himself, you reward him with . . . well. I'm sure you'll figure out something creative."

Chloe's button nose wrinkled. "It sounds like an awful lot of work. Did you have to teach Nico how to kiss?"

I smiled. Chloe said sourly, "That's what I thought."

From across the yard, a voice called, "Girls!"

Chloe and I turned to see Nico standing at the back of the house, where the living room opened to the pool terrace. He was barefoot, wearing faded, holey jeans and a Led Zeppelin T-shirt so old it was almost transparent. His hair was mussed and he hadn't shaved in a few days, and his smile was as brilliant as the sun.

As it always did when I saw him, my heart fluttered like a hummingbird's. I'd never, ever get used to the fact that that beautiful creature was mine.

"Come and eat! We're takin' a break!" He waved, then disappeared inside.

Chloe watched me watch him go. When I looked back at her, she was grinning from ear to ear. "It's good to see you happy, Kat."

I hesitated a moment before I answered her. I hadn't breathed a word about the reality of Nico and Avery's relationship to anyone, including Chloe and Grace. I never would; that information I'd take to my grave. But sooner or later I'd have to tell them about Nico's proposal. If I'd been hiding it from the world, I'd been hiding it from them, too. In my heart of hearts, I knew it was fear that kept my mouth shut.

I was still waiting for that other shoe to drop. But the waiting was getting awfully lonely.

I blurted, "He asked me to marry him, Chloe."

Her squeal was deafening. She leapt from the chaise longue, dropped her iced tea, and grabbed me, hugging me tightly. "Ohmigod Kat that's unbelievable, I'm so happy for you I could *scream!*" It came out in one burst, followed immediately by, "Where's the ring? Is he having it made? Did you pick it out together? Oh God, I'm dying! *Dying!* This is the best news I've heard in years!"

When I didn't respond, she pulled away and looked at me sharply. Slowly, horror dawned over her face. She sank back to the chaise, her blue eyes huge and round. "Please don't tell me you said 'no.'"

"I said 'yes.' But we're not really telling anyone yet. Only his brother knows, and now you. We've agreed to keep it a secret for the time being."

She looked relieved for a split second, then worried again. "Okay, it's a secret. But you said 'yes'! So why are you not happy?"

I looked at the spectacular house, at the shimmering pool, at the incredible view. Then I looked back at Chloe. "Because there's a very persuasive voice in my head that keeps telling me this is all too good to be true."

"That voice belongs to Grace," said Chloe dismissively.

"I don't know, Chloe, I just feel like . . . " I took a breath. "Like life can't be this good. Not for any extended period of time. Things like this aren't meant to last."

Chloe gazed at me pensively for a while, a little wrinkle appearing between her eyebrows. "All right. Let's play this out. Say for some reason in the future—you and Nico have a huge fight, he gets hit by a bus as he's crossing the street, whatever—your relationship ends."

My stomach tightened. Chloe merely shrugged.

"Yeah, it will be painful. It will really suck. But it won't be the end of the world, Kat. It won't kill you. And it won't lessen how wonderful it is now, or how wonderful it would be if you *let* it be. Relationships end. People die. But the world doesn't stop turning. You know that better than anyone. So for now, just enjoy every moment of what you have with Nico. If it's meant to end, it will end. You have no control over that. But you *do* have control over yourself. How you act, what you say, how you show him your feelings. Just live for today and be happy, because in a way, you're right. Everything eventually ends. We all eventually die. That's why every day we have is so special. The fact that we only have a limited amount of time is what makes life precious."

Chloe leaned over and took my hands. "What you have with Nico is a gift, no matter if it lasts the next ten minutes or the next fifty years. Don't screw it up with what-ifs. Your past is just that: past. Let it go and be happy. You deserve it."

I stared at her with my mouth open. "Holy shit, Chloe."

Her eyes sparkled. "Don't let my blonde hair and bubbly personality fool you. I'm a Zen *master*, girlfriend."

"Apparently. And here I thought Grace was the smart one."

She pretended outrage. "Hey! Just because I'm a babe doesn't mean I'm dumb!"

"Obviously. Though I had no idea Zen masters had such high opinions of themselves."

Chloe adopted a yoga pose, legs folded beneath her, thumbs and forefingers in circles, eyes lifted to the heavens. "The truth has no ego, my unenlightened friend."

I snorted, and she dissolved into laughter.

"Okay, Yoda, let's go get something to eat."

"Definitely," she said, rising and tying her hair back into a sloppy ponytail. "Though, technically, Yoda was a Jedi master, not a Zen master."

We gathered our towels and sunscreen, then linked arms, smiling like loons, and went into the house.

Which is when things got really interesting.

Chapter 27

Apparently, whoever ordered lunch thought there should be enough food to feed a mob. Nico laughed at the look on my face as I stopped short in the kitchen, staring at the platters taking up every inch of space on the island.

The island that was about the size of my dining room table at home.

"Are we having a party I don't know about?" I counted twelve aluminum trays. There were sandwiches, cold cuts, tacos, fruit, lasagna, an enchilada casserole, and BBQ wings piled high, along with a basket of dinner rolls and a veggie and dip platter.

Nico pulled me against him and kissed the top of my head. "This is what happens when you let A.J. order. He'll end up eatin' most of this himself." He dropped his voice and murmured, "And I'll end up eatin' *you*, darlin'. That bikini should be illegal."

I blushed and looked down at myself. The bikini in question was one of Chloe's, a turquoise number with sequins on the bra.

She loved sparkly stuff. I'd asked her to bring a spare when I invited her over that morning because most of my clothes were still at my house. Needless to say, my girls were spilling out of the bedazzled top. Chloe's B cups were no match for my cleavage.

Nico's appreciative gaze swept over me, and his eyes heated. "Would you think I was bein' an overprotective asshole if I asked you to go change before the boys came up?"

I smiled, loving that he wanted me all for himself. "Since you asked so nicely, Mr. Nyx, no, I wouldn't think that at all." I rose up on my toes and gave him a kiss. His smile warmed me all the way through.

"Chloe, you want to come with me to change?" I tore my gaze from Nico to see Chloe already grazing through the food. Chewing on a wing, she nodded, then held up a finger.

"One sec. I'll be right behind you. I just need to murder a few more of these first. I'm *starving*."

Chloe was always starving. She had the metabolism of a jack-rabbit. As further proof of the unfairness of the universe, she never gained an ounce, no matter how much she ate. Though she was my best friend, I had to admit my jealousy of her slender, athletic build. To me she looked like what God must have had in mind when he created Eve. Even with no makeup and her hair in a sloppy ponytail, shoving food into her mouth like a starving animal, she managed to look both glamorous and lovely.

I sighed. Then Nico pinched my ass.

"Hey."

I looked up at him. His grin nearly melted me. He bent to whisper into my ear. "You're the most beautiful girl in the world, Peony. Don't forget it."

"Peony?"

"Yep. Exotic. Rare. Smells like heaven. Brings good fortune. Peony. That's you."

It was my turn to grin at him. The man was excellent for my ego. "Have you been spending your spare time on the internet surfing flower sites?"

"Nah. Just a little somethin' your florist friend here taught me the day I went into her shop for your birthday."

"Oh, really?" I tried to sound put out. "So you went with roses for my birthday present instead of the exotic and heavenly peony, hmm?"

Nico's smile grew even wider. He gazed down at me, his hair falling into his eyes, happy and so handsome it hurt. "Peonies are also a symbol of a happy marriage. I was savin' those up for when I got you the ring."

My heart flip-flopped inside my chest. "Are you for real?" I whispered.

He brushed his thumb across my cheek and squeezed his other arm around me. "Real as a heart attack, baby. Now go get changed before the boys get up here and get a look at you in that bikini and I have to do some murderin' of my own. And not of chicken wings."

He released me, lightly slapped my ass, leaned into the counter, and jerked his chin in the direction of the doorway. "Get."

I rolled my eyes. "You're lucky that order was preceded by some sweet talk, mister, or I'd—"

"Yeah, I know exactly what you'd do." Voices and footsteps echoed down the hall from the direction of the recording studio, and Nico glowered at me. "Now, *get* woman!"

I couldn't help it. I laughed. Quickly gathering my towel and the bag I'd stashed my sunglasses and lotion into, I skipped out of the kitchen and went upstairs to change, leaving Chloe sucking BBQ sauce from her fingers and Nico shaking his head.

When I came back downstairs no more than ten minutes later, I walked into what can only be described as a standoff.

Leaning against the counter in the same spot I'd left him was Nico. Right beside him was Brody, dressed casually like Nico in a T-shirt and jeans. Standing across the other side of the kitchen were Ethan and Chris. Propped on a bar stool he'd dragged across the kitchen was the recording engineer, Ray, an older guy with long, gray hair and round glasses. Everyone seemed a little confused.

In the middle of the room, glaring at each other across the island and trays of food, stood A.J. and Chloe.

"Because I'm her best friend, that's why," said Chloe, sounding defensive.

A.J.'s brows were drawn down, shadowing his eyes. The sneer in his voice was as unmistakable as the one on his face. "You two attached at the hip?"

"Yes, we're attached at the hip." Chloe's voice was thick with sarcasm. "The cord is just invisible."

"Too bad *you're* not," A.J. instantly shot back.

Chloe's mouth fell open. Nico and Brody exchanged looks.

"Quit bein' a dick, A.J." Nico sounded as if this was something of a regular occurrence. "She's my guest. And what's your problem with her bein' here anyway?"

Chloe put her shoulders back and lifted her chin. "Yeah, A.J. What *is* your problem? Considering this isn't the first time you've been an unprovoked dick to me, I think I have a right to know!"

For a moment I was startled; Chloe had just called someone a name. That was unprecedented. And she seemed so fierce she reminded me of Grace. But then I saw her trembling hands, and knew it was all for show. Whatever A.J. had against her, it really hurt her feelings.

Feeling protective on her behalf, I stepped into the kitchen. "What's going on here?"

A.J. cut me a lethal look that would have done a serial killer proud. He remained silent. Looking back to Chloe, his cold amber gaze flickered over her, taking in her bikini, her tanned skin, the look of anger in her eyes. His jaw worked. For a moment, he wore an odd expression of satisfaction, then his face closed down. "Fuck it. I don't need this shit. I'm out."

He turned on his heel and stalked out of the kitchen. A few seconds later, the front door slammed so hard the living room windows shook. There was an awkward moment of silence until Nico spoke.

"Sorry about that, Chloe. Don't take it personally. A.J.'s not exactly what you'd call a people person."

"He's not exactly what I'd call a *person*," she said, her voice shaky. She looked over at me. "I didn't even do anything! I was just standing here, minding my own business, when he came in and started giving me grief!"

"He's probably just agro about the tour," said Brody, shrugging. "Brother always gets twitchy before we go on the road."

My gaze shot to Nico. My legs became rooted to the floor. "Tour?"

"Yeah," he said, watching me warily. "About that."

"Just got confirmation this morning," chimed in Ethan, smiling. He obviously wasn't agro about going on the road. He looked positively gleeful about it. "Forty dates in thirty cities over two months. Kicks off in October in New York. Then we go all over Europe. Denmark, Sweden, Spain, Italy, Germany, you name it. Winds up in Paris on New Year's Eve."

"October? Europe?" I repeated, unable to process what I was hearing. Nico was leaving for Europe for two months? When had he been planning on telling me?

"Can't wait to see if the Krugermann twins will be at the Munich show again this year," said Chris. He and Ethan shared a high five and a snicker that told me all I needed to know about their special relationship with the Krugermann twins.

It felt as if all the air in the room had been sucked out.

Ethan strolled over to the food as if nothing out of the ordinary had just happened. Chris and Ray followed, and soon the three of them had plates in hand and were piling them high.

Chloe intervened, knowing full well I was on the verge of a meltdown. "I think I'll go change now. Come with?"

I tore my gaze from Nico. "Sure," I whispered.

"Kat."

"I'll be right back, Nico. Just give me a few minutes," I said over my shoulder as Chloe and I left the room. It had grown very quiet behind us.

Once in the master bedroom, I sank slowly to the bed, dazed.

"I'm sure he was going to tell you." Chloe went to the pile of her clothes she'd left on the top of the dresser when we'd changed to go to the pool earlier. She dragged on her shorts, pulled a pretty coral-colored shirt over her head, slid her feet into a cute pair of blingy flip-flops, then came and sat next to me. "They only found out this morning, right? So he just hasn't had a chance to tell you yet."

I avoided her sympathetic gaze. It only made me feel worse. "They only *confirmed* it this morning. It must take, what, six months or something to plan a world tour? He had to have known this was coming. He had to have known for *a long time*."

"I did." Nico stood in the doorway with his arms crossed, leaning against the frame, staring at me. "I've known since May."

May. Long before I even met him. He'd known about the tour for the entire time we'd been together.

I was beginning to feel queasy.

Nico pushed away from the door and moved toward us.

Chloe stood. "Um, I think I'll head on out now. Thanks for having me over, Nico. Kat, call me later?"

I nodded. She gathered up the rest of her things, then came and gave me a hug. Into my ear she whispered, "Go easy on him. He looks worried."

My smile was tight. He *should* look worried. Lucky for him, there weren't any sharp objects in the immediate vicinity.

Chloe murmured a good-bye to Nico, and then we were alone.

"You're mad." He said it as a statement of fact.

Since it was true, I didn't bother to deny it. "I just thought we were on this whole 'no more secrets' train together. Considering that's what I was told." I looked at him pointedly.

He moved closer, watching my face. "Well, there's a difference between secrets and surprises, am I right?"

Oh, goodie, we were back to the wordplay. I crossed my arms over my chest and kept quiet. My silence made him smile.

He stopped in front of me. When I refused to look up at him, he tilted my chin up so I was forced to meet his eyes.

He said softly, "We're goin' on tour. For two months. To Europe. Surprise."

"Gee, it's almost better than Christmas morning! Have a lovely trip. I'm sure the Krugermann twins will keep you very entertained."

His soft laugh irritated me further. What the hell was so funny?

"No, darlin', you're not listenin'. *We* are goin' on tour. Not just Bad Habit. Us. Me and you. That's the surprise. You're comin' with me."

Whatever look I had on my face amused Nico no end, because he threw his head back and laughed.

"Whoa. Wait. I can't go to Europe for two months."

Nico knelt in front of me, and took my face in his hands. "Course you can. Where I go you go, remember?"

"But I have to work. I can't afford to take that much time off. Let alone the price of airfare, hotels, meals—"

"Christ. Here she goes."

"No, I'm serious Nico. I can't afford any of that—"

"I can," he said calmly. "Everything's already paid for. Flights, hotels, everything. Your name is on all the tickets. Band's havin' a little pre-tour party next Friday, and I was gonna tell you then. It was supposed to be a surprise. You're comin' with me, Kat. We'll be in Barcelona for Thanksgiving, Florence for Christmas, Paris for New Year's Eve."

I stared at him in disbelief. "B-but my mortgage! I don't have enough savings to pay that in advance for a few months. I used half the money from the video shoot to pay down the loan principal and the other half went to credit card balances—"

"Said everything was paid for, didn't I? That includes your mortgage."

My face went hot. I blinked rapidly, sure I'd misheard him. "I'm sorry, I must be hallucinating. I thought I just heard you say my *mortgage* is paid for."

Nico leaned in and kissed me. "House is still yours, of course. Keep it, sell it, do whatever you want with it. You just don't have to worry about payin' for it anymore is all."

"How . . . you . . . *what*?" I couldn't form a coherent sentence.

Nico grinned. "I might have written down the account number from a statement I saw lyin' on your dinin' room table. And then I might have written a check to the bank."

I couldn't believe it. I simply could not wrap my head around a word he was saying. It must have been obvious I needed more explanation, because he readily provided it.

"The day the paps showed up at your house. You and the girls went in your bedroom to pack. Your mail was on the table." He shrugged. "I couldn't resist."

My eyes bugged out. "You went through my mail?"

"Don't look at me like that. I didn't open anything. That statement was just lyin' there on top of the pile, beggin' any passersby to have a look-see." His grin grew wider. "Further provin' my innocence, I didn't even *touch* the envelope from Magic Moments Sex Toys and Lingerie. Looked like a pretty thick invoice, sweetheart."

"I can't . . . Nico . . . I can't accept that."

He pushed me back against the bed and hovered above me, gazing down with a look of amusement. "No? And why's that?" He dipped his head and drew the tip of his nose up my neck, from my collarbone to beneath my earlobe. I tilted my head to better accommodate him.

We were in the middle of a quasi argument, but I wasn't insane.

"It's too much! That's *your* money, that you earned!"

He chuckled against my throat, making me shiver. "Case you haven't noticed darlin', I got plenty of money. And it's not like I'm throwin' it away; told you before, real estate's a good investment. For either one of us." He gathered my wrists in his hands, pinned them over my head, and settled his weight between my legs. "Next argument?"

I tried to sound very stern. "I'm a grown up. I should be responsible for my own bills."

"You are responsible." He nibbled on my earlobe, sending a spike of heat through my core. "And you're a hard worker. Neither of which has any bearin' on whether or not I should be able to give you a little gift if the mood strikes."

"Little gift! Paying off someone's mortgage is more than a little gift! It's an act of reckless abandon! I think you could be committed for less! Eight hundred thousand dollars is—"

"Less than I make in a week, baby."

I'm no genius, but it didn't take me long to do the math. I sat on this new knowledge for a moment, as my lungs slowly deflated. "Oh."

He smirked. "Yeah, *oh*. Next argument?"

"No, wait. Let's stay on this topic for a minute. This is an interesting topic."

Nico started to hum "Gold Digger" by Kanye West.

I shoved against his chest. "What I'm *saying* is that it's really surprising how rich you are." I eyed the threadbare Zeppelin T-shirt beneath my palms. "Considering your wardrobe."

His brows shot up. "You got somethin' against the greatest rock band of all time? And before you answer," he added quickly, "you should know that if you say 'yes,' I'll have to strip you down to your skivvies and do very, very bad things to you."

Lord, how I adored that wicked glint in his eye. And how I adored him. My sweet, badass, generous, volatile, infuriating, wonderful man.

"Yes," I answered seriously, looking him dead in the eye. "Yes. A thousand times, *yes*."

Nico pursed his lips and shook his head, pretending to be disappointed. "Well, I did warn you, baby. Prepare for the worst."

Then he lowered his lips to mine, and for several hours thereafter, he proceeded to make good on his promise.

We remembered to lock the bedroom door this time.

Chapter 28

I awoke to a dark room, dragged from a vivid dream in which Nico and I were getting married on the beach on a tropical island. Lying on his back beside me, he breathed steadily, still asleep. His face was shadowed, but his bare chest gleamed in a bright wedge of moonlight that spilled through the bedroom windows.

We'd returned downstairs after an extended absence to a good-natured chorus of hoots and wolf calls from the boys, who'd made easy work of all the food, proceeding thereafter to consume enough liquor to get a Russian army drunk. Brody sang "Afternoon Delight" with backup from Ethan and Chris, who, according to Nico, did an excellent job of proving why they weren't allowed to sing backup on Bad Habit's albums. Then everyone, including me, went back into the studio to tinker and play for several more hours as I gazed on in awe and fascination.

Watching Nico work was amazing. He was a genius with lyrics. Starting with a bare-bones idea, he'd make things up as he went along, doing take after take with a new line here, a different way of vocalizing there. The band was a well-oiled machine, following his lead, the guys playing off one another, having as much fun as they were working hard. When finally they'd get a track just right, they'd record it. Most of them would be re-recorded to master in the record company's studios, but the band seemed to prefer that the initial creative process take place in the informality of Nico's studio.

And it worked. Seeing Bad Habit make music was nothing short of magical. Each one of them was a virtuoso in his own right, but it was Nico who was truly breathtaking. I couldn't take my eyes off him the entire time. He played the guitar like he was making love to it. And every time his gaze met mine, he'd smile a slow, secret smile that I'd feel from the top of my head to the bottom of my feet.

We'd gone to bed after midnight. I wondered what time it was now.

I listened into the quiet for a moment, wondering groggily what had awoken me. I didn't have to use the bathroom. I wasn't thirsty, or uncomfortably cold or hot.

Had there been a noise?

I stretched beneath the covers. Turning my head, my gaze wandered around the darkened room. Hmm. Maybe it was that slight throbbing in my temples that had woken me. I'd had quite a few glasses of red wine during the recording—

With a strangled scream, I bolted upright.

Someone was standing just outside the open bedroom door.

"What is it?" Instantly alert, Nico bolted upright next to me. "Kat, what's wrong?"

"S-someone's there!" Shaking, I pointed to the doorway.

I might as well have just told him Al-Qaeda was waiting in the living room. In a blur of movement so fast it seemed superhuman, he'd thrown back the covers, bent and retrieved a shotgun from beneath the bed, stood, and cocked it.

Chh-chh!

It was a sound that froze my blood to ice water.

Nico hit a switch on the wall beside the bed, and the room was flooded in light. The doorway was empty.

"Someone was just there," I whispered, trembling all over. I pulled the covers up to my chin. "I'm sure of it. They were right there."

Nico's voice was steady. "How many?"

I swallowed, tasting the sour bite of fear. "One."

We both listened hard for a moment. No sound came from beyond the doorway. The hallway was dark.

"Get into the bathroom and lock the door. Take the portable phone from my nightstand and call 911."

I moved as fast as I could, crawling over his side of the bed. "What are you going to do?"

"Get in the bathroom. Lock the door. Call 911." His voice was low and hard.

Terrified, I obeyed him without further question. I grabbed the phone, stumbled in blind panic into the bathroom, and shut the door, locking it with fumbling fingers. My hands shook so badly it took several tries for me to dial 911.

"Nine-one-one, what's your emergency?"

Trying to keep my voice low, I hissed into the phone, "Someone broke into our house!"

The operator read off Nico's address. "Is that correct, ma'am?"

"Yes! Please send someone as soon as possible!"

"Can you describe the situation for me please, ma'am?"

I gave the operator as much information as I could recall. It wasn't much. I'd just seen a dark figure in the doorway. There hadn't been enough light to make out what kind of clothing he was wearing, let alone describe his features.

"How can you be certain it was a male, ma'am?"

That stumped me for a moment. "I just thought from the size of the person. The height. It didn't seem like a woman."

The operator made a sound that indicated she didn't think a person awakened from a dead sleep in a dark bedroom could be trusted on the matter of whether or not the intruder in her home was a man or a woman. "Do you wear corrective lenses, ma'am?"

I'd been pacing, but stopped short. There was something about this operator . . . something in her attitude . . .

"Wait. Were you working the morning of Saturday the twenty-third last month?"

A faint, weary sigh. "Let's get back to your emergency, ma'am. Is there anyone else in the home with you? Any minor children or—"

"Oh my God! It *is* you! You're the lady who took my call when I was being attacked by the paparazzi!" I recognized her now. That faintly bored, put-upon tone. The I'd-rather-be-anywhere-but-here sigh. I'd know that voice anywhere.

Jesus Christ, what were the odds? Ten million to one?

"I need to talk to your manager." I began pacing, chewing my thumbnail.

The operator had the audacity to sound insulted. "Ma'am, please try not to panic—"

"I'm not panicking!" I shouted, exactly like a person who is panicking.

"A unit has been dispatched to the address, ma'am," said my nemesis firmly. "Now I need to get more information from you so that when the officers arrive they won't mistake anyone else who might be on the premises for the intruder."

A brief, horrifying vision of Nico being shot dead by police made my jaw snap shut. I managed to control myself, but only just. "Okay, yes. Ask me, ask me. What else do you need to know?"

There followed a laundry list of questions, which I answered to the best of my frazzled ability. When she started asking about weapons, I grew even more panicked.

"Uh, yes. We do have a weapon. My boyfriend does, I mean. A shotgun."

"Is your boyfriend the homeowner, ma'am?"

"Yes."

"His name, please?"

"Nico. Nico Nyx."

There followed a silence so total I thought the line had disconnected. Then the 911 operator cleared her throat. "I'm sending additional units, ma'am. What is Mr. Nyx wearing?"

I knew it! This broad gave preferential service to famous people! If I ever had to call the police again, I'd say I was Kim Kardashian. I'd probably have five hundred cops on my lawn in three minutes.

"Black boxers. But the police will know it's him because he'll be the one holding the really big gun."

That tidbit didn't faze her. Now that she knew who she was dealing with, she had her game face on. "Please stay inside the dwelling in a safe spot until the officers arrive. If you see the intruder again, do not attempt to engage him. Where are you inside the house, ma'am?"

I told her. She asked a few more questions, each more detailed than the last, until she'd apparently exhausted all of them.

"Would you like me to stay on the line with you until the officers arrive?"

"No."

"All right, then, ma'am—"

She kept talking, but I'd already hung up. I had no desire to speak with her for one second longer.

Within ten seconds, the phone rang. I jumped, heart pounding. "Hello?"

"This is nine-one-one, to whom am I speaking, please?"

"It's me! Kat Reid! You just talked to me!"

"Ma'am, are you all right?"

I stared at my reflection in the mirror. My eyes were wild. My hair was mussed up. I looked like I'd been on a three-week bender. "Of course I'm not all right! There's some kind of weirdo in the house and my boyfriend is chasing after him with a loaded shotgun!"

I heard a sound like fingers drumming on a desktop. "You shouldn't hang up on nine-one-one, ma'am. We don't know if it's because you're in imminent danger and have to put down the phone—"

"Nobody called me back the day we hung up on you when the paparazzi were stalking me!"

She didn't have a pithy comeback for that one. "If you need to hang up, please let me know."

I ground my teeth so hard I thought they might shatter. "I'm hanging up on you now. Okay?"

She sniffed. "Okay. Thank you, ma'am. Please remember to identify yourself to officers—"

"Good-bye!" I clicked off the phone. Well, at least I wasn't afraid anymore. I was just pissed.

I heard sirens.

Unfortunately, the view on this side of the house overlooked the city. If I wanted to see the cops pull up, I'd have to go out of the master bedroom and cross the hall into one of the other rooms that overlooked the driveway. But I had no idea where Nico was at the moment . . . or where the intruder might be, either.

I decided I wanted to stay right where I was.

Five minutes passed. Then ten. After twenty minutes, my nerves were shredded. I was just about to throw open the door and make a run for it when Nico knocked on the closed bathroom door.

"Baby. Open up."

When I did, Nico pulled me into a brief, hard hug. "You okay?"

I nodded. "What did the cops say?"

"They wanna talk to you for a minute. Put somethin' on."

Hurrying to the clothes I'd left in a pile on the floor beside the bed, I dressed quickly while Nico pulled on jeans and a T-shirt.

"Did they find anyone?"

"No." He paused to run a hand through his hair. "Went through all the rooms. Nobody's here but us. You sure you saw—"

"One thousand percent sure," I said firmly.

"Okay, baby," he murmured, drawing closer. He gave me another hug. "C'mon downstairs."

Nico took my hand. I followed him silently through the house, which was now lit up like a Christmas tree. Lights blazed in every room, making me feel safer, if not entirely safe. Even though Nico assured me no one was in the house but us, I was still frightened.

What if they'd forgotten to check a closet? Or behind a bathroom door?

A cluster of uniformed officers were conferring in the foyer. They turned when we neared. One of them, the one in charge I gathered, nodded to me. "Miss Reid?"

"Yes."

Nico stood behind me, his chest touching my back, his hand warm support on my hip. I leaned into him, grateful for his strong presence.

"Reynolds." The lead cop offered his hand, and I shook it. Then he got right down to business. "Can you give us any information about the intruder's appearance? Clothing? Height? Anything like that?"

Officer Reynolds looked like he'd been on the job a hundred years. The others with him were much younger, but he had a weathered face, iron gray hair, and sharp eyes that didn't miss anything. I trusted him immediately.

"It was too dark for me to see much of anything. He was just standing there right outside the door." I swallowed. "Watching us."

"You're sure it was a male?"

"Women don't stand like that. Legs open, arms a little away from the body, like a bodybuilder. Plus with the height and build . . . it was a man."

Reynolds nodded thoughtfully. He glanced at Nico. "How many people have your alarm code?"

"No one. Just me."

Reynolds's gaze snapped back to mine. "Well, you got a problem, then, son. We just spoke to your alarm company. They said someone disabled the system by entering your code into the keypad in the garage. Got the code right on the first try."

As Nico cursed, my hand flew to cover my heart. I went cold with fear. "Wouldn't a break-in to the garage have triggered an alarm?"

Nico's voice was dangerously hard. "There's a ten-second delay after an outside door's opened. The alarm only sounds if you don't enter the code."

Reynolds nodded. "We'll review the video feeds from around the property. Should be able to get back to you shortly to let you know what we find. In the meantime, call your security company and reset the code. We'll keep a unit posted at the gate." He paused. "The gate code different than the house code?"

Nico replied that it was.

"Change that too. Whoever it was didn't come through the gate, but you can't be too careful. Might want to think about getting a dog, too."

"Hundred-thousand-dollar security system and I have to get a fuckin' dog," muttered Nico. His hand around my hip tightened. His other arm wound around my waist.

"Your system's one of the best, Mr. Nyx, but no system is foolproof. Especially if you know the disable code."

A horrible possibility struck me. "Do you think it could be someone from the security company? How else would the intruder know what to enter?"

Officer Reynolds shook his head. "Can't rule out any possibility, but I doubt it. More likely the company was hacked, or you were. Or it could be someone who knows you well enough to know what numbers you'd choose."

His steady, penetrating gaze held mine while that sunk in.

Someone who knows you. My body erupted in chills.

Officer Reynolds promised to be in touch as soon as they looked at all the videotapes and assured us again there would be a unit at the end of the driveway just outside the gate. He shook hands with Nico, then left, along with the others.

Leaving Nico and me alone in the vast, house-with-a-million-perfect-hiding-spots house.

"There's nobody here but the two of us," Nico assured me gently. He hugged me close and kissed me. I snuggled against his chest.

"The two of us and your shotgun, you mean."

"Well, technically, if you're gonna count the guns . . . " I glanced up to find him smiling grimly at me. "There's quite a few of us here."

Oddly, that made me feel better. Up until that moment, I'd never had a fondness for guns.

"I suppose it makes sense, you being from the sticks and all."

"You callin' me a hillbilly, darlin'?"

I didn't have the energy to banter, so I just shook my head and hid my face in his chest.

Nico immediately became serious. He took my face in his hands. "No one is ever gonna hurt you, Kat. Not while I'm around. I'd die before I'd let anyone hurt you. Understood?"

I nodded, loving the possessive look in his eyes. We stared at one another for a moment, until Nico suddenly bent and swept me into his arms. He walked us through the foyer and began to ascend the stairs.

"Not the elevator? Brave man." I kissed his neck and rested my head on his shoulder.

He pretended to have trouble breathing. "I need the workout."

This time I bit his neck. A laugh rumbled through his chest. He carried me all the way to the bedroom without passing out, a feat I had to admit was impressive, then laid me down on the bed. He pressed a tender kiss to my lips. "You gonna be able to sleep?"

"As long as you're right next to me."

He smiled, pulling his T-shirt over his head. His jeans came off next, along with his boxers, and I was treated to the sight of a body that could have made the David weep with jealousy.

"I'll always be right next to you, baby," he promised, then proceeded to remove all my clothes. When I was naked, he pulled me against his side in bed, adjusting the covers over us. I snuggled against his warmth, drawing strength from his solidity, from the steady beating of his heart beneath my cheek. Even though all the lights were still on, and I never thought I'd be able to, I eventually began to drift back to sleep.

"Just out of curiosity," I asked groggily a few minutes later, "what was the security code?"

Nico's chest rose and fell on a long, thoughtful exhalation. "Amy's birthday."

Chapter 29

I came instantly wide awake.

"When you say 'Amy,'" I began carefully, but Nico provided clarification before I could go any further.

"I mean Amy. Not Avery. Her alter ego had a fake birthday, along with a fake name."

Oh shit. That could only mean one thing.

Nico felt the tension in my body. "Yeah. When Officer Reynolds said 'someone close to you,' he was spot fuckin' on."

"Michael?" I whispered. Images of our one and only meeting came back to haunt me with startling clarity. The look of hatred in his eyes. The way he'd stood so close to me at the funeral. His inexplicable accusation, followed by his even more bizarre about-face.

That kiss.

Nico's voice was harsh. "He's the only one that makes any sense. Though why the fuck he'd be standin' outside my bedroom door in the middle of the night starin' at us while we sleep is anyone's guess." His arm drew tighter around me. "Be findin' that out first thing tomorrow mornin', though," he growled softly, touching his lips to my hair.

"Okay, I'm going to say something, and I don't want you to get mad."

Nico's entire body fell still. "Say what, exactly?"

If I didn't know him as well as I did, that tone alone might have shut me up. But I did know him. And, knowing me, I barged ahead full force without thinking too clearly about what damage I might do by not controlling my mouth.

"That you think it's Michael actually makes me feel a lot better."

Before I could draw another breath, I was on my back, pinned under Nico's substantial weight. He stared down at me in cold, controlled fury, his eyes blazing.

Deadly soft, he said, "For future reference, baby, that's not the kind of thing a man likes to hear his woman say when she's naked in his bed."

"I just meant—"

Nico flipped me onto my belly, yanked the pillow out from under my head and tossed it aside, gathered my wrists in one of his hands, and set a knee between my legs and nudged them apart, all before I could react to what was happening with more than a squeal of surprise.

He leaned over me. His hair tickled my cheek. His voice came even softer, but no less scary for all its quiet control. "And it's especially not something a man likes to hear his woman say about his *brother*, when she's naked in his bed."

"Nico—"

"The brother who had his mouth on you."

Normally this display of irrational alpha-male jealousy would have made me incredibly mad. For some reason, possibly because I was relieved we weren't dealing with a psycho fan, or a serial killer, or some other degenerate, it made me want to giggle.

We were just dealing with a degenerate relative. Pretty much everyone had one of those.

So the situation was bad, but it could have been way worse.

So giggle I did.

Bad idea.

Crack!

I sucked in a huge, shocked breath. My legs jerked. My back bowed. My head snapped around, and I stared at Nico over my shoulder. I shouted, "Do *not* tell me you just slapped my ass! Don't you *dare* tell me that you just manhandled me to get me facedown on this mattress, and then spanked me like a misbehaving two-year-old! Tell me that didn't just happen!"

I knew it had happened, though, because my ass stung like hell. It was beginning to throb. I was sure there would be a giant, Nico-sized handprint on it if I looked in the mirror.

The anger I'd managed to initially avoid over his display of jealousy had come on in full force. I was barking mad.

Nico said, "Want another, baby?"

It was clear from his tone that he would love for me to say "yes."

It was also clear from his tone that he was laughing at me.

Oh, the *nerve*! I hissed, "Let me guess. You've been planning your revenge since the second you saw him kiss me."

He smoothed his palm over my stinging backside, caressing it. He moved his hand to my other cheek, pinching my flesh softly. I shuddered involuntarily as his fingers drifted down the cleft of my ass to the crease between my thigh and sex. His voice still held the amusement, but now it was thick with desire. "No. Won't hold grudges against you, baby, not ever. Once a fight's over, it's over. But

I'd put money down that you'll never again mention another man in my bed."

His fingers stroked my entrance, feather light. My breath hitched at the sensation.

"Am I right?"

I closed my eyes and bit my lip to try to stifle my soft moan as his fingers delved gently inside me, then pulled out and stroked upward to my clit, spreading my wetness around as he swirled his fingers. This time I was unsuccessful at stifling my moan. I let it out on a long, low breath, arching into his hand. His soft, pleased chuckle followed.

"Yeah. I'm right."

Still holding my wrists, he directed, "Up." The pillow nudged my hip. I lifted my hips and he slid the pillow under my stomach so my ass was propped in the air.

He moved, and between my legs I felt his erection, stiff and ready. His hands tightened around my wrists. "You're gonna take me hard, Kat. You're gonna take whatever I wanna give you."

God, his voice alone made me even wetter. Commanding. Demanding. Hot.

"You're gonna do that to make up for sayin' somethin' without thinkin' that twisted my heart and made me want to break every piece of furniture in this house. And tellin' me not to get mad about it. And then laughin', no less."

I'd hurt him. With my stupid words, and my stupid giggle, I'd hurt him. Knowing that, my chest squeezed tight.

His voice darker, Nico said, "Say 'yes' now, Kat."

I whispered, "Yes."

He thrust inside me. I cried out. His free hand curved around my hip, steadying me. "Say you're sorry, baby." He thrust again, harder than the first time, the force of it slamming the headboard against the wall.

I felt every glorious inch of him, all the way in and out. "Nico, sweetie—"

Crack!

Shocked, furious, incredibly turned on, I groaned.

The other cheek now had a matching handprint to its twin.

He did it again and again as he fucked me from behind, varying the intensity and the location of the blows, so that I didn't know what to expect, and couldn't anticipate what was coming. I'd never liked it before, when other guys thought it would be cute to try and spank me. On the few occasions it had happened—most notably with lingerie man—it had been awkward, and not at all sexy. Somehow it had seemed distasteful, as if I was giving someone permission to hurt me, which felt weird, and wrong.

This didn't feel weird. This didn't feel wrong.

This felt *empowering*.

I was submitting to this of my own free will, to a man I knew loved and cherished me, and would never harm me. This was a way for him to communicate his displeasure with something I had done. A physical way, because he was a physical man. He showed his feelings with his body and his actions, with the intensity in his eyes.

It was also a way for me to make it up to him.

It was raw, definitely. But it was also honest.

Nico didn't sulk, or punish me with silence or withholding his affection, or try to make me jealous by flirting with another woman. He wasn't passive-aggressive. He was completely up-front with his emotions, with what he felt and wanted, from the very beginning.

He was all in. He had been from the start. It had always been me who was holding back, second-guessing, waiting for something bad to happen because I couldn't believe my good luck.

That sunk in, hard. Chloe had been right. The entire time I'd been with Nico, I'd held my breath. Held on to the not-so-fantastic past. Held on to the certainty that I didn't deserve to be this happy.

I'd been robbing us both.

I turned my face to the sheets, stifling a sob.

Nico immediately stilled. He leaned over me, planting a fist into the mattress near my head. He panted, "Baby?"

Pain made my voice thick. "I'm s-sorry, Nico. That was so s-stupid of me."

That's as far as I got. Nico pulled the pillow out from under me, withdrew long enough to flip me over and settle between my thighs, then pushed inside me again, his fingers tight against my head.

"Yeah, baby," he said softly, staring into my eyes. "But it's not the end of the world. It's over now."

He flexed his hips, sinking deeper inside me. I turned my head away and closed my eyes, trying not to let him see me cry.

"No," he said firmly. "When a fight's over, it's over. No hangin' on to it. No rehashin.' No dredgin' it up in the future.

He flexed his hips again to drive his point home.

I opened my eyes and stared up at him. With tears still leaking from the corners of my eyes, I whispered, "Have I told you how amazing I think you are? Because I think you're the most amazing man I've met in my entire life. And I love you so much it hurts."

His face did a funny thing. His eyes got all crinkly at the corners, his lips twisted as if they weren't sure whether to curve up or down, and a big furrow dug its way between his brows.

His voice came rough. "Right back at you, baby. Right back at you."

Then he lowered his mouth to mine and gave me everything I'd never knew I needed, and then some.

I loved him. God, how I loved him. And he loved me, too.

Which was ultimately what ruined us.

Chapter 30

For eight days, Nico tried to contact Michael. Phone calls, email, texts, even a series of faxes, of all things. He went so far as to have Barney drive up to San Francisco and pound on his door, but Michael wasn't home. And didn't come home for the entire twenty-four hours Barney waited on the doorstep for him.

Michael had disappeared.

I wondered if he was hiding somewhere in Nico's house.

That chilling thought didn't hold a candle to one other piece of news provided by the police, however. When they tried to review the footage from the security cameras installed all over Nico's property, they found nothing. The digital file for that day had been erased. As had the backup. Whoever had done that had known exactly how to breach the security company's firewall without being detected, which meant that not only was he an expert at breaking in to real houses, he was an expert at breaking in to virtual ones.

Which consequently meant that Nico's tendency to be overprotective exploded into a state of full-blown paranoia.

"I have to go to work!" I insisted for the tenth time, trying to keep the aggravation from my tone. It was eight o'clock Monday morning, and Nico was blocking my exit from the bedroom with his body. Getting past him with physical force would prove impossible, so I was trying to talk my way past.

I wasn't having much luck.

Glowering down at me, he shook his head. "No way, baby. You're not leavin' this house until we know what we're dealin' with. I'm not takin' a chance with your safety."

I crossed my arms over my chest. My foot tapped a staccato rhythm against the floor. "Nico. Sweetie. I love that you're worried about me, but I can't hole up like a scared rabbit because your brother found his way into the house."

I'd avoided saying the name "Michael" since I'd been given a red ass for speaking it in Nico's bed. I might be dumb, but I wasn't stupid. "It's already been over a week, and I've missed way too much work. Besides, it's not like he's going to do anything to hurt me, he's just a weird peeping—"

"We don't know that, Kat. We don't know what his motivation is for anything." Nico paused. "Or what he might be planning."

A tingle of fear swept down my spine. "Planning? What's that supposed to mean?"

Seeing the fear on my face, Nico stepped toward me. He unfolded my arms and wrapped them around his shoulders, pulling me into a hug. "I told you before. Michael doesn't do anything without a reason. And the fact that he's not answerin' my calls or emails means he's avoidin' me, which means he's up to somethin'. I know him, Kat. This is more than just a one-time thing. I didn't want to scare you by sayin' anything earlier, but . . . that little midnight visit of his was probably just the beginning. He can hold a grudge like a motherfucker."

My heart began to race. Michael had looked at me with such anger in the kitchen the day of Avery's wake. Was I in danger?

Nico guessed my thoughts. He pressed me into the warm solidity of his chest and kissed my temple. "You're safe as long as you're with me, baby. So work is gonna have to wait for a few more days until I can find out where my brother is and deal with this shit."

There was only one problem with that plan: what if Nico never found him?

I pulled away and gazed up into Nico's face. He looked tense, and I hated seeing him that way. I caressed his cheek, rough with stubble, and stood on my toes to give him a soft kiss on the lips. "Okay. I get that you're worried about me. And I get that you want to keep me safe. But we can't live our lives around what someone else might do. So how about this."

Nico's brows pulled together. "Ask away, baby, but if it involves you leavin' this house, the answer's 'no.'"

I chose to ignore that. "What if Barney drives me to work?"

A chuckle from Nico. It was a sound without humor. "No."

Shit. Today I had a really important job, one I couldn't miss. I had a client I'd worked with for years, an aging film and television actress who was up for a part as the love interest in George Clooney's new movie. She was scheduled to do a screen test, and was freaked out about the face-lift scars around her ears; they were still healing and were red. One of my specialties was hiding plastic surgery scars. This skill alone had often kept me booked solid for months.

And if I screwed her over, the word that I was unreliable would travel fast. She'd referred me to dozens of her friends, many of them celebrities. I couldn't flake. Not today.

"Barney could hang out with me on set. He'd probably love that, right? He wouldn't be in anyone's way." As Nico's mouth thinned, I hurried to add, "And he could stay with me the whole time. You know how tight security is at the studios—"

"Not tight enough. The answer's '*no*,' Kat."

Frustrated, I pulled out of Nico's arms and walked away to look out the wall of windows. "This is ridiculous, Nico. Your brother hasn't threatened me. I know you think he's up to something, but I can't live my life around what-ifs." Grasping at straws, I added, "Maybe he just took a vacation, and that's why you can't get in touch with him."

"Nice try," said Nico sourly. "But drug dealers don't take vacations."

Stunned, I spun to look at him. "A drug dealer? Oh my God, Nico, he's still doing that? And you still *talk* to him?"

"Yes, he's still doing that. And no. I don't talk to him. Before Avery's funeral, we hadn't talked for five years." He paused, looking at me as if he was choking down a sudden violent anger. Anger and something that might have been anguish.

My intuition buzzed exactly the same way it had the minute I'd first laid eyes on Michael. "Why? What happened five years ago?"

Nico's lips parted. Before a word left his lips, someone shouted from downstairs.

"You're going to be late for the meeting, man! We gotta get a move on!"

Barney.

Nico closed his eyes, and squeezed his forehead. "Fuck. The fuckin' meeting. I completely forgot."

"What meeting?"

With a heavy sigh, Nico dropped his hand and gazed at me. "With my label. All the bigwigs. They love to get their face time, especially before a tour. I'll be gone for at least a few hours."

I seized the opportunity in front of me. "Great! Barney can drop you off at the meeting, then come with me to the studio! I'll only be working for a few hours, so we can pick you up when we're done!"

Nico scowled. "Baby. Forget it."

Sensing a chink in his armor, I drew closer. "I happen to know that your record company's offices are in Hollywood, sweetie, which, coincidentally, is also where my job today is. As a matter of fact, I think Paramount is just down the block, isn't it?"

Nico watched me move toward him, his gaze alternating between my face and the twitch I'd put in my hips. I always dressed a little more businesslike when I went to the studios, and this morning I had on a cute black pencil skirt and a pair of nude heels that I knew made my legs look longer.

"Kat," he said. But his warning tone wasn't as convincing as his eyes, which were eating me up.

"So we'll be right next door to each other." I flattened my palms on his chest and blinked up at him, smiling coyly. "And then we'll be back together, lickety-split."

Nico pulled me against him, winding his arms around my waist. My breasts were crushed against his chest. In a voice like a growl, he said, "Hearin' you say anything with the word 'lick' in it just makes me wanna fuck you, woman, so take care. And quit tryin' to manipulate me with those big goddamn eyes. It's not gonna work."

But I could tell it *was* working. He'd gone from 'absolutely not' to 'maybe you could convince me,' even if he didn't realize it himself.

I whispered, "Okay. No manipulating you with my eyes. How about this?"

I tilted my head and softly licked the spot where his jaw met his neck, just beneath his earlobe. I knew I'd hit the jackpot when

I heard the low grumble he made in his chest. His arms tightened around me. He dipped his nose into my hair and inhaled.

"Not takin' any chances with your safety."

I sucked his earlobe into my mouth, then ran my tongue lightly around the shell of his ear. "No. Definitely not. I'll be very, very safe with Barney." I wound my arms up around his neck, pressed myself tighter against him, and trailed kisses over his jaw until I reached the corner of his mouth.

Warily, he watched me with hooded eyes. "I know what you're doin'. Forget it."

With the tip of my tongue, I licked the corner of his bottom lip. "Please?"

He groaned.

I flexed my hips into his. Suppressing a smile at how hard he already was, I said, "Pretty please? With a cherry on top?"

He cupped my bottom and ground me against him, digging his fingers into my ass. "The word 'cherry' leavin' your mouth does the same thing the word 'lick' does, darlin'. You askin' for trouble?"

"No trouble," I said, sugar sweet. "Just negotiating."

He snorted. "In my experience, negotiations usually end with both parties gettin' screwed outta what they want."

"No, honey. This is a win-win negotiation. I get what I want, which is to go to work, and you get what *you* want, which is for me to be safe. Because I will be, because I'll have Barney the ex–special ops ex-cop with a Taser trigger finger. See? Total win-win."

He stared at me silently. I smiled what I hoped was a brilliant, irresistible smile. After a long moment he shook his head and sighed, resigned. My smile grew wider.

"Don't get too excited yet," he warned. "You're gonna need to give me some additional terms before we close this deal."

The cool tone of his voice made me worry. "Oh? Such as?"

His gaze dropped to my lips. His voice was a husky rasp. "Mouth. Now."

My worry disappeared in a poof; he'd been playing with me. The desire in his expression made me feel melty all over. I stood on my tiptoes, bringing my lips close to his. "That's another win-win honey," I said, then gave him what he'd asked for.

He drank deep, threading a hand into my hair to hold my head in place as he explored my mouth with his tongue. I loved the way he kissed, the way he held me still and took what he wanted, giving me what I needed in return. I loved his warm, sleepy male scent, the stubble on his chin that tickled me, the way his heart raced when I made a small noise of surrender in my throat.

Most of all, I loved the way he looked at me when he broke the kiss. The wonder. The desire. The way it seemed nothing else in the world existed to him except my face.

He was right when he told me he'd ruin me for any other man. Nothing could compare to the way his eyes showed me what he felt. At that moment, I pitied every other woman on earth.

"You taste so fuckin' good," he whispered.

I had to smile. "Yeah?"

"Yeah. Sweet as sin, baby. Sweet as sin."

"You should remember that, superstar, because the next time you're dismissive of my livelihood, I won't resort to feminine wiles to get what I want. I'll just kick your ass six ways from Sunday and go on my merry way, and you won't be getting any sweetness from me for who *knows* how long."

His brows rose. "Don't mistake me worryin' about your safety for not respectin' your work, baby. Know it means a lot to you, just as much as mine means to me. I'm proud you're such a hard worker and so responsible."

"Thank you, honey," I said, pleased.

He continued as if I hadn't spoken. "Which has absolutely nothin' to do with me needin' to make sure you stay safe. Which I'll continue to do, no matter how much flak I get for it."

I sighed. We'd come to an obvious impasse. "Well, I suppose you'll just have to be prepared to have your ass kicked, then."

His smile in answer was wry. "Suppose I will. Though if you wanted to throw in a few feminine wiles while you were doin' it, I'd be grateful."

I had to press the smile from my lips. I knew I'd won this particular battle, but was far from winning the war.

Barney's voice drifted up from the bottom of the stairs. "Nico? We ready?"

Nico's expression hardened. "You're not to be out of his sight, understood? Not even for a minute."

"What if I have to pee?" I teased.

Apparently he didn't think that was funny, because it earned me a swat on the ass.

"Not that again!" I wormed my way out of his embrace, but he didn't let me get far. He grabbed my wrist and pulled me back into the circle of his arms.

"Kat. I'm serious. Don't fight me on this. Be safe."

I searched his face. His eyes had closed off, and he wore an expression I interpreted as worry mixed with a dose of anger. Along with his repeated warnings, it was very uncomforting.

"You're scaring me with all this. What don't I know about Michael that makes you so concerned for my safety?"

There was a long, tense pause, until Nico sighed and smoothed a hand over my hair. He kissed me on the forehead. "Other than that he's a drug dealer, and they're not exactly known for their compassion and reliability?"

I sensed he was sidestepping the question, but I didn't want to jeopardize our tenuous agreement, so I let it slide. I'd ask him about it later. Probably in bed.

I had no scruples whatsoever about using every tool available to me to get the information I wanted. And I had every confidence I'd get it.

"Good point. Okay, I promise. Now please don't spend all morning worrying about me. You know Barney will take good care of me."

"He better," Nico muttered, taking my hand and leading me out of the bedroom. "Or I'll have his fuckin' head."

It was a good thing I followed behind Nico, because if he'd seen the way I rolled my eyes, my ass would have, no doubt, been as red as a tomato.

Nico was tense the entire drive to the studio. He stared out the window of the Escalade, holding my hand tightly, his jaw muscle jumping. Beside him in the backseat, I squeezed his hand, trying to be reassuring, but he only glanced at me, smiling briefly, before turning back to the view, preoccupied by his thoughts.

I met Barney's gaze in the rearview mirror. He gave me a slight upward tilt of his chin, which I took as recognition of Nico's mood, and his attempt to relay that everything would be all right. He'd never been much of a talker.

Barney turned into the underground parking lot beneath the record company's office building. We passed through a security gate, then stopped in front of a glassed elevator lobby.

"Here we go, boss."

"Barney." Nico's voice was quiet.

Barney turned in the seat and looked at Nico over his shoulder. "Yeah, boss?"

"Don't let her out of your sight."

Something passed between them, and an unspoken understanding flickered in the depths of Barney's eyes. Seeing it caused a flutter in my stomach. What was going on here? What was I missing?

Barney pressed a hand to his coat pocket. "I've got her covered, Nico. We're good."

There was a bulge beneath the coat of his black suit that I hadn't noticed before. Holy crap, was he carrying a gun?

"Um, Barney? They do a pretty good search of bags and things when we go through security at the studio. I'm not sure you want to bring anything . . . extra . . . in with you. I don't want you getting in trouble."

Nico and Barney both smiled. They shared another loaded look.

"You let Barney worry about that, baby. He knows how to take care of himself." He leaned over and kissed me softly. "And he'll take care of you, too. Just be good, and don't get a wild hair up your ass to go anywhere other than straight back here when you're done, okay?"

"Okay."

Nico studied my face. "That seemed too easy."

I sighed. "Go, will you? I'll be done by noon, and we'll come back and pick you up, and then we'll go home and I'll make my world-famous chicken enchiladas."

Nico raised an eyebrow. "You cook?"

"Just because we've been living on takeout recently doesn't mean I can't cook," I scoffed. "I'll have you know I've mastered at *least* four dishes."

Nico's brows climbed higher.

"The number could actually be as high as six. Let me see." I started a count on my fingers. "There's the aforementioned world-famous enchiladas, there's the less famous, but no less fabulous, turkey burgers, there's a chili casserole that is so spicy it will curl your hair, and there's a grilled fish taco dish with mole sauce. All of which go very well with margaritas, in fact."

When Nico grinned, I added, "Not that that has anything to do with anything."

"Of course not." He lifted my hand to his mouth for a kiss. "But that's only four. What happened to the other two?"

Grateful his mood seemed to have been lifted by the shocking revelation that I could cook—limited though my skills were—I said, "I'm not giving away all my secrets at once, mister! You'll just have to wait and find out."

He said something under his breath that sounded like "living dangerously," and I swatted his shoulder. Whereupon he pulled me close for a quick, hard kiss.

"Noon." The way he said it was both warning and promise. He looked at Barney, who nodded.

"Okay, now that we're all settled on the time, go! I'm going to be late!" I shooed Nico away. He gave me one last kiss before climbing from the car and reluctantly closing the door.

He stood at the elevator lobby, watching us drive away, until we rounded the garage corner and he fell from our sight.

As it turned out, Barney had no trouble at all getting through security at the studios. He had a quiet conversation with the head of security when we arrived, showed him some paperwork, dropped a few names, shook hands, and that was that.

Apparently being a former cop, former military badass, and current bodyguard of a famous person—and having a license to carry a concealed weapon—gave you some serious cred.

He stayed in the background while I worked, out of the way but within eyesight. My client was so worried about her face she barely even noticed he was there. The time flew by, and when I was finished with the job, we still had over an hour left before we needed to pick up Nico. Which gave me an idea.

"I want to make a quick stop by my house, Barney."

I sat in the front seat with him as we exited the studio lot, because being by myself in the backseat as he drove just seemed strange. He sent me a pained look.

"No can do. You heard what Nico said. We have to go straight back to—"

"I know, I know, but we've still got an hour before we're supposed to meet him, and I need to get some clothes. I've been wearing the same three outfits for over a week. C'mon, it'll only take a few minutes. I'll just run in and run out."

His hands gripped tighter around the steering wheel. "Don't make me choose between him and you, Kat."

I knew where he was going with that. Obviously I wouldn't come out on the winning side of that coin toss. I had to try another angle. "Look. Nico wants you to make sure I'm safe, right?"

A curt nod. Barney could tell I was up to something.

"And the only way to really make sure I'm safe when I'm not with him is if I'm with you, right?"

Barney adjusted his tie, and stroked his thumb and forefinger over his tidy goatee.

"And I think we both know that it would be much better for you to accompany me to my house to get some clothes, than for me to drive there myself. Say, in the middle of the night. When you're not around, and Nico is sleeping."

Barney's eyes widened. "Why the hell would you do something like that?"

"Because I need to get my stuff! And nobody seems to know how to find Michael, so I have a bad feeling I'm going to be stuck without most of my clothes for the foreseeable future, because Nico basically has me under house arrest."

"Just ask him to take you to your place later, then."

I didn't mention I'd already tried that tactic. Nico had responded by saying he'd hire a personal shopper to come to the Shack to get all my measurements so I could get a new wardrobe.

I didn't want a new wardrobe. I wanted the one I already had.

"But we can take care of it right now, and won't have to inconvenience him at all. And I'll make sure he knows you didn't want to," I hurried to add as I saw his expression sour, "but I forced you to do it when I said I'd sneak out of the house anyway. So you're actually doing *both* of us a big favor."

Barney tapped his thumb against the steering wheel. He looked at me sideways. He shook his head, and I thought I'd lost, but then he turned the car in the direction of the freeway.

I squeezed his arm. "Thanks, Barney. You're the best."

"Yeah. Don't forget to tell that to Nico when he's got my head on the chopping block."

"Don't worry, it's all going to be fine. Ten minutes and I'm out. Easy peasy."

Barney grumbled, shaking his head again, clearly not happy with the position he was in. I felt a twinge of guilt, but I still thought Nico was being over the top about this whole safety thing.

Until, that is, I swung open the front door of my house, and looked inside.

Chapter 31

Disaster.

Overturned furniture littered the floor. The coffee table lay on its side in the living room, glass top smashed, legs kicked in. The sofa spewed pale stuffing from ragged, gaping slashes. My bookcase lay on its side, its contents spilled in rainbow colors over the rug. In the kitchen, my wood dining table had been destroyed, smashed to a splintered mess. The refrigerator door stood open, shelves empty, everything once inside now scattered over the tile floor, comingled with all the plates and glasses from the cabinets, which were shattered into jagged pieces.

I cried out in shock, stumbling forward with my hand clapped over my mouth.

Directly behind me, Barney cursed. He pushed past me, set a hand on my shoulder, and said, "Stay here." He reached into his coat pocket and pulled out a small silver handgun, then quickly searched each room in the house. When he found no one, he made a brief phone call, his voice low and indistinct from the other room.

All I could focus on was the feeling of extreme violation eating through my guts. How could someone do this?

And why?

In my bedroom, the duvet and sheets had been ripped from the mattress and tossed into a corner. The mattress itself was slashed from corner to corner, the cuts forming an x. Broken glass crunched underfoot as I moved forward in a daze, smelling a potent confusion of flowers and musk lingering in the air.

All my perfume bottles on the bathroom vanity had been shattered, thrown hard against the mirror. They lay in piles on the marble and in the sink. Everything from the drawers beneath the sink had been dumped into the bathtub.

In the master closet, my clothes hung in shreds.

Someone had taken a knife to every piece of clothing I owned.

Stunned, I began to violently shake. My heart twisted, my stomach knotted. All that paled in comparison to what I felt when I turned and saw the blown-up black-and-white photograph stuck to the wall above the dresser with a carving knife.

The picture was of Nico and me, kissing.

It had been taken by the paparazzi the night we'd met, when he'd come to Lula's and sat at a table with Chloe, Grace, and me. Featured on the cover of *Star* magazine, it was the picture captioned by the awful tagline, "Nico Nyx and His Harem!"

An angry, red marker line was slashed across our faces. Because my face had been obscured by shadow, whoever did this knew that the woman Nico was kissing in the picture was me. Every nerve humming with fear, I sank to the ruined mattress. For the first time, I understood that Nico's concerns were founded on more than mere paranoia.

He must know exactly what his brother is capable of. He must have proof.

"Kat." Barney stood in the doorway, his expression grim. "Let's go."

My head was a fog of jumbled thoughts. "But . . . I need to . . . there's paperwork here . . . my things . . . I can't just leave it like this."

"I'll come back later and get whatever you need. Right now we need to go. It's not safe for you here."

Tears welled in my eyes. I whispered, "It was him, wasn't it? It was Michael."

Barney nodded. "Most likely."

"Why would he do this?"

Barney crossed the room, took my hand, and gently pulled me to my feet. With an arm around my back, he ushered me out of my ruined bedroom. "Because he's damaged, Kat." His voice darkened. "And damaged people are dangerous."

I stumbled through the mess in the living room, leaning heavily on Barney's arm. "We have to tell Nico—"

"Already called him," Barney cut in. Something in his voice told me in no uncertain terms that it hadn't been a wonderful conversation.

In the distance, sirens wailed.

Barney said, "Gonna have an escort back to the house, at Nico's insistence. They'll talk to us there."

"Oh, God." I knew what that meant. I could only imagine how ballistic Nico would be when we arrived home.

Nico was pacing in front of the fountain in the driveway when Barney and I pulled up at his house. His head snapped up, our eyes met through the windshield, and I went cold.

"Shit," muttered Barney. "Brace yourself, Kat. This won't be pretty."

Barney cut the engine. The two squad cars parked, one ahead of us, one behind, and the officers got out. They headed toward Nico, but he was already striding toward the Escalade, his hands clenched to fists. His dark hair was in disarray, as if he'd been pulling at it.

He yanked open the passenger door. Nostrils flared, chest heaving, he stared at me in silence. He cut a burning glare to Barney.

"It wasn't his fault," I said. "I made him. He didn't want to go. If you're going to be angry, be angry with me, not him."

Nico's gaze sliced back to me, sweeping quickly over my body. "Are you hurt?"

"No." I didn't dare add anything else.

Leaning across my body, he unsnapped the buckle on my seat belt. I smelled the cigarette smoke in his hair. He removed me from the car as if I were a wild animal that might bolt at any moment. With his hand wrapped firmly around my upper arm, he strode toward the house, taking me with him.

"Shouldn't we talk to the police?" I ventured, hurrying to keep up with him in my heels.

Nico didn't answer. I looked over my shoulder and saw Barney talking with the two officers, one of whom I recognized as Eric Cox, Chloe's new guy. He shot me a sympathetic look, right before Nico opened the front door, then slammed it shut behind us.

He whirled on me. I was so surprised I jumped. I retreated until I could go no farther, my back flattened against the door.

"Don't be afraid of me," he snapped.

"I'm not."

"I can see it on your face, Kat!"

I wondered how it was possible for him to speak without moving his jaw. I moistened my lips, trying to breathe steadily so my heartbeat would slow down. "Well, I know you'd never hurt me, but honestly, you're being scary."

He whispered, "I'm fuckin' scary? *I* am?" His blue eyes blazed. He towered over me, bristling, his voice growing louder with every word. "I'm the man who would lay down his life to keep you safe, Kat! I'm the man who would do anything to ensure no harm ever comes to you! I'm the man you promised to come right back to after work!"

Looking up at him, I bit my lower lip.

I didn't want to fight with him. And I knew anything I said would only make the situation worse. I didn't have Grace's talent of gently speaking to someone in an agitated state, so I just had to let him get his anger out of his system.

If I'd learned anything about Nico, it was that his temper flared fast, but it burned out faster.

He paced away from me, looking around the entryway as if he'd like to find something to smash, then just as abruptly turned back. "Do you have any idea what I went through when I got that call from Barney? Do you have any idea how worried I was? What if Michael was still there, in your house? Barney told me the fuckin' place was trashed! What do you think it would have done to me if you'd been hurt?"

I swallowed, chest tight, aching to reach out for him, wanting desperately to reassure him. I knew it was futile. I'd fucked up.

"Jesus, I got a room full of record executives who think I'm a fuckin' madman, Kat! I must've shoved ten guys to the ground on my way outta that meeting! I didn't even have a car—I had to take a cab, almost got thrown out when I kept screamin' at the guy to go faster!"

With a guttural snarl, Nico spun away again, hands clenched in his hair. He stood with his back to me for a long moment, breathing hard, the muscles in his arms clenched tight, his posture rigid.

I went to him. It was pure instinct. I needed to hold him, and he needed to hold me.

He could yell at me later. Right now, I really just needed a hug.

Wrapping my arms around his waist from behind, I rested my cheek against his broad back. "I'm sorry, Nico," I whispered. "I'm sorry I made you worry. I'm sorry I talked Barney into taking me there. I promise I won't do anything like that again. I didn't really think I was in danger. I thought you were overreacting, but now I get it. I get how crazy Michael is."

A tremor shivered his body. He dropped his hands to his sides, and bowed his head. "No. You don't. And I hope to God you never do."

Hearing that, my skin crawled. Whatever made him tremble, whatever his brother had done that made Nico's voice sound so hollow and hopeless, I needed to know.

"Why don't you tell me?"

Nico turned and faced me. His beautiful blue eyes were so fraught with pain, I wanted to kiss his entire face just to make that awful look go away.

"You don't need to hear every ugly detail, Kat. I don't want you carryin' that shit around in your head like I do. Just trust me when I say you have to stay away from him. Understand?"

I wound my arms around his waist again, slipping my hands beneath his shirt so I could feel the warmth of his skin, needing the contact. "If you thought he was so bad, why did you let him come to the funeral?"

Disgust crossed his face. "My mistake. We hadn't talked in so long, and I thought he needed . . . " Nico swallowed. His voice dropped. "I thought he would need to say good-bye. I thought it might help him. Obviously I was wrong."

"So now what? We have to look over our shoulders for the rest of our lives?"

In Nico's beautiful blue eyes I saw cold determination. "Now you let me do what I need to do. I'll find him. I'll fix this. And you won't ever have to worry about him again."

The vehemence in his voice frightened me. "'*Fix* this'? And what would that involve, exactly?"

Taking me in his arms, he squeezed me against his chest. His heart pounded against mine. "I'd spend the rest of my life in prison if I knew it meant you'd be safe."

Oh God. Was he talking about doing something . . . permanent?

"No!" I cried, pushing against his chest. "That's not what I want! Yes, he's a crazy fucker who watched us sleeping and trashed my house and I'd love to see you kick his ass, but not—not—"

"Kill him?" he interrupted, his voice flat.

I yanked away. Crossing my arms over my chest, I glared at him. "Don't even say that as a joke!"

"Do I look like I'm joking?"

Panic washed over me in a hot, huge wave. "You can't possibly mean that, Nico."

Silent, he stared at me.

"Jesus! Let the police handle him! That's what they're for! They'll find him, we can press charges—"

"They *won't* find him!" Nico cut in. "He's too smart to be found if he doesn't wanna be. He's lived off the grid his entire life, Kat. He's a fuckin' drug trafficker who's never once been picked up by the cops. He's never even gotten a fuckin' speeding ticket! He's got three different identities—that I know of—you think he doesn't know a thousand ways to hide?"

Reeling from this new information, I had to grip the edge of the glass console table beside the door for support. "A trafficker. A drug *trafficker.* That's a bit different from a dealer, Nico. How the hell can one of the most famous men in the country have a drug trafficker for a brother, and no one knows?"

His reply was instantaneous. "The same way he can have a sister everyone thinks is his girlfriend: lies that go so deep, nobody can find the roots."

I stared at him, rocked to my core by the realization that perhaps I was only seeing the poisonous flowers of this plant of deception. What else could be festering underground in the dark?

My voice shaking, I asked, "How many other lies are there, Nico? What else don't I know?"

He took a step toward me, eyes fixed on mine. "You know me. You know all the important things about me. Don't start second-guessing that."

"Considering I just this moment found out your brother's real occupation, I think that's a stretch."

Anger darkened his face. "That's a matter of degree, not a lie. I told you before the business he was in."

"There are no *degrees* of truth, Nico! Something is either a lie, or it's not!"

"Blacks and whites don't exist in my world, Kat. Everything is shades of gray."

"And I'm just supposed to accept that? Accept whatever you tell me without question? Especially now that I know you think it's okay to give me the barest pencil sketch of reality?"

He stared at me long and hard, tension radiating off him in waves. "If you're thinkin' that I'm bein' a macho dick, or tryin' to get away with somethin' by withholdin' information, you're wrong. I'm only tryin' not to expose you to shit that's ugly and fucked up, and can't be changed anyway. I'm tryin' to protect you, Kat."

Furious, frustrated, I shouted, "And it never occurred to you that I might want all this ugly, fucked-up information before I agreed to marry you?"

Nico's face turned chalk white. He looked as if I'd slapped him. He growled, "What the fuck does *that* mean?"

The front door opened, and Barney stuck his head inside. "Boss? A word?"

Nico and I stared at each other in burning silence.

Barney cleared his throat. "Uh, Nico. Officer Cox here would like to speak with Kat. Take her statement. Is that okay?"

Looking at Nico, I spoke, my voice icy cold. "You can ask me, Barney. Nico doesn't get to decide whether or not I speak with the police. And yes; it's okay." Lower, for Nico's ears only, I said, "And thanks for asking how I'm coping with having everything I own destroyed. I guess you're the only one around here whose feelings matter."

Nico's eyes flared. I could tell he was grinding his teeth together by the flexing of the muscles in his jaw.

I turned away, and went to face the police.

Chapter 32

"Any idea who might've done this? You have any enemies, get into any fights with anyone recently?"

Officer Cox looked at me expectantly, a furrow between his brows. He was smart, and efficient, jotting down the answers to all his previous questions in smooth shorthand on a form on a clipboard, but I kept getting distracted by the vision of him slobbering kisses all over Chloe.

I looked away from his mouth, debating how to answer. Considering I'd just given Nico a lecture on degrees of truth, I was now faced with a dilemma. If I told the police I thought it was Nico's brother who was behind the destruction at my house, the entire can of worms would be opened. If, however, I lied to the police . . . well, then I'd be a liar. And a hypocrite to boot.

Being with Nico was testing every conviction I had.

Barney stood discreetly to one side of the front door, pretending to watch a bird circling in the sky. Nico had stayed inside. He was probably breaking things.

"Actually I did get into a fight with someone recently, yes."

Barney's head snapped around. Officer Cox raised his brows. "Oh?"

I nodded. "There was a girl, a guest of A.J.'s—"

"A.J.?" Officer Cox's pencil hovered above the form.

"The drummer for Bad Habit. I'm sorry, I don't know his last name." I looked to Barney for confirmation.

"Edwards," said Barney. "The initials stand for Alex James." His voice was smooth and untroubled, but I knew from the look in his eyes he was uneasy with where I was going with this.

"Yes, Edwards, that's it." *Alex James Edwards*, I thought. *What a perfectly American name for a guy who's trying to hide a James Bond villain accent.*

"Anyway, there was a small gathering here a few weeks ago, and this girl of A.J.'s—honestly I don't know her name, either, you'd have to ask him—well, she sort of got in my face when she found out Nico and I were dating. I guess they used to have a thing."

Officer Cox prompted, "And? What happened?"

I looked him directly in the eye when I answered. "I slapped her."

Barney coughed into his hand, hiding a laugh.

Officer Cox frowned at me. "Did she retaliate?"

"No. I mean, she tried to, but the guys separated us before it went further. I only did it because she was about to hit Nico, so I acted before she could. It was stupid, and I wasn't thinking, and she left right after that, but," I shrugged, "that's what happened."

Officer Cox scribbled on his pad. "Okay. We'll look into it. Anything else?"

My mouth went dry. It was a calculated risk, but I had to do it. "Yes. There was an intruder here, eight days ago. Someone broke in to the house in the middle of the night."

Almost imperceptibly, Barney stiffened. Officer Cox perked up like a dog when it hears the word "treat."

"I heard about that. Officer Reynolds was on duty, correct?"

I nodded. "It was too dark for me to see the person's face, unfortunately."

Officer Cox had an unusually direct, unblinking gaze. I began to wither under the weight of it. He said, "Nothing was taken? No damage was done?"

"No. We filed a report, though. Everything is in the report."

"Hmm." He inspected my face for so long I grew uncomfortable. "Hmm."

One "Hmm" seemed okay. The second seemed suspicious. I was operating within a very tight loophole here, and I hoped he wasn't about to figure it out. If he asked me the right question, my loyalty to Nico would be put to the test.

A cold trickle of sweat slipped down my back.

Officer Cox tucked his pen into the shirt pocket of his uniform and from it withdrew his card, which he handed to me. I took it, trying not to let my fingers tremble.

"You're attracting a lot of attention, Miss Reid. You've been in the tabloids, you've been tagged as a person of interest by the paparazzi, and you've been in a very popular music video." A faint hint of a blush colored his cheeks. "Nice job in the video, by the way."

"Oh. Thanks."

"The guys down at the station think you look like a brunette Anna Nicole Smith."

He'd obviously said it without thinking, because his blush deepened, and he stammered when he spoke next. "M-my point is that there are a lot of crazy people out there. People who can become obsessive. When you're a celebrity, you're also a target."

I was a celebrity now? How awful.

"So just be careful. Call me if you need anything. I'll be in touch."

He turned to walk away, and I felt as if my knees would buckle from relief. Until he turned around again.

With a sideways glance at Barney, he drew nearer. "Would you mind if I asked you one more question?"

I had the fleeting, horrible thought he was going to ask me for my autograph.

"Has Chloe . . . well, she uh . . . I don't know. Things started out so well, but now it seems like she's backing off. And I can't figure out why. I know you're her best friend and all, and I thought maybe you would know what the problem is." He looked sheepishly at his boots.

I breathed, "Oh, Officer Cox—"

"Eric. Please, call me Eric."

Over his shoulder, Barney stared at us in confusion. He obviously didn't know that the good officer and I shared a friend in common.

"Uh, well, Eric." I cleared my throat. How the hell was I going to tell him? No, I couldn't. This was unbelievable.

When I hesitated, he glanced up and saw the look on my face. His own went beet red.

"Shoot. I'm sorry. I know I shouldn't put you in this position. Forget I said anything, this was really dumb of me—"

"Promise me you won't tell Chloe." I reached out and touched his arm.

His brows drew together. "Well, Miss Reid—"

"Kat, please."

"Okay, Kat. I want to know, but I won't lie to Chloe. And if what you're going to tell me is something I'm going to need to talk to her about, I can't promise I won't tell her."

Shit. Of course not. Black/white, lies/truth, deceit/disclosure. The universe was trying to tell me something today.

But if I were in his shoes, I'd want to know. He was a good man. I could see he really cared for Chloe. And from what she'd told me, she cared for him, too. Except for this one little thing.

"Have you ever had a massage?" I blurted.

Eric blinked, taken aback. "Like a happy ending thing, is that what you mean?"

"No! Oh, God, sorry, no I mean a real massage. Like a sports massage."

Relieved I wasn't going in a weird direction, Eric relaxed. "Yeah, of course. I used to play football in college. Got sports massages all the time, helps with muscle recovery."

"Okay, good. And you know how, sometimes when you're getting a massage, the masseur can go a little overboard, get a little too . . . er . . . enthusiastic, and it winds up hurting more than it feels good?"

His brow crinkled. Even his dimples looked confused.

I sighed. "What I'm saying so badly is that sometimes less is more. With massages, and also with . . . kissing."

There was a beat of silence before he got it. Then, like a glass being filled from the bottom, he turned red from his chin to his hairline and groaned. He covered his eyes with his hand. "Oh, geez. Oh, boy. Ouch."

"I'm so sorry. This is awkward. I shouldn't have told you."

He waved my apologies off. "No, you're doing me a favor, trust me. That's not the first time I've heard it." He grimaced. "My last girlfriend dumped me after three months because she said she couldn't imagine having to eat my tongue for every meal for the rest of her life."

"Oh, God. That's terrible!"

He shrugged, looking at his feet again. "I kinda thought she was just being mean, but apparently it's an issue."

An uncomfortable silence followed. I shifted my weight from one foot to another, eager to end the conversation. "Look. I know Chloe really likes you, okay?"

He looked at me with big puppy-dog eyes. "She does?"

"Yes," I said emphatically, nodding. "She does. She said you two have a lot in common, and you make her laugh, and she thinks you're really hot."

He beamed and stood up a little straighter, puffing out his chest.

"And I really think that if you just, um, make an effort to be a little more, uh . . . "—*holy hell this is so freaking uncomfortable*—"gentle, everything will work itself out. Maybe you could even let her take the lead. Let her show you what she wants."

By this time, my face was as red as his had been moments before, but I thought it would all be worth it if he and Chloe could figure out a workaround to this problem.

God knew there were worse things they could be dealing with.

Officer Cox held out his hand. Surprised, I shook it.

"Thank you, Kat. I appreciate you telling me about this. And now that I know what it is, I promise I won't tell her we had this conversation, if you still don't want me to."

I could tell by the look on his face he was hoping no one would ever bring it up again. I made a zipper motion across my mouth. "My lips are sealed."

He grinned, and I had to admit he was handsome. And charming. And sweet. I really hoped they could work it out, because he seemed light years better than any other guy Chloe had been with.

"Deal. And I owe you one." He dipped his head in farewell, and turned and walked to the squad car and his waiting partner, a new spring in his step.

Barney ambled over as they drove away. Watching the back of the squad car disappear down the long slope of the driveway, he said mildly, "Well. He seems like a good sort. And it never hurts to have a cop who owes you a favor."

A cop who owes you a favor.

A thousand unsaid things screamed out around those few, simple words. I felt the weight of every single one of them, and knew what they all really meant.

This, too, was a test. Barney wanted to know where my loyalties lay. He wanted to know if he could trust me. If Nico could trust me. If they both could trust me to keep the secrets that had held them together for so long.

And how far I was willing to go to do that.

Though unspoken, the question had been asked. My gut responded with an answer. Instantly, without fanfare or much emotion, I knew something about myself I hadn't known before.

"He's the one who did me a favor," I said, still looking at the empty driveway. My hand lifted to the gold charm nestled in the hollow of my throat. My fingers rested on it, feeling its shape and solidity, my pulse beating softly beneath.

"How's that?"

I turned my head, meeting Barney's intense gaze. "He just taught me what my priorities are. With how I chose to answer his very first question. With what I chose to put in, and leave out."

He studied me. "And what are those priorities, Kat?"

Without hesitation, I pointed at the door. "Every single one of them is inside that house."

I turned and went inside to find Nico.

Chapter 33

I found him without searching, without wondering, just using a hunch so strong it felt like a premonition. I stood outside the shower in the master bathroom and watched him inside, palms flat against the wet tile, leaning with his head bowed and eyes closed, unmoving, letting the water pound over his naked body.

He was beautiful. Like a sculpture.

Stepping out of my heels, I unbuttoned my blouse and let it fall to the floor. My skirt came off next, then my panties and bra, every piece of clothing dropped to the tile as quickly as my hands could remove it. I opened the shower door. A billow of steam lifted my hair from my shoulders, kissed moisture all over my skin in warm beaded drops.

Nico raised his head. His eyes blazed when he saw me, and he straightened. He opened his mouth to speak.

"No." I touched my fingers to his lips. "No talking. It doesn't matter. Nothing else matters but this."

I kissed him.

He responded instantly, groaning into my mouth. He pinned me against his chest with an arm like an iron band around my back, pulling my head back with his other hand fisted in my hair. Breathing hard, trembling all over, he pressed me against the smooth tile wall and ravaged my mouth.

I knew what he needed. This was how we communicated best. Pounding heartbeats and desperate kisses and skin on heated skin, we surrendered without thought or hesitation to the thing that always burned between us, the aching desire and greedy, dark need.

"Kat." His voice broke when he said my name. "I'm sorry. Of course your feelings matter—"

"Shh," I whispered. "I know. I already know."

I turned in his arms, flattened my palms against the slick shower wall, leaned forward, and looked over my shoulder. Nico's hands gripped my hips. His erection pressed against my bottom. He licked his lips and stared at me in silence, waiting. I'd never seen such a look of lust.

I placed my hand on his, and slid it down my hip, to my bottom. Nico's avid gaze followed the motion, then snapped back to mine. Water dripped down his brow. Caught on his long lashes, a single drop fell to his cheek like a tear.

Voice husky, barely audible above the spray of the water, I said, "Do it."

His lashes fluttered closed. When they opened again, Nico's expression held a new, dangerous edge.

He slapped my ass, hard.

Pain, stinging hot, exploded like a firework over my skin. I jumped and sucked in a breath, but I'd been expecting it.

He slapped me again. This time I moaned. The pain was brighter, sharper. My back arched. My eyes slid shut. He steadied me with his fingers curved firmly around my hipbone.

When his hand made contact with the tender flesh of my ass a third time, the pain was so strong I went up on my toes, gasping.

"Take it," he said in a low, raw voice. "Take it for me, Kat."

Heart pounding, I bowed my head between my raised arms. I whispered, "Yes."

Seven more swift, merciless blows, and it was over.

Nico's arm snaked around my waist. He pulled me against his chest, and pressed his lips to my ear. "Beautiful," he breathed and slid his hand between my shaking legs.

My head fell back against his shoulder. My heart was pounding so frantically I could barely catch my breath. With his strong fingers stroking through my wetness, he lifted his free hand to my breast and gently pinched my nipple. Sensation sizzled through me, hot as the steam billowing around us. I made an incoherent sound of pleasure.

Nico turned me around, and pushed me against the shower wall. He dropped to his knees in front of me, and buried his face between my legs. Hot water rained over his back, splashing up onto my stomach and breasts, onto my hard, aching nipples.

"Please!" I begged, arching into his mouth. My bottom throbbed, my nipples throbbed, my blood screamed through my veins. It felt as if the whole world would explode.

Suckling my clit, Nico slid his fingers deep inside me. I came, crying out his name.

My knees buckled, but before I could fall, Nico picked me up in his arms. He kicked open the shower door, strode through the bathroom into the bedroom, and set me gently on the bed. He found a condom in the nightstand drawer, and rolled it down the length of his beautiful hard cock as I watched, trembling, emotion overwhelming me. He knelt on the mattress and spread my legs, running his open palms down my thighs, his dark gaze on mine. Rivulets of water dripped down his chest.

Silently, watching my face, he eased inside me. Stretching around his girth, I shuddered, exhaling a soft moan.

He lowered his body to mine so our chests were pressed together, and put his hands on either side of my face. He rocked deeper into me. I flexed my hips in response, needing every inch of him inside. When his thrusts gained speed, I folded my legs around his waist and hooked my ankles together, my heels pressed to his spine.

We didn't speak. It felt even more intimate because of it. We stared into each other's eyes, our bodies moving together, our ragged breaths drawn together, our hearts beating in time.

Nico lowered his head, took one of my nipples in his mouth, and sucked. Close to another orgasm, I moaned again. The sound made Nico growl softly against my breast and suck harder. With just enough force to make me jerk, he bit down on my nipple.

Filled with a sudden, violent need, I sank my fingers into his wet hair and gripped his head.

I knew he felt the change in my body, knew he understood my wordless plea. I knew because he slid one hand around my throat and squeezed lightly, then bit down harder on my nipple as he began to fuck me with stronger thrusts, and greater speed.

My body bowed. *Yes.*

"Not yet."

Hearing his husky command, I groaned my frustration. I couldn't hold back much longer. My fingers twisted tighter in his hair. I squeezed my eyes shut, biting my lip.

Nico made a sound like a hiss. All the muscles in his arms and back tensed. He thrust into me three more times with almost violent force, then grunted, "Now, baby! Now!"

The orgasm ripped through me, stiffening my entire body, curling my toes. I screamed. Nico's answering groan was broken, guttural. Deep inside me, he throbbed. Delirious with pleasure, I ground my pelvis against his, my fingers digging into the bunched muscles of his arms. Bucking and crying out beneath him, I rode every thrust, milked every twitch of his cock.

I didn't want it to stop. I wanted him inside me forever.

His arms sagged. I drew him down against me and kissed him recklessly, mindless of our clashing teeth. He kissed me back just as savagely, his mouth crushed to mine, his tongue invading. I tasted salt and rust and knew he'd drawn blood, or I had. A primal thrill had me sinking my nails into his back.

Breaking the kiss, he laughed, a sound thick with satisfaction. "Little tiger," he panted, pressing his forehead to mine. "My fierce, sweet, beautiful Kat."

Nico looked down at me with so much emotion in his eyes, I wanted to cry, but I steeled myself against it.

I realized at that moment that there would be no jumping off this speeding train to land in safety on the ground. It was going too fast. A jump would break me.

And so might staying aboard to discover our final destination.

I turned my face away from Nico's, and stared out the wall of glass to the city glittering in the afternoon sunshine below, wondering how badly this was all going to end.

It would only take another twenty-four hours to find out.

Chapter 34

The House of Blues on the Sunset Strip is a funky, rock 'n' roll mash-up of a bar, nightclub, restaurant, concert venue, and eclectic voodoo art gallery. In the members-only Foundation Room on the top floor, exclusive guests can revel in high-class debauchery and feast on southern-inspired cuisine, while downstairs in the music hall patrons can listen to some of the most famous bands in the world play live, while rubbing shoulders with the biggest A-list celebrities.

As soulful as it was sinful, it was the perfect venue for Bad Habit's EuroTrash tour kickoff party.

"After what happened yesterday, I'm surprised you're in the mood for a party."

Grace's voice on the other end of the line was neutral. She knew full well I was in no mood for a party, just as well as I knew she was in no mood to hang out with the band. I was hoping she'd come as a favor to me; right now, I really needed my girls. Chloe had already agreed to come, and she was even bringing Eric. I had high hopes about what that might mean.

"Believe me, it's the last thing I want to do. I spent all morning at my house trying to clean up the mess. I'm exhausted."

"Then why go? Stay home and soak in a bubble bath with a bottle of wine."

I debated for a moment, then dismissed the idea. "If I don't go, Nico won't go, and then there won't be any party. I don't want to ruin it for everyone else just because I'd rather bury my head in the sand."

"Which is a perfectly reasonable response to major trauma," Grace quipped, "even if it's not ultimately useful. Cut yourself some slack, Kat. You're going through a lot right now. It's normal to feel overwhelmed."

I made a noncommittal noise, not really wanting to delve too deeply into the dark state of my psyche. Monsters lurked in there.

"And speaking of overwhelmed," Grace continued briskly, "I can't believe security at the House of Blues can possibly be counted on to keep out the kind of riffraff that's sure to be stalking Bad Habit." Her voice turned cutting. "Not to mention the riffraff that's stalking *you*."

I'd told her the whole story about Michael. Our encounter at Avery's wake, the night I'd awoken to the figure in the bedroom door, the wreckage at my house. She'd been furious with me when I admitted I hadn't told the police my suspicions about Nico's brother.

She'd been even more furious when I told her about the engagement. Her anger took the form of a long, frozen silence that chilled my ear right through the phone. She'd kept her word about keeping her opinions to herself, though. She simply offered a polite, "Congratulations," and we'd moved on to the subject of the party.

It must have been hell on her to bite her tongue. I was going to give her a huge hard hug when I saw her next.

"Nico's got so many cops coming you won't be able to walk ten feet without bumping into a man with a gun. And Barney has a bunch of his freelance undercover buddies scheduled to be there, too. Security will be tighter than a nun's snatch. If anyone so much as sneezes the wrong way, he'll have ten cops up his ass before you can say 'God bless.' "

"What lovely visuals," said Grace with distaste.

"Those are Nico's words, not mine."

"Naturally."

We shared a small laugh, then fell into tense silence. After a moment, she sighed. "I'm worried about you."

"I know, Grace. And I love you for it."

When I didn't add more, she sighed again. I imagined her tapping her perfectly manicured nails on the mahogany desk in her office, staring at the PhD in psychology from Stanford framed on the wall, wondering how she'd wound up with such a train wreck for a best friend.

"All right. I'll go to this party of yours—"

"Bad Habit's," I corrected.

"—whatever. I'll go to this party, and be nice, and pretend to have a good time, because I love you, too." Her voice turned thoughtful. "And it might be mildly amusing to observe the hero-worship dynamic in collective. It's fascinating how adults can idolize entertainers as if they're gods—"

I cleared my throat. "Yes, that's very interesting, Doctor Freud. Now can we please talk about what we're going to wear?"

"Aside from a liberal coating of anti-bacterial hand cream? Of course."

"I'm pretty sure you won't have to shake anyone's hand, Grace. It's not exactly a business meeting."

"And I'm pretty sure one can catch a virulent strain of gonorrhea from the toilets in places like the House of Blues."

"Well then you'll be putting that anti-bacterial cream somewhere other than your hands, won't you?"

She laughed. "I suppose I will. Do you think anyone will notice if I just wear a full-body condom instead of a leather miniskirt?"

It was my turn to laugh, and it felt good. "Girlfriend, I think if you show up in a leather miniskirt half the men at the party will drop dead of heart attacks."

"Please," she scoffed. "Give me some credit. With my legs, I'd kill off at least three quarters of them."

"Well, if it helps you decide, I'm wearing a red dress so short my coochie will probably be waving hello to everyone."

Grace said drily, "You always were a class act."

"It's not *my* fault! Nico sent over a personal shopper from some boutique in Beverly Hills. I've never seen such an abundance of stretchy, shiny, *tiny* dresses."

"Did you get the clear heels?"

"Okay. I think this conversation has continued long enough. What time should I meet you there?"

"Nico said he'd send a car for you. They'll pick you up at eight."

Grace made a small, indistinct noise. "Did he now? Isn't that gentlemanly of him."

Smiling, I had to shake my head. Grace was the only person I knew who could convey disdain, pleasure, irritation, gratitude, and about a dozen other conflicting emotions, all in under ten words. "Love you, Gracie."

"Love you, too, Kat. See you tonight."

"Can't wait."

"And Kat?"

I cocked my head, arrested by the new, urgent tone of her voice. "Yeah?"

With quiet conviction, she said, "If you're happy, I am, too. No matter what." Then she hung up before I could say another word.

The afternoon passed quickly. I busied myself with list making and obsessing, trying to figure out how I'd get my house back in shape before leaving for Europe with the band. I only had a week in between the kickoff party and the flight out, and was a little panicked at the thought of leaving without everything being back in order. If I was going to be gone for two whole months, I needed to know I wasn't leaving a mess behind.

I'd already arranged to have my upcoming jobs covered by a girl I'd worked with before, another makeup artist I trusted to take care of my clients, and not steal them from me. She was thrilled to have the extra work, and I was happy with the arrangement as well. I definitely wanted to continue working when I came home. After Nico and I were married, I planned on working, too.

I just hadn't told him that yet.

Since we'd made love the day before, he'd been in a strangely quiet mood. Honestly, I hadn't felt much like talking, either, with the black cloud of Michael hanging over our heads. But I sensed Nico's quietness wasn't only about Michael. Something else was bothering him.

Something big. Or bad.

Or both.

He'd risen early, before me, and had since been prowling around the house like a caged bear, checking windows, locking and relocking doors. The security code on the alarm had been reset, and he'd hired twenty-four-hour guards to roam the property in addition to installing more video cameras, but he still wasn't satisfied I was safe.

Hence his having clothes brought to the house, instead of allowing me to go out shopping. Hence his standing over me scowling, Barney and cops in tow, as I retrieved important files and documents from my place, groaning in distress at the mess.

Hence his insistence on being glued to my side like a barnacle.

That barnacle was now rooted against me in the backseat of the Escalade, his big hand wrapped tightly around mine. We were cruising down Sunset Boulevard, Barney driving, on our way to the party at the House of Blues. It was dusk, and the sky outside glowed orange and purple in the deepening twilight.

"You're quiet," I said, squeezing Nico's hand.

He glanced at me. Wearing his trademark painted-on jeans and black T-shirt under a leather jacket, his dark hair in finger-combed disarray, a thin leather cord around his neck and a silver ring on his left thumb, he looked sexy as hell . . . and distracted.

"How're you doin', Kat?"

His soft question took me by surprise. As did the serious look on his face. "I'm okay. As well as can be expected under the circumstances, I guess."

He studied me, sweeping his thumb back and forth across my knuckles. "No second thoughts? Not regrettin' meetin' me?"

There was an underlying subtext there. Some tension ran through his words. It made me nervous. "Why? Are you regretting meeting me?"

His stare pierced me. "That's not an answer."

"Neither is that."

In the front seat, Barney reached to turn up the volume on the radio. He was trying to give us some privacy, but it wouldn't work. He was sitting too close.

Nico looked away and ran a hand through his hair, a gesture I easily recognized as one of frustration. He didn't push for another answer, and I wasn't much in the mood for conversation, so we spent the rest of the ride in tense silence.

It felt shitty.

When we pulled off Sunset onto the side street where the entrance to the House of Blues's parking lot was located, I felt even shittier.

A line of police cars blocked traffic from the street from below. Uniformed officers conferred in small groups along the sidewalk. Burly bouncers checked guest names off a list before cars were allowed to enter the parking lot, and a host of security guards wandered up and down the block with flashlights and walkie-talkies. A crowd had gathered beyond the line of police cars, hoping for a glimpse of their favorite band, and even more bystanders watched from across the street. Everywhere lurked men with cameras.

A scream went up from the crowd when we exited the car. They recognized Nico.

"What?" he asked, watching my face carefully.

"I don't think I'll ever get used to that," I muttered, shooting a glance over my shoulder.

Nico's face turned a shade darker than it had been in the car. He tugged on my hand, and we went inside.

"Oh my God, they're amazing!" shrieked Chloe above the blare of the music. She and I, along with Grace and Eric, stood in the wings offstage as we watched Bad Habit rock the House. Nico was so fucking sexy, strutting and stomping his way around the stage, thrusting his hips as he played his guitar, singing with his head thrown back and his eyes closed, sweat dripping down his brow. The music hall only held about fifteen hundred people, but he sang as if there were a hundred and fifty thousand screaming out his name.

Even Grace was transfixed. She stared at the band, blinking rapidly, her hand at her throat.

Bad Habit finished the song with a hammering drum solo, and the room erupted in deafening screams and applause. Nico laughed, pumping his fist in the air. I caught his eye as he turned away from the mike and smiled. He grinned back at me and winked.

Fanning herself, Grace said, "I don't know about you ladies, but all that testosterone has strangely made me need to pee. I'm off to the loo."

"I'll come with." Chloe gave Eric a kiss on the cheek. Adorably, he blushed.

"The three of you need an armed chaperone," he said, eyeing our outfits in alarm. "You're in danger of causing a riot on the way to the ladies' room."

Chloe wore a pale green, sleeveless minidress that complemented her golden tan and hair to perfection. I wore one of Nico's Beverly Hills boutique dresses, a tight, crotch-grazing number in fire-engine red, with heels to match. Grace wore the killer leather mini, as promised, paired with a glittery purple camisole top, and was attracting a lot of attention. Contrasted with her vivid hair and pale skin, the purple was incredible. I'd even seen a few girls send her admiring glances.

"Puh!" Grace waved her hand. "Thanks for the offer, Eric, but I won't have you following us around and ruining my chances of finding a hot roadie I can do the nasty with tonight and never see again."

"Grace!" Chloe was scandalized. The thought of a one-night stand was about as shocking to her as the thought of murder. It was just one of those things a lady didn't do.

Grace rolled her eyes. "I didn't wear this skirt for nothing, Chloe. I'm fishing for a man tonight, and this is what you call *bait*. Now off with you, Eric, we'll be back in five. Or Kat and your girlfriend will. If I go missing, don't come looking for me."

I think Eric was too distracted by Grace calling Chloe his girlfriend to protest. He wore a dazed smile as we left, his gaze glued to her retreating back. The band launched into another song, and we took the private elevator to the top floor.

The ladies' room upstairs was in the private club. Decorated by someone with a fetish for red velvet and gilt, it looked like something out of a nineteenth-century bordello. The incense that burned in a little jar in one corner was probably meant to cover the smell of bleach, which it didn't.

I wondered if Grace had been right about the toilet seats.

"I have to admit," said Grace, leaning over the sink and staring into the mirror while applying lipstick, "watching Bad Habit play live has given me a much better understanding of how people become enamored with musicians. They practically *oozed* sex. It was very powerful, if I do say so myself. Almost mesmerizing."

"You've never seen a band play live before?" asked Chloe from inside the stall. The toilet flushed, and she came out to wash her hands. "How is that possible?"

For a moment, Grace froze, her hand to her mouth. Then she looked down, slowly recapped her lipstick, and put it back into her clutch. Quietly, she said, "I don't actually know if I've seen a band live before. I just know I haven't in the past twelve years."

"Oh crap." Chloe's voice and expression reflected her regret over her choice of words. She laid a hand on Grace's shoulder. "I'm sorry. I always forget."

Another bad choice of words, but at least Grace had the, well . . . *grace* to smile. "Me, too. And don't worry about it. You've got enough to worry about with your new man and his little, ahem, *problem*."

Apparently Chloe had also told Grace about her dissatisfaction with Eric's overly enthusiastic kissing style. I hadn't heard an update since my little talk with Eric the day before. "Yeah, how's that going, Lo? Last time we talked you were thinking of breaking up with him."

Chloe blushed even deeper than Eric had minutes before. "You guys, I have no idea what's gotten into him, but it's like he's taken *lessons* or something. I mean, all of a sudden the prehensile tongue is gone, and he's, like, *gentle*. As a lamb."

"Awesome!" I said a little too loudly. Grace looked at me strangely. "I mean, he's such a great guy, Chloe. I really think the two of you are the perfect couple."

"Really?" she asked shyly. "Because I think you and Nico are the perfect couple."

"Oh dear God," muttered Grace, fluffing her hair. She spun from the mirror and looked down her nose at us. "All right, you two, enough of that. I'll gain five pounds just from breathing in all the sugar in the air. Can we please go back downstairs now so I can find my own Prince Charming and not have to listen to you two hens clucking over your roosters?"

"I'm pretty sure you'd scare the crap out of Prince Charming," Chloe said, smiling.

"And his horse," I added.

"Shut up," Grace said good-naturedly. "Even though you're probably right. I can't see myself with a man who wears white gloves and epaulets."

She and Chloe moved to the door, their steps muffled on the thick, blood-red carpet. Chloe asked, "What's an epaulet?"

Grace sighed.

Noticing I was hanging back, Chloe asked, "You coming?"

"I think I'll hide out in here for a few minutes longer." Feeling a headache coming on, I sank into the red velvet chair beside the row of sinks. "Big parties were never my thing."

Grace was concerned. "Are you feeling okay?"

I nodded. "Yeah, just . . . need a few minutes alone, maybe. These past few weeks have been insane."

Standing near the door of the ladies' room, Grace narrowed her eyes at me. She was about to say something when Chloe beat her to it.

"We'll be outside when you're ready, okay? At that bar we passed on the way in. Then if you want we can go back downstairs and watch the band from the balcony. It'll give you a different angle to ogle your man from."

I smiled. "Deal."

Before Grace could protest, Chloe dragged her from the room, and I was left alone with my thoughts. I dropped my head into my hands and contemplated the rug.

I hadn't admitted it to Nico, but I was worried about the tour. What would life on the road be like? What if I hated it? What if I got homesick? It seemed both exciting and terrifying. And what was going on in Nico's head the past few days? Why had he been so remote?

What about Michael?

The more I thought about everything, the more my head began to spin, and the more distracted I became. Which was why I didn't hear anything when the door opened and closed. I only looked up when I heard the lock on the handle turn with a sharp *snick*.

The man in the doorway smiled at me. It was the most frightening thing I'd ever seen.

"Fancy meeting you here," said Michael as he stepped into the room.

Chapter 35

Heart pounding, I sucked in a breath and leapt to my feet. As Michael stepped closer, I backed away on shaking legs.

"How did you get in here?" I whispered, terrified.

The expression on his face was indescribable. His eyes held the flat killer gaze of a shark. Even his smile was shark-like. "You mean, how did I evade all the security and police Nico hired to try to keep you safe tonight? I came in with the dinner crowd last night." His smile grew wider. "And never left."

The realization that he'd been lying in wait for me like a patient predator stalking its prey since *yesterday* made my skin crawl and my blood run cold. I backed up another few steps until I hit the wall. I couldn't go any farther. I inhaled a breath, readying a scream.

"Scream and I'll make you regret it," he snapped.

My shaking hands curled to fists at my sides. My mind flew in a million scattered directions. "What do you want, Michael?"

He cocked his head. His eyes roved hungrily over me. I shuddered, which made him laugh. "I'm many things, but a rapist isn't one of them, Kat. Your virtue is safe with me."

"But my house apparently wasn't!"

His laugh settled into a chuckle. His similarity in physical looks to Nico was truly eerie. They were even dressed the same: boots, jeans, and a black leather jacket. I wondered if it was coincidence or just another weird fetish, like standing outside a darkened bedroom and watching his brother sleep.

"That was just to get your attention. Take down that smug self-confidence of yours a notch. I see it worked."

There was a deafening roar in my ears. I wasn't sure which I wanted to do more, run or lunge at him and gouge his eyes out. "*What* do you *want*?"

The smile faded from Michael's face. His gaze turned haunted. "Amy. I want Amy back."

Something about the way he said it, some odd inflection in his tone, rang an alarm bell in the back of my mind. The way he spoke her name was perversely possessive. "I can't do anything about that, Michael. No one can."

His throat worked. His voice came in a low, choked rasp. "I loved her."

What the hell is he talking about? What the hell does he want? "I know you did—"

"No you don't!" Michael shouted suddenly. His face flushed with color. "I told you at the wake: you don't know anything!"

I flinched. Fear screamed along my nerve endings, scraped cold fingernails down my back. Every sense honed. His rage was so palpable I almost tasted it. I held myself perfectly still as Michael struggled to get himself under control, flexing his hands open and closed over and over, his chest rising and falling with his ragged breaths.

He said, "I *loved* her. I was *in love* with her. And she loved me. We were more than just brother and sister, Kat. We were everything to each other. We were best friends." His voice cracked. Tears spilled down his cheeks. He whispered, "We were lovers."

I gasped, feeling sick and shocked and repulsed, all at once.

"She tried to fight it. That's why she ran away with Juan Carlos; she thought another man would make a difference. She thought distance would make a difference." He laughed. It was a harsh, ugly sound in the quiet room. "And boy, did it. But not in the way she thought. Three years, she whored for him, locked up like a bird in a cage. And when the day came that some filthy john passed out on top of her with his cell phone in his shirt pocket, who do you think she called? *Me.* She called me. Because I was the only one who ever really loved her, Kat. And she knew it. She knew I'd do anything to get her away from him. Anything."

With growing horror, I remembered what Nico had told me about the phone call Avery made to him from Brazil, when she said she was coming home. He had said he knew Juan Carlos was dead . . . and he thought his sister had something to do with it.

"It was you," I whispered. Goose bumps broke out all over my arms. "*You* killed Juan Carlos."

Like a cornered animal, Michael bared his teeth. "You're goddamn right I killed him! She told me where to find her and I hunted down that bastard and killed him like the insect that he was! Then I brought her back, and Nico barely even noticed I'd been gone, he was so wrapped up in his own bullshit!" His voice gentled, became stroking and strange. "So Avery and I were together again, only this time both of us knew it was for good. It was meant to be. And we were happy."

My stomach twisted. I felt an almost overpowering urge to throw up. "Happy? My God, Michael! She was an addict—she was molested by your father, she was forced to work in a brothel—how could you do that to her? How could you take advantage of someone so damaged in that way? She was your *sister*!"

He screamed, "She was my *life*!"

Terrified, I jumped. On a gut level, I knew he was a grave danger to me. One wrong move, and I'd be dead.

He prowled slowly closer. My hands were ice. I couldn't breathe. My mind hurtled through space at a thousand miles per hour, but my body was rooted in place.

Michael's voice dropped to just above a whisper. "And when Nico found out about us, he took away the only thing I ever loved and threatened to kill me if I ever went near her again. He told her I was sick, I was just like our father, and she listened to him. They cut me off, and I never saw her again until the day they lowered her fucking coffin into the ground!"

I now understood with bloodcurdling clarity why Nico had been so upset when he'd seen Michael kiss me, and when I'd told him I was glad it had been Michael watching us that night at the house and not some stranger. Here was the reason Nico hadn't spoken to his brother in five years. God only knew how he'd found out. I hoped with all my heart Nico hadn't walked in on the two of them together.

Michael reached into the waistband of his jeans. He produced a shiny black revolver, and pointed it at my heart.

My face flushed hot. My entire body began to shake. I almost fainted with terror. "Killing me won't bring her back."

"Of course it won't," he answered through gritted teeth. "This isn't about *you*, Kat. It's about *him*. After we came to LA, his entire life was handed to him on a silver platter. Money, fame, success, now love . . . he has everything. And I have nothing. I want him to suffer like he made me suffer. I want him to know exactly what it feels like to be thrown away by the person you love more than anything else on earth. I want to watch that."

I blinked. *Watch that?*

His face twisted into an ugly grimace. "I'm not really interested in killing you, Kat. That would hurt my brother, but in the end, he'd have closure. It would be over too quickly. It would be too clean. Also, I have no interest in going to prison. So that only leaves one other choice."

I didn't understand. Wordlessly, I slowly shook my head.

Michael said, "You're going to leave him."

"No!" I said it instantly, without thinking. He ignored me and kept talking, a wild glint shining in his eye.

"If you *leave* him, if you tell him you've changed your mind, that you don't really love him and turn your back on him, it'll tear him apart. I know him. He'll never get over it. He'll pine over you for the rest of his life. He's never been in love before. Ridiculous, isn't it, for a man his age? A man with beautiful women throwing themselves at him left and right as he walks down the street?"

He nodded, agreeing with himself. "Ridiculous. I almost didn't think he had it in him. But, lucky for me, he does. And now I finally have my chance to prove to him that there are far worse things in this world than death. Do you know what's worse than death, Kat?"

Swallowing back the bile rising in my throat, I stared at him.

With chilling softness, Michael said, "*Abandonment.* Rejection by the person you love more than life itself. Death is nice and peaceful compared to that. Death would be a relief! So I won't kill you. Instead, we're all going to suffer together." He cackled. "For as long as we all shall live."

I realized then that Michael wasn't only dangerous. He was insane. *Think, Kat. Think!*

"And if I refuse? If I tell Nico every word you just said?"

Michael smiled. "Then I'll tell the whole world our ugly little family story, beginning with how Nico pushed our father down a flight of stairs—only omitting how much of an incestuous, drunken bastard daddy dearest was—and ending with an illicit affair between two siblings. Only I'll change it up a little. I'll say it was Nico who was having the affair with our sister, not me. And that when Daddy found out, Nico killed him."

I made a choked sound of horror. Michael merely smiled and smiled, the gun still pointed at my chest.

"You know they'll all believe it, too, the way Amy insisted on pretending Nico was her boyfriend." His smile drained away, replaced by a scowl. "She was always trying to make me jealous with that shit."

I had to do something. I had to figure out a way to get out of this, to change his mind. "Michael, let's just talk about this for a minute—"

"No. We're done talking, Kat." Michael's voice was stone cold, to match the look reflected in his eyes. "Here are your choices: Leave Nico. Do it loud, and do it tonight. Make it embarrassing for him. Make it public. Have a screaming fight over dinner, slap him silly in the bar, whatever. Just make him believe it's over, make everyone watching believe it's over, and then walk away, for good.

"Or . . . " his wild eyes glittered. "Don't leave him, or leave now but get back together with him at any point in the future and I'll sell my story to the highest bidder. Which means Nico's life will be ruined."

I already saw the headlines. Worse, I knew that even if I insisted to anyone who'd listen that Michael had set this all up, Nico might be charged with the murder of his father. I had no doubt that, if questioned by the police, he'd admit to pushing his father down the stairs, especially if he was trying to clear his name of false accusations regarding his relationship with Amy. But any protestations he might make about Amy's abuse at the hands of their father could never be proven now that she was dead. And being Nico's fiancée, I probably wouldn't even be a credible witness.

And though Michael wasn't exactly a credible witness, either, the press would have a field day with the story. Ultimately, it would be Michael's word against Nico's.

It would be a bloodbath.

Michael was carefully watching my face. He said, "I have nothing left to lose, Kat. I might even tell the police Nico had his way with *me*." Before I could recover from that fresh horror, he added, "And there's the small matter of the disappearing photographer. Did he tell you about that?" He waited a beat and saw confirmation on my face. "Of course he did. He's told you everything. Personally I think with the right judge, Nico could be spending a very, very long time behind bars."

There was no way out. I couldn't say anything. I couldn't do anything. I could only stare at him, mute, spinning, devastated, my heart thrashing like a dying animal inside my chest.

"It's your decision. I'll give you eight hours. If I don't read on all the stalkerazzi blogs that Nico Nyx got dumped in a highly humiliating way by," he checked his watch, "six o'clock tomorrow morning, I'm blowing it all up."

I made a helpless noise of disbelief. For a moment, Michael seemed to take pity on me.

"Think of it as the lesser of two evils, Kat. You can save Nico from career suicide, massive public ridicule, and prison, but only by breaking his heart. If you care for him at all, it shouldn't be such a hard decision."

Through the chaos wreaking havoc inside my head, I managed one final rational argument. "And if I do break it off with him? What guarantees do I have that you won't go to the press with your story anyway?"

Michael gazed at me, his eyes filled with darkness. His voice fell to a ragged rasp. "I could have done this years ago. I could have ruined him as soon as I realized he'd poisoned Amy against me. But I didn't. I waited until he had something he'd rather die for than give up. I can see it in his eyes when he looks at you. I can hear it in his voice. You're his Achilles' heel. Did you know he's been writing songs about you? That Bad Habit's next album is going to be titled *Thunderstruck*, for how he felt when he first saw you? That's how much he loves you. Losing you will break his *soul*. He'll have to live in the same place I live, in this bottomless black hole of pain. He'll stay out of prison, he'll keep everything he's worked for, but he'll be broken. He'll be empty, like me. That's all I want, Kat. An eye for an eye. It's only fair."

All the speeches over, he lowered the gun to his side. We stared at each other in silence.

The magnitude of the situation hit me with the force of a wrecking ball. I had to do what he'd asked or Nico's life was over.

Michael turned and walked slowly toward the door. He paused for one last look at me, his hand resting on the doorknob. "Do the right thing, Kat. Let him go. You can still have a life. You can find your happiness with someone else. But there are no happily-ever-afters for people like Nico and me. We were cursed from birth."

He unlocked the door, opened it, and disappeared. Trembling violently, I sank to my knees on the floor.

I knew exactly what I had to do next.

Chapter 36

Sick and shaking, I walked slowly from the bathroom. From downstairs came the thumping bass of music, rumbling through the floor. At the bar, Chloe and Grace waited for me, drinks in hand, laughing with a long-haired guy in head-to-toe leather. As soon as Chloe caught sight of my face, her laughter died.

"Kat?" She rose from the bar stool. "What's wrong?"

"I have to get out of here."

Michael was nowhere to be seen. He'd melted back into the night as quickly as he'd appeared.

"What?" Grace twisted in her seat to stare at me as if I were insane. "What are you talking about?"

I couldn't explain. I could never explain. I strode past them to the elevator and pressed the button for the ground floor.

Abandoning their drinks and their companion, Chloe and Grace came up behind me. "Kat, what the hell is going on? Your face is white as a sheet, and you're trembling! Are you sick?"

I closed my eyes. *You have no idea, Grace.* I whispered, "I just can't take this anymore. I'm done with all of it. And I have to go."

Chloe gripped my arm. "Wait, are you talking about Nico? You're done with him?"

The elevator doors opened. I shook off her hand. I stepped inside, stabbed my finger to the button, and slumped into the corner, looking at the floor. The girls crowded in with me, peppering me with questions, but I didn't respond, except to beg, "Please don't ask me anything. I can't talk about it. I have to go."

When the doors slid open on the ground floor, I bolted.

I ran down the shadowy hallway, pushing past couples making out and guys sharing a joint, the acrid haze of pot smoke hanging low in the air. The music was louder down here. The band was still playing, but they were almost finished with their set. They were going to play, then eat, drink, and be merry with all their friends and family who'd come, the favored inner circle of roadies and agents and managers, the hundreds of others who'd helped them along the way.

I made it to the side stage where I'd been standing earlier just as Bad Habit finished the final song. I watched, panting and holding back tears, as they high-fived and hugged. The crowd screamed with happiness.

Then Nico turned and saw me standing there. Before I could call him offstage, he did something that made me choke on my own breath. He began to play a tune on his guitar. A mariachi song: "La Canción del Mariachi."

Our song.

He smiled at me from the stage, the lights shining on his hair. He leaned into the mike and said to the crowd, "Anybody here ever been in love?"

The response was deafening. Nico's smile was exultant. He turned his gaze back to me. "C'mon out here, Kat!"

Time slowed. The noise of the crowd faded to a dull roar. Every beat of my heart sounded like thunder in my ears. His hand extended, Nico beckoned to me. Someone behind me nudged me forward, and I moved toward Nico on feet I could no longer feel.

As I stumbled onto the stage, bright lights seared my eyes. Color and motion and noise hammered me from all sides. It was then that I noticed the flowers. Massed low in a long row of fluffy white, peonies lined the entire length of the front edge of the stage. From offstage I hadn't been able to see them.

Peonies are a symbol of a happy marriage. I was savin' those up for when I got you the ring.

My stomach lurched. I thought I would vomit. Frozen, my eyes wide, I stared ahead blindly, the room a watery waver. Nico strode over, took my hand, and pulled me center stage. He handed his guitar to Brody, who winked at me, then Nico pulled the mike from the stand. Into it he said, "Got somethin' I wanna ask you, baby. And this time I'm gonna ask it right."

Nico got down on one knee.

The crowd erupted into a screaming, jumping riot.

No. Oh, God, no. Not like this.

I should have known. His distraction, his question in the car on the way over, the way he always did everything over the top, loud as could be. If I thought I'd ever felt pain before in my life, I'd been wrong. What I felt staring down at the man I loved as he reached into his jacket and pulled out a black velvet box was nothing short of devastating.

Someone handed me a wireless mike. My fingers curled around it in a death grip. I no longer knew how to blink, or breathe.

Gazing up at me with adoration, Nico said gently, "I love you, Kat Reid. I wanna spend the rest of my life with you. You said I couldn't propose right without a ring, so . . . "

He cracked open the black box. An enormous diamond glittered at me, mockingly bright. Over the screams of a thousand people, Nico asked, "Will you marry me?"

I couldn't speak. Everything inside me clamored *yes yes yes*! But I couldn't say it. I couldn't say anything at all. From my mouth came a small sound, a wordless noise of anguish, and the speakers shrieked with a sudden burst of feedback from my mike.

Nico winced. The noise of the crowd died down. There was a long, drawn-out moment of tension in which I stared down at Nico, he stared up at me, the crowd stared at the two of us in our horrible spectacle on stage, until I found a strength I didn't know I had, and opened my mouth.

In a voice clear and strong, I said directly into the mike, "I can't. I'm sorry, but I can't."

Cries of shock. Gasps of disbelief. Even a few snickers. Someone near the front of the crowd muttered, "Man, that's some cold shit right there." Nico, still down on one knee, stared at me in stunned incomprehension, his blue eyes flared wide.

I imagined I heard the sound of Michael's laughter in the distance.

The mike dropped from my fingers. It hit the stage with a thud. Nico shot to his feet, his face twisted in shock. I backed away a few steps, then turned and ran.

He followed me. As I shoved past flabbergasted Chloe, Grace, and Eric standing in the wings, I heard Nico shouting my name, heard his feet pounding the floor. I ran with no idea of direction, through the twisting backstage corridors, until Nico caught up to me around a corner. He grabbed my arm from behind, and pushed me against the cold cement wall with so much force my breath left my lungs in a grunt.

"What the fuck?" he shouted into my face.

"Just let me go, Nico! I can't do this anymore!" I shoved him, my hands flat on his chest. It was like trying to move a mountain.

He screamed, "*What the fuck?*"

A sea of rotting garbage tossed inside my stomach. As I began to get a clearer picture of what my sacrifice might actually involve, of the days and weeks and months and years I would now have to survive, drawing breath from dead lungs, seeing out of dead eyes, walking around in a corpse's body, I almost, *almost*, told him the truth.

Then he let me off the hook by being an asshole, and the moment was gone forever.

"Did you *know* I was gonna do that? Is this some kind of fucked-up *test*? Humiliate me in front of everyone who's important to me to see just how much I'll put up with, to prove how much I love you? Are you that fuckin' insecure?"

"No!" I shouted. "I just finally realized I don't love you enough to be your wife!"

I might as well have stabbed him through the heart. His face turned white. His mouth dropped open. He recoiled from me, staggering back a few steps to stare at me as if I were the demon who'd just ripped his soul from his body and gobbled it down.

I swallowed back the bitter bite of bile rising in my throat, trying to catch my breath. I guessed I had about thirty seconds of bravado left before I'd crumble, and he'd know it was all a giant pack of lies.

"I'm sorry, Nico. I wish it wasn't true, because you're an amazing person, and I do care for you. But—"

"You said you loved me. You said you'd be mine for as long as both our hearts were beating." His voice was hoarse and breaking. Looking at his face was like watching a building burn to the ground.

"Nico, I—"

"I told you everything about me, all my secrets, all my darkest shit, and you fucking *said* you *loved* me!"

There wasn't any air. There was nothing supporting my weight. I felt as if I were being sucked hard against the ground, and it might at any second swallow me whole. Nico stared at me, shaking, red faced, a vein in his temple throbbing like mad.

I whispered, "You promised me you'd let me go if I ever wanted to walk away."

His eyes welled with tears. He shook his head, a violent jerk that sent his hair flying.

"Yes. You promised. And now I want to walk away. I can't take it, Nico. Your lifestyle. Your past. Your possessiveness. This craziness with your brother. I want out. Now. Tonight. I'm sorry it had to be this way, but I'm done."

His throat worked. His gaze darted all over my face. He stood there a few feet away, breathing hard, looking as if he'd like to scream, or smash my face in with his fists. As best I could, I kept my expression a cold mask.

He just shook his head back and forth, in complete disbelief. Even wrecked, his face wet and his lips pulled back in an ugly snarl, he was still the most beautiful thing I'd ever seen.

He lunged for me suddenly, grabbed my face and crushed his mouth to mine. "You love me! I know you love me!" He cried it against my mouth as he held my head trapped between his hands. I twisted away, fighting back, until finally I found enough space to slap him.

His head snapped back. When he snapped it back around, he stared at me with his hand against his cheek, panting and wild-eyed.

I shouted, "I don't love you! I never did, all right? Stop being such a child! I only said it because that's what you wanted to hear! You knew I was never really committed to you, you said so yourself! I'm always running away, remember? I'm always comparing you to some other dickhead, remember? That's because you were never the right thing for me, and we both know it!"

I saw the change as it happened. Fury took the place of disbelief, and for a moment I thought he would lunge at me again, only this time to curl his hands around my throat.

Instead he reached out, ripped the chain he'd given me from my neck, and threw it to the ground.

The room wobbled. I had to get away from him before I fainted, or cracked apart with the screams of anguish bubbling up inside my throat.

I turned and walked quickly away. After ten feet, I stopped. Over my shoulder, I said, "I won't tell anyone about you. About Avery and Michael." I bit back a sob. "And I'll pay you back for the house."

There was a moment's silence. Then Nico said bitterly, "Don't bother. I usually pay my whores a lot less, but you earned it. That was the biggest mind fuck of all time."

His angry steps pounded down the corridor. Once they faded and he was gone, I leaned over and threw up all over my shoes.

When Chloe and Grace finally found me, I was crumpled in a corner, sobbing like a baby, clutching the broken necklace to my chest.

Chapter 37

It didn't take anywhere near eight hours for the entertainment news to begin reporting what would soon become the hottest story of the year.

By midnight, the internet had exploded with eye-witness accounts of the lead singer of Bad Habit's epic rejection. One particularly nasty piece, titled "Life Imitates Art," a reference to how I'd left Nico at the altar in the video for "Soul Deep," crucified Nico for his ruthlessness in not only finding a new girlfriend, but also proposing to her so soon after Avery Kane's unfortunate death. I'd anticipated this kind of thing, which was one of my main reasons for wanting to keep our engagement quiet for as long as possible.

What I hadn't expected was the tsunami of hate that would be directed my way.

I was a ruthless gold digger. I was a conniving slut. I was the reason Nico and Avery broke up. I was the reason she overdosed. A whole galaxy of conspiracy theories arose in which I had not only plotted to oust Avery from her role in the video, but I had plotted to push her to the edge by flaunting my relationship with Nico in her face. A few of my more rabid detractors went so far as to outright blame me for her death.

Apparently I was also plotting to break up the band. In some corners, that was considered worse.

I read every story. I obsessed over every detail. In the days that followed, I hunted through papers and magazines and stalked online bloggers, hungry for news, for any mention of Nico and how he was doing in the aftermath of the atomic bomb I'd dropped on his head.

Unfortunately for me, there was plenty of news to be had.

"I don't know why you keep doing this to yourself," snapped Grace, snatching the copy of *US Weekly* magazine from my hands. The cover picture showed Nico and a busty brunette staggering through the lobby of the Four Seasons Hotel in Beverly Hills at two o'clock in the morning. His arm was slung over her shoulder; his head was bent as he said something into her ear. Her skirt was so short it was almost a belt.

Not even a week and I'd been replaced. I was so depressed I couldn't even muster the energy to feel sorry for myself.

I snatched the magazine back, returning to the page I'd been reading. "It's called self-flagellation," I muttered. "I've heard it's good for the soul."

Grace huffed, "There's nothing wrong with your soul, Kat. It's your *brain* that's the problem!"

I'd been staying with her again, hiding in the cocoon of her controlled-access building since the prior weekend. Chloe was hysterical with worry, mainly because she was convinced I was headed for a trip to the hospital due to the sheer amount of liquid that had been exiting my body through my eyes, but Grace was her usual tough-as-nails self, ordering me to eat when it was time, ordering me to sleep, ordering me to take a shower. It was good she was around, because if not for her influence, I wouldn't have done any of those things.

I would have simply existed on a steady toxic diet of tabloids, watching the love of my life fuck his way through every brunette in town.

To say I was surprised by that unexpected development would be akin to saying the dinosaurs were surprised when that giant meteor first touched down.

I wasn't surprised. I was fucking *annihilated*.

"This is ridiculous, Kat. None of this even makes sense. If you were so convinced you were done with him, if you were so over it that you had to break up with the poor guy like *that*, why the hell are you acting like *this*?" Grace's narrowed gray eyes drilled into me.

"It's complicated. And by the way, that 'poor guy' has had his dick inside at least two dozen women in the past week! I think he's doing just *fine*." In an attempt to escape her relentless stare, I tossed aside the magazine and burrowed deeper into the safety of her couch. The snuggie I was wrapped in was no match for her burning gaze, because I felt its heat right through the Barbie-puke-pink fabric.

"*If* the tabloids are to be believed. And considering their track record with UFOs, mutant human-alien hybrids, and Oprah Winfrey secretly being a government-controlled robot, they're not."

She had a point. It counted for exactly zero on the "Make Kat Feel Better" scale.

I said, "You'll never convince me Quentin Tarantino isn't a mutant human-alien hybrid. Have you seen his forehead?"

Grace sighed.

"And why are you sticking up for Nico anyway? I know you never liked him!"

A stony silence. I looked up to find Grace staring down at me, scary as an axe murderer. Her tone was as severe as her expression. "You know I'm not stupid, right?"

"Um. Yes?"

"Good. Because you're acting as if I'm too dull to figure out something else is going on here that you're not willing to talk about."

I opened my mouth to protest. Grace put up a hand and said, "Shush."

I shushed.

"I won't push you to tell me what it is, but I want you to know that *I* know you have a ridiculous tendency toward unquestioning self-sacrifice. You'd be first in a line of Hindu widows to throw herself on her husband's burning funeral pyre. You'd be the only virgin in tribal history to willingly jump into the volcano to appease the gods. You're that soldier who would fall on a grenade to save his buddies."

I was touched. "Thanks, Gracie."

"It's not a compliment, for God's sake! What I'm saying is that you have no sense of self-preservation! You're too worried about saving everybody else! How about if, just once, you thought about what *you* wanted first?"

I said, "What I want, more than anything else in the world, is for Nico to be happy. That's all. So in a way, I *am* being selfish by letting him go."

Grace stared at me as if I were insane. "Kat, if you think that man is going to be happy without you, you've never been more deluded in your life. He's going to self-destruct. What do you think all these women he's suddenly with are about?"

"They're about to score him a nasty case of genital warts, that's what," I grumbled.

She snapped, "Don't be flippant! When you're talking about flushing true love down the toilet, you don't get to be flippant. Not in front of me."

I was astonished. "And here I assumed you thought true love existed in the same place as unicorns and the tooth fairy."

She swallowed, looking away. "Well, you're wrong. It's rare, but it happens. It's what every single person I see in my practice really wants. Underneath all the bullshit, it's what everybody longs for." She looked back at me. For the first time since I'd known her, Grace's eyes shone with tears. "And if you throw it away like a piece of trash, I will never forgive you."

She stood abruptly. Crossing to the dining room, she snatched her handbag from where it hung on the arm of a chair, then proceeded to walk out of the apartment and slam the door shut behind her, all without looking at me once.

In the bedroom, my cell phone rang.

I flew down the hallway, my heart in my throat. But when I fished the phone from my purse, it was a number I didn't recognize. It wasn't *him*.

"Hello?"

"Hello, Kat. It's Barney."

My heart leapt, then plummeted. I clutched the phone as if my life depended on it. "Oh God, Barney, has something happened to Nico? Is he all right?"

Barney paused. In a strange voice, he said, "He's been through worse. It's not the end of the world, it's just an adjustment."

Goddamn, drive a stake through my heart, why don't you? I had to put my hand on my chest to press against the piercing pain his words evoked.

"I'm calling because I have some of your things here that Nico packed up, and he's anxious to get rid of them. I went by your house to give them back to you, but you weren't home. Where would you like me to bring them?"

Now he sounded businesslike and impersonal. I supposed I was lucky he wasn't calling me the c-word. I gave him Grace's address.

I thought we were going to hang up, but then he said offhandedly, "You know the band leaves tomorrow night for the tour."

"Of course I know."

"Well, I thought you should also know that Nico's bringing a few . . . guests with him. A few special guests, that is. Of the female persuasion."

Was he fucking kidding me? My face went hot. "Gee, thanks, Barney. I really needed to know that. I appreciate your honesty. I'm sure it will help me sleep much better tonight."

There was a distinct shrug in his reply. "I'm only telling you because I don't want you to feel badly about how you ended it. You did him a favor, really. He realizes now your relationship was just sort of a temporary insanity. He's been laughing about it. He's going to chalk it up to hard experience. Boot camp, so to speak. As you can see, he's already moved on."

I stood there with my mouth open, blinking rapidly, unable to come up with a single reply that didn't involve threatening to disembowel a man I had previously respected and liked.

"I mean you must have known, Kat. I love Nico, he's like a brother to me, but he's a musician. Honestly, they're unreliable. There's always something more important to them than you."

He hung up without waiting for my reply. I stood motionless in the living room with the dead phone to my ear, replaying the conversation over and over in my head, wondering if I was going insane.

Boot camp.

It's not the end of the world.

He's a musician. Honestly, they're unreliable.

I'd heard all that before.

When the front desk called the house phone twenty minutes later to announce a guest in the lobby, I was prepared.

I'd put on actual clothes. (They were Grace's, and they didn't fit right, but who cared.) The snuggie had been rolled up and shoved in the closet. I'd brushed my teeth, combed my hair, and consumed a fortifying shot of tequila.

"Send him up," I said to the concierge, and sat down to wait.

Three minutes later, a knock came on the door. I opened it, not knowing what to expect, but it was only Barney with two lumpy duffel bags, standing in the doorway with his calm smile, his crisp suit, and the bulge of his gun beneath his breast pocket like some kind of assassin Buddha.

"Barney," I said cautiously.

"Kat." His gaze dropped to the hollow of my throat. A ghost of a smile lit his face, then disappeared.

"Come in."

He ambled into the foyer of Grace's elegant apartment, looked briefly around, then set the bags down beneath a mirrored console. He turned back to me. His gaze flickered to the light fixture in the ceiling, to the oil painting that hung on the wall in the hallway, to the phone on the console where he'd set the bags.

"Nice place," he said and set a finger to his lips.

All the hair on the back of my neck stood on end. *Holy shit, is he telling me what I think he's telling me?* "Uh . . . yep."

Barney nodded slowly, his gaze meaningful. He glanced at the bags. "That should be everything. Nico didn't have time to bother with it, so I did my best to find whatever of yours was lying around."

"Okay."

Barney and I stared at each other. His gaze dropped again to the hollow of my throat. "Sorry about all this, Kat. You always struck me as a nice girl. I hate to see him acting like such a dog so soon after you broke up."

My voice shook with emotion when I answered. "Well, it's like you said. He's a musician. There's always something more important to them than you."

Those were the exact words Barney had said to me on the phone, which were also the exact words I'd said to Nico the day I walked out on him before Avery's death. I remembered the other things, too: when I'd told Nico about how I thought life was a boot camp, and when Grace had said I'd been through worse the day the paparazzi first showed up at my house. Put together, they were much more than coincidence.

They were a code. Nico was telling me something. But what?

Barney stepped closer. He reached out and touched the chain around my neck. I'd had it repaired the day after Nico had torn it off. Looking into my eyes, he said, "Take care, Kat," and he tapped the gold pendant twice.

And I understood what he was really saying: trust.

I had to shove my fist in my mouth to stifle my gasp. Barney nodded, holding my gaze, then turned and let himself out. As the door closed behind him, I dove at the bags he'd left on the floor near the console and tore open the zippers. In a frenzy, I dug through the contents of one bag until I reached the bottom. In it were only clothes, some makeup, a few pieces of my jewelry. I tore into the other bag, crushed when I didn't find anything, thinking the entire thing was in my head, manufactured from desperation and denial, but then my fingers brushed a smooth surface, and I froze.

A folded piece of paper lay at the bottom of the bag.

I picked it up with shaking hands and read.

Phones tapped. House(s) bugged. Barney's waiting for you downstairs, parking garage level two. PS – I'm gonna give you such a goddamn spanking.

Sweet relief flooded me. I laughed and sobbed at the same time, tears springing to my eyes. I found a pair of Adidas in the mess of clothes on the floor and tugged them on, not bothering with the laces, then dashed off a note for Grace, and left it on the console. When I got to the lower parking level, Barney leaned out the driver's window, impatiently waving me over to the Escalade.

I sprinted to it as if I were being chased by a herd of stampeding elephants, jumped in the passenger seat, slammed the door behind me, turned to Barney, and shouted, "What the hell is going on?"

His response was a curt, "Seat belt."

Without waiting for me to comply, he threw the car into drive. We burned rubber around a corner and leapt up the incline to the first parking level. The force threw me back against my seat. Deciding now would be a good time to follow Barney's instructions before I cracked my head against the dashboard or the window, I fumbled with the strap of the seat belt as we screamed around another corner, roared down a straight section, and blasted past the parking attendant hollering at us to slow down.

We flew out into the street. Barney made a hard right, and the Escalade fishtailed for a moment before righting itself. Barney stomped on the gas pedal and the SUV jumped forward with a spine-tingling bellow. An intersection loomed ahead, which, judging by our current speed, we would be barreling through just as the light turned red.

"Christ, Barney, slow down!"

I turned my head to shout at him again, but the words died in my mouth as I looked past him, out the driver's window.

I just had time to scream before the other car smashed into us, dead-on.

Chapter 38

Blackness. A crushing weight on top of me. A high-pitched buzzing in my ears. The stench of smoke and gasoline stinging my nose.

I opened my eyes and saw light in flickering flashes, like a strobe light in a disco, pulsing and disorienting. Everything looked wrong. Smashed and upside down. Moving my head sent pain shooting through my neck. I moaned and tasted blood in my mouth.

We were in an accident. The car's upside down. Someone hit us. Someone . . . someone is saying my name.

I turned my head toward the voice. I was dreaming, surely. That hand could not really belong to that arm, to that body, to that face. I was mixing it all up. Everything was jumbled in my head.

The hand fastened on my wrist and pulled. It hurt. The weight on top of me didn't budge. I tried to focus on the weight and realized it was Barney, unconscious and bleeding from a cut on his forehead, his body slanted across mine. Another hand wrapped around the back of my neck. The hands dragged me from beneath the motionless body of Barney, through the smashed window, onto the asphalt of the street. I saw flashes of blue sky and green trees, a high-rise glinting in the afternoon sun. My body screamed in pain, but I was too weak to give voice to it.

Then Michael lifted me onto his shoulder, the pain crescendoed, and the world fell black once more.

The first thing I became conscious of was the fresh, bracing scent of salt air.

I held perfectly still, aware in every cell of my body that I was in danger. I remembered what had happened. More important, I remembered who had taken me. I could only guess as to why.

After a moment, I stopped trying to guess because everything I envisioned ended with me lying facedown in a pool of my own blood.

When I opened my eyes, I was surprised to find myself in a grand, unfamiliar room. It had vaulted ceilings and acres of white carpeting, and, through a glistening wall of glass, a sweeping view of the sea and distant mountains. Some time must have elapsed, because the sun had begun to sink below the horizon. The sofa beneath me was plush and comfortable, the feather pillow under my head was thick and soft.

Where the hell was I?

"It's Amy's house," said a quiet voice to my right. I turned my head to find Michael standing a few feet behind the sofa where I lay. Hands in the front pockets of his jeans, he stared pensively into the darkening sky beyond the wall of windows. "She bought it for us. I spent the happiest days of my life here." His gaze flicked to mine. "Before."

My head throbbed. I felt sick to my stomach. I was almost certain I'd broken something in my right ribcage area because every breath was stinging, searing misery. Trying not to breathe too deeply, I asked, "Are you going to kill me?"

His brows flew up. My bluntness had surprised him. "Are you so ready to die?"

"Just thought I'd cut to the chase. I hate drawn-out suspense; it's so nerve-racking."

"Sorry," he said unremorsefully. "Prepare to be racked."

When I tried to sit up, a spasm of pain speared my side, making me gasp. Michael watched me struggle into an upright position with a detached, faintly hungry expression, as if I were the lobster he'd chosen to be boiled for his dinner from the deli case. I noticed the only mark on him was a red rash on one side of his face, possibly the result of an airbag deploying.

He said, "Careful. I don't want you any more bruised than you already are."

That was even more chilling than his expression. What did he have planned for me?

Without warning, his hand shot out. He grabbed my hair and yanked my head back. I cried out, trying to twist away, my hands curled around his wrist, but I didn't have the strength to escape. Every part of my body throbbed with pain.

"Stop!" he spat, and gave my head a firm shake.

I stilled. Breathing hard, my hands wrapped around his wrist, I looked up at him looming over me. He planted his other hand next to my head and leaned down to speak into my ear.

"At first I didn't get it. Had I read him wrong? Had I misjudged the situation?" His pupils were dilated unnaturally large, leaving only a thin ring of blue surrounding a pool of black. Our faces were so close I saw the tiny red veins shot through the whites. His hand in my hair shook so hard my teeth rattled.

I'd seen people on drugs. If I was afraid before, now fear turned my blood to ice water.

"But then I realized I hadn't read him wrong at all. It wasn't him I'd misjudged." His voice turned to a hiss. "*It was you.*"

He yanked me to my feet with brutal strength, using only that hand fisted in my hair. I screamed, clawing at his arm. He dragged me backward over the couch. I fell to the floor with a bone-crunching thud, the wind knocked out of me. I lay there gasping for air, curled into a ball, until Michael began to drag me across the floor by my hair. The pain was like being mauled by a tiger, from the inside. He dragged me down a long, tiled hallway and into a master bedroom, where he dumped me unceremoniously at the foot of the bed.

As my head hit the floor, something in my neck popped. Black dots danced in the edges of my vision.

Michael prowled to the opposite wall of the room, where a camera on a tripod stood, along with one of those large black umbrella halogen lights used in photo shoots. He flipped a switch, illuminating the wall in a wash of brilliant white, then turned to me.

"You told him, didn't you Kat? You broke our deal. You lied to me, and you told him. I have to admit, I'm really disappointed."

My fake cool from before vanished under the sudden crush of near-death adrenaline. "I don't know what you're talking about! I didn't tell him anything!"

I tried to roll to one side, to get upright again, but couldn't manage it. The pain was too much. My head was spinning. I knew I was about to pass out, and fought it, biting my tongue to keep me awake.

For the first time, I noticed how cut and bloody my hands were. One of my shoes was missing. On my left leg, the black trousers I'd borrowed from Grace had been shorn apart and a ragged gash ran the length of my inner thigh. Blood dripped down my leg in long red streams.

Michael stalked toward me. He grabbed me beneath my armpits, hauled me to the lit wall, and threw me against it. Unable to hold myself upright, I slumped sideways to the floor.

Michael sighed. He came back and propped me up carefully, arranging my limbs as you would a doll on a shelf. The room took on a dreamy, hazy quality. I moaned and let my eyelids drift shut.

"It's no use, Kat. I know you told Nico about our little talk. And even though I've been listening in on all your conversations, and nothing *sounded* amiss, I finally realized he wouldn't have acted the way he did afterward if you two hadn't cooked up some silly scheme to try to throw me off. But, as you can see, I wasn't. And now you've forced me to do something unpleasant. You only have yourself to blame."

I opened my eyes. As he came into focus, I whispered, "Listening in?"

So Barney was right.

"Did you think that nighttime visit of mine was some kind of voyeuristic jerkoff?" Michael sounded insulted. "Please. I was there with a specific purpose: to ensure you'd uphold your end of the bargain I was going to propose to you. Bugging phones is just one of the many talents I've picked up in my travels. I'm sure you've figured out by now I'm pretty good with hacking computers, too."

High, unsmiling, he stood over me looking like something the Boogeyman would run from, then stepped back, cocked his head, and stretched out his arms. With his hands, he made a frame. He looked at me through it. After a moment, he grinned.

I understood with bone-chilling clarity what was about to happen.

"You have such eloquent eyes, Kat. Like a silent movie star's." Michael's tone had turned almost tender. "It's too bad you're short.

With that face, you really could have been a model." He dropped his arms and stared at me. "Well. At least this once, you will be."

He went to the tripod. He looked into the camera and adjusted the lens. "Say cheese."

A flash went off. Then another, and another. Michael was photographing me, bloodied, semiconscious, splayed against the wall in his dead sister/lover's bedroom. He was taking the final photos of my life.

I knew who he'd be sending them to.

Well, brain, I thought frantically, *now's as good a time as any to prove your existence.*

"Amy told me about you. The day we met." My words sounded a little slurred to my own ears, but they must have been perfectly clear to Michael, because he froze, then stood ramrod straight, his eyes wide.

"What?"

I nodded, licking my lips, surreptitiously looking around the immediate area for a weapon. Any kind of weapon. "I was hired to do the makeup for the band's video—"

"Yes, yes, I know. And?" Michael held so still he might have been a statue. His gaze on my face burned.

"Well . . . she seemed a little sad . . . so I asked her what was the matter." *Ceramic cat statue on the dresser. Lamp on the nightstand. Framed photo of Avery on the wall.* In spite of my head and my pain and the direness of the situation, I had to smile. That would be a bit of poetic justice if ever it existed, smashing in Michael's skull with a picture of his sister.

"What did she say?" prompted Michael impatiently.

I heard a noise. A creak, or a pop. Most likely it was something inside my own body. I whispered, "She said . . . " Was that a shadow creeping down the hallway? No, my eyes were playing tricks on me. "She said . . . she said she really wanted . . . "

Michael moved toward me. He shouted, "What? What did Amy say she wanted?"

From the doorway, a deep voice snarled, "*Peace*."

Michael spun around. He pulled a gun from the waistband of his jeans. A shot rang out, then another. As blood sprayed crimson against the wall above my head, Michael staggered back, cursing, but didn't fall.

With the last remaining ounce of my strength, I lunged to the dresser, grabbed the ceramic cat statue, then smashed it against the back of Michael's head on my way back down to the floor.

Michael crumpled to the floor beside me. He didn't move again.

Then Nico was kneeling above me, his eyes tortured, his face red with fury. The whine of sirens rose far off in the night.

I whispered, "Glad you could make it, superstar. Hope I didn't interrupt a hot date."

"You said, 'I can't,'" growled Nico. Beautiful and fierce, he cradled my face in his hands, staring down into my eyes with so much love in his own it took away what little breath I had left.

"What?"

His words spilled out in a rush. "When I asked you to marry me, you didn't say 'no,' you said, 'I can't.' I didn't realize it until later because I was too fuckin' *crushed*, but then someone said they saw me walkin' out the back door at the House of Blues when I hadn't walked out the fuckin' back door, and I knew it was him, and he'd gotten to you somehow, and you'd promised to do somethin' crazy like break up with me to protect me, because that's exactly the kind of fucked-up thing he would ask you to do, and exactly the kind of fucked-up thing you *would* do instead of talkin' to me about it, and I should've known in the first place because you lie for shit, always have, told you that the first fuckin' day I met you. Entire time you were tellin' me you didn't love me and you wanted to leave, your eyes were sayin' you were dyin'. Been kickin' my own ass over that for a week."

The room above his head careened like a roller coaster. The ground beneath me lurched like a stormy sea. The pain in my body grew more intense, along with the sharp, unwelcome appearance of nausea, but I managed sarcasm in spite of it all. "You mean in between sticking your dick in every available hole?"

"Don't be fuckin' dense, woman," Nico murmured, tenderly stroking my cheeks with his thumbs. "Already told you, you ruined me for anyone else. All those others were a cover. I thought Michael'd leave you alone and come after me when he saw his plan didn't work. Obviously that backfired 'cause he knew me better than I thought he did, and that fuckup is one I'll never forgive myself for. You left me for real, I woulda dug myself a ditch, crawled into it, and never crawled back out."

Oh, wonderful feeling. What lovely, lovely relief. No dick. No holes. Just Nico trying to create a diversion and save me from his evil brother.

I whispered, "He said he'd tell everyone about what happened with your father. And that *you* and Amy had a thing . . . and about that photographer you made disappear. He said you'd go to prison. That's why I did it. I wanted to keep you safe, too."

"Oh, baby," Nico said softly. "I didn't make the photographer disappear. Wanted to, but Michael beat me to it. As for prison, I got some new insurance against that. Apparently Amy kept a diary her whole life. Made a video diary before she died, too, as part of her therapy in rehab. Gave it all to Kenji for safekeeping. After the funeral, he gave it to me. Guess they were a lot closer than I realized."

So the diaries were what must have been on Kenji's mind at Avery's funeral. No wonder he'd been so distracted.

"Speaking of funerals, is he dead?" I tilted my chin toward Michael.

"Unfortunately, he's still breathin'. Think I only got him in the arm. Though he's gonna have one motherfucker of a headache when he wakes up, thanks to you." Nico glanced back at me, and suddenly it was as if he was seeing me for the first time. He jerked away, eyes widening.

"Jesus, fuck, baby, you're bleedin' everywhere!" His voice broke over the last word. He tore off his leather jacket, then his T-shirt, and ripped the shirt right down the middle. He gingerly wound the piece of fabric around my upper thigh, tied it into a tourniquet, then pressed the rest of the shirt against the ragged wound.

As pain scorched through me, the room grew dim. The sirens were right outside. Someone shouted from the front of the house. Nico shouted back, "In here!" Then a dozen cops burst into the room, led by Officer Eric Cox and a very bloody and disheveled Barney, shakily gripping his gun.

I whispered, "Oh, fun, the gang's all here," and that's the last thing I remember before I passed out for good.

Chapter 39

The E! *True Hollywood Special* that aired two months later was the highest-rated episode in the network's history. Nico refused an interview, but there were plenty of other people eager to tell what they knew about Amy Lynne Jameson aka Avery Kane.

Neighbors. Teachers. Friends from school. It seemed everyone in the shitty little Tennessee town the Jameson kids had fled remembered something. How the mother had abandoned them. How the two boys would show up at school bruised and silent. How pretty Amy was. How strange and wild she grew as she changed from a child to an adolescent.

How the kids had run away, and the town never heard from them again. Only the town had, but it just didn't know it.

The network had also scored interviews with everyone from her agent, the snake-eyed Ethan Grossman, to Gloria Gentry, the head of the National Council on Child Abuse and Family Violence, who weighed in with solemn statistics about child abuse and neglect, and reminded the viewers at home of the warning signs of possible abuse.

After they played the segments of Avery's video diary where she detailed the horrors she'd suffered at the hands of her father, Ms. Gentry answered the interviewer's follow-up questions with tears in her eyes.

Nico and I watched it from the penthouse suite of the Four Seasons Hotel George V in Paris on New Year's Eve, silently sipping champagne together in the massive king-sized bed, until he couldn't take it any longer and turned the television off. He set his champagne on the nightstand, took mine from my hand and did the same, then pulled me down against him to the satiny, pillowed heaven of the mattress, and buried his face in my neck.

"What did you think?" I whispered, running my fingers through his hair.

He inhaled deeply against my skin, hiding a few moments longer, then reluctantly withdrew, and propped himself up on an elbow. His gaze was solemn. "I think it's what she wanted, or I never would have allowed it to be shown. It's not how I wanted people to remember her."

I kissed his bare chest.

We were both naked, having made love for the second time that night. He was still being gentle with me—much to my irritation, I'd never received that spanking he'd promised months ago in his note in the duffel bag—and touched me as if I were fragile as porcelain. Which I think I'd proven I wasn't, considering the size of the bump I'd put on the back of Michael's skull.

Also considering how quickly I'd bounced back after sustaining a serious concussion, breaking three ribs, fracturing the maxillary bone of my eye socket, and losing a potentially life-threatening amount of blood from the laceration on my thigh.

The scar was already kick-ass. I felt like I'd done battle with a saber-toothed tiger and won. The tour only had to be pushed back three and a half weeks before I was well enough to travel.

Naturally, pushing the tour back was Nico's idea. "Where I go, you go," and that was that.

I sighed, running my fingers over the new tattoo of my name inked on his chest, right above his heart. It was big, surrounded by thorns and roses, and almost as kick-ass as the scar on my leg. "I wish I could have known her better. She was brave, doing that video. Wanting to make sure she helped you if you needed it."

"She did it for other abuse victims as much as for me. There was no way she could have predicted this shit with you, but during one of her lucid moments, she must have realized Michael would eventually snap. Maybe she thought he'd even do something to hurt *her*. Either way, her intentions were clear: she wanted the world to know what she'd gone through, and who she really was." His voice grew soft. "I think she was just as tired of all the lies as I was."

Don't let something awful someone does to you make you feel like you don't deserve love, she'd said in the video, staring straight into the camera, her blue eyes fierce with unshed tears. *Don't take that on yourself, like I did. Don't let the bad guys win.*

"So you're not sorry the truth is finally out about who *you* really are?"

"I'm only sorry for all the attention it's brought us. I know how much you hate that shit."

I made a small noise of agreement: I did hate that shit. Newspapers and the tabloids had picked up the story long before E! aired it, and it had gone viral. On the plus side, once the general public knew I wasn't the cause of Avery's overdose or breakup with Nico, the death threats against me died down. There was, however, a thriving online community convinced the entire thing was a conspiracy to boost Bad Habit's record sales and generate buzz for the tour.

Not that they needed it. The tour had sold out the day tickets had been released. Apparently people didn't care if Nico Nyx was really Nico Jameson, or if he was from Mars. They just wanted to watch him play music.

As for the threat of Nico going to prison because of what happened that fateful night with his father when he'd taken his two younger siblings and fled town, the police had told us that Amy's video testimony—self-defense, she said—combined with eyewitness accounts of teachers and friends from that time who vouched for the violent alcoholism of their father, were enough to convince them not to bring a case, in spite of the story Michael had been telling in prison.

Maybe Eric had something to do with that, as well. Like Barney said, it never hurts to have a cop who owes you a favor.

And, as it turns out, the word of a drug trafficker who'd been under investigation by the FBI for several years doesn't hold much water. In addition to being extremely pissed off he'd tapped all our phones and houses with software only the NSA was supposed to have access to, the FBI had found out about the hacking of the security company's computers and the murders of Juan Carlos and the photographer. The list of Michael's transgressions was so long I doubted he'd ever be released from prison.

Which suited me just fine. All in all, things were looking up.

"How do you think Barney's doing? I'm a little worried about him."

Nico's deep chuckle vibrated his chest. "Why, because he's followin' you around like your shadow or because of his back?"

He'd sustained injuries to several of the discs in his back from the car crash, and now walked with a distinctive limp. So far it hadn't deterred him from making himself a complete nuisance, sticking almost as close to my side as Nico did. I had a pair of bookends beside me wherever I went.

"Because he takes his job too seriously. The man has no private life, and he never takes time off. Don't you think that's unhealthy?"

"We're the only family he has, Kat," said Nico softly, trailing his fingers up my arm. "He considers me his brother, and he loves you like the little sister he never had. Him bein' the way he is, he feels responsible he didn't figure it out sooner that Michael had everyone's places bugged."

"But he *did* figure it out, and not only that, he turned it to your advantage! He has nothing to feel guilty for. He's awesome."

I didn't understand all the technical particulars, but somehow Barney had used the software Michael had installed in our phones in reverse to track Michael's location. When he tapped in to listen to a call, Barney could see where he was. Which was how when Chloe called me that morning to see how I was doing, Barney discovered Michael was lurking right down the street from Grace's. Barney had never gone to my house first, like he'd told me. He just knew Michael was listening to our conversation, and hoped to smuggle me out of the house before Michael decided to make a move. Nico had been waiting to pounce with the police nearby, but Michael, with his suspicious nature, figured out the clothes drop for the red herring it was and beat him to it.

"Hmm," said Nico, sounding disgruntled. "So Barney gets all the credit for comin' to your rescue, does he? Your man thinkin' to track you to Malibu usin' the GPS on your cell phone doesn't count for much in the knight in shinin' armor department?"

I snuggled closer to the heat and safe solidity of Nico's body, inhaling his warm, spicy scent. I trailed my foot up his calf. "Yes, it definitely gets you credit, sweetie." I paused. "Though to be honest, I still might be a little pissed about all those brunettes. And that everyone in the world thinks I took you back without a fuss after you'd gone on a humping rampage across Los Angeles."

"Not like they could blame me, after the shitty way you dumped my ass."

I shoved at his chest. "Nico!"

He dipped his head and playfully bit my shoulder. "Kat!"

Pretending to pout, I rolled away. Nico prevented my escape by grabbing me around the waist and hauling me atop his naked body.

Just as I'd planned.

I grinned down at him. "You're so easy, sweetie."

"Oh yeah? 'Cause I'd describe myself as hard." He flexed his hips to underscore his prominent erection. I'd nicknamed it Mr. Happy due to all the joy it evoked.

"Speaking of which . . . we never did take one of those baths you told me you liked so much." When I coyly batted my lashes, he laughed, and squeezed me.

"Oh, yeah? Twice in two hours and she's still not satisfied? Now she wants to do it in the bathtub?"

I rolled my eyes. "If you're going to start with the 'she' business again, you won't get lucky at all, mister."

He pinched my bare behind. "And if you're gonna start with the smart mouth again," he said in a husky voice, "you won't be sittin' right for a week, woman."

I nearly squee'd in glee. "Promises, promises."

Nico's eyes grew hot. "You tellin' me I haven't been takin' care of business, darlin'? You missin' out on somethin' you been needin'?"

I bit my lip and made my eyes go big and dreamy, in the way I knew he couldn't resist. "Let's just say I've been very, very bad. And I need you to make it all better."

Faster than I could blink, Nico scooped me into his arms, and tossed me over his shoulder. He headed for the enormous master bathroom with its spacious infinity tub. "Careful what you wish for, baby," he said, and gave my ass a brisk swat.

I held out my hand, enjoying the sparkle of the enormous diamond on my ring finger, and grinned.

Yes, things were *definitely* looking up.

Epilogue

"Come on, lovey, suck it in! You know the drill; it's not like we haven't been through this before!"

I stared at Kenji's reflection in the wall of mirrors as he stood behind me in the dressing room of the bridal salon, tugging in frustration at the reluctant zipper of the elaborate gown I was trying on. "I hate to disappoint you, Kenji, but I'm not wearing anything to my wedding that even slightly resembles that sausage casing you stuffed me into for the band's video. This zipper is trying to tell us something. As in, give it up, sister, the carbs have finally won."

His scoff sounded as if he was trying to expel something lodged in his throat. "I won't be defeated by twelve inches of tiny metal teeth! You're wearing Monique Lhuillier when you walk down that aisle, Kitty Kat, or nothing at all!"

Grace, with crystal champagne flute in hand, sat beside Chloe on a white tufted sofa nearby, her feet propped on a mirrored coffee table covered in bridal couture books. Smiling, she said, "Somehow I doubt Nico would object to that."

Chloe frowned. "I'm still unclear on this. Why exactly is wearing a Monique Lhuillier dress so important?"

Hands on hips, Kenji straightened and glared at the offending zipper. "Because that's the designer Kat wore the day she met Nico. It's good luck."

"I thought the good luck was supposed to be, 'Something old, something new, something borrowed, something blue'?"

Kenji waved his hand. "Those, too. But in the theater community it's considered good luck to wear the same thing for a callback that you wore to the original audition. So I'm including as many good-luck superstitions as I can for this wedding. Because if this morning is any indication, we're going to need as much help as we can get."

Chloe snorted. "In that case, Kat should be wearing flip-flops, a denim mini, and a shirt that's losing the fight with her cleavage."

"Thank you, Joan Rivers." I turned to and fro on the carpeted riser, examining my reflection. It was too bad about the zipper, because the dress was incredibly beautiful. But I was determined to be comfortable on the happiest day of my life, even if I *did* have to wear a denim mini.

"You're welcome, Dolly Parton," replied Chloe. To Kenji, she said with interest, "You used to be in the theater?"

He turned to look at her with raised brows. "What, you thought I used to be a mechanic?"

She looked him up and down, examining his red silk vest, leopard-print tie, and white skinny jeans. "I was thinking more along the lines of magician. You have the look of a man who could pull a rabbit out of his hat."

Though I wasn't convinced it was a compliment, Kenji beamed. "Oh, honey, that's so sweet!"

Grace hid her smile behind her glass of champagne.

Into the pristine dressing room glided a saleswoman so thin she'd be invisible if she turned sideways. She had a slash of crimson lips, blonde hair scraped into a severe bun at the nape of her neck, and so much mascara it looked as if two hairy tarantulas were perched on her eyelids. "And how are we doing? Anything else I can get you? Different selections? More champagne?"

Looking at my rear end, Kenji muttered, "Spanx?"

Grace said calmly, "Shut up, Kenji, or I'll hide your lip gloss and tell everyone those Prada boots you're wearing are knockoffs from Payless."

He gasped.

I ignored them both. "Unfortunately, the last few dresses I've tried on have been a bit too tight, so maybe I could try a few more one size larger? This same general style?"

The tarantulas on the saleswoman's eyelids fluttered. "Of course. I'll be right back." She turned and silently glided out.

Chloe watched her go. "Poor thing. When was the last time she's eaten, do you think?"

Grace laughed. "I don't know about eating, but hearing Kat say, 'one size larger,' looked as if it might drive her to drink."

I gathered the heavy silk skirts of the dress and stepped off the platform. "Speaking of, give me some of that champagne. I'm going to need it to get through the rest of this afternoon. Shopping for wedding dresses is about as much fun as getting a Brazilian wax."

The four of us had already been in the swanky Beverly Hills salon for hours. Nico and I had finally chosen a wedding date—August fifteenth, the one-year anniversary of the day we'd met—and the preparations were quickly moving forward. It had been a month since Bad Habit's wildly successful EuroTrash tour had ended and we'd returned home to LA, and those weeks had been the happiest of my life.

Today excepted. I'd never been a clotheshorse, and I'd guessed—correctly—that finding a wedding dress I could stand, sit, eat, and dance in, while simultaneously flattering my figure, would be like the quest for the holy grail. On top of that, the guest list had somehow swelled to close to four hundred people. I'd already floated the idea of eloping to Vegas to Nico, who gave me a look I correctly interpreted as "over my dead body." He had his heart set on a grand, romantic, fairy-tale white wedding at the Hotel Bel-Air, complete with a horse-drawn carriage for my arrival, an orchestra to serenade us as we said our vows, and a dove release at the end of the ceremony.

I thought his enthusiasm was adorable. He was even interviewing photographers and pastry chefs himself, determined to make sure every detail was perfect.

I was happy to let him go crazy with the planning, but I'd put my foot down about the horse-drawn carriage. It was way too Disney princess for my taste. We'd compromised on a stretch limo. That way I could arrive with my three bridesmaids in style; Kenji was already obsessing over how he was going to accessorize his outfit to coordinate with the gorgeous sage-green gowns Chloe and Grace would wear. I had a feeling he might end up rocking one of those gowns himself.

Now if only I could find a wedding dress that didn't pinch, pucker, or require me to hold my breath for eight hours, we'd all be good.

Guzzling the remainder of Grace's champagne, I wondered if Juicy Couture made wedding attire. Getting married in velour sweatpants was starting to sound like a fabulous idea.

Kenji's cell phone rang. He looked at the screen, then answered it with a shout. "No! Absolutely not! It's bad luck!"

Chloe, Grace, and I shared a look.

Kenji listened for a moment. He glanced in my direction. Finally, looking resigned, he sighed. "You're right outside, aren't you?"

"Yep," said a voice I recognized from just beyond the doorway to the dressing room. Holding his cell phone to his ear, Nico peeked around the corner, caught sight of me, and broke into a huge grin.

"Ah, yes, the relentless stalker strikes again," said Grace, rolling her eyes.

Chloe smiled. "I'm actually surprised it took him this long." She said to Nico, "That was, like, three hours Kat was out of your sight. Were you already having withdrawals?"

Sliding his phone into his back pocket, Nico stepped into the room. His gaze swept over me. His cocky grin softened to a tender smile. "Can you blame me? Look at her. This woman's picture is next to the word 'beauty' in the dictionary. I still can't believe I get to wake up next to her every day."

"Sweet talker." I smiled back at him.

He murmured, "God's honest truth, baby. I'm the luckiest man alive."

Chloe sighed in happiness. Grace rolled her eyes again and took another swig of her champagne. Kenji took the opportunity to swat Nico on the arm and chastise him for intruding on the sacred female ritual of wedding dress shopping.

"You're here, brother. Pretty sure your parts don't qualify you as a female." Nico strolled over to me. I held out a hand and he kissed it, then laid a swift, potent kiss on my lips.

"My *parts*, as you so eloquently put it, have absolutely nothing to do with anything. You should know well enough by now that Kenji will not be defined by something so limiting as gender stereotypes. We refuse to be shoved into such a dreary conventional box."

I squeezed Nico's hand. "Uh-oh. Referring to himself in the third person *and* the royal 'we.' You've really pissed him off now, sweetie."

Nico chuckled. Before anyone could say another word, there was a grumbling noise from the next room, followed by a loud, irritated voice. "No, I don't want a glass of fucking champagne! And eat a hamburger, woman, a stiff breeze could blow you away."

Grimacing, Chloe looked at Nico. "Great. You brought Prince Charming with you."

"Yeah, well, Prince Charming has agreed to be my best man, so I thought it would be a good idea if you girls and A.J. got to know each other better."

"The best man? He's going to be *in the wedding*?" Distressed, Chloe looked to me.

Nico and I had only just agreed yesterday, after a long discussion, that A.J. would be the best man. I hadn't managed yet to bring it up to my bridesmaids. I had my doubts about him, but the entire time the band was on tour, he'd been nothing but polite to me, if distant. Nico had made it clear that I had the final word, but if A.J. was his choice, I didn't feel it was right to object simply because we'd had one strange encounter at Avery's funeral, a day that *everyone* had been out of sorts. And I'd made Nico promise to talk to him about being nicer to Chloe.

My fingers were crossed that A.J. could play nice. Judging by his current mood, I was having my doubts.

"You don't have to walk down the aisle with him, Chloe."

Grace said, "I guess that honor's reserved for me, then." She didn't sound particularly concerned. I knew she could handle him.

"Well, you can bet he's not going to want to walk down the aisle with *me*," said Kenji, examining his manicure, "seeing as how he'll look like an unchained beast by comparison."

Nico raised his brows, and Kenji shrugged. "You know I love him, Nico, but honestly the man has all the style of a gorilla."

"And the charm," muttered Chloe, crossing her arms over her chest.

"He'll probably show up in head-to-toe leather," continued Kenji breezily, "in which case I will personally wring his neck."

"Good luck with that, Pixie Dust."

Dwarfing the doorway, A.J. stood just outside the entrance to the dressing room, gazing at Kenji with a faint smile hovering at the corners of his mouth. Or maybe I'd just imagined the smile, because as soon as his amber eyes flicked in the direction of Chloe, his face hardened, his body stiffened, and he tilted back his head, looking at her down his nose.

Chloe paled, but Kenji didn't seem to notice the change. "I do adore it when you call me by your pet names, lovey, but 'Pixie Dust' is a tad hostile, even for you."

A.J. turned his attention back to Kenji. His faint smile returned. "Would you prefer 'Tinker Bell'?"

For some reason, Kenji blushed.

"Don't tease him, A.J.," said Nico, hiding his own smile. "I doubt you'd like it if I shared with everyone the nickname Heavenly calls you."

I said, "Am I missing something here?"

Nico wound his arm around my waist. "Seems everyone's favorite stylist went and found himself a special friend while we weren't lookin'."

Grace said, "A special friend who calls you Tinker Bell?"

Chloe said, "*Heavenly?*"

Kenji shrugged, looking bashfully at the floor. "London and I met the night of the party at the House of Blues."

"I don't remember seeing you at all that night," I said.

"Well, lovey, we met on the way in." He paused. "And then we turned around and went back out."

Grace laughed. "Oh, my. It seems Nico and Kat aren't the only ones who found love at first sight."

Kenji's blush grew deeper, spreading from his cheeks to his ears. "Well, I wouldn't go that far." He giggled. "Lust at first sight, definitely. In fact, you could say London had me at herro."

"Ugh. That one was a real groaner, Kenji."

"Speaking of groaners," piped up Chloe, "I'm betting anyone named 'Heavenly' has the market cornered on that. What do you think, Grace?"

A.J. snapped, "She probably thinks anyone named 'Chloe' has the market cornered on stuck-up, frigid rich girls who wouldn't know a dick if it hit them in the face."

Chloe managed not to holler, but only just. "Which I'm guessing is probably how girls named 'Heavenly' spend most of their time!"

A.J. stepped inside the dressing room, Chloe shot to her feet, and the two of them squared off and started to hurl insults at each other. The saleswoman appeared in the doorway holding several gowns. She took one look inside, turned around, and went back the way she came. I sighed, Grace watched the back and forth in amusement from her spot on the sofa, and, beside me, Nico shook his head.

"Well," he said, tightening his arm around me, "I can see that talk I had with A.J. on the way over had zero effect. Should be an interestin' next few months."

"Interesting is one way to put it. Insane is another."

My mouth dropped open when Chloe threw the remains of her champagne in A.J.'s face. She stormed out of the room through the main door. Cursing, A.J. barreled through a door at the back.

With a flourish, Grace finished her champagne, looked at Nico and me, smiled broadly, and said, "Kids, this is going to be *so* much fun."

Acknowledgments

When I was halfway through writing this book, my father died. Logical and pragmatic, acerbic and loyal, taciturn and tenacious, he was the smartest, fairest, most reliable person I've ever known. In the chaotic aftermath of his death, I stopped writing. I was unable to write for weeks. When I picked up my pen again (I was still on a contractual deadline), the book veered off into dark territory, reflecting my state of mind.

Kat developed terminal breast cancer. She and Nico did not have the happy ending they deserved.

The chapters I wrote during that time were powerful, black, and very confusing. I wasn't sure which direction I was headed with the manuscript. I wasn't sure what I was doing at all. So I reached out to my author group at Montlake Romance, described my predicament, and asked for advice. They responded with such wonderful words of support and encouragement that it helped me forge a path forward that steered clear of disaster for my beloved characters. A special, sincere thank you to my fellow Montlake Romance authors for their kindness, wisdom, and clear-eyed advice. I appreciate you.

Equally important, thank you to Jay, for everything. There is no me without you.

Thanks to Maria Gomez, my editor, to Kelli Martin for assisting during transitions, and to the copywriting and proofreading teams, cover artists, and marketing department at Amazon Publishing.

Always, THANK YOU Melody Guy. You get me, you make me better, and I love you more than any other person I've never met.

Hugs and high fives to Geissinger's Gang, my street team! You guys rock.

To my readers, family, and all those who supported me through a difficult year, thank you.

About the Author

Joyce "J.T." Geissinger is an award-winning author of paranormal and contemporary romance featuring dark and twisted plots, kick-ass heroines, and alpha heroes whose hearts are even bigger than their muscles. Her debut fantasy romance *Shadow's Edge* was a #1 international Amazon best-seller and won the Prism award for Best First Book. Her follow-up novel, *Edge of Oblivion*, was a RITA© Award finalist for Paranormal Romance from the Romance Writers of America, and she has been nominated for numerous awards for her work. She resides in Los Angeles with her husband.

Website: www.jtgeissinger.com
Twitter: www.twitter.com/JTGeissinger
Facebook: www.facebook.com/JTGeissinger
Goodreads: www.goodreads.com/JTGeissinger

Made in United States
Cleveland, OH
08 February 2025

14165148R00225